Sex on the Slopes

sex
on the
SLOPES

SUSAN LYONS

Heat | New York

THE BERKLEY PUBLISHING GROUP
Published by the Penguin Group
Penguin Group (USA) Inc.
375 Hudson Street, New York, New York 10014, USA
Penguin Group (Canada), 90 Eglinton Avenue East, Suite 700, Toronto, Ontario M4P 2Y3, Canada
(a division of Pearson Penguin Canada Inc.)
Penguin Books Ltd., 80 Strand, London WC2R 0RL, England
Penguin Group Ireland, 25 St. Stephen's Green, Dublin 2, Ireland (a division of Penguin Books Ltd.)
Penguin Group (Australia), 250 Camberwell Road, Camberwell, Victoria 3124, Australia
(a division of Pearson Australia Group Pty. Ltd.)
Penguin Books India Pvt. Ltd., 11 Community Centre, Panchsheel Park, New Delhi—110 017, India
Penguin Group (NZ), 67 Apollo Drive, Rosedale, North Shore 0632, New Zealand
(a division of Pearson New Zealand Ltd.)
Penguin Books (South Africa) (Pty.) Ltd., 24 Sturdee Avenue, Rosebank, Johannesburg 2196,
South Africa

Penguin Books Ltd., Registered Offices: 80 Strand, London WC2R 0RL, England

This book is an original publication of The Berkley Publishing Group.

Copyright © 2010 by Susan Lyons.
Cover design by Diana Kolsky.
Cover photo of "Muscle Man" copyright © Yukmin / Getty Images; cover photo of "Snowflakes" copyright © Keren-seg / Shutterstock; cover photo "Mountain" copyright © Alexander Chaikin / Shutterstock.
Text design by Kristin del Rosario.

PRINTING HISTORY
Heat trade paperback edition / December 2010

Library of Congress Cataloging-in-Publication Data

Lyons, Susan.
    Sex on the slopes / Susan Lyons.
        p. cm.
    ISBN 978-0-425-23701-4
    1. Whistler (B.C.)—Fiction. I. Title.
PR9199.4.L97S496 2011
813'.6—dc22
                        2010023001

PRINTED IN THE UNITED STATES OF AMERICA

10   9   8   7   6   5   4   3   2   1

ACKNOWLEDGMENTS

This book owes its existence in part to Allison Brandau, my former editor at Berkley. After I wrote *Sex on the Beach* (January 2010), we brainstormed ideas for my option book and decided it would be fun to take the same concept—three secret romances at a destination wedding—and set the story in spectacular Whistler, B.C. So it is thanks to Allison that I developed the proposal.

Thanks, too, to my current editor, Wendy McCurdy, for buying that option book, and for being so great to work with, and to editorial assistant Katherine Pelz for so efficiently handling the administrative details.

As always, thanks to my wonderful agent, Emily Sylvan Kim at Prospect Agency.

My critique team helped me bring the initial concept to realization. I couldn't have done it without them. Thanks to Betty Allan, Michelle Hancock, Nazima Ali, and the Novelistas: Christina Crooks, Delilah Marvelle, and Lacy Danes.

I'm also very grateful to Susan McFee Anderson and Loreth Anne White for Whistler hospitality, and to Loreth for research assistance.

I ran a contest to find the recipe for the "Sex on the Slopes" signature drink. All the recipes submitted were great, and my tasting team enjoyed them thoroughly on a cold December night in Vancouver, B.C. Thanks so much to Carol Woodruff for providing the winning recipe, a true classic for a romantic winter night by the fire.

I love to hear from readers. You can e-mail me at susan@susanlyons .ca or write c/o PO Box 73523, Downtown Postal Outlet, 1014 Robson Street, Vancouver, BC, Canada V6E 4L9. Please drop by my website, www.susanlyons.ca, where I have excerpts, behind-the-scenes notes, discussion guides, reviews, contests, a newsletter, recipes, articles, photos, and all sorts of good stuff.

CONTENTS

Sex on the Slopes

Recipe provided by Carol Woodruff

INGREDIENTS

1 cup strong, full-bodied coffee
1 tbsp. or ½ single serving pkg. cocoa mix
(the richer and more decadent the mix, the better!)
1 oz. Kahlua

INSTRUCTIONS

Combine ingredients in an Irish-coffee glass. Top with lots of whipped cream. Garnish with shaved chocolate, shaved peppermint-stick candy, a maraschino cherry, or whatever else tickles your fancy.

Fire and *Ice*

Fire and Ice Cocktail

INGREDIENTS

1 oz. Goldschläger cinnamon schnapps
1 oz. Baileys Irish cream liqueur

INSTRUCTIONS

Pour the cinnamon schnapps into a shot glass. Using a bar spoon (or long-handled spoon), let the Irish cream run down the back of the spoon to form a layer atop the schnapps.

Chapter 1

WHAT the hell? Andi Radcliffe bolted upright in bed as a clanging noise shattered the night. A fire alarm? Was this for real or the usual false alarm?

Wait a minute. She wasn't at home in her Vancouver apartment where they got a false alarm every couple of months. On this January night, she was in a cozy guest room at the Alpine Hideaway in Whistler.

And she, as the wedding planner, was responsible for the bride and groom and fifty guests. She scrambled out of bed, thrust her feet into Chinese silk slip-ons, and grabbed the filmy thigh-skimming robe that matched her sheer, slip-style nightie. Holding the robe to her chest, she rushed over to yank open the door. When she stuck her head out, the hallway was flameless, deserted. She blew out a sigh of relief and turned back toward the duvet-covered bed.

But, wait. From the ground floor below came the sound of shouts.

And when she breathed in again, the air had a hint of smoke that bit at the back of her nose and throat.

She gasped, and her eyes widened. Fire!

Down the hall, a door opened, and Maddie, the groom's mid-twenties younger sister, emerged, pulling a fluffy pink robe over flannel pj's. "Is this really a fire?"

"Yes! Smell the smoke." Heart racing, instinct told Andi to flee. But she couldn't leave. She'd organized this event and booked the chalet. She was responsible, and she had to make sure everyone was safe.

Galvanized into action, Andi rushed across the hall, shrugging into her robe, then pounded on the door yelling, "Fire!" From there, she ran down the hall, rapping on doors and shouting in a noisy duet with the alarm. As guests emerged, she cried, "Hurry! Down the stairs, don't use the elevator. Get outside right away!"

She should have listened to Shelley. The bride had suggested a ritzy hotel in Whistler's Upper Village, but Andi had said a picturesque alpine chalet would create the warm, intimate atmosphere the wedding couple wanted. When she'd said *warm*, fire definitely wasn't what she'd had in mind.

Above her head, she heard footsteps thudding on the floor, reminding her there were two floors above her. The bride and groom, as well as both sets of parents, were on the top floor.

Heading for the stairwell, she passed Maddie—now wearing red gumboots below her pink robe—helping a pair of elderly guests. The girl grabbed her arm, eyes wide with worry. "Have you seen my family?"

"I'm going up now. I'll make sure they're okay."

"Thanks. Hey, you need warmer clothes."

"There's no time." Lives were at stake. Forcing herself to breathe through her panic, Andi hurried up the stairs, shoving her way through guests who were rushing down. A motley group, they were shrugging into bathrobes and jackets, zipping jeans, all asking each other what was going on.

Fortunately, the bride and groom and both sets of parents, the occupants of the luxury suites on the fourth floor, were among them.

The groom's dad caught her arm. "Andi, have you seen Maddie?"

"She's on her way downstairs."

Andi darted out the door to the third floor. Relieved to still see no flames or smoke, she ran along the hall, hurrying stragglers. She banged on closed doors, keeping up a duet with the alarm as she yelled, "Fire! Everyone out!"

As she reached the end of the hall, a siren whooped outside, competing with the jangle of the alarm. Thank God! She sprinted for the stairs.

The stairwell was empty, and so was the second floor when she poked her head out to check. Or, at least, it was empty of people. Tendrils of smoke floated like ghostly dancers, beautiful but terrifying, searing the back of her throat and making her cough.

With the bitter taste in her mouth, she fled down to the first floor. The smoke was thick here, pouring in a black cloud from one open-doored room and—oh, God—flames licked out the doorframe, crackling as they consumed the wood and advanced across the ceiling.

A few minutes longer, and they'd engulf the hall and cut off her escape.

Coughing, raising her hand to her nose to try to block the smoke, she raced past the flames toward the front door and flung it open.

Giddy with relief, she ran into the safety of a snowy winter night strobed by the flashing red and blue lights of a fire engine. Huge firefighters in turnout gear carrying axes and hoses rushed toward the front door.

Sucking in fresh air hungrily, she moved away from the chalet. Coughing again to clear her throat of smoke, she looked around for Gord and Inger Jacobs, the middle-aged owners of the Alpine Hideaway, who lived in a wing off the ground floor. Not seeing them, she rushed over to a group of guests who huddled together. "Did everyone get out?"

In reply, she got stunned glances, a few strange looks, shrugs.

Then a muttered, "I think so," from the dazed-looking father of the bride who had his arm tight around his wife.

Someone had to take a head count. And Andi was best equipped, having studied the guest list more than a hundred times in the past months. Besides, she couldn't relax until she knew for sure that everyone was safe.

Wrapping her arms around herself, shivering with cold and tension, she made mental note of all the people in this group, then moved to the next group to do the same. There she saw Inger Jacobs, dressed in boots, sweatpants, and a ski jacket over what looked to be a pajama top. Her pretty face was strained and her graying blonde hair tousled.

"Andi, there you are," the woman said in her lilting Norwegian accent, face brightening. "Thank God. We couldn't find you. But are you not frozen?"

"I'm fine." She'd survived fire. What was a little cold? "Did all the guests get out?"

As she asked the question, a car with flashing lights drove up, with an ambulance right behind. Had someone been hurt, or was this just standard procedure? The two women exchanged anxious glances.

"I hope everyone is out," Inger said, her face again creasing into worry lines. "We didn't think to get the register, so we have nothing to check against." Pale blue eyes wide with dismay, she stared at the chalet.

Andi touched her arm and turned to look, too. Normally the Swiss-style Alpine Hideaway was welcoming and charmingly picturesque with its gables, eaves, and balconies with carved wooden railings. Now, firefighters hurried about purposefully, barking terse comments. A hose, taut from water pressure, ran through a first-floor window. Psychedelic patterns of blue and red from the engine's lights flashed over banks of snow, white-boughed evergreens, and the crystalline fringe of icicles decorating the eaves.

"What could have happened?" Inger asked. "We have the wiring inspected regularly."

"I don't know." Andi's teeth chattered, and snowflakes brushed her face with icy fingers. Regardless, she needed to carry on with her mental head count, so she turned toward another cluster of guests.

Before she'd taken two steps, strong arms hoisted her like a baby.

She gaped upward as a firefighter, his face covered by a helmet and visor, gathered her against his smoky-smelling turnout jacket and stalked off with her like a Neanderthal.

She was so stunned she couldn't react. Then she began to struggle. "Put me down. I have to make sure everyone's safe."

He clutched her tighter. "Lady, there's guys doing that right now, and the fire's under control."

He was a firefighter. She could trust him. It was over, and everything was okay. Relief flooded her as he headed for the fire engine and hoisted her onto a seat.

"What are you doing?" she asked.

"The lieutenant saw you, told me to take care of you."

"I'm f-fine." Just too cold to form words properly.

"You're frozen." He pulled off his helmet, ran a hand through hair dark as night, and shot her a heated gaze from silver gray eyes.

For a moment she forgot her worry and discomfort. That was one good-looking guy, strong-featured and supremely masculine.

"Are you nuts coming out in the snow and ice dressed like that?" His tone was a mix of frustration, disbelief, and . . . yes, arousal as his gaze took a leisurely tour of her body.

Shivers racking her, Andi glanced down. Oops. Her nightwear was definitely more suited to a tropical night than a snowy one. Her silk slippers were thin and soaked through. The skimpy nightie, which she wore over a pair of tiny panties, barely cleared her butt. Both it and the matching thigh-length robe—a deep violet that brought out blue mauve tones in her gray eyes—were made of semi-sheer, clingy fabric trimmed with lace.

Her body was covered in goose bumps, she was shivering like crazy, her feet were so cold she couldn't feel them, and her nipples were as hard as miniature steel cones under the arms she'd wrapped around herself. If her blood hadn't been frozen, she'd have blushed.

But she wasn't going to apologize for putting the guests' safety first and not taking time to change into something warmer. She curled her frozen feet under her almost-bare butt, crossed her arms more tightly over her chest, and forced words out between chattering teeth. "Do you have a guest list? How do you know everyone is out?"

The firefighter, who'd been staring at her as if mesmerized, gave a start. "Leave this to us. It's not the first fire we've responded to." He peeled off his gloves, then his heavy jacket, which he tucked around her like a blanket.

The coat reeked of smoke but held the warmth of his body, and she huddled inside it gratefully. Mmm, this was even better than sinking into a nice hot bath. And the sight of him, strong and muscular in a blue T-shirt, with that midnight hair and gleaming silvery eyes, would warm any girl up.

"Are you okay?" he asked. "Any trouble breathing? Any medical conditions?"

She shook her head. "No. I'm just worried. I'm responsible for all these people. This is my wedding."

The spark of appreciation that had lit his eyes dimmed. "You're the bride? Then where the hell's the groom?" Those handsome, blatantly male features were marred by a scowl. "Why isn't he looking out for you?"

"I'm not the bride; I'm the wedding planner."

"The wedding planner," he repeated, lips beginning to curve, eyes igniting again. Great eyes, fringed with long lashes as thick and black as his wavy hair.

Warmth tingled through her, an effect of his burning gaze and extreme hotness as much as the jacket she clutched around her. Her chilled blood was definitely heating up.

Had she ever reacted so quickly to a man? She was twenty-six, and she'd dated a fair bit. She and her friend Sarah—now her business partner—had always joked that Sarah, a Barbie lover, was looking for the ideal Ken, and Andi wanted a white knight to sweep her off her feet, to woo and win her. Though she hadn't had a serious relationship in a while, Andi knew one day she'd meet that perfect man, a man who'd put her first in his heart. When Sarah had recently married, she'd hurled her bouquet directly into Andi's hands and said, "Your time is *now*, girlfriend."

When it came to perfection, it would be hard to beat the firefighter in front of her. Now he was tucking a blanket around her, so she was doubly cocooned by it and his jacket. She must look ridiculous, yet he was still staring at her as if he wanted to eat her from head to toe, paying special attention to the goodies in the middle.

It wasn't his *heart* speaking, she knew darned well. No, he was motivated by a quite different body part, one she had to admit she was more than a bit curious about. In fact, her corresponding female one felt a tug of sexy response that told her she was well on her way to thawing out.

Normally, she was sensible, responsible. But tonight, she could have died in a fire or frozen in the ice. Tonight, she should have what she wanted. And what she wanted was right in front of her. Chances were, he wasn't her white knight—though he'd done a fine job of swooping her up and rescuing her—but he was very male and very hot.

She lifted her left hand from the shelter of the coat and blanket and wiggled her ringless fingers. "And the wedding planner," she said, glad her teeth were no longer chattering, "happens to be single."

STANDING beside the fire truck, Jared Stone stared at the bundled-up woman on the seat: a damned cute, sexy woman with a highly developed sense of responsibility and amazing taste in nightwear. She'd been so worried about the wedding guests, she'd dashed out into an icy night in only those erotic scraps of thin, lacy fabric.

When the lieutenant had told Jared, "Take care of the woman over there," he'd immediately turned to obey. And he'd seen a sight straight out of a lingerie ad, a sexy one. He was responsible for the woman's safety, so he shouldn't have been noticing the taut nipples almost poking their way through two layers of lace or the shadow of barely-there panties beneath the filmy fabric. But hey, he was a guy.

A fact—in the sexual sense—that he'd almost forgotten in the three years since Beth died. Truth was, attractive women hadn't been on his radar, so it was disconcerting that tonight, when he was on duty, his hormones would suddenly roar to life. He was in a T-shirt in the snow, and all he could see of her now was her head, yet heat pounded through his veins and swelled his cock.

"Single, eh?" he muttered, knowing he shouldn't respond to what was pretty clearly a come-on. But how could he resist? Her smoky eyes were pure, sultry seduction, and he had to curl his fingers into fists to stop from touching her tousled shoulder-length curls, the same rich dark blonde as wild honey. Her scantily clad body might be hidden now, but the memory of her cradled in his arms was etched in his mind. Oh yeah, she was hot.

She made him feel horny and protective, annoyed that she'd risked exposure, yet admiring that she put others' needs ahead of her own. It was a crazy mix of feelings blending together in an over-whelming desire. He wanted her: hard and fast and *now*.

He fisted his hands tighter, and his voice came out gruff. "Want me to go inside and get you some warm clothes? The guests won't be allowed back in until the fire inspector says so."

"No, thanks." Her eyes danced, as if she knew the effect she was having on him. "I'm plenty warm."

Jared stifled a groan. Hot, so very hot. "Then I need to go see what the lieutenant wants me to do next."

Her eyes widened. "Oh my gosh, of course you do. I'm sorry for keeping you."

"Don't be sorry." He was the one who'd crossed the line, staring at her as if he wanted to fuck her.

"You'll need your coat." She thrust aside the blanket then shoved at the heavy jacket.

When he lifted it away from her, he saw another tantalizing flash of creamy curves in purple lace before she wrapped the blanket back around her. "Here, better have another one," he said, though he wanted nothing more than to unwrap her again. He found another emergency blanket and draped it over her. Words came out of his mouth, ill-advised but unstoppable. "I'm single, too. In case you wanted to know."

Her lips, soft and pink, curved. "Mmm, that's useful information."

Adrenaline always raced during a call-out, but the fire at the Alpine Hideaway had been small and easily dealt with. No, it wasn't the fire that was responsible for the crazy energy surging through him. It was the woman.

Whatever she read on his face, it made her eyes widen and her lips part.

Before he did something insane, he forced himself to turn away, shrugging into his jacket, which carried the heat of her body and a faint scent that reminded him of summer flowers.

Gord Jacobs hurried toward them. "Andi," the chalet owner said worriedly, "are you all right? What happened?"

Andi. Now he knew her name.

"Yes, I'm fine. I rushed out without getting properly dressed, but I'm warming up nicely." Her cheeks flushed.

Forcing his gaze away from Andi, Jared greeted the other man. "Hey, Gord." He'd gone to school with the man's son and had a lot of respect for Gord and his wife Inger.

The stocky middle-aged guy, dressed in jeans and a hooded jacket, rested a heavy hand on Jared's shoulder. "This is a hell of a thing. The chief says they've checked every room; everyone's out and healthy except the couple who were in the room where the fire started. They walked out under their own steam, but they did inhale some smoke, so they've been taken to the hospital. Should be all right, though."

"Who was it?" Andi asked.

"A man named Randy Brown and his wife Deena."

"The bride's cousins," she said.

"Randy was talking," the chalet owner went on, "even though the paramedics told him not to. He was blustering, said it couldn't have been his fault. He said he was sure he put out the cigarette."

"He was smoking?" she asked. "We made it completely clear there was no smoking."

"I know. But he did it anyhow, in one of those big overstuffed chairs. He dozed off, then woke up and went to bed. He and his wife woke up a couple hours later with the alarm going off and smoke pouring out of the chair. Guess it had smoldered for a while."

Listening, Jared agreed, though it wasn't his place to state an opinion. That would be up to the fire inspector. Nor was it his place to say what he was thinking: that this Randy guy was an asshole who'd endangered the lives of everyone in the Alpine Hideaway.

"Will we be able to go back in?" Andi asked. "Or do we have to find alternate accommodations for fifty people?"

"No, we're okay," Gord said. "The chief says they put the fire out quickly, and the inspector's going through the place to make sure there's no, uh, fire extension?" He raised his eyebrows in Jared's direction.

"Right," he said. "Need to make sure the building's completely safe."

The chief came over to join them. "Mr. Jacobs," he said, "the inspector's given the all clear. You can go back inside. Your guests can go to their rooms to change if they want, and they need to open up all the windows. Then gather them somewhere, like your lounge, for an hour or two until the rooms are thoroughly aired. The people in the rooms on either side of the fire source won't be able to sleep there, but everyone else should be okay in their rooms."

"I'll go tell Inger," Gord said, "and we'll get everyone organized."

"I'll help," Andi said. "I'll run back inside and change."

"You're not running anywhere in slippers," Jared said.

The chief nodded. "You get her inside safely." Then he walked away, and Gord followed.

"You heard the chief." Jared scooped Andi off the seat and into his arms, blankets and all.

One blanket slid off, and she gasped and grabbed the other before it could fall, too, holding it around her as she snuggled against his chest. He hadn't fastened his jacket, so she was right up against his T-shirt, so close he could feel her warmth.

What a sweet armful. One of his arms wrapped around her shoulders, and the other was under her curvy butt and thighs, his fingers just inches from paradise. Thank God turnout pants were bulky, because he was getting a serious hard-on.

He strode through lightly falling snow as guests also made for the front door. Inside the Alpine Hideaway, he asked, "Where's your room?"

"Second floor." Her head was tucked under his chin, her breath a seductive kiss against his neck. "I could walk now." The teasing lilt in her voice suggested she didn't want to any more than he wanted to put her down.

He started up the stairs with her firmly clutched to his chest. She got to him, the way no woman had in three years. But damn, he was on duty.

When she directed him, he carried her into an attractive, homey room with a queen-sized bed, the covers rumpled invitingly. Reluctantly, he let her down, and she stood in front of him, hanging on to the blanket so it concealed her body.

"You need to put on some warm clothes, Andi, then open the window." Fortunately, the smell of smoke wasn't unbearably strong here.

Her eyes searched his face. "You'll need the blanket back." She could have gathered clothing and headed for the bathroom, but she didn't move.

"Yeah," he said roughly. He should have turned his back to let her change, but his legs wouldn't budge. Instead, he just stared into her eyes, knowing there was no way he could conceal his hunger. The snowflakes that had landed on his face must be sizzling with the heat he was giving off.

Her lips parted, quivered. She stepped past him and closed the door. Then she thrust the blanket away from herself and held it out. And there she was, creamy skin and slender curves clad only in lace-trimmed scraps of seduction.

Something caught the back of his throat, and he couldn't breathe. His cock surged against the confines of his underwear.

Her body trembled. From cold? Nervousness? Or lust, like him?

He took the blanket from her outstretched hand, and their fingers brushed. Heat arced between them. His cock pulsed again.

She gave a little gasp.

His entire body ached with the need to touch her, and it took every ounce of willpower to restrain himself. If he hadn't been on duty, she'd have been in his arms.

"I want . . . " she started. "I've never . . . Oh, damn it!" With one quick step, she closed the distance between them and flung herself at him.

He dropped the blanket, caught her as her arms came around his waist under his jacket, and then his arms were around her shoulders, pulling her close.

She went up on her toes, full breasts pressing against his chest. He smelled her sweet, summery scent, felt the heat of her breath, and then her lips were on his.

The fire in the room downstairs had probably smoldered a couple hours before finally bursting into flame. This kiss was the opposite. It went from spark to ignition in a second flat.

Her tongue was in his mouth, and no way could he stop himself from chasing it back and mating with it. He thrust a hand through her hair, finding it as silky as it looked. Their lips pressed, sucked, nipped greedily. He tasted smoke, knew she'd be tasting the same. Not usually the sexiest flavor, but it was smoke that had brought them together.

And where there's smoke . . .

Heat raced through Jared's veins, speeded his pulse, thickened his cock. The woman in his arms fueled the fire with each wet, hungry kiss, each erotic moan. Burning, he managed to shrug out of his jacket.

She slid out of her skimpy robe and his hands caressed her bare skin. He stroked her shoulders and her upper back. He felt soft skin, a band of lace, and delicate fabric as his hands moved downward.

Silk slid over the twin curves of her butt, rising high as she stretched up. He cupped her firm cheeks, clad only in a scrap of barely-there fabric.

She was so lush, so female. He hadn't held a woman, touched a woman, in well over a year, and she felt incredible.

She made a noise that sounded like a cat—no, a tiger—purring.

Then, because she got to him in a way he hadn't believed possible, he slid one hand down between her legs.

The crotch of her panties was soaked.

He wanted in there so bad. His cock stood rigid against his belly, so hard he ached with the need to find release.

From the way Andi squirmed against his hand, she felt the same.

He wrenched down the thin strip of fabric, stroked her slick folds, then slid a finger inside her.

Chapter 2

ANDI moaned with pleasure. Oh, he felt good!

She'd never been the kind of woman who hopped into bed with a guy on the first date. She liked romance and foreplay. A man had to woo her before he got into her panties.

Now she'd thrown herself into the well-muscled arms of a stranger, and her panties were gone. As she ground down on the firefighter's finger, her body tingling and pulsing on the edge of orgasm, all she knew was pleasure and need. "More," she begged.

"Oh, yeah." Another finger stretched her, going deep, pumping in and out in a seductive rhythm.

Out of her mind with lust, she rode his fingers, throwing her head back.

His thumb found her clit and pressed lightly.

The delicious heat gathered, built, and she gasped for air, pushing against him.

He circled, rubbed gently, reading her signals. So good, that achy, on-the-edge feeling. So intense. She wanted, needed to come.

He nuzzled her neck, and soft beard stubble caressed her sensitive skin. "Come for me, Andi." And then he nipped her earlobe lightly.

The climax crashed through her in surging waves of pleasure and release that made her cry out.

It was wonderful, but it wasn't enough. She wanted this man inside her. His firefighter pants were heavy and bulky, but they hadn't totally camouflaged his massive erection.

She shoved down his suspenders, hands brushing the cotton of his shirt and feeling the hard muscles beneath, and reached for the waist of his pants.

His hands were already there.

A knock sounded on her door, and Inger Jacobs's voice called, "Andi? Are you all right?"

Oh, shit! She froze. Panting for breath, she gaped up at her companion.

He stared down at her, strong features rigid with tension. "Fuck," he muttered softly but vehemently.

"I'm fine, Inger," she called, voice rough as she stared back at the firefighter, seeing her own frustration and confusion mirrored in his face.

"Then do you think you could help us get people organized?" the chalet owner said through the door.

"Of course. I'll be out in a moment." What had she been thinking? She'd totally forgotten about the guests, about her own responsibilities. All she'd wanted—and still wanted—was to get her rocks off with the hot guy in front of her.

The firefighter groaned and yanked his suspenders back up. "I'm on duty. I don't know what got into me."

"Me, too. This was insane." He was so out of place, so ruggedly masculine, in this cozy, charming room. His yellow turnout pants were garish, his broad chest stretched his navy tee, his bare forearms . . . Mmm, they made her fingers itch with the need to touch. And then there was the bulging erection that even the heavy pants couldn't completely hide. Talk about itchy fingers.

"I've never done anything like this before," he said gruffly.

Though she didn't know him at all, she sensed he wasn't the kind of man who screwed around on the job, any more than she was the kind of woman who ignored her duty. "Nor have I."

A sparkle lit his silver gray eyes. "There's something to be said for insanity."

She had to grin. "Oh, yeah." He was so temptingly firm-bodied, she wanted to step back into his arms. Instead, she forced herself to take a step away. "This is so embarrassing. People will see you leave my room."

His lips, so sensual and kissable, quirked. "It's not like we were in here very long."

Her cheeks burned. Yeah, he'd given her an orgasm in under five minutes. That was a first. And she knew it had very little to do with the fact that she hadn't had a man-induced orgasm in a really, really long time, and a whole lot to do with the man in front of her. If he was that good with his fingers, she could just imagine how his cock would feel embedded inside her. She stifled a whimper and forced herself to say, "I have to get dressed, and you have to go."

"Yeah." He picked up his jacket. "If anyone asks, say I needed to make sure your breathing was okay."

She chuckled. "As in, hot and heavy?"

"You're not the only one." He studied her for a long moment, then he said firmly, "This isn't finished."

It should be. But the pulsing heat in her body said it wasn't.

"Tomorrow," he said.

"Tomorrow . . . " Could she? This whole . . . *thing* was crazy, fueled by danger. Fire and ice, an irresistible combination. She craved more of this man. "I, uh . . . "

"I'll come over before I go on shift again at six."

"Here? You can't come here." At this chalet, she was supposed to be all work, responsible for the wedding guests, not to mention a diva bride who liked to be the center of attention.

"You're right. Uh . . . " Again, he stared into her eyes. "My place?"

No invitation for dinner or even coffee. But what had she expected, when she hurled herself into his arms? They had unfinished business, sexy business. "I want to, but . . . " Outside the door, the sound of footsteps and people chatting reminded her again of her job. "I have to go. Let me call you."

He nodded and wrote down two phone numbers, home and cell. Then he shrugged into his jacket. "Tomorrow, Andi." He strode toward the door, all masculine and powerful.

And she realized something. "Wait!"

He turned.

"What's your name?"

He laughed softly. "Jared. Jared Stone."

And then he was gone, closing the door firmly behind him.

"Wow," she murmured. That had been explosive and crazy, and the most fun she'd had in a very long time. As she hurried over to the dresser to find clothes, the door opened, and he came back in, closing it behind him.

She glanced around. "Forget something?"

"Yeah." He strode over. "This." He bent to press a quick, searing kiss across her lips.

Oh, my. She barely had a chance to react before he was gone again. Her body tingled from head to toe. But right now wasn't the time to relish that feeling. Tomorrow. She could see him—*do* him—tomorrow.

Hurriedly, she shed her nightwear and dressed in jeans, a cotton turtleneck, and a sweater, then flung open the window to air her room. She stepped into the hallway and went hunting for Inger Jacobs, determined to act like an efficient wedding planner rather than a woman who'd just had her world rocked by a sexy firefighter.

She found the co-owner of the Alpine Hideaway at the end of the hall, talking to some guests. "Gord's lit a fire"—the woman said, wincing slightly—"in the lounge so we can be cozy. Sigrid's making hot chocolate and snacks." Sigrid, Inger's niece, worked at the chalet. "Can you help round everyone up?"

"Of course. Have you seen Shelley and Tom?" The bride and groom were her top priority.

"They went upstairs."

"I'll start on the fourth floor, then."

As Andi took the stairs, she shivered, remembering racing up and down them earlier, terrified by the fire. Halfway up, she met Shelley and Tom on their way down.

The groom, a good-looking guy, lean and fit in jeans and a navy sweater, looked at Andi with concern. "Are you all right? We saw that firefighter carry you in."

"I'm fine."

Shelley, sleek in a turquoise après-ski outfit that complemented her golden hair and tanned skin, smiled. "I'm glad, Andi." Then her brows drew together. "So, what was all that drama with the firefighter?"

Drama. A word that was more typically applied to Shelley. The American, only twenty and a gold-medal skier from the 2010 Olympic Games, was definitely a princess and didn't like sharing the limelight.

"No drama," Andi assured her, trying not to flush. "When the fire alarm went off, I was so worried about everyone's safety that I didn't stop to pull on heavier clothes or boots."

Shelley winked. "Well, if you had to be rescued by a firefighter, you did pick a hot one."

Tom gave a good-natured huff.

His fiancée hugged his arm. "Come on, babe. Let's go get some sex on the slopes."

Mmm, that sounded good. Especially with Jared Stone. They'd melt the snow. Andi held back a grin.

In fact, Sex on the Slopes was the Alpine Hideaway's specialty drink, a yummy blend of chocolate, coffee, and Kahlua, topped with whipped cream and shaved chocolate.

As Shelley and Tom headed downstairs, Andi continued on up to make sure all the guests were obeying the fire inspector's instructions. As she chatted to guests and reassured them, Jared was never far from her thoughts. What a change—a pleasant one—it had been to for once be the one being rescued. Usually, it was the other way around.

Her family called her Rescue Girl. As a child, she'd brought home a constant stream of wounded birds and animals, not to mention kids who the others at school teased and bullied. As an adult, she was still the one who took care of others. Mostly, people were appreciative; sometimes she got taken for granted; and occasionally she'd been burned. Only once had the burn been third-degree, though. She'd dated a traumatized divorced guy and fallen hard for his aura of tragedy. She'd thought he might be the one for her and believed she was the woman who could heal him. And she had, well enough that he'd fallen in love—with someone else. Andi had been heartbroken.

Lesson learned. In order to truly fall in love, both parties needed to start out heart-whole.

Finished checking all the rooms, she went downstairs to find the guests settled into the couches and chairs grouped around the huge stone fireplace. She helped hand out hot drinks then claimed a mug of Sex on the Slopes and sat down with a group of guests.

The fire'd had a side benefit. Everyone had shared a scary, exciting experience and survived, and now relatives and friends of the bride and groom who hadn't met before this weekend were bonding.

Except for Logan Carver, an old friend of the groom's and a last-minute addition to the wedding party. Dark and sexy, he had a bad-boy vibe some women found fascinating. He'd annoyed her by blowing off the welcome dinner, and he'd only returned to the chalet after the fire. Now he sat apart. Disdainful? Or . . . Hmm. Studying him now as he watched Maddie, her brother Tom, and the vibrant Shelley, she got a sense of loneliness, the same way she had with the schoolkids she used to befriend, the ones who stood on the outside looking in, pretending they didn't care yet secretly yearning to be welcomed.

Her Rescue Girl instincts stirred, and she began to rise to go talk to him.

He must have felt her gaze, because he glanced her way. If there'd been vulnerability on his face, it was gone now. His expression was hard and chill as granite.

Okay, scratch the loneliness thing. The man was tough, and he was letting her know it.

When she'd finished her drink, she checked her watch, then went to confer with Inger. Together, they slipped out to see whether the rooms were well enough aired.

When they returned to the lounge, Maddie had joined Logan, sitting on the arm of his chair, so close she was almost in his lap. And her brother Tom was glaring at the pair. Interesting. He might be friends with Logan, but he sure didn't want the man messing with his little sister.

Andi stepped in front of the fireplace and called out, "Okay, folks. Inger and I have checked your rooms." As conversation died down, she lowered her voice. "They're aired out, and you can go back to bed, but leave your windows open a crack."

Yawning and stretching, people rose. A few guests had volunteered to take in friends or relatives whose rooms had been badly smoke-damaged, so everyone had a bed for what remained of the night.

Andi said her good nights, then went into her own room. Leaving the window open a crack, she snuggled into bed, this time wearing sweats rather than lacy nightwear, and settled her laptop on her lap. Normally, she'd e-mail her partner Sarah, but Sarah was off on her honeymoon. The Happily Ever After office was in the hands of Gwen, the assistant they'd recently hired.

A few years older than Andi and Sarah, Gwen used to be a conference planner but had been out of the work force for a couple of years, looking after her very ill husband until he died. She said she'd been with her husband so long and so intensively, she'd kind of forgotten who she was, and now she was keen to find out. Andi and Sarah had both taken to her immediately. She didn't wallow in her loss—which, while being totally understandable, would have been a really depressing quality in a wedding planner—she just dove into life.

Andi started an e-mail to her, first reporting on the fire and how well everyone was coping.

> So, everyone's sleeping in and going to take it easy today, which was more or less what I'd planned for the first day anyhow. No major plan adjustments, thank heavens.

Then she turned to the fascinating subject of Jared Stone. First she told her friend how they'd met and that they'd shared a scorching kiss. She didn't yet know Gwen well enough to confess the orgasm.

> The chemistry, wow! Spontaneous combustion!!! But it might have been fueled by circumstances. Danger and skimpy lingerie. LOL.
>
> I'm so tempted to see him again. But I'm here to work, not play, and Shelley'd be pissed off if she thought she wasn't my top priority 24/7.
>
> It's so crazy, though. I don't know him; he doesn't know me. He probably thinks I'm a total slut! Which, actually, tonight I was <g>.
>
> And on that note, I'm going to bed. You don't have to actually reply to this crap. I'm just used to venting/ processing with Sarah, and what with her off honeymooning, sorry, you're getting it!

Chapter 3

THIS time the sound that brought Andi out of sleep with a start was only the familiar peal of her alarm clock. She tossed aside the duvet, stretched, and went over to the window.

Leaning her forehead against the chilly pane, she gazed out. Sunshine sparkled off a fresh fall of snow that had covered all traces left by the fire vehicles. Gord Jacobs, whistling, was shoveling the path from the road to the door of the chalet. A squirrel scurried along the branch of a snow-covered tree, discharging a shower of what looked like fairy dust in the glinting morning light, and Andi smiled.

What was she going to do about Jared? If last night had been fire-and-ice-fueled insanity, then her excuse was gone, because now it was the bright light of day. Yet that didn't diminish her desire to see him.

She hurried through her morning routine then turned on her laptop and checked e-mail. Gwen had responded.

Not reply? Give me a break, how could I not reply to that???

First, that's awful about the fire. I'm so glad everyone's okay. And that Bridezilla wasn't a total bitch about it!

As for the firefighter . . . Whew!! You're reminding me that I used to know what sex was like, and it was pretty wonderful. I say go for it. I bet he'll let you play with his hose—and I'm guessing he has a BIG one! LOL. (Being a slut isn't necessarily a BAD thing!)

Andi spluttered with laughter. Oh yeah, from what she'd felt, Jared did have a lot to offer in the hose department. She toyed with the slip of paper where he had written his phone numbers.

What was the downside? She'd make sure seeing him didn't interfere with work, and she'd keep Shelley from finding out. Maybe it'd just be a quickie, a chance to discover whether the sex could possibly be as fiery as she imagined.

On the other hand, maybe Sarah had been right when she tossed that bridal bouquet and told Andi her time was now. A girl could always dream.

JARED put the handset of his home phone back in the stand. Good thing he'd been optimistic enough to buy condoms this morning. Andi was coming over. For sex.

At least, he hoped that was what she had in mind. It wasn't as if they knew each other, and she'd been the one to come on to him. Likely, they had nothing in common except mutual sexual attraction.

And he sure as hell did feel horny. He'd had a cold shower, he'd jerked off, and still all he could think of was Andi. Those barely concealed curves, her summer flower scent, the gleam of her golden curls, the way she'd gasped as he slid his finger inside her and her wet heat engulfed him. Oh yeah, she was what his body craved.

His body. This was purely physical. But they hadn't actually clarified that or discussed expectations. He'd have to talk to her as soon as she arrived to make sure she didn't want more from him than he could give. The truth was, his heart belonged to Beth.

Shit, was he doing the right thing? In the three years since his wife died, he'd only slept with two other women, once each, and both times had been disasters. Oh, he'd completed the act, even brought his partners satisfaction, but he'd felt like crap, more lonely than ever and as guilty as if he'd cheated on his wife. But it had been more than a year now, and the chemistry between him and Andi was amazing.

He made a quick check of the kitchen and living room, making sure everything was neat and tidy. Photos of Beth sat everywhere. She belonged in this room.

She'd cluttered the place up with her books and magazines, her latest quilting project, cast-off scarves. The house had felt warm and lived-in. Kind of old-fashioned.

But then, he was an old-fashioned guy at heart: a skier rather than a boarder, the kind of man who paid off his mortgage, the kind who believed you married once and it lasted for life.

Their marriage would have, too.

Gently he tucked the pictures into a drawer, feeling guilt bite into him. Never before had he brought a lover to this house. The two times before, he'd met tourists in bars and gone to their hotel rooms. Andi had been right that the Alpine Hideaway wouldn't work, not with his friends the Jacobses there, and the guests Andi felt so responsible for.

He walked down the hall, closing the door to the room he hadn't touched in two years and went into the bedroom. He tucked the wedding photo on the dresser into a drawer and picked up the picture that sat on the bedside table. This was one he'd taken on their honeymoon in Hawaii, and Beth—who was a quarter Chinese—looked almost Hawaiian herself. A strip of colorful fabric wrapped around her gracefully, leaving her tanned shoulders bare. She'd tucked a flower in her long, shiny black hair.

For a moment she'd seemed exotic, almost a stranger, then she'd grinned her big Beth grin, the one he'd captured in this photo, and she was the girl he'd known and loved all his life. The only woman he could imagine ever loving.

He touched his wife's cheek through glass, feeling the ever-present ache in his heart. "Sweetheart, this isn't about you. You know that. You're my love. You'll always be my love."

They'd been young when her car was totaled by a drunk driver. Only twenty-seven. They'd never imagined dying, never talked about what would happen if one of them went first. He knew her, though. She'd have said he should get on with his life.

And he had. When he wasn't on shift as a firefighter, he did home renovations, went skiing, had dinner with his parents, hung out with the guys. He knew she'd say he should start dating again, but he couldn't. Even his two quickies had felt like a betrayal.

Would this time be different?

He slid Beth's picture into the drawer and went to the bathroom, where he opened the condom box. He stuffed one in the pocket of his jeans and tossed a couple on the bedside table where his wife's picture usually sat. Could he really do this? Did he want to?

Frowning, he headed for the front of the house and glanced out the window. Andi was right on time, climbing out of a CRV. Casual in jeans and a blue and purple jacket, she glanced around and then walked up the path he'd shoveled.

When she climbed the steps, he opened the door. Sunshine turned her hair to a rich, summery gold. When she gazed up at him, her eyes, gray flecked with purply blue sparkles, dazzled him. Despite the nippy air, arousal warmed his blood.

"Nice house," she said softly. "It's not what I expected."

"Thanks. I've done some work on it." All he and Beth had been able to afford was a fixer-upper, but now it was a home to be proud of. It was a home he'd created for her, even after she was dead.

Shit. Arousal and guilt didn't mix well. He should have booked a hotel room. "Come in," he said gruffly. If they were going to do this, he had to make sure they were on the same page. Hell, she was a wedding planner. Maybe she saw every relationship in terms of its hearts and flowers potential. Though, last night, she'd been hot for him without even knowing his name. "I need to talk to you."

Her gaze met his for a long moment, then one corner of her mouth kinked. She walked through the doorway and past him into the entrance hall. "A man who wants to talk? Last night you struck me as more a man of action."

He closed the door, the paned window splitting the sunlight into separate shafts. "Yeah, well. It's just . . . You need to know, uh . . . "

"Let me guess," she said evenly. "I think I know how this talk goes. You don't want me to think this is more than it is?"

"Yeah. Right."

"More than . . . ?" She tilted her head, eyes smoky and enigmatic.

"More than right now. Today." This close to her, even though she was clad in warm winter clothing rather than scraps of silk, he again found himself falling under her spell. His body tightened with need as he remembered how hot they'd been in her room, and he remembered why he'd invited her here. Why—hopefully—she'd come. "Sex." That one syllable came out husky with need.

Her eyes sparked. "Last night we started it, and today we finish. Casual sex."

She was so pretty, glowing in the warm light that poured through the window in the door. Her scent, like sunshine on summer flowers, was intoxicating. *She* was intoxicating, and now he was more confident. He nodded. "Great sex."

Her lips twitched. "Is that a promise?"

"You got any doubts?" He put one finger under her chin, drew a line down her neck to the collar of her jacket, and took hold of the zipper tab.

Color tinged her cheeks. "No, can't say I do." Her pink lips remained parted, as if she was anticipating a kiss.

He gave it to her, because he couldn't survive any longer without doing it. At the same time, he tugged down her zipper.

She met his kiss with matching hunger.

If he'd had any thoughts that the sparks between them last night had been fueled by the fire, any worries that she wasn't sure she wanted this, they vanished in that moment.

Fiercely, he took her mouth, needing to own it. Her lips were full and firm, and her tongue invaded his mouth in turn, thrusting and parrying with his. She bit his lip—maybe intentionally, maybe not—and he tasted blood. In a moment, they were back where they'd been last night, passion exploding fiercely between them.

As they kissed, they tugged at each other's clothing. Her jacket hit the floor. Under it, she wore a turtleneck sweater. He cursed, drew away from her, yanked it over her head, then yanked off his own hoodie as well.

As he got back to kissing her, her hands were at the fly of his jeans, unbuttoning, then unzipping. She shoved his jeans and boxer briefs partway down, enough to free his erection. He hadn't even realized how achingly hard he was until his cock sprang free into her hands.

She gripped it, and he groaned with pleasure at the touch of her fingers, still slightly chilled from being outside, on his sensitive flesh.

He managed to free himself of his jeans and, naked now, reached for the back of her bra, needing to see and to feel her breasts. Her hands, exploring his shaft, stroking urgently from base to crown, shot tingles of pleasure straight down to his balls. Damn, he wanted to be in her.

He fumbled urgently with the bra clasp and finally got it unhooked.

She moaned against his mouth as her bra loosened, then she struggled out of it.

He stared, transfixed by the sight of her in the sun—firm, creamy breasts, tipped by pale brown areolas and rosy budded nipples. Before he could touch them, she'd pressed herself hard against his chest.

He wanted all of her, those rosy nipples between his lips, her steamy pussy hugging his cock, the brush of her silky hair against his skin. Every single bit of her, right this instant. He couldn't wait much longer, or he'd explode in her deft hands.

"Shit, Andi, you're so hot," he panted.

"I want you," she moaned, eyes dark and glazed with passion. "Now, Jared."

Somehow, between them, they got her jeans off, and he retrieved the condom he'd stuffed in his pocket. A moment later he was sheathed, lifting her.

She grabbed his shoulders, her legs hooked around him, and her heels pressed into his ass. "Now," she demanded.

He backed against the wall, bracing himself. Balancing her weight with one arm under her butt, he reached between their bodies, found her moist heat, and they both moaned.

Adjusting position, he gripped his swollen shaft, nudged the head between her slick labia, and then—hell, yes—he slid into her in one hard, deep thrust that made her gasp. His fingers had traveled this path before, but this was ten times better. A hundred times better.

She was soothing dampness, burning heat, incredible pressure and friction around his aching cock. His chest constricted so he could barely breathe. When she grabbed his head in both hands, pulled it down, and kissed him, he couldn't answer back. Then he gasped for breath, and his hips pumped compulsively, driving both of them toward their primal goal. Their bodies slapped wetly together, and her heels thudded against the wall behind him.

Andi tore her mouth from his, moaned, and squeezed her eyes shut, a look of intense focus on her face. Panting, she muttered, "Oh, yes. Yes. So good."

She was beautiful, face flushed and dewed with sweat, riding out their mutual passion. Sex in the entrance hall wasn't what he'd expected when she walked through his door, but man, was it incredible.

She tossed her head back, tendrils of sunlit hair dancing across her cheeks and neck. Her body arched; spasms rose inside her. Gripping his cock, she milked him, insisting that he come along with her.

Pressure built at the base of his spine, tightened his balls. He pulled out almost all the way and felt her opening quiver around his crown.

And then he let go, and with a wrenching cry he plunged deep, pouring himself into her as she convulsed around him. Sensation ripped through his body, straight to the top of his head. His orgasm was so deep, so intense, his knees almost gave out. If it hadn't been for the support of the wall behind him, he'd have collapsed to the floor, taking her with him.

Gradually, her body went limp and heavy in his arms, shuddering as she gasped for breath.

Her back was arched, and he gazed at her breasts, the pale skin mottled with a rosy flush, her nipples deeper pink and beaded. The sight gave him new energy. In fact, he could feel his cock, so recently satisfied, swell again inside her.

As his breath came back, as his arousal grew, so did the strength in his legs.

When Andi finally lifted her head, looked him in the eye, and murmured, "Oh, my," he said, "It ain't over yet. Not by far." He shoved away from the wall and, with her clinging to him, headed for the bedroom.

Then reality hit, and he stopped in his tracks. It wasn't safe to keep a condom on and have sex again. He would never run the risk of making a woman pregnant. "Damned condoms." He pulled out of Andi and lowered her to the floor, then stalked toward the hallway half bath.

Chapter 4

MOUTH open, Andi stared after the man who'd dumped her unceremoniously out of his arms. Then she shook her head in rueful amusement. No, Jared Stone was certainly not a white knight.

Though he did have a knight's strong body. Muscles rippled in his shoulders and his firm butt flexed with each step. She wished he'd turn around so she could see the front view.

She knew he'd gone to dispose of the condom and would soon be back. All the same, abandoned stark naked in his hall, she felt self-conscious. What was she supposed to do now? Normally, she had sex in a bed with a man she knew after a relaxed evening of conversation over dinner and a bottle of wine. And after the lovemaking, she'd curl up in his arms all soft and mellow, and they'd hold each other, share the intimate secrets of lovers.

Yeah, right. Jared had said all he wanted was sex.

How could he be so sure, when he barely knew her? When they were totally hot together?

The door opened, and he came out, still naked. "Sorry. Should have shown you the bedroom."

"Mmm." What had he said? All her attention was on the view. The man was solid muscle, in all the right places. Rippling muscle, as he walked toward her. Dark hair was scattered across his chest, arrowing down, down. Her gaze followed, to the thick curls at his groin.

His cock was swelling, beginning to lift.

Her sex clutched in response. She wanted to run her fingers over those rippling muscles, through those dark curls, to take his cock between her lips.

But that wasn't all. She wanted to get to know him. He'd said all he wanted was casual—great—sex, and if that was all it turned out to be, then so be it. On the other hand, why not be open to possibilities? Maybe Sarah'd been right when she aimed that bridal bouquet at Andi.

She realized Jared was staring at her not only with hunger but a kind of wonder, almost as if he'd never seen a woman before.

"You're beautiful, Andi. Beautiful and sexy." He tugged her into his embrace, and then they were kissing, and the passion flared again. He hoisted her into his arms and strode down the hall and through a door.

His bedroom wasn't the typical bare-bones bachelor one. It had a cozy, almost old-world feel that made her wonder if a woman had helped him decorate it. His mom or a sister? An ex? A woman who'd meant more to him than just casual sex?

He put her down on the side of the bed and leaned forward to tug the duvet down.

How many women had he brought here? A man as virile as Jared couldn't survive long without sex. Self-conscious again, she slid between the sheets, holding the top one across her chest.

One corner of his mouth quirked. "The woman who went outside in her underwear is shy?" He didn't seem the least bit self-conscious about standing by the bed naked, with a rising erection.

"It wasn't my underwear. It was a nightie *and* a robe."

He grinned. "I like your taste in sleepwear, though it's not very warm."

That grin relaxed her enough to tease him. "What do you wear? Flannel pajamas?"

He chuckled. "Too confining."

"Hmm. So now I know two—no, three—things about you. You're a firefighter, you don't like to be confined—in pajamas or a relationship, and you have a lovely house."

"Not four? No comment on my sexual prowess?"

She gave him a mischievous look. "One hand job and one quickie orgasm? That's not much to base an opinion on."

He laughed, then flicked the sheet off her and sat down on the bed, nudging her over with his hip. "Then I'll just have to give you more."

She pulled the sheet back up to cover herself. "It does seem like the only way I'm going to be able to form a fair opinion."

He dove under the sheet, and next thing she knew, he'd grabbed one of her feet. "Just checking that you thawed out," he said, voice muffled by the sheet.

Fingers tickled her sole, making her squirm and giggle. "Is this part of a firefighter's job description? Follow up the next day to make sure there's no frostbite?"

"Only in special cases."

Was she special? If so, wouldn't he want more than casual sex?

She knew so little about this man, and it was starting to drive her nuts. Well, she was a big girl; if she wanted something, she should go after it. Just as she had last night, when she kissed him.

She started with an easy question. "You like being a firefighter?"

"Yup." He caressed her leg and planted a moist kiss behind her knee.

"Did you always want to be one?"

"Yup." More kisses trailed up the inside of her leg, the pace slowing as he neared the top, each one becoming more sensual, more lingering. Each resonated in pulses of arousal between her legs. She'd not only thawed, she was going to start steaming if he kept this up.

She was less thrilled with his answers to her questions. This time, she'd ask one that required more than a yes or no answer. "Why?"

He groaned, yanked down the sheet, and looked up at her. "D'you always ask a bunch of questions when you're having sex?"

"No, I usually ask them over the lovely dinner the man buys me *before* we have sex."

He snorted. "So you're a closet romantic."

"I'm not a *closet* romantic, I'm a blatant one. This thing with you is the exception."

He sighed, then slid up the bed to lie beside her, both on their sides so they faced each other. She put her leg over his, and he bumped her belly with his cock. "Why're you making an exception, Andi?"

How about that? A real question.

It was one she had no good answer to. "Because of the way we met? Because you're hot, and I can't resist you?" Because it had been too long since she'd had sex or even met a guy she wanted to sleep with?

She gazed into his silvery eyes and saw genuine curiosity, maybe concern. "And perhaps," she admitted, "because my best friend got married last month." And she promised Andi would be next. "And you're—" She couldn't tell the truth, that she wanted to find out if Jared might be her special guy. "You're my consolation prize."

One corner of his mouth kinked. "Not sure if that's a compliment or an insult."

"Me, either." Then she gave him a wry grin. "But hey, you get sex out of it."

"True."

She expected a jab about how he wished she would be content with sex and not demand conversation, but he was quiet.

After a moment, he said, "I take it you want to get married?" He stroked her hip, following the curve. Down then up, then down again, circling a little. It was partly arousing, partly soothing. There was a strange intimacy to the way they were lying together—a greater intimacy in some ways than when they'd had sex.

"Yes, I do. When I find the love of my life. I'm a wedding planner. Of course I believe in marriage."

His hand stilled, and his words surprised her. "Yeah, me, too." Then he said, "But I'm not that guy, Andi. I can't be."

Well. That certainly told her where she stood. She couldn't help but feel disappointed and hurt. What the hell was wrong with her? Or maybe it wasn't her; perhaps he was a confirmed bachelor who only believed in marriage for other people.

Now what? She took a breath and reflected. If he'd never be more than a consolation prize, at least he was an exceptionally sexy one. Gazing at him, stunning in his nudity, there was no way she wanted to leave this bed. She thought about Gwen's comment that being a slut wasn't necessarily a bad thing.

"Okay, you've made yourself clear," she said. "I think it's time for my consolation prize to start earning his keep."

A slow grin curved his lips and lit his eyes. "You got it, Andi." And then he slid down the bed.

A romantic would have given her a long, lingering kiss. On the lips. Jared instead went for her breast.

Not that she was inclined to object. She shivered with delicious sensation as he cupped and molded it in his large hand, caressed it gently with his fingers, then ran his tongue lightly around the areola. Her breath quickened, and her body tightened and heated.

JARED gazed at the beautiful female flesh in front of his eyes. The way Andi's areola puckered and her nipple beaded under the touch of his tongue was amazing. Oh yeah, this was good. Very good.

Being with a woman—this woman—felt great.

He was glad they'd gotten things straight and that she still wanted to be here. For one disconcerting moment, he'd almost wanted to tell her about Beth. But Beth was . . . private. He didn't want pity. Nor some woman trying to replace his wife. No complications.

Breasts, now, they were uncomplicated. Beautiful, responsive. He turned his attention to Andi's other one, sucking her sweet nipple into his mouth and teasing it with his tongue. His cock, pressed between his belly and her thigh, hardened.

Her back arched and she murmured, "Oh, yes." Her hands fisted in his hair, pressing him tighter, and her pelvis twisted demandingly.

He slid a hand down her soft belly, brushed through a patch of tight curls, and found the damp heat between her legs.

She moaned with satisfaction as he slid his finger back and forth, caressing her, then opening her and sliding inside. He stroked in and out, and her muscles contracted around him with gentle suction.

He needed to taste her, so he eased down the bed and climbed off the end. Then he gripped her ankles and tugged her down the bed as she giggled in surprise.

Kneeling on the floor, he lifted her lower body, hooking her legs over his shoulders. What a great view. An intimate one of her lush pussy framed by creamy thighs, and beyond it a whole landscape of beautiful woman: sleek tummy, the lift of her rib cage and swell of her breasts, then her flushed face framed by tousled hair.

He pulled her up so his face was between her legs.

"Jared, I—" She stopped abruptly when he licked along the same path his finger had taken. A shudder rippled through her. "Oh yes, that's good. More."

Hell, yeah.

Hands gripping her hips, he held her exactly where he wanted her. In this position, she couldn't touch him, could barely move. He was in control—of her pleasure.

His cock throbbed, urging him to seek release between her soft thighs, inside the pink folds slick with moisture. He ignored its demand, wanting to focus on her.

Flattening his tongue, he pressed firmly as he stroked back and forth, laving her swollen folds, teasing the slit between them. He read her response in the honey that seeped from her body, the ohs and whimpers she let out.

He slid his tongue inside her to caress her inner flesh, thrusting it in and out as he'd done earlier with his fingers, and her body trembled.

Slowly he eased out and found her clit, engorged and sliding boldly from its hood. He circled it with his tongue and flicked it softly.

"Oh God, yes," she panted.

Gently he suckled the firm bud, alternating swirls of his tongue, a rhythmic suck-and-release pressure from his lips.

"So good . . . I can't stand it."

He released her clit, swiped long strokes against her labia, then returned to her clit. And this time, when he sucked her, she came apart with a cry of release.

His own body clenched in response, aching with need. With light touches of his tongue, he kept her there, spasming and moaning, until finally she twisted away, gasping, "Enough. I can't."

Carefully, he eased her legs down one by one so they bent over the bottom of the bed, with him still kneeling between them, painfully hard.

Neither he nor Andi moved or spoke for several long moments; then she pushed herself up to a sitting position. "That was amazing." Looking dazed, she shook her head. "Like, wow."

He rose to his feet, and her gaze sharpened, focusing on his rigid cock where it thrust up his belly, only inches from her face. "Now, there's a tempting sight."

"You know the best thing to do with temptation?" he asked.

She shot him a mischievous grin. "Give in to it." Then she reached out to grasp his shaft. With one hand she held him at the base as if she was worried he'd move away.

Not in this lifetime.

With the other she stroked upward, sliding her fingertips over his skin gently but with enough pressure to be wickedly arousing. She formed a circle with her thumb and forefinger, gripping under the crown, and when she gave a tiny tug, his cock jumped in her hand.

He fought the impulse to thrust, waiting to see what she'd do next.

A soft fingertip circled his crown, making him throb with sensation. She captured a couple drops of pre-come and spread them, circling faster, intensifying the sensation. His breath rasped, but he managed to say, "Oh yeah, Andi, that's good."

A sparkling glance slanted up at him. "If that's good, then how about this?"

She leaned forward to lick the same path her finger had been following, and then she opened her lips and took him inside the sweet, wet heat of her mouth.

Holy shit, that felt fucking amazing. If he'd been able to find words, he'd have told her so, but all he could manage was an inarticulate groan. He gripped her smooth shoulders with both hands and locked his knees so he didn't collapse in a heap at her feet.

She seemed to get the message, because she sucked him in, her tongue and mouth pulsing around him in alternating waves of pressure and release. Her hand worked his shaft, sliding up and down, moving faster and faster as he grew slick from her saliva.

If she was trying to drive him crazy, bring him to climax, she was doing a fine job of it.

Gazing down, he saw the top of her head, the tumble of honey-colored curls as she moved back and forth on him. He watched the base of his shaft appear then disappear again each time she moved forward. So sexy, the sight of her combined with the feel of that skilled mouth on his sensitive flesh.

He tensed his muscles, fighting the rising need to climax. Gently, he tugged on a curl of hair. "Stop now," he gasped.

When she didn't obey, he squeezed his eyes shut and gritted his teeth. It would be so easy to let go, to explode in her mouth. But hell, that wasn't the way he wanted this to go. He wanted to be inside her, buried deep, the two of them moving together and bringing each other to orgasm.

So he gripped her head in both hands and forced himself to step back.

She gazed up, her lips slick, pink, a little swollen. "It's okay, Jared. It's your turn."

Those lips, her offer . . . How could a guy resist? But there was something he wanted even more. He shook his head. "It's *our* turn."

He tugged her up so she was standing in front of him, then he leaned down and, because those lips were irresistible, kissed her. When his tongue dipped inside her mouth, she tasted different than before, muskier. He was tasting himself. His hips thrust, lodging his cock firmly against her belly.

She broke the kiss, giving him a questioning glance. "You're still obsessing about impressing me with your sexual prowess?"

He took a couple of deep breaths, bringing his body under control. "Nah, I—" He what? Wanted them to merge together? That would sound almost romantic and give her the wrong idea. He tried for a casual shrug. "If I'm your consolation prize, you should get some decent sex."

Her lips twitched. "Guess I can't object to that. Okay, Mr. Stone, bring it on. Give me some decent sex." The lip twitch turned into a teasing grin.

What could he do but smile back? "Never said I had much of a way with words." Action was his forte, so he'd show this woman some action she couldn't complain about.

His body might want nothing better than to drive to a quick, hard orgasm, but he'd damned well be patient if it killed him.

Killed him with pleasure, that was, he thought as he wrapped his arms around Andi and tumbled them both onto the bed with him on the bottom.

She rose on her elbows, and he captured her mouth for another quick kiss, then he put his hands on her shoulders and gently pushed her away from him. "Sit up, Andi, and let me see you."

She took a condom from the bedside table. "Can I sit anywhere I want?" she asked flirtatiously. Without waiting for an answer— after all, what man would say no?—she unwrapped the condom and sheathed him.

Then, taking her sweet time about it, she lowered herself onto him, inch by inch, enveloping his swollen, aching flesh in the only place in the world that was sweeter than her mouth.

She was deliciously tight, but the dampness of her arousal eased his way, and the soft moans she gave were definitely pleasure, not pain.

The heated grip of her pussy, those earthy moans, and the scent of her overwhelmed Jared's senses. It took all his willpower to lock his muscles and not thrust, to let her do this her way.

Her full breasts bounced gently, and he reached up to cup them, to stroke her petal-soft skin, to delight in the way her areolas and nipples puckered and budded under his caress.

She whimpered and moved restlessly, arching her back and tossing her hair, her pelvis rocking against him. Then she lifted, easing slowly up his shaft, almost to the top, and came down again, still slow and easy, like she was getting to know the feel of him.

He tweaked her nipples and she made an *mmm* sound and her pace picked up a little.

His hips wanted to lift, to thrust hard, but he forced himself to lie still as she took her sweet time torturing him with the gentle, seductive friction of flesh sliding against flesh. Each soft rub sent arousal throbbing through him, and when her breathing quickened and her chest flushed, he couldn't hold back any longer. He began to pump, slowly and steadily, rising to meet her each time she came down. "You feel great, Andi."

"You . . . too." Her mouth was open, the words coming out between pants for breath. Her eyes squeezed shut in concentration, and each time she came down, her hips gave a little grind, pressing their bodies together.

He ground back, thrust harder, stopped fighting the growing spiral of orgasm, and let the pressure build again.

Her head tossed. "Oh . . . oh, yes."

He released one breast and dropped his hand to where their bodies joined, slid through the slick curls of her hair, and found her swollen clit.

Gently he rubbed it while, with his other hand, he tweaked her nipple.

She cried out again, so wonderfully responsive. Her internal muscles clenched and held for a long moment.

The instant she released again, he surged into her, letting everything inside himself loose. One hard thrust, another.

"Jared!" She broke in rhythmic surges around him, and he poured himself deep inside her, groaning with relief and pleasure.

His chest heaved as he gasped for air. His eyes were shut, and behind his lids he saw hot, fiery colors. Firm, warm female legs gripped his hips. He hadn't felt this good in a very long time.

Andi's weight shifted, and she lowered herself to lie atop him.

He opened his eyes lazily. "That was—" He broke off, surprised to find her staring into his face with an unreadable expression.

"Decent sex?" She said the words lightly, but there was something odd in her voice.

"Great sex. At least for me. You're a wonderful lover."

Her brows drew together. "Gee, thanks. You're pretty good yourself." She pulled herself off him and lay down on her back beside him.

Chapter 5

BY the time Jared had dealt with the condom, Andi had pulled the sheet up to her shoulders. Her arms were crossed over her chest, above the sheet, anchoring it. Shutting him out, it seemed to him.

"Andi? What's wrong?"

"Nothing." She stared at the ceiling and didn't even dart a glance in his direction. "Everything's fine."

Body language didn't lie. He could just say, "Great," because her issues weren't his responsibility. But that didn't feel right. "It's not fine. What's wrong? I thought you were okay with, uh, casual sex."

"Mmm." Gaze still fixed on the ceiling, she said, "I guess you do this all the time. Hook up with tourists."

Suppressing a sigh, he slipped under the sheet, too, and lay on his side, wondering if he should touch her. "No, I don't."

"Just when it falls into your lap, like it did with me."

He squeezed his eyes shut then opened them again. She was still staring at him. "Guess it fell into both of our laps," he said. "Neither of us was looking, but it happened." A thought struck him, and he tried out a smile, reaching out to coil a curl of her hair around his finger. "Kind of like that fire. Unexpected and, uh, fiery."

Her jaw tightened. "Gee, and you said you didn't have a way with words."

He grimaced and released the curl. "Guess I don't have much experience with this kind of conversation."

She sighed. "I'm sorry. I don't mean to be a bitch. I get it that this is casual, and that's fine. The sex is great. But I guess I need something to make it personal so it's Andi and Jared, not just two anonymous bodies."

Slowly, he nodded. "Yeah, okay. It is." Andi Radcliffe could never be just an anonymous body.

She gave a rueful chuckle. "Thanks, oh ye of few words."

"No, I mean . . . I know who I'm with. Who I want to be with. You're the wedding planner. The one with such an overdeveloped sense of responsibility she'll run out in the snow in her nightie. Her very sexy nightie, that's the same purple as her eyes."

Her lips curved. "My eyes aren't purple, they're gray blue. But when I wear purple, it makes them look like they're mauve."

A difference only a woman would care about, but he wouldn't say that. "You're the woman who smells like sunshine on flowers, the not-so-closet romantic who deserves more than a consolation prize."

"Oh, Jared. Thank you."

For a long moment, they gazed into each other's eyes, not speaking, and he felt an unusual sense of peace. This conversation might be a little awkward, but he didn't feel empty inside, the way he had with those other two women. There was something about Andi that kind of seeped into his lonely spaces.

He felt a twinge of guilt, as if he'd been disloyal to Beth, and he looked away from Andi. Here he was, in the bed he'd shared with his wife, not only having sex with another woman but feeling . . . connected to her.

The silence was broken when the grandfather clock in the hall—a decrepit one he and Beth had picked up at a garage sale and he'd gotten working—chimed four o'clock.

"I need to go," Andi said. "People will be gathering for drinks, then we're all going for dinner." She slid from the bed and headed for the en suite bathroom.

The door closed, and he heard the shower go on. Clearly, he wasn't invited. And that was fine. He was feeling unsettled, and it would be good to be alone in the house, just him and his memories of Beth, before he headed out for tonight's shift.

Jared retrieved their clothes from the front hall and pulled his own on. A few minutes later, the bathroom door opened, and Andi emerged, pink-cheeked, wrapped enticingly in a towel. "I need to get my—"

He handed her the armful of clothing and her purse, and she disappeared back into the bathroom.

The next time she emerged, she was fully dressed, still flushed, and biting her lip. "Well, Jared, it's been, uh, a nice afternoon."

"Yeah, really nice." Andi was complicated, and so was the way she made him feel. But it was good, and not just because of the sex. "Let's get together again. Tomorrow?"

She nibbled her freshly lipsticked lip some more. "Oh, Jared . . . I wish . . . But I'm not here on holiday. I have to organize activities for fifty people. This afternoon was different, because the guests were doing their own thing, so I wasn't really needed."

Seemed to him she was babbling. Nervous, or had she decided to give him the brush-off? He opened his mouth to ask, but she was carrying on.

"Tomorrow there will be ski lessons and other things going on, and details to firm up with Shelley and Tom—that's the bride and groom—and Inger and Gord, so—"

He held up a hand to stop the flow of words. "You trying to say you don't want to see me again? If so, just spit it out." After all, it wasn't like they were emotionally involved.

"I, uh . . . " She raised her own hands and rubbed them over her face. "This really was fun, but I am going to be awfully busy."

Well, shit. She really didn't want to see him again.

That thought settled for a moment, like a lump of lead in his gut.

What could he say to change her mind? And why was it so important that he do so?

He was pondering that when the phone rang. "Hang on a sec," he told her. "Don't go."

He scooped up the phone, and to his surprise heard Gord Jacobs's voice. "Gord? What's up?"

Andi's eyes widened and she made a panicky *Don't tell him I'm here* gesture.

Nodding to her, he listened as the older man said, "Seeing you last night got Inger and me to thinking how long it's been. You should come over for drinks and dinner." For some reason, Gord sounded kind of awkward.

"Sounds good."

"Tonight?"

After a day of dealing with smoke damage and a chalet full of wedding guests? Weird timing. "I'm on shift."

"Darn it, that's too bad." Gord must have half covered the phone with his hand to talk to someone else, because Jared heard him mutter, "He's working."

A moment later, a female voice with a Nordic lilt said, "Jared?"

"Hi, Inger."

"I hear you're working tonight, so here's what we'll do. You come by tomorrow morning after your shift ends. There'll be a big buffet breakfast. It's been too long, and I feel bad that we've been neglecting one of our son's best friends."

The thought crossed his mind that she might be trying to match-make him with her niece Sigrid. When Beth had died, his friends had fed him and tried to cheer him up. He'd appreciated the company, just as long as people let him find his way back into the world at his own pace. Recently, he'd been getting some pressure to start dating again. Hell, didn't folks realize no woman could replace Beth?

"Young man, I'm not taking no for an answer. I'll see you for breakfast just as soon as your shift ends tomorrow."

A thought struck him. If he did go to the Alpine Hideaway for breakfast, he'd see Andi. He didn't have to push things now; he'd get another chance.

"Okay, Inger, that's a deal. Thanks."

He hung up the phone and turned to Andi. Should he tell her or let her be surprised?

"Gord and Inger?" she asked. "What was that about?"

"Just saying it'd be good to get together." No, he'd keep it a secret and see how she reacted when she saw him in the morning. Besides, by then he might have had second thoughts.

He put an arm around her shoulder and steered her toward the front door. "I know you need to go, so I don't want to keep you."

At the door, she stared up at him for a long moment. "Okay, I guess I'll head off."

"Drive safe." He dropped a quick kiss on her full lips and resisted the urge to linger, then opened the door. "See you round."

THE next morning as she dressed for breakfast, Andi was still upset over Jared's behavior yesterday. He'd asked to see her again, then when she'd waffled—unsure whether it was a wise idea—he'd dropped the idea so quickly it was insulting.

He'd said he believed in love and marriage—yet he'd made it clear he'd never be the man for her.

What was so wrong with her? He didn't want to know her better; he didn't even seem to give a damn about having more sex with her. Despite the incredible sex, she was beginning to regret that she'd ever hooked up with him in the first place.

A brisk knock sounded on her door. "Andi?"

The voice was Shelley's. Most brides were excited, nervous, and demanding, but this one defined the term *high maintenance*. She wasn't a total Bridezilla, but she was definitely a princess.

"I'll be right there." Andi pulled on a camel-colored cardigan and went to unlock the door. "Good morning. What can I do for you?"

The girl breezed into the room, tossing her blonde ponytail. She was slim and sleek in black ski pants and a pink top with a sponsor logo on it. "I couldn't sleep a wink. I was going to come talk to you earlier, but Tom said not to wake you up."

Bless his heart. Though in fact Andi had probably been awake herself, fussing about Jared. "What's the problem, Shelley?"

"The flowers are all wrong. Didn't you hear Brianna last night, talking about that enviro-wedding she covered on *The Scoop*? We shouldn't be having hothouse flowers, just seasonal local stuff."

Thirty-something Brianna George was the creator and host of *The Scoop*, a soft journalism TV show based in Vancouver. The show had started out local and expanded nationwide. Tom, Shelley's fiancé, worked for her. Brianna and Tom had become friends, and she was the only person from *The Scoop* who'd been invited to the pre-wedding week. Andi wished she'd kept her thoughts about weddings to herself.

Still, after months of working with Shelley, Andi'd had a lot of practice controlling the urge to roll her eyes or throttle the bride. Instead she said, "What a lovely idea. But, hmm, since it's the middle of winter and the ground's covered with snow, that would mean no flowers at all. Just stuff like pine boughs. Wouldn't that feel more like Christmas than a wedding?"

"Hmm." Shelley's eyes narrowed.

"Besides, think about the ivory and rose color scheme. Everything's coordinated, the dresses, flowers, wedding cake. If you re-thought the flowers—"

"We'd have to rethink everything." Shelley waved a hand. "But we could do that. This is Monday, and the wedding's not until Saturday."

No, Andi would absolutely not grind her teeth. "We could do it if you were willing to settle for an off-the-rack dress and—"

As she'd expected, a gasp interrupted her. Shelley's tanned face went pale, and she sank onto a chair. "Off the rack? No way!"

"You're right. This is your special day, and you deserve the best of everything. Including flowers. Everything's going to look so lovely in the wedding photos."

"It is, isn't it?" Now Shelley's eyes were dreamy.

"And remember what Brianna said. They're going to have you

and Tom on *The Scoop*. This is a big deal, an Olympic gold medalist wedding one of Brianna's most valued team members. They'll include wedding photos, and you don't want anything to look less than perfect."

Nor did Andi, because it would be fabulous promo for Happily Ever After.

"No, of course not." Shelley rose and gave Andi a quick hug. "Thanks. You're the best. Now, let's go get breakfast."

Whew. The first crisis of the day had been averted. Knowing Shelley, it wouldn't be the last. It wasn't that Shelley meant to be difficult; she was just young, self-centered, and spontaneous. On the plus side, she was warm, generous, and appreciative.

Andi walked downstairs with her and paused in the doorway to the chalet dining room as Shelley went to join Tom.

Sunshine brightened the spacious room, and a dozen guests were already there, lining up for the buffet or munching and chatting. The mingled scents of coffee, bacon, sausage, and baked goods made Andi sniff hungrily. Yesterday's breakfast had been hit or miss, with everyone tired after the fire and guests straggling in over the course of several hours. Today, the Alpine Hideaway was back to normal. The fire and smoke damage in the hall had been repaired, and the culprits who'd started the fire were back safe and sound, though Shelley'd had a few sharp words with them.

Andi was about to head for the coffeepot when, across the hall behind her, the front door opened, and a drift of brisk, wintery air made her shiver. She glanced over her shoulder, then swung around. "Jared!"

He looked as fresh and appealing as the crisp, sunny morning, and the mere sight of him raised her temperature—and her hopes. He'd decided to pursue her after all. But he shouldn't be here. "What are you doing here?" she demanded in a whisper. She didn't want the wedding group—and especially the bride—knowing she'd taken time out from her duties to have hot sex with a near stranger, much less that just looking at him made her long for a second round.

Inger bustled from the kitchen wearing an apron. "Jared, dear,

I'm so glad you could make it. It's good to see you in so much happier circumstances than the other night." She gave him a hug and stretched up to peck his cheek.

Andi's eyes widened. *Ooh!* He hadn't come to see her after all.

Arm still around him, Inger turned to Andi. "Andi Radcliffe, Jared Stone. I know you've met, but I'm not sure you've been introduced. Jared, the woman you rescued the other night is the wedding planner who's organizing the week's festivities."

Eyes glinting with humor, he stuck out a hand. "Pleased to officially meet you, Ms. Radcliffe."

At least he was keeping her secret. She took his hand and shook it in a businesslike fashion, trying to ignore the sexy rush that tingled through her at his touch. So what if that hand had explored her body in the most intimate of ways? So what if those gray eyes had gone silver with passion? So what if she'd had his cock in her mouth? None of those things would happen again.

"Mr. Stone," she said coolly.

"Come now, no need for formalities," Inger said. "It's Jared and Andi."

"What's *Jared* doing here?" Andi asked with a polite but totally fake smile.

"I invited him for breakfast."

So that's what the pair of them had arranged on the phone yesterday, and Jared hadn't bothered to mention it? Could it be any more obvious that he didn't want to see her again?

"Oh," she said with fake sweetness, "is it firefighter appreciation morning?" Not that she was going to spend another single moment appreciating anything about the man's strong body in his jeans, gray cotton turtleneck, and down vest.

He choked back a laugh, and Inger gave a trilling one of her own. "No, no, Jared's an old friend. Gord and I realized how long it had been since we'd seen him, so we asked him to drop over for breakfast."

"For breakfast?" Shelley spoke from behind Andi and stepped up to join them. "With my family and friends?"

Andi shot Inger a warning look. The entire chalet had been booked for the wedding party. "He's a family friend of our hosts, Shelley. I'm sure he'll be eating with them."

Then she said, "Jared Stone, meet Shelley Williams, the lovely bride. Not to mention the gold medalist in the downhill at last winter's Olympics." Shelley did like having her ego stroked.

"Pleased to meet you," he said with a charming smile. "I saw that race, and you were terrific. Sorry to intrude on the pre-wedding festivities. I'll stay out of your hair."

Shelley tilted her head. "I know you. You're the firefighter." She shot a piercing glance at Andi. "You're *her* firefighter."

At her sides, Andi clenched her hands and then forced herself to relax them. "He's the one who kept me from getting frostbite. What a coincidence that he's an old friend of Inger and Gord's. But I guess Whistler's a small town in a lot of ways, isn't it?"

"Sure is." Jared's voice joined with Inger's.

"Shelley, hon," the groom called. "I dished out eggs for you like you asked, and they're getting cold."

"Be right there." She cast another quizzical look between Jared and Andi, then went back into the dining room.

"And I have muffins in the oven," Inger said. "Jared, I guess you and Gord and I had best eat in the kitchen with Sigrid and the staff. You come along when you're hungry. And Andi, would you mind coming in to talk to me about the menu for the rehearsal dinner?" She bustled away.

Hadn't they already settled the menu a month ago and confirmed it on Saturday? Oh well, there was nothing wrong with an excess of caution. But she'd talk to Inger *after* Jared had gone. She glanced at him. "You should go eat."

"Sorry I didn't tell you yesterday." He kept his voice low. "You'd gone all businesslike, saying you were too busy to see me again."

"It's not like you were overly anxious to get together again," she reminded him.

IIis brows drew together in a puzzled expression. "Hey, I asked. You blew me off. What was I supposed to do? Beg?"

Oh. So that was how he'd viewed it. And of course he wasn't the kind of man who'd need to beg for a woman's company.

"I do want to see you again, Andi," he said softly. "That's why I accepted Inger's invitation."

"Really?"

He nodded. "Yesterday was great. Best time I've had in a long time. I thought about you all night."

He'd thought about her. Her, not some anonymous sex partner. He'd had the best time with her. The words, the gleam in his eyes, his sheer masculine presence softened her. Her body heated and swayed toward him.

She pulled herself back, remembering she was in the hall at the Alpine Hideaway.

Maybe he hadn't really meant it when he'd sounded so adamant about not being the man for her. Would he be pressing to see her again if he didn't think they might have something special? "I want to see you again, too," she admitted. "But I really am tied up during the days and through dinner, and you're on night shift, so how can—"

"Nope, last night was the last for a while. I've got some days off, then I'm on day shift with evenings free." He reached out and caught her hand. "See, I'm flexible." His wink gave the word a double meaning.

She couldn't help but grin. "You are, are you?" The sexy wink, the heat of his hand, and the vision of their bodies twined together made her flush.

"Try me out," he said seductively.

A whimper of need threatened to escape, but she forced it back. "I have to go." She tried to tug her hand free, but he held on to it.

"Say you'll see me again." His gaze was intent, compelling. Irresistible.

"Yes, I'll call you when I get a chance. But Jared, don't tell anyone. Shelley thinks my attention should be focused on her, one hundred percent."

He nodded and let her go, then headed toward the kitchen.

She turned to go back to the dining room.

And there was Brianna George, the TV host, leaning in the doorway. She was elegant as always, in figure-hugging pants, a patterned sweater that could only be cashmere, and a matching vest and boots trimmed with faux fur. A Native Canadian, she wore her black hair short, gorgeously styled, and highlighted with amber streaks that gleamed in the light. Her expression was speculative. "Andi, is that your boyfriend?"

"No!" she said, maybe too vehemently. Had the other woman overheard their conversation? Surely not; they'd kept their voices low. But she might well have seen their linked hands. She shrugged casually. "He's the firefighter who helped me the other night. Turns out he's a friend of the Jacobses, and they invited him for breakfast. He was just asking how I was, and I was thanking him again."

"I see." But her brown eyes remained curious.

"Well, I'm dying for a cup of coffee and some breakfast." Andi headed into the dining room, and Brianna came with her. To change the subject, she asked, "Are you coming for ski lessons this morning, Brianna?" Andi had arranged group lessons for the guests, with instructors lined up to teach beginners and intermediate skiers, and help the pros further hone their skills.

The other woman wrinkled her nose. "I think I'll pass. I've never understood the point of skiing."

Point? Did every activity need a point? "How about fun, exercise, the great outdoors, exhilaration?" Andi wasn't a particularly skilled skier, but she did enjoy the excitement of swooping down a snowy slope at high speed, sort of in control but not entirely, always vulnerable to an unseen bump, a patch of ice, a lapse in concentration that could send her tumbling.

Hmm. She'd never taken that approach to her dating life, but the description kind of applied to her relationship with Jared.

Chapter 6

AFTER breakfast, Andi went in search of Inger, as the woman had requested her to do. Inger and Sigrid were bustling around the kitchen, and there was no sign of Gord or Jared. "You wanted to talk about the menu for the rehearsal dinner?" Andi said.

Inger put down a towel. "Let me get it."

Together they sat and went over it one more time, without making the tiniest change. Inger really was being conscientious.

When Andi stood to leave, Inger caught her arm. "Have a cup of coffee with me. Jared's down in the basement with Gord, and he should be back any minute."

Aha. Was this a matchmaking attempt? How funny was that? Tongue in cheek, Andi said, "That's all right. I don't need to see Jared."

"He's a good man," Inger said. "I've known him since he was a boy. He and his wife went through school with my son."

Wife? She'd slept with a married man? Oh, shit. "Jared's married?" The words came out tight and choked. He'd told her he was single, the bastard.

"Was." Inger shook her head sadly. "Beth was killed by a drunk driver, let me see, it was three or four years ago now. She was pregnant, too. A real tragedy."

Stunned, all Andi could do was stare at her, her lips forming a silent *Oh*. How terrible.

"He's had a hard time. They were so in love; he was devastated."

Andi managed to nod. No wonder he'd said he believed in love and marriage. "The poor man."

"It's time he started dating again," Inger said.

Sigrid, passing by with a jug of milk, laughed softly. "You've been saying that since I came here two years ago, Aunt Inger. I don't think Jared agrees."

"He hasn't been dating at all?" Andi asked.

The two women, a generation apart, shook their heads in identical motions. "If he was, he'd tell me," Inger said. "Just to keep me from matchmaking."

"If he was," Sigrid added, "everyone would know. Believe me, if you go out in public with someone, the grapevine starts working." She carried the milk over to the counter.

Heavy footsteps sounded on the stairs leading up from the basement, accompanied by male voices. "I need to go get the guests organized for skiing," Andi said and fled toward the kitchen door. She couldn't face Jared now. She needed time to digest the news about his wife.

It sounded as if he'd married his childhood sweetheart, then lost both her and their unborn child. Her heart went out to him. Now, things made sense, from the homey house with its female touches to his bald statement that he wanted nothing more than sex from her.

He hadn't even been dating. Maybe just, occasionally, hooking up with a woman to meet his sexual needs.

Well, he'd done that with her last night, but it had been more than just a hookup. He'd said it was the best time he'd had in a long time. He'd thought about her all night and wanted to see her again.

It had been three years since his wife died. Might he be ready to move on? She had to see him again and find out.

*   *   *

AS Andi had feared, her duties kept her busy all day Monday. By ten thirty Tuesday night, she was itching to see Jared. Not only did she want more of that mind-stunning sex, but the man's tragic past tugged at her heartstrings. She wanted to know him better, to find out how he was doing and how he saw his future.

She and a group of guests had returned to the Alpine Hideaway after dinner in Whistler Village. Most of the rest of the younger crowd had stayed in the Village with Shelley and Tom, enjoying the nightclub scene.

To the dozen or so people lazing about the chalet's lounge, Andi said, "Good night. Enjoy the rest of the evening, everyone."

She hurried to her room to collect a jacket, then downstairs, where she slipped silently down the hall and out the front door. As she went down the steps toward the parking lot, headlights flashed once from a far corner. When she'd called Jared to tell him she could get away, he'd insisted on picking her up, saying she shouldn't drive at night when she didn't have experience with snowy roads.

Used to being the one in charge, it was odd but rather nice to have someone act protective.

She hurried over and hopped into a silver 4x4.

The ceiling light didn't come on. He'd paid attention when she said she didn't want anyone to see her meeting him. Perhaps he didn't either, given what Sigrid had said about the local grapevine.

He stared at her for a long moment, his face partly in shadow, lit only by the dull gleam from a streetlight. He looked a little mysterious and very male, very sexy, but . . . she really didn't know this man at all. He'd been a husband and had lost a wife and unborn child.

Then he smiled, and his face softened. "Andi, you look even better than I remembered."

This was the man she'd been dreaming of during every sleeping and waking hour. "You, too." She slid closer, needing to touch him, to kiss him.

His arms closed firmly around her, their lips met hungrily, and she gave herself up to the demanding heat of his mouth, the warm strength of his body beneath a light wool turtleneck.

The kiss grew into something fierce and fiery that made her heart race and robbed her of breath. Finally she had to pull away to gasp for air. "Wow." No man had ever kissed her that way, like he wanted to devour her.

"Yeah." He looked breathless himself, almost startled, and his hair was disheveled from where she'd dragged her hands through it.

When he didn't seem inclined to move, she said, "We should go somewhere."

"Right." He shook his head as if to clear it. Then he flashed her a grin. "Though at the moment, the idea of parking sounds pretty good to me."

"In the snow?" She chuckled. "I don't think so."

"I'd keep you warm."

That was for sure. She was tempted, but before she had sex with him again, she really wanted to know more about his wife. He hadn't mentioned his marriage. Would it be rude of her to ask?

"Hey, don't look so worried," he said, turning the key in the ignition. "I was joking. I have something more comfortable in mind."

As they left the parking lot, a car approaching on the road flicked its headlights from high to low beam, then pulled into the driveway they'd just left.

It was a taxi, and under the light from a streetlamp she saw Brianna George alone in the backseat. Her head was tilted down, so hopefully she hadn't seen them. Brianna hadn't joined the group for dinner, saying she had work to do. No doubt she'd been researching a story; the woman was a workaholic.

They didn't pass any other vehicles as Jared drove down the snow-dusted road of the White Gold subdivision. "How are things going with the pre-wedding stuff?" he asked. "Sounds like you have a lot of activities happening."

She nodded. "Destination weddings are a challenge. The bride and groom have the naively romantic idea that it'll be fun to gather their friends and family together for a week. It's inevitable that not everyone gets along. But the destination is usually someplace wonderful, with lots to see and do."

"So you keep people too busy to fight?"

"Pretty much. If people are active and happy, there's not as much chance for tensions to build. Besides, I figure they ought to get the best Whistler experience they possibly can."

"And how about you?" He stopped at a traffic light and reached over to squeeze her leg, high on the inside of her thigh. "Are you getting the best Whistler experience you possibly can?"

Her pussy pulsed, wishing he'd move those couple of extra inches. "It's improving moment by moment." Yet, despite the arousal he awakened in her, she couldn't forget about his sad past.

She moistened lips that suddenly felt dry and rested her hand on his shoulder. "Jared, Inger told me about your wife. I'm so sorry."

His shoulder tensed, then he released his breath, and it relaxed. "Yeah. So'm I." He was quiet for a long moment, and she didn't know whether to offer more sympathy, ask a question, or keep quiet.

Finally he glanced over at her, gray eyes bottomless and unreadable in the dim light. "The other night, you said you wanted to find the love of your life? Beth was mine. I knew it from the day we met, back before we even started school."

"Wow." Imagine that kind of certainty and the security of growing up in love with someone. She'd had strong feelings for the divorced man she'd dated, but never that certainty.

He stared out at the road. "When you find a love like that, you grab on to it." His throat muscles rippled as he swallowed. "And hope you never lose it."

Her hand still rested on his shoulder, and now she squeezed lightly. "I'm so sorry."

He shot her another quick glance. "Beth's a part of me. I'll always love her."

"Of course you will." A love like that should always be honored. But that didn't mean a person couldn't find a second love.

After a few minutes' silence, she said, "Inger said you haven't been dating."

He shook his head. "It would feel like trying to replace Beth, and that's never going to happen."

Never? He intended to stay single, loving only his dead wife, for the rest of his life? That was tragic, and it was just plain wrong. Surely one day he'd come to realize that a person who had loved deeply and truly was capable of loving again. Maybe not in the same way, but in a way that could create a happy, caring relationship. One day he'd realize, but it sounded as if that day was a long way off.

"That's why I needed to be clear with you," he went on, "that this is just . . . you know."

And now he couldn't even say the word? "Sex," she supplied clearly. "Great sex. Sex that isn't anonymous but isn't leading to a relationship."

"Uh, yeah." Another sideways glance. "Is that okay?"

Andi studied the man beside her, from his hard thighs in jeans to the powerful torso clad in slim-fitting black wool, to the strikingly masculine face. Yes, she was disappointed that Jared didn't see any possibility of anything more for the two of them, but at least she knew where she stood. He wasn't her perfect guy, her white knight. But neither were any of the other men she'd been involved with.

"Andi?"

Sex with a good man, purely for mutual pleasure, with no expectations. "Oh yeah, that's just fine."

The heater was on in his truck, and she was plenty warm, so she wriggled out of her jacket. Under it, she wore the designer jeans and semi-dressy mauve blouse she'd worn for dinner.

Cautiously she said, "Have you seen anyone else, since . . . ?"

He shrugged. "Not really. Two times, but it was a long time ago. Didn't work out."

"You dated, and it didn't work out?"

"God, no." He shot her a horrified look. "Didn't date. Just, you know, met someone in a bar, chatted, and, uh, went up to her room."

Jared had invited her to his house. And, she guessed from the direction he was driving, he was taking her there again.

"Did you see them again?"

"No. Just the once."

"So, why me?"

"It's different. Before, the sex was, uh, flat. And after, I'd lie there and feel . . . hollow. Couldn't wait to leave."

"You didn't feel hollow with me?" Even though she'd gone kind of strange on him, getting insecure and wanting to make sure the sex wasn't anonymous.

The corner of his mouth moved. "Hard to feel hollow when you kept me busy talking." Then he gave a quick headshake. "Sorry. I mean . . . I don't know how to describe it. Just, I didn't feel alone."

"I know what you mean." Yes, she'd lain in bed with a lover after sex and felt distanced and lonely. That's what had happened with her last boyfriend. On paper, they'd matched perfectly, she'd liked him, and the sex had been pretty good. But they hadn't had a true connection. She hadn't felt a sense of intimacy.

She felt a connection with Jared, and it seemed as if it went both ways. That was good, so long as she didn't romanticize it. But didn't he realize that he'd taken a big step, from unsatisfying one-night stands to what they shared?

"I know what you and Beth shared was special. Still, don't you think that one day you'll want—"

He cut her off, speaking brusquely. "Can't imagine being with anyone other than Beth."

She felt a twinge of regret and nodded, accepting his feelings. Then she shared her own. "It's lonely though, isn't it? When you're not in a relationship. You miss the simplest things, like holding hands, getting a hug after a bad day."

"Yeah." He said it gruffly.

For a few minutes, they were both quiet, and then he pulled into his driveway. She unbuckled and hopped out.

A few flakes of snow whispered down on her head as she gazed at his house. It was such a *home*, softly blanketed in snow, lights glowing from the front porch and a curtained window. If things had gone the way they were supposed to, there'd be a child, maybe two, inside that home, and a loving wife waiting for Jared.

"Your house looks as beautiful at night as it does during the day," she told him as they went in the front door.

"Thanks." He ushered her into the living room, where he touched a match to a fire he'd already laid in the big stone fireplace.

She glanced around, noting furniture that begged to be sat in and framed photographs of Whistler during all seasons. No pictures of Beth, and there'd been none in the bedroom, at least not on display. They existed, though. She was sure of it. What did it mean that Jared had tucked them away, separating his past and his love for Beth from his . . . whatever this thing was with her?

Trying to relax, she snuggled into the corner of a cinnamon brown couch. The fire began to crackle, and Jared put on music—a sultry, jazzy instrumental. "Nice," she said.

The man himself looked very hot as he moved around the room, his powerful body shown off by old jeans and a light wool turtleneck that was as midnight-black as his hair. His face, framed by his hair and the neck of the sweater, was particularly striking. Her fingers itched to touch him. She'd dated good-looking men, but never one with such pure and unaffected masculinity. And yet he fit so naturally in this cozy room.

Nervously, she rubbed her hands together. This felt awkward, the two of them here in the house he'd shared with Beth, after that conversation in the car. "It's good to be in out of the cold," she said.

He gave a quick grin. "I can warm you up in a hurry."

"I bet you can."

He chuckled. "That, too. But first, how about a shot of Fire and Ice?"

"That's a drink?" The name reminded her of how they'd met: the fire, her standing in the icy snow, the way Jared had swept her up in his arms and the sparks that had ignited. "Sure." Alcohol should ease the awkwardness.

He left the room, then came back with two shot glasses. Inside was a layered drink, clear on the bottom and creamy on top. "Glad you're here," he said, his voice a little rough as he raised his glass to her.

"Me, too." She touched her glass to his and then lifted it to her lips. The scent of cinnamon drifted into her nostrils, and she noticed, in the firelight, something sparkling in the bottom layer. Aha. Goldschläger cinnamon schnapps. The gold flakes made it popular for weddings.

She sipped, making sure to get a taste from each layer. "Nice." A zip of spicy heat raced through her, but the creamy liqueur mellowed the taste. "Goldschläger and cream liqueur?"

"Uh-huh. Baileys."

Silence fell. She gazed at him as he stared into the fire. Jared wasn't into dating, yet tonight had the trappings of a date. When she'd first hopped into the truck, passion had flared and, if they'd been assured of privacy, they might have had sex right there. Now, she didn't know what was supposed to happen next.

Fortunately, he answered the question by putting his glass down, taking hers and doing the same, and hooking his arm around her shoulders to pull her closer. "Let's try that kiss again, a little slower this time."

Anticipation quickened her pulse as she tilted her face toward his.

But he didn't kiss her right away. Instead, he studied her, appreciation warming his gray eyes. Then, with the rough fingertips of a workingman, he smoothed curls of hair back from her temple. "You're so fresh and natural," he said. "You make me think of . . . sunshine."

Guys had told her she was pretty, even beautiful. Jared's compliment, such an original one, meant even more. "Thank you."

He lowered his head, and his lips touched hers. The sensation was so purely blissful she closed her eyes and gave herself up to the kiss.

In the truck, their lips had been hasty and hungry, but now, as if she and Jared took their cue from the smoky jazz, they kissed more lazily, tasting, savoring, exploring: a lick here, a nibble there, tongues teasing each other, twining, then retreating.

At the same time, arousal twined its way through her body, building slowly and deliciously.

Humming approval in her throat, she settled more comfortably in his embrace. One arm curved around his taut waist, her other hand stroking down his back, enjoying the play of muscles under the thin sweater.

Jared's hand moved down her throat to the open neck of her blouse and fingered her amethyst pendant. "Pretty." He undid another button or two, his fingers brushing her skin, making her quiver.

Her nipples tightened as his hand slipped inside her blouse and brushed across the silky camisole she wore over a lacy bra. Through two layers of filmy fabric, he grazed her nipple, and she moaned against his mouth, wordlessly asking for more.

He brushed back and forth with his palm, more firmly each time, as she grew even more achingly hard. He caught the firm bud between thumb and index finger and squeezed, then he said, "I want to see you, Andi."

"I want to see you, too."

Fumbling a little, he undid the rest of her buttons and slid the blouse off her shoulders, smiling when he saw her revealed in her camisole. "Very nice view," he said, "but I know there's a better one." He tugged up the hem of the camisole, pulling until the garment rose over her head and she was free of it.

"You, too." She reached for the bottom of his sweater.

As the tight neckline pulled over his head, it messed up his hair, but the tousled look suited him, as did the rippling muscles, golden in the light of the fire.

She ran her hands over him, pressing firmly, feeling his strength. She remembered the effortless way he'd lifted her, first when he'd rescued her from the snow and then two days ago at his house. He was so strong, so attractive, so sexy, and she wanted him so badly.

An erection strained against the front of his jeans. Needing him naked, she reached for the button at his waist.

He caught her hand. "Why don't we go someplace more comfortable?"

She glanced toward the fireplace and the gleaming hardwood floor topped with only one thin, braided rug. "In front of the fire? I love the firelight. Do you have a rug, or maybe the duvet?"

He stared toward the fire for a long moment then pushed himself to his feet. "Uh . . . okay. Hang on a minute."

When he left the room, she realized what she'd done. Probably, he and Beth had made love in front of that fire. But then, they'd made love in the bedroom, too. For Jared, there'd be no escaping the memories.

He returned with the duvet from the bed, which he tossed to the floor, and a couple of pillows that went atop it.

A nest. A cozy nest for lovers. She tried to push the thought of Beth aside and hoped he could do the same. "Perfect."

He came over to her and held out his hands to pull her to her feet. She went quickly, pressing her near-naked torso against his firm, bare one in an attempt to erase all memories and doubts. God, the man felt so good.

She'd left her boots at the door and now quickly peeled off her socks and jeans. Clad only in her lacy bra and thong, she sank down on the cushiony, featherlight duvet. There, she struck a sultry pose, weight backward on her hands, back arched so her breasts thrust out, one knee up and bent. "Hey, sexy. Care to join me?"

Oh yeah, he was back in the mood, already yanking off his jeans. In a moment he lowered himself beside her, clad only in black boxer briefs that barely contained his hard-on.

Her mouth watered, and her sex clenched with the need to feel him inside her. "Jared Stone, you're so damned hot." She went up on her knees, wrapped her arms around his neck, then, laughing mischievously, used her weight to topple him backward.

"Andi Radcliffe, you're . . . " He caught her head between both hands and pulled her down for a kiss, and laughter flamed into passion.

She squirmed, rubbing her sensitive breasts against him, grinding her pelvis against his erection, needing to get close, and closer still.

His hands were on her back, stroking, then undoing the clasp of her bra.

She sat up, letting her bra fall free, and before he could reach for her breasts, she lifted herself off him and tugged on the waistband of his underwear. Why was it that firelight made everything even more erotic?

As she peeled the briefs down, his erection sprang free, thrusting enticingly toward her. His briefs were rolled around his thighs, but she abandoned them and bent to wrap her lips around his cock.

"Wait," he said. "Jesus, Andi, give a guy a chance to get undressed." He groaned as she darted her tongue around his shaft, sucked on the head of his cock, fondled his balls. "Oh shit, that feels good."

It did. Taking him in her mouth made her sex ache with the need to be filled up, to feel him plunge in and out. She made hungry, needy sounds as she lapped him. He tasted like man: a little salty, a little musky, totally yummy.

He thrust himself to a sitting position and tugged on her hair, urging her to stop. "Too good, too much."

When she let him go, he yanked his underwear the rest of the way off. "I need to touch you, Andi." He stroked the crotch of her panties, the brush of his fingers against her labia, her clit, tantalizing through the thin barrier of fabric. He gave a growl of satisfaction. "So hot, so ready."

She squirmed against his hand, her dampness, her heat, her uncontrollable movements sending him a silent message. But just to make sure, she said, "Make me come, Jared, I need to come."

He pulled off her panties. "Hell, yeah." Then he was between her legs, his tongue lapping her as if he was starving and she was the only thing that could satisfy his hunger.

Long strokes, short ones, a dip inside, a flick across her clit, each sending tingles of heat pulsing through her. He aroused her the way no other man ever had, but this wasn't the time to pause and wonder why.

Her hips twisted; she pressed against his face and whispered, "So good."

Gently, he sucked her clit, toying with it, two fingers thrusting into her and rubbing her G-spot, creating blissful, intense sensations. Oh, God. Her breath caught. Yes, just like that. Exactly, perfectly like that.

Her body arched and spasmed as a delicious orgasm rushed through her. She hung there, quivering, caught in a daze of sexual pleasure.

He held her, lips gentle against her most sensitive, private flesh, until she could catch her breath. The climax had been great, but she wanted more: more connection—his lips on hers, his hardness sliding deep inside her core. "I want you inside me, Jared. Now."

She lay back on the duvet, panting, while he moved away to sheath himself, then knelt between her thighs, his body strong and beautiful in the flickering light.

Wanting him with every fiber of her being, she spread her legs and opened her arms. "Come here."

He obeyed, thighs brushing the insides of hers, cock painfully hard against her groin, lips soft and tasting of her as he kissed her. As his tongue thrust in to claim her mouth, he reached between their bodies, and she felt the head of his penis brush her clit.

Oh yes, this was good, right, perfect. A fresh thrill of arousal raced through her, then he was slipping between her slick folds, sliding into her channel.

For the past two days, she'd been remembering this, imagining the feel of Jared inside her again, and now, reality was even better. His body fit hers perfectly, as if he'd been designed to give her maximum pleasure.

If the rapid pumping of his hips and the moans of pleasure he gave were any indication, he was enjoying this as much as she.

She closed her eyes, grabbed his firm butt, and hung on for the ride as he drove both of them higher and higher. Inside her, another climax was building, close to exploding, when his buttocks clenched and he let out a hoarse groan.

He plunged deep, hard. Once, twice. And now she was coming with him, crying, "Jared!" as he drove into her one final time.

For long seconds their bodies were locked together, shuddering with pleasure, gasping for air.

Andi opened her eyes to see that his were squeezed shut, his face sleek with sweat, his shoulders heaving. Finally, with what seemed to be a lot of effort, he lifted his weight off her and flopped down beside her. Gray eyes opened and met hers, crinkling at the corners as he smiled. "That was worth the wait."

She laughed softly. "It sure was."

He rose. "Be right back. Want a glass of water?"

"No thanks."

Propping herself up on her arms, she enjoyed the view of his strong back, long legs, and especially the shift of powerful butt muscles as he walked away. Then she summoned enough strength to retrieve her shot glass and take a sip. Cinnamon, gold, and cream; a crackling fire, sultry jazz, a duvet on the floor—it was all pretty darned romantic.

Except, of course, for the fact that Jared wasn't into romance. He'd been there, done that.

She brushed the thought away and told herself to stop thinking and enjoy the moment. The here and now was very, very fine.

Chapter 7

JARED dashed cold water on his flushed face. That had been in-credible, him and Andi.

In front of the fire.

When they'd arrived, he'd felt strange. They'd had that conversation in the truck about Beth, then Andi was in his living room. It wasn't like having friends over for a drink or two, a game of cards, or to watch football on TV. Alcohol had helped; a heated kiss had helped. He'd been totally in the mood. And then she'd wanted to have sex in front of the fire.

It had reminded him of the times he and Beth had done the very same thing.

For a moment, the memories had thrown him. But then he'd focused on Andi again, and the memories were gone. When the two of them got together, it was like a flashover. Heat built and built, then suddenly everything burst into flame, hot and hard.

Now, after an orgasm that had made him see stars, he ought to be able to slow down and explore her sexy body at leisure—and with a little finesse. She deserved finesse.

Not that he'd heard any complaints.

He swallowed a glass of cold water then returned to the living room.

She was sitting in front of the fire, one hand clutching a fold of the duvet up to her chest, a provocative image to go along with that sultry jazz and the languid dance of the fire.

"Cold?" he teased, knowing that if she was, she'd have wrapped the duvet around her.

"Demure," she said, the mischievous sparkle in her eyes telling him it was a lie.

Thinking how lucky he was to have her here to warm a lonely winter night, he poked the fire until it crackled, then tossed another log on. He wasn't looking forward to taking her back to the chalet and then returning here alone. Normally, his house suited him just fine, but it would feel empty after she'd gone.

Brushing aside the errant thought and a twinge of pain in his chest, he dropped down to sit facing her. She was here now, and that was what mattered. "Hope you don't mind that I've got no clothes on. You being so demure and all."

She chuckled. "You're not exactly hard on the eyes." The double meaning must have struck her because she giggled, then her gaze boldly surveyed his body. "Well, not at the moment, but I bet I could make you hard in a minute or two."

"You know it. But before we do that, I think there's a pretty body under that duvet that needs some attention."

"You think? Hmm. Let's see." And she let the duvet drop.

She was all cream and peach and gold in the light of the fire: slim curves, pale skin, a brush of rosy color across her cheeks and chest. Golden hair tumbling to her shoulders and tawny curls at the apex of her thighs. Pink polish on her fingers and toes, echoing the natural shade of her lips.

"God, you're beautiful." He'd seen her in sunlight and firelight, and she was equally dazzling in both. She was natural, too, not all fussed up with makeup and some fancy hairdo.

She reminded him of Beth.

What? How could that be? Beth had been dark and petite at barely five feet tall, where Andi was fair and had a good six or seven inches on her.

No, it wasn't about looks; it was personality. They were both natural, warmhearted, and fun to be with. Both believed in true love and happy endings, as he once had himself.

"Jared? Is something wrong?'

He realized he was frowning. Since he'd met Andi, he'd been thinking things, doing things, that were out of character.

"Not a thing." Again, he tried to refocus on the moment. "Just wondering where to kiss first." He leaned in to nuzzle her neck, breathing in a scent that was summer flowers and sex: ripe, lush, sensual.

She arched her neck, murmuring approval as he kissed along the clean line of her jaw, then teased her earlobe with his tongue. Andi was so great; why was she still single? Were the guys in her life completely crazy? Or, more likely, they weren't good enough for her. She deserved someone special. He pressed kisses to the satiny skin of her neck and felt her pulse throb under his lips.

Her fingers wove through his hair, and her other hand caressed his shoulder, stroking, digging in gently, kneading the muscles. Her head dipped, and she pressed a kiss into his hair. "You smell like snow and woodsmoke. I like it."

"What can I say? I'm a Whistler guy."

"You are. Were you born here?"

"Yup. Me and a younger sister. She married and moved to Toronto. My folks are still here, though."

Andi lay back on the duvet, taking him with her. "Lots of changes here since you were born. But you still like it?"

Whistler was all that he knew: family, friends, Beth, and now the memories of Beth. He'd never wanted to live anywhere else. "It's home. Yeah, it's changed, but lots of us have been here a long time. The residents are a whole different community than the tourist scene."

She nodded. "Vancouver's a big city, but I have my own community within it, especially Sarah, my best friend since we were little kids. We're business partners now."

Her hand rested on his shoulder as he kissed the top slopes of her breasts, breasts that were rising and falling more quickly now, the nipples beginning to pucker despite the heat from the fire.

"Sarah's the one who got married?" With his tongue, he circled her areola, staying on the outside, watching her nipple get harder and harder as if it was begging to be touched.

His cock was swelling again, but the need was less urgent than before. Caressing her slowly, even chatting about this and that, felt easy and right.

"Mmm, that feels good. Yes, Sarah met Free—Freeman—when she organized a wedding in Belize." She chuckled, and her breast moved softly against his mouth. "He was the groom's best friend, and he was hell-bent on stopping the wedding."

He lifted his head. "Really? Why?"

"He had the misguided idea the bride was a money-grubber, and he had to save his buddy. But he finally realized the truth, and all was well. And Sarah got her own happy ending." She gave a gentle sigh, making him remember how Beth used to love those sappy Hallmark movies.

His wife would have liked Andi. In fact, he knew exactly what Beth would have told her, and he said it himself. "You'll get yours, too."

Her mauve eyes gazed into his for a long moment, as if she was trying to see behind his words. Then she nodded. "I will."

The thought of her with someone else gave him a twinge of . . . regret?

Another odd feeling to brush aside. Right now, she was his. He was the guy who got to enjoy her beauty and sexiness, her sense of responsibility and caring for others, her romantic side and her teasing, and her habit of talking during sex.

He dipped his head again and licked across her nipple, making her gasp. A few more licks, then quick, hard flicks with the tip of his tongue, then he sucked her nipple. Andi was so responsive, so sensitive, and her body's reaction guided him.

Speaking of responsive, his cock, resting alongside her hip, was now rigid and growing impatient.

He moved to her other breast, and at the same time slipped a hand down her body, grazing her silky stomach, drifting over the tangle of curly pubic hair, finding a home between her legs—a wonderfully warm, moist home.

Her thigh muscles clenched, holding him there. Not that he had any intention of escaping.

The CD had ended, and she'd stopped talking, too, only giving little sighs and whimpers. Still teasing her nipple with his lips and tongue, he glanced upward to see that her eyes were shut and her face was taut with concentration.

She was caught up in the sensations, her focus inward rather than on him. Her questions had stopped, and he missed them. They'd made the sex more personal, and for the first time since Beth, that was a good thing.

He slipped a finger between her slick labia and felt her grip him. Slowly, he moved in and out, adding a second finger, his cock pulsing in a rhythmic echo of his fingers' movements.

Her lips curved. "Mmm, I love the way you touch me, Jared." Her eyes opened, glazed with sexual heat, and met his.

Oh yeah, this was personal. Even with her eyes shut, with tension mounting in her body, she knew it was him. He didn't know why that should matter, but it did.

His fingers circled inside her, his thumb found her clit, and he sucked a little harder on her nipple. The soft whimpers, the sweet scent, the toss of honey blond hair as her head moved restlessly, they were all Andi. Very personal. Very arousing.

Her hips lifted, twisted, each movement brushing his now-rigid cock, and she began to pant. "Yes, oh yes," she whispered. "Like that, just like that. Oh . . . oh!"

Inside her, muscles clutched him, then released as she cried out and spasms of orgasm broke around him.

His own body ached with need, but he forced himself to hold still, to hold Andi until she went limp.

He eased his fingers from her and lifted up so he could drop a soft kiss on her lips. Then he moved down her body, kissing his way across the thrust of her rib cage, the dip of her waist. Firelight danced across her skin, giving it a peachy glow. He dallied in her navel, so soft and sweetly feminine.

When he began to move down again, she shifted under him, putting her hands on his shoulders and gently shoving him away so she could sit up. "I want to play, too," she told him.

His cock pulsed hopefully.

"Lie down," she said.

He obeyed, lying on his back, stacking his hands behind his head, waiting to see what she'd do. Hoping she'd zone right in on his erection.

Instead, she leaned over him and ran her hands lightly over his shoulders, then down his arms, just grazing the fine hairs.

For some reason, the simple touch was erotic. Or maybe it was the fact that the woman touching him was naked and lovely in the firelight.

Those soft fingers drifted over his chest, covering every inch, leaving a trail of tingly heat. It was almost as if she were blind and seeing him, memorizing him, through touch.

"What are you doing?" he asked.

"Appreciating you. Learning your body. Is that okay?"

"Feels good. Really good." His cock grew impossibly harder with each touch.

When she reached his waist, both hands cruised out to one hip, avoiding the center of his body. They continued to the top of his leg where one hand, smoothing over his inner thigh, lightly brushed his balls, making him shudder with need.

But she moved away and down his leg. His calf muscles flexed under her touch, and when she reached his feet and stroked the soles, he pulled away. "Ticklish."

"Aha. Good to know." But for now she had mercy on him and switched over to the other foot, not touching the sole, just stroking the top then moving up to his ankle.

At the same leisurely, exploratory pace, she worked her way up the second leg until now, finally, she was at the top of his thigh. Again her hand grazed his sac, but this time—oh, God, yes—she didn't draw away.

He propped himself up on the pillows so he could watch.

Expression intent, she cupped and fondled his balls, caressed his ultrasensitive perineum, and made him gasp with pleasure. Then she was stroking his shaft, softly, deftly. She paused to moisten her fingers with saliva, and now her hand wrapped him, sliding up and down slick and fast, pumping until—

"Shit, Andi." He grabbed her hand and pulled it away. "Stop. Stop, or I'll come."

"I want you to." She tugged her hand free, and steady eyes met his. "I want to watch."

"Oh, Jesus." How sexy was that?

"Or you could come in my mouth. But Jared, I'd really like to watch. I've never . . . " Color flooded her cheeks, and she ducked her head.

"Never seen a guy come?"

She shook her head. Not looking up, she said, "Never wanted to before. But you're . . . so male and virile and sexy. I want to make you come, and I want to watch."

Gently she touched the head of his cock, where drops of pre-come glistened. She spread them, circling around and around, then she bent and licked her way down his shaft, coating him with saliva.

He groaned with pleasure.

Then she circled him with one hand, and with the other she tugged one of his hands over so it rested atop hers. "Show me. Show me how you like it."

"Believe me, you're doing fine."

"Then do it with me."

He stared down at his cock, circled by her slim, delicate fingers, which were almost hidden by his larger, darker hand. She began to slide her hand up and down his shaft, taking his along for the ride. Oh shit, it looked so erotic, felt so damned good.

He pressed down on her hand, tightening her grip just a bit and guiding her as together they increased the pace.

When more pre-come leaked out, she used the fingers of her free hand to spread it around the head of his cock. The round, smoothing motion was such a seductive contrast to the steady pumping of their joined hands.

Her hand was hot, deft, the strokes on his shaft reaching deep inside him, pulling—demanding—a reaction.

His breath rasped as the need to come built, tightening his balls.

He glanced at Andi's face, saw the flush on her cheeks, the glitter in her eyes as she watched what they were doing. Seeing her getting turned on only heightened his own arousal.

He had to come. Now.

He tightened the grip of their hands, guided her to make the strokes longer, faster, harder, and then, yes! His cock jerked in climax, foamy come jetting out to land on his belly.

It coated their hands, making them slick, as together they stroked again, and once more, until finally he'd released everything he had to give.

He sank back on the pillows. "Oh, man, Andi."

"That was so sexy." Her eyes glittered with need.

He grabbed the boxers he'd tossed aside and haphazardly swabbed off the semen. Then he urged her forward until she was kneeling above him, one knee on either side of his head.

After admiring the view of her slick, rosy pussy, he put his hands on her hips and eased her down until his tongue, his lips, could taste that sexy landscape. Wanting to give her the same kind of pleasure she'd bestowed on him, he sucked and licked her until she moaned and squirmed against him and finally shattered in orgasm.

After, when she collapsed beside him, he circled her shoulders with an arm, and she curled into him, head on his shoulder, one arm around his waist, a leg thrown over his.

He breathed a deep sigh of contentment. This was about as good as life got.

Wait. Life was good? He was actually thinking life was good?

For the first time since Beth had died. Should that thought scare him?

He breathed in the summery scent of Andi's hair and wondered what was happening to him. And then he had another realization. Something was missing. "You're not talking. Tired?" Hopefully that was all it was, not that she was upset about something.

"No." Her voice was muffled against his shoulder. "Well, a little, but I'm used to late nights. It's just . . . I'm afraid you think I talk too much."

He smiled against her hair. "Guess I'm kind of getting used to the chatter."

"Oh, well, in that case"—she eased from his grip so she could lie on her side, facing him—"I was going to warn you. Inger's into matchmaking."

"Yeah." He stroked her shoulder, her arm, then rested his hand on her hip. "I know."

"Every time she's seen me in the last couple of days, she's been singing your praises."

"Same about you at breakfast yesterday."

She raised an arm and pillowed it under her head. "I told her I'm sure you were great, but I was in Whistler to do a job, and Shelley'd throw a major hissy fit if she thought I was canoodling on the side."

He cocked an eyebrow. "Canoodling?"

She grinned. "My grandma's word. It's more polite and less explicit than *screwing around*. So, what did you tell Inger?"

He smoothed his hand over the firm, warm curve of her hip. "That I was sure you were a wonderful woman, but if I wanted to date, I could handle it myself." At the time, he'd figured it would be a very long time before that would happen. Now, lying here with Andi, dating didn't seem like such a bad idea. Dating her, that was.

That was another thought that should be scary. He loved Beth. She was the love of his life.

"Inger cares about you," she said. "So does Gord."

"I know. And so do my folks, and my sister who nags long-distance, and a bunch of old friends from school."

"But it's your life. We each do things at our own pace. I just hope . . . "

"What?"

She glanced away from him, then back. "That one day you'll be open to letting someone else into your life. To letting happiness into your life again."

"Happiness." Yeah, when people asked how he was doing he always said he was fine, and it was true. But Andi was right. Happiness hadn't been a part of his life.

Until, maybe, now, with her.

ANDI saw the frown on Jared's face, and he was quiet far too long. She'd offended him, pushed too hard. "Sorry. I'm being like all the other nags. It's none of my business."

His face cleared, and he touched her cheek. "No, Andi, that's okay."

Hmm. So what had the frown been about? She smiled at him. "You deserve happiness, Jared. We all do." She shivered slightly and realized the room had cooled off. Glancing past him, she saw the fire had burned down, no longer flaming or crackling, just glowing. It was late—very late.

She sighed. "I need to get back and catch a few hours' sleep." No way could she stay over; she had to be at the Alpine Hideaway at the crack of dawn in case Shelley needed her. Besides, Jared hadn't invited her. She was sure he wasn't ready to have a woman—a lover—sleep over.

"Yeah, it's late," he agreed. "I'll get dressed and warm up the truck." Suiting action to words, he rose and pulled on his clothes, not bothering to go down the hall for a clean pair of boxers, just pulling his jeans on commando style.

She sat up to watch, draping the duvet around her for warmth. "You don't have to drive me. I can call a cab."

"No way." He bent to drop a kiss on her forehead. "Get dressed and give me five minutes or so, then the heater should be working."

Considerate. Sweet as well as sexy. The man had so much going for him. If he was heart-whole . . .

But he wasn't. She dropped the duvet, shivered again, and gathered her clothes. A quick trip to the bathroom, and she was ready, though it might be nice to take the duvet and pillows back to the bedroom.

She bundled them in her arms and carted them down the hall, then reached for the doorknob. The room was dark, so she flicked the light switch by the door and—

She gasped. This wasn't the bedroom. This room held a crib and rocker, a table with a sewing machine, and a basket full of fabric. Her fascinated gaze roamed from object to object, each a testament to Jared and Beth's dreams.

Then she gasped again. What if he caught her here? Hurriedly she turned off the light, closed the door, and scurried back to the living room, where she dumped the duvet and pillows on the floor. She rushed to the entrance hall, where she pulled on her boots and jacket. Then, making sure the door was set to lock, she hurried out into the freezing-cold night.

When she climbed into the 4x4, the heat of the cab was welcome, but she couldn't meet Jared's smile with one of her own. Instead, she busied herself doing up the seat belt. Nothing had changed, she told herself. Nothing, except that she'd seen physical proof of what he'd already told her: that he was nowhere near being ready to move on.

As he backed out of the driveway, she yawned and leaned her head against the headrest. "I'm so tired. It just hit me." Tired, and a little depressed, for no good reason.

"Sorry about that. I wish there was a better time to get together."

"I do have a crazy schedule. It's day and night, at a destination wedding."

"Hope it's not too crazy. I'd like to see you again."

Oh yeah, there was a good reason for her depression. She wanted to see him, too. Jared Stone was special. A man it would be easy to care for. But that wasn't what he wanted. Sex, and maybe friendship, that was all he had to offer.

It was good, but was it enough? He brought her Rescue Girl instincts to the fore. She wanted him to heal, to be happy, to love again. If she could help him do that . . . But she'd learned her lesson with her divorced lover. She'd sworn to only get seriously involved with men who were heart-whole. So, could she enjoy being with Jared and not fall for him?

"Forecast calls for snow tomorrow night," he said. "We could sit out in my hot tub in the snow."

He knew how to tempt her, but she needed some distance and perspective. "Let me see if I can get free. I'll call you."

When he turned the truck's headlights off and stopped in the parking lot, she leaned over to give him a kiss, letting her lips linger in case it turned out to be the last one. "I had a great time."

"So did I." As she opened the door and began to climb out, she heard him add, "Andi, is everything okay?"

Pretending she hadn't heard, she closed the door.

WHEN Jared walked into his house, it felt as lonely as he'd anticipated. He tidied the living room, returned the duvet and pillows to the bedroom, then took the photo of Beth from the drawer by the bed.

Carrying it, he walked across the hall, opened the door, and went in. He hadn't changed a thing here, in this room he and Beth had been fixing up so she could share her quilting space with their baby. He sat in the rocker and gazed at her photo.

"Sweetheart, I love you so much. I've always loved you." He smiled into her eyes. "All the way back to day care, when you were this tiny little thing with a huge grin and sparkling black eyes who made every day fun."

With one blunt finger, he touched her through glass. "I'll always love you. But now . . . I've met this woman, Andi. She's . . . "

For a moment, Andi's image flashed into his mind, replacing Beth's: blonde curls like sunshine, mauve eyes like flowers. "She's like you, Beth. Sweet and fun, caring. I . . . like her. Like being with her."

Beth's smile, the one he'd captured on film, didn't falter.

"But I feel guilty," he admitted. "When I'm with her, I feel almost . . . happy. But how can I be happy when you're gone?"

Her eyes, gazing at him with so much love, answered him. *Darling, I want you to be happy. To move on. Yes, love me, as I'll always love you, but you can't live in the past.*

The past. A room with the quilt she'd been working on, the crib they'd assembled together. "It's who I am, Beth. You and the baby are part of who I am."

Of course. And you can take us with you, wherever you go.

His lips formed a kiss, sending it to wherever his wife might be. "Thank you, sweetheart. You've given me a lot to think about."

He rose, walked to the door, and turned off the light, then went back to the bedroom where he put Beth's photo back on the bedside table where it belonged and undressed for bed.

Chapter 8

THE next morning, Andi slept through her alarm, couldn't get her hair to look right, and discovered a stain on the pants she'd intended to wear.

Finally dressed, she arrived downstairs later than usual and took a seat at a table with the bride and groom, his sister Maddie, and his boss and friend Brianna George. Five or ten minutes later, she realized she'd been brooding over the widowed firefighter rather than listening to the conversation. She took a long swallow of tepid black coffee and forced herself to focus.

Tom and Shelley were talking, Brianna and Maddie listening, and there was definite tension in the air. What was going on?

"Tell me more about this coach," Tom said, not sounding pleased.

Andi leaned toward Maddie and whispered, "Coach?"

"A couple of ski instructors told Shelley about some top-notch European coach who's relocated to the U.S.," she murmured.

Shelley was raving about how great the guy was and how many Olympic medalists he'd trained.

"And he's moved where?" Tom asked.

"Utah," Shelley said. "I know he'd take me on." She grinned. "Gold medal and all."

"But we agreed you'd work with a coach in Whistler." Tom dragged a hand through his hair. During all the wedding planning, as Shelley fussed, took center stage, and bossed him around, he'd been even-tempered and indulgent. Now, though, his voice was rising. "We've got a mortgage on a condo in Vancouver and a lease on one up here."

"Things change." She waved a hand airily. "You know my skiing always comes first."

The words dropped into a pool of silence, and Andi, shocked, saw the same emotion on the faces of Maddie, Brianna, and poor Tom.

"Oh man, sorry," Shelley said quickly. "That came out wrong. I mean after you and me, of course. But, Tom, this is a great opportunity. I can't afford to pass it up. The next Olympics are only three years off."

"And what about the next great opportunity?" he asked darkly. "Where the hell's that one going to be, Shelley? And when? Next year, or a couple months from now? Are you going to want to pack up and move to France? Switzerland?"

"Well, I . . . Who can look that far ahead?" she said with childish defiance.

Andi could almost see the steam rising in Tom, and she could definitely sympathize. Shelley was immature, spontaneous, and she changed her mind constantly. The girl couldn't even commit to what topper she wanted on her wedding cake.

Damn. Was the wedding about to fall apart? So often, there were jitters, spats, even flat-out fights in the days leading up to the ceremony, and she and Sarah had become experts at coping.

Their business was about happy endings, not strong-arming or manipulating a mismatched couple into getting married. The question always was, did this particular pair truly belong together? Were they genuinely in love, only in lust, or in love with the idea of love?

With Tom and Shelley, she honestly didn't know.

She glanced over at Maddie and saw indecision on the groom's sister's face.

It was Brianna who broke the charged silence. "Shelley," she said crisply, "Tom has a career, too, a good career with lots of potential. And it's in Vancouver."

"You're being selfish," Shelley shot back. "You just don't want to lose him."

"No, I don't," she replied evenly. "Because I value him. Maybe I value him more than you do."

"Ooh! You just keep your cougar paws off my man!"

Brianna winced. "That's not what I meant."

"It's disgusting when a middle-aged woman goes after a younger guy."

Andi expected Brianna to respond, but the woman's dark face paled, and she rose abruptly and walked away. Wow. That was the first time—including the night of the fire—that Andi'd seen the TV host lose her composure.

Was there truth to Shelley's accusation? Andi hadn't picked up on any vibes between Brianna and Tom. Likely, Brianna was just pissed off and restraining herself from exchanging childish barbs with Shelley.

"Don't be ridiculous," Tom was saying fiercely to his fiancée. "You owe Brianna an apology."

Shelley gave him a wounded-Bambi look. "How can you take her side over mine?"

He let out an exasperated sigh. "Because she's *right*."

"Ooh!" Now it was Shelley's turn to leave, which she did with a dramatic flounce.

"Shit." Tom scrubbed a hand over his jaw. "I'll go talk to her."

"Wait," Andi said quickly, just as Maddie put a hand on his arm and said, "No."

Andi glanced at Maddie. "Tom, you both need time to cool off."

Maddie nodded. "She's right. You know Shelley; she's a mood-of-the-moment person. Right now, this Utah thing is a whim, and she's all excited. She'll calm down and think it through."

He let out a sigh. "You're right about her moods. She's . . . spontaneous, enthusiastic. It's one of the things I love about her. Usually."

"You balance each other well," Maddie said. "You're steady, and she's impulsive." She put her arm around him and gave him a hug. "I love you, big brother, but before you met Shelley, you could be kind of dull. She's lightened you up, made you more fun. And you've steadied her, which is something she really needs."

"She's been a superstar athlete from the time she could walk," Andi said reflectively. "That's not exactly a steady life. She's used to being the center of attention. Used to the pressure of having to train and work crazy hours, to travel and competition, to the high of winning and the low of losing."

Tom nodded. "And she's only twenty. Seven years younger than me. She's mature in a lot of ways—like having the discipline to achieve what very few people have—but immature in others. She's never had a normal social life or even a proper family life."

Maddie gave him a warm smile. "Not like us. We kind of take it for granted, but our family's always been great." Then she said, "I like Shelley, and I think you guys can work this out. I'm going to go talk to her mom. She's crazy about you. Maybe the two of us will go see how Shelley's doing."

She hugged her brother again. "Chin up, bro, things'll work out." Then she, too, left the table.

Andi was left alone with the groom. Quietly she said, "Tom, are you sure? As you said, Shelley's young. When a couple gets married, they should believe their love will last. You have so much ahead of you, your careers, decisions about where you'll live, kids. Do you truly believe the two of you can deal with those things together and still love each other?"

He had the loveliest hazel eyes. Normally, they were warm and clear. This morning, though, they were cloudy. "I thought so when I asked her to marry me. And we've gotten through all the wedding preparations, we found the two condos, made plans. But now . . . "

"Most couples have pre-wedding jitters. Perhaps that's all this is. But Tom, if you're really not each other's true loves, it's better to find out now."

He bit his lip. "She's not perfect. Me, either. But I do love her, Andi. Couples always have to make compromises, right? There's no such thing as a perfect couple."

"They're rare." She'd seen one or two and envied them deeply. From what she'd heard about Jared and his wife, it sounded as if they might have been one of those couples. Even when—if—he was ready to love again, what woman could compete with what he'd shared with Beth?

She and Tom left the table together, and she wished him luck as he headed upstairs. Andi was scheduled to take the guests skating on Green Lake and was pretty sure Tom and Shelley would be missing that expedition, so she popped into the kitchen to have a private word with Inger. She alerted the other woman to the fact that there'd been a slight lover's spat, so she'd be sensitive to the situation and deal appropriately with Tom and Shelley.

Then Andi went to her room to make a quick call to her colleague Gwen.

When she'd told Gwen about the quarrel, the other woman said, "Oh no, that's awful. What do you think will happen? Do you think Shelley's really in love with Tom?"

Standing by the desk, Andi stared out the window, noticing clouds in the sky. Sunshine would have been nicer for the skating trip. Gloomily, she said, "Is she old enough to know how she feels?"

"How can you ask that? Think of that Hawaiian wedding you just did. They were what, twenty-two? And it was clear they were meant to be together."

"You're right. But they were more mature than Shelley. She has some growing up to do."

They were both quiet for a minute, then Gwen asked, "How's it going with your firefighter?"

Andi sighed and leaned her forehead against the cool double-paned glass. "Not so good. He's a special man. But he's widowed and still loves his wife. They'd been in love forever."

"Oh, that makes it more complicated." She paused. "But, Andi, that doesn't mean he can't love again."

She pushed away from the window and flopped down in the chair. "One day, perhaps."

"Why not now, with you? You've got so much going for you."

"He actually said that, too. In the context of, 'Of course you'll find a great guy one day.'"

"Ouch."

"Yeah." She surveyed the sky again. Didn't look as if it was going to clear any time soon. "He has this closed-door room in his house with her sewing stuff still spread out, and things for the baby."

"A shrine. A few reminders are normal, but a shrine isn't good. And I bet there are photos of her all over the place? I know how hard it was to get rid of Jonathan's clothes and put away most of the pictures, but I couldn't move on until I had."

"I haven't seen a single photo of Beth. It's eerie. I know they're there, somewhere. They have to be. I don't know if he's hiding them out of consideration for me, or because he feels guilty, like he's cheating on a woman who's been dead for three years."

"You're right. It's healthy to have a few pictures, to share some memories."

They were both silent for a long minute, then Gwen said, "I'm sorry, Andi. Sorry about Jared, and sorry Sarah's away. She'd have better advice to offer."

Andi missed Sarah, too. Normally, she'd have phoned and e-mailed her a dozen times, obsessing about Jared. But a woman's honeymoon was a sacred thing. Besides, if there was anyone who could relate to Jared, it was her widowed colleague. "You have helped," she told Gwen. "I can see what moving on looks like, and it's not what Jared's doing."

"Each person is ready at a different time. You can get in a rut with grief. You wallow in it, and it's not pleasant, but it's like a worn-out old blanket you can't bear to abandon. Then one day, something happens."

Outside, the vans had arrived to transport the guests. Andi should go downstairs, but she had to ask, "What was it for you?"

She heard a quavery breath, then a trembling laugh that hinted of tears. "A blanket. Literally. It had been on Jonathan's bed all the time he was sick. After he was gone, I'd wrap that old thing around me. One day, a friend phoned and asked me out for lunch, and I said no, then I realized I was sitting at the kitchen table, huddled up in that blanket like it was some kind of armor against the cold, cruel world. Except, the world wasn't cold and cruel. I had friends, interests, job skills. The world could be a good place if I only had the guts to go back out into it.

"So I threw out the blanket," she said, "and called my friend back to accept the invitation. Then I got my hair done, got a mani-pedi, bought some new clothes, and started searching the job ads."

"And you found Sarah and me. I'm glad, Gwen. Thanks for sharing that story." She wondered if that moment of enlightenment would ever come for Jared.

After saying good-bye, she hurriedly donned warmer clothing, her mind still on Jared. She knew that being with her was helping him deal with his grief. She also knew what Sarah would say: that Rescue Girl had to look out for her own heart. Andi'd been burned once, helping an emotionally wounded man heal.

Should she see Jared again or not?

That decision would have to wait, because she was running late. She rushed down to join the guests who had gathered in the entrance hall and spilled out the front door. No surprise that Tom and Shelley weren't there. Fortunately, none of the guests but Brianna had witnessed the spat, and Brianna was, as usual, heading off someplace on her own. The woman was such a hard worker; she'd earned every bit of success and celebrity.

When Andi told the guests that the bride and groom were taking a little alone time, everyone assumed they preferred their bed to a frozen lake. She could only hope it was true.

Despite the cloudy weather, the expedition to Green Lake

proved a success. More than a few butts landed on the ice, but everyone laughed it off. The groom's parents skated together like young lovers, and one of Shelley's friends turned out to be a skilled figure skater who held everyone spellbound.

The group was chilled but exhilarated when they arrived at Passionate Pizza, where Andi had organized gourmet pizzas for lunch. Enough beer and Chianti were consumed that most folks just wanted to head back to the chalet for an afternoon nap.

There, Andi went looking for Inger. "Any sign of Shelley and Tom?"

"They're together in their room. They asked for soup and sandwiches to be sent up for lunch." Inger winked. "And a bottle of wine."

"That's a good sign."

Andi went up to her room, leaving her door open, and pulled out the spreadsheet that detailed all that went into putting together a wedding rehearsal and wedding. Staring at it, she bit her lip and thought of everything that would need to be canceled, all the needless expenditures, if the wedding was called off. Neither the bride's nor the groom's parents were wealthy, and it had been a stretch for them to give Shelley and Tom the wedding celebration they wanted. The guests had paid most of their own travel and accommodation costs.

Mostly, though, she worried about Tom. His heart would be broken.

When she and Sarah had been girls, they'd assumed love would be easy. You'd meet Mr. Right, and it would be smooth sailing to the altar and beyond. Since they'd been running Happily Ever After, they'd sure smartened up.

Hmm. It sounded as if Jared and Beth had experienced the smooth sailing kind of romance. No wonder he was so devastated, so ill equipped to deal with her death.

A knock on the door interrupted her thoughts. Tom came in, closing the door behind him. The poor guy looked exhausted as he sank into the overstuffed chair by the window. He gave her a smile, but it was definitely at low wattage.

"How are things going?" Andi asked sympathetically, turning the desk chair to face him.

"Not too bad. We're talking." For a moment, his eyes lit with humor. "More than we've talked in the year we've known each other. Turns out, neither of us is very good at it. But we're trying."

"That's great."

He nodded. "Inger said something when she brought us lunch. She said people are so busy these days, with work, play, all the constant inputs from cell phones, e-mails, and so on. We think we're communicating, but it's so quick and superficial. She said we need to slow down, shut out all the inputs. Think about what we really feel and share it with each other."

Andi nodded. "Good advice." The bride and groom seemed to be on the right track. "So, what do you and Shelley want to do now, Tom? We have sleigh rides scheduled for late this afternoon, and a fondue dinner." Not to mention a wedding rehearsal in less than two days, but he was as aware of that as she.

"I know." He stood slowly, as if it was hard work dragging himself out of the big chair. "We'll be there. We don't want anyone to know we've been having problems, because we really think we can work things out."

"My fingers are crossed for the two of you. Let me know if there's anything I can do."

"Sorry to put you through this," he said ruefully. "Must make your job hell."

"Hey, this isn't about my job; it's about you and Shelley. That's all that matters."

TOM looked more rested when, a couple of hours later, he and Shelley appeared, holding hands, to join their guests for the sleigh rides. And, when everyone reached the departure point, the couple claimed a sleigh built for two, as did three other couples. The rest piled into larger sleighs, all of them pulled by beautiful, impressively big Percheron horses and equipped with piles of warm blankets.

Andi cast a wistful eye at the romantic sleighs for two and wished she and Jared could do something like that, but there were two strikes against it. First, it was out in the public eye, and they'd agreed their relationship would be a secret. She didn't want to be seen fooling around on the job, as it were, and he didn't want the gossips of Whistler believing he was dating. And that brought her to the second strike. Their relationship was about sex, not romance.

She noticed Maddie, who was sitting with a girlfriend, also gazing over at the small sleighs with a longing look. Interesting that she wasn't sitting with Michael, a single friend of Tom's. The two had seemed to be hitting it off, yet now each was alone and looking lonely.

Maybe that troublemaker Logan Carver had gotten between them. She'd seen him speaking to Maddie a time or two and sensed a spark between them. Hopefully, the girl had better sense. Logan couldn't be bothered hanging out with the wedding party, and he and Tom had had words more than once. She could see the groom regretted inviting him, but Logan wouldn't take the hint and leave Whistler.

The driver shook the reins, made a clucking sound, and they were off. Bells jingled on the horses' harnesses, everyone's breath steamed in the crisp air, and Andi breathed deeply and tried to relax. Tom and Shelley had made up, and Logan was fine so long as he kept his distance. The smoker who'd caused the fire had vowed never to smoke inside the chalet again.

Maybe the rest of the week would go smoothly.

It was already getting dark, and trail lights glinted appealingly along the side of the track they were following. A few small snowflakes drifted down, and she lifted her face to them, snuggling up under her blanket.

Jared had suggested they enjoy his hot tub. A hot tub in the snow sounded magical.

Romantic, too, but she couldn't let herself think that way. So, bottom line, what was she going to do? She still hadn't phoned him about tonight.

"Be nice to be sharing this with a special guy," one of the young women across from her said wistfully.

"Be nice to be sharing this with *any* guy," the groom's divorced aunt said wryly.

Andi chuckled along with a couple of others. That comment put things in perspective, though. She'd dated lots of men, slept with several, thought a few were special. For whatever reason, all the relationships had broken up. She'd survived, because the guys clearly weren't right for her. Jared was just another guy, not her perfect white knight. What was wrong with having a little fun—sharing a hot tub in the snow—rather than staying home alone?

As soon as she could find a moment's privacy, she'd give him a call.

Chapter 9

A few hours later, after a delicious fondue dinner at a rustic log restaurant, the bride and groom had returned to their room, and everyone else had found something to occupy them. Andi made her excuses, then hurried out into the snow where Jared was again waiting in his 4x4.

Going into his arms was feeling too much like coming home. Home to a sexy haven she might never want to leave. She had to cling to the perspective she'd worked out during the sleigh ride and remind herself he was just another guy, albeit a really sexy one.

"The hot tub's heating," he told her. "You still up for that?"

Mmm, that sounded so appealing. "Oh, dear." She widened her eyes theatrically. "Silly me, I forgot my bathing suit."

He chuckled. "Then you've saved me the step of taking it off you." His eyes gleamed. "Not that I'd have minded seeing you in a bikini. Maybe a thong bikini . . . "

"A thong bikini?" She snorted. "Only in your dreams. Now, get going, drive. We're wasting time."

When he'd pulled away, she said, "How was your day? I realize I don't have a clue what you do when you're not working days."

"Sleep, work on the house, ski. Right now I'm helping my parents renovate their spare room. How about you? Everything shaping up okay for the wedding?"

She groaned. "I can only hope."

"What's wrong?"

"Just between us?" When he nodded, she told him about Tom and Shelley's quarrel. "She's only twenty. I'm not sure she knows what she really wants."

He shrugged. "Doesn't necessarily have to do with age. Sometimes you just know." He glanced at her, and in the dim light of the 4x4's cab, his expression looked a little odd. Thinking about his wife, she thought, feeling irked. Damn it, he was with *her*.

One day, a man would look at her, and he'd know. And so would she. These feelings she was developing for Jared were . . . like a rehearsal. She'd feel them again for another man, and they'd grow deeper and stronger. "How do you know?" she asked softly.

Again he glanced over with that unreadable expression. Then he turned back to the road. She thought he wasn't going to answer, then he said, not looking at her, "I guess . . . it's a feeling."

"Well, yeah," she teased gently.

"I mean, it's not about your brain. It's not about what you think you're looking for or not looking for. It's about how you feel when you're with someone."

Like, they were a sexy haven? They felt like home? If so, she was in trouble.

JARED pulled up in front of his house, thinking how good it felt to have Andi by his side. How right. He sensed Beth would approve.

When he'd been with other women, he would look at them and wish they were Beth. That didn't happen with Andi.

A few minutes ago, they'd talked about love. All afternoon, as he'd sawed and hammered at his parents' house, he'd wondered if that was what he might be starting to feel for Andi. He'd told her that sometimes you just know you're in love, and that was how it had been with Beth. When kids were old enough to have the slightest concept of what love was, he and Beth had known that was what they felt for each other.

He opened the front door for Andi, and they shed their boots and jackets in the entrance, then he led her through to the kitchen.

For the last three years, his heart had been shut down, or, rather, it had been totally devoted to Beth. Since he'd met Andi, it felt to him as if it was cracking open, thawing. The feeling was good, but scary. She lived in Vancouver, had her own business, was bright and beautiful and fun. She had all those dreams about finding the love of her life, and what were the chances a guy like him, with so much baggage, could be that man?

All he could do was see how things played out.

She had walked over to the fridge, where a magnet held up a picture of him and Beth at a picnic with his parents. "Beth?"

"Yeah, and my folks." Before, he'd hidden all the pictures away. After the last time Andi had been here, he'd taken a few out again. Not all of them, just some favorites. He figured Beth would be okay with it and only hoped Andi was.

"She's lovely," she said softly. "Great smile."

"Yeah. It's one of the first things I noticed about her." He handed her a big towel. "And with you . . . let's just say, it wasn't your smile I noticed first. Even though you have a great one, too."

She gave him a smile now, one that looked pleased and a little surprised.

"Hot tub's out on the deck," he told her. "You'll want to leave your clothes in here so they stay warm and dry."

"Okay." She began to pull off her sweater, then noticed he wasn't taking his clothes off. "Aren't you coming?"

"You go on out. I'll get us something to drink and be right there."

Hurriedly she scrambled out of her clothes, giving him only an enticing flash of nakedness before she'd bundled the towel around herself and headed for the door. She glanced over her shoulder, and he thought her expression was uncertain. "Don't be too long, Jared."

Only long enough to mix a couple of big mugs of Sex on the Slopes. In Whistler, there were all sorts of hot winter drinks: the classic hot chocolate with a marshmallow on top that Beth had loved, the Fire and Ice his mom favored, his dad's classic rum toddy, and a bunch of exotic concoctions. Jared figured Sex on the Slopes was perfect for the hot tub.

He stripped off his own clothes and, not bothering with a towel, went outside. Though his skin immediately pricked to goose bumps, he paused a moment to enjoy the view. The wooden deck was lit by a couple of dim carriage lights. The hot tub steamed, and lightly drifting snowflakes glowed in the light. Andi faced him, immersed to the neck, hair pulled haphazardly back and secured with some kind of clip.

The scene was perfect, expect for a hint of reserve in her eyes when she smiled up at him and said, "Come on in; the water's fine."

"And the air's freezing." Quickly he handed her a mug, then lowered himself gratefully into the hot water. "Man, that feels good."

He sat across from her. The tub was small enough and his legs long enough that they tangled with hers. His blood hummed at the thought of her nakedness, concealed by the bubbly water.

"This is magical." She lifted her mug in a toast, then sipped. "Oh, yum."

He toasted her back. "Thanks for coming." And yes, the evening was magical, but that was because of her, not the hot tub and snowflakes.

Many times, after a shift at the fire hall, he'd climbed into the hot tub and tried to soak the smell and feel of fire out of his pores. Then, the tub was functional and relaxing, never magical. The only problem was that, despite her words and smile, Andi seemed to have something on her mind.

He was about to ask what was going on when she put her drink down, sighed, and gazed across at him. "I know what we agreed to, Jared, but I'm having trouble with it." She twisted her mouth ruefully. "I guess I'm not built for casual sex, for relationships with no prospect of a future. Or at least"—she took a breath—"not with you. You're special. You have so much to give, but you're not ready to give it because of Beth."

She had feelings for him. That was the reason she kept pulling away, because she thought he was still back where he'd been their first time together. A big grin split his face, and he sat up. "Andi, you're wrong. I was wrong. This is more than casual sex." He reached under the water and secured both her hands in his. "You make me feel . . . " He searched for the words.

Finally, those mauve eyes had brightened. "Yes?"

"Happy. For the first time in three years."

"Oh." It was just a tiny, surprised sound. And now her eyes went luminous. "That's . . . I'm . . . Wow."

She got it. Knew what a big thing this was for him.

He released her hands, handed her her mug, and picked up his own. Then he offered a toast. "To you, Andi. And to that stupid jerk who was smoking when he shouldn't have been, because without him, we wouldn't have met."

She clicked her mug to his. "That's the oddest toast I've ever drunk, but okay, here's to Randy."

"And to you," he insisted.

Her lips curved. "And to me."

They drank, kissed gently, then settled back against the sides of the hot tub, smiling at each other. It was another of those life-doesn't-get-much-better-than-this moments. Except, it could. He stretched out his legs, deliberately brushing hers in the process. Then he ran one foot up the inside of her leg, not stopping until it had lodged firmly against her crotch.

"Mmm." She squirmed against it. "Two can play that game."

"So I was hoping."

The pink tip of her tongue flirted suggestively with the whipped cream atop her drink. Then, under the water, her foot began to explore. He was already hardening by the time her toes tickled his balls.

The subzero air nipped his face and shoulders, pulsing jets of hot water massaged his back and sides, and the taste of chocolate and coffee lingered on his tongue.

Andi's toes danced a clumsy yet erotic pattern on his cock as it swelled.

Across from him, she was smiling, cheeks pink, blonde curls damp at the edges. She opened her mouth and stuck out her tongue to catch a snowflake, eyes sparkling.

What would it be like to come home from his shift and climb into the hot tub with Andi? Then to wrap themselves in robes, stroll inside for a snack by the fire, make love on that feather-soft duvet . . .

"Jared?"

"Sorry. Did you say something?"

"Just asked what you were thinking. You looked kind of dreamy."

He snorted. "Guys don't get dreamy. I was relaxing and enjoying this." With his big toe, he gently probed the folds between her legs. "And this." Her wet heat merged into that of the hot tub; it was hard to tell where one ended and the other began. But her reaction guided him.

When she was giving little *oh*s and whimpers, he slipped away from her teasing toes and found the condom he'd brought outside. A minute later, he'd pulled her onto his lap, sliding easily between her legs as she came down.

"So good," she murmured as they began to move together.

The water was too hot to allow anything very energetic, so their movements were small, focused, deeply intimate.

Her sheath was like the water, steamy and pulsing as her internal muscles squeezed and released. He thrust slowly, deeply, filling her to the core then gradually easing out only to slide back in again.

Circling her shoulders with his arms, he pulled her closer for a kiss. Their lips, their faces, were cool, damp with melted snow, while beneath the surface of the water their bodies were scorching hot. The contrast was unbelievably sexy.

He kissed her more deeply, needing her to know how much she meant to him. That she was sex incarnate, but so much more as well.

That she was the woman who was healing his soul and giving him hope.

This time, when they made love, she didn't close her eyes but gazed into his with a combination of tenderness and passion that warmed his lonely heart.

He reached down, gently fingered the pearl of her clit, and slowly they rocked together to a climax that seemed to go on and on.

After, when they'd finally untwined their bodies and caught their breath, he kept an arm around her shoulders and said, "Stay the night."

Her eyes widened, glowed. "Oh, Jared." Then she shook her head slowly. "I wish I could. But if I stayed, people would find out, and we agreed we didn't want that."

"Maybe that would be a good thing. For me, anyhow."

"Really?"

"For three years, everyone I know has been worrying about me. I want to show them I'm okay." He gazed steadily into her eyes. "That I've found someone special."

"Oh, Jared," she said dreamily. "That sounds so good." Then she sighed. "But not this week, okay? Things have been touch and go with the lover's quarrel, and I don't want anything else to set Shelley off. Let's wait until the wedding's over."

She'd be back in Vancouver. Long-distance dating would be a hassle, but with Andi it'd be worth it. "I can drive down to Vancouver when I have days off. And maybe you can come up on weekends sometimes?"

"I'd like that."

"We can get to know each other. Out in public." He nudged her bare leg with his. "As well as in private."

"That sounds wonderful." Then her brows pulled together in a slight frown. "Jared, I need to ask. What about Beth?"

He tensed. "What do you want me to say? That I'll forget her? Stop loving her? Because I won't."

"No. No, you shouldn't. I wouldn't want a man who'd forget the woman he loved."

"Thanks." He should have known she'd understand.

"But . . . Are you really sure you're ready to move on? You've been saying all you wanted was casual sex, and now you've done this about-face."

"I know it seems sudden. I don't know how to explain it. It just feels right to be with you."

She looked unconvinced, so he tried again. "I loved Beth with all my heart, and I thought that meant I'd never love again. Never want to love again. But this week I've realized that isn't true."

"Really? Then . . ." She bit her lip and stared into his eyes. "Have you cleared out that room?"

"That room?" he echoed stupidly, though he knew exactly what she meant. How had she found out about the room?

"I opened the door by mistake, Jared. Last night, I was going to take the duvet back to the bedroom, and I opened the wrong door. I'm sorry, I didn't mean to pry. So, I need to know if you've cleared out that room."

He'd given Beth's clothes to her favorite charity. All of them, soon after her death, because he hadn't been able to bear going through them. But he couldn't bring himself to give away the quilting she'd so enjoyed, nor to change the nursery they'd worked on together. They'd shared so many hopes and dreams in that room.

"No," he said shortly. "I can't."

"Can't?" Regretfully, she said, "You're not ready to move on."

"I *am* ready," he snapped.

"Jared, it's good to have memories, to keep some pictures around, to talk about Beth. But that room's a shrine."

Of course it was. "What the hell's wrong with that?"

She shook her head slowly, her eyes huge and impossibly sad. "She still owns your heart. You're not ready to love again. And that's not good enough for me."

"Shit." He glared at her. After three years of loneliness, he'd found a woman he could care about, and had the guts to tell her, and she was second-guessing him. Throwing his feelings back in his face. Telling him how he should act.

Telling him to get rid of the room where he felt closest to Beth and their unborn child. How dare she? Who the hell did she think she was?

He lurched out of the hot tub and stalked inside, where he didn't bother to dry off, just struggled to pull his clothes over his damp, chilled skin. Behind him, he heard Andi come in, heard her moving around putting on her own clothing. But he didn't look at her. "I'll drive you home."

"You don't have to," she said stiffly. "I can get a cab."

He turned to face her. So beautiful. The woman who'd touched a heart he had believed was beyond repair, only to batter it again. He couldn't bear to be with her any longer. "Sounds like a good idea."

He picked up the phone, dialed a cab company, and gave them his address. "They'll be here in five minutes," he told Andi, then added bitterly, "Good luck finding the guy who's good enough for you."

"Jared, I didn't mean it that way." She touched his arm.

He shook off her hand and stalked away, heading straight for the room with the closed door.

ANDI stared after Jared, tears beginning to spill over. Down the hall, she heard a door open and close again. She knew exactly which door it was. He'd gone to Beth.

She picked up her purse and made her way to the front door.

As she rode back to the Alpine Hideaway in the taxi, swiping tears away with a tissue, she thought back on all the things they'd said. Then, in her room, she sat on the bed, piled pillows behind her back, and picked up the phone. Gwen wouldn't mind being woken.

Between sniffles, she explained what had happened. "Everything seemed so perfect, but I had to ask about the room. Had to know. Am I right that he's not ready for a relationship?"

"It sounds as if he's getting there," Gwen said tentatively. "He's already done things with you and said things to you that he never has with anyone else."

"That's what I thought." She twisted restlessly against the pillows, trying to get comfortable. "But until he clears out that room . . . "

"Yeah." Gwen paused. "Let me ask you, if he was ready, how would you feel?"

"Excited. I'm really falling for him." She had been, from the moment he swept her off her feet in the snow. "Nervous, too," she admitted. "His life is here, and that life has been built around Beth since he was a little kid. How could I ever fit in? Compete?"

"It's not about competing. Each relationship is unique. You know that, Andi. You've seen second and third marriages."

"True. But Beth sounds so perfect."

Gwen chuckled. "No woman is perfect." Then, no longer laughing, she said, "Though sometimes we idealize people after they die."

Andi rubbed her dripping nose with a tissue. "Thanks a lot. Competing with another woman's bad enough. Competing with an ideal is impossible."

"Why not take it slow? Be patient. Spend some time together and see how it goes."

"I think he's written me off." She rubbed her temple, where a headache was building. "Besides, every time I see him, I fall harder. If it didn't work out . . . " Did she want to set herself up for heartbreak?

"Sorry, Andi. I wish I could be more help. But you know there aren't any magic answers. It's a tough situation. But then, that's love."

Love. Was it?

Chapter 10

THE next morning, Andi put on a red sweater to try to cheer herself up, present a bright facade, and disguise the fact that she'd barely slept and felt like crap.

It obviously didn't work, because when she met up with Shelley and Tom in the downstairs hall, Shelley gazed at her with concern. "Hey, are you okay?"

Andi's surprise at the self-absorbed bride noticing, much less caring, must have been reflected on her face, because Shelley frowned. "I'm not completely selfish, you know."

"Of course not," Andi said quickly, as Tom gave a quick snort of laughter.

Shelley shot them both an annoyed look, then a grin quirked her lips. "Okay, so I tend to know what I want and say so. I don't think that's so bad." She hooked her arm through Tom's and shot him a teasing glance. "If everyone did that, we'd all know where we stand."

He gave her ponytail a tug. "Yeah, yeah, I'm learning. You can't read my mind any more than I can read yours."

"You don't have to read mine, because I always tell you what I'm thinking." She planted a kiss on his lips then turned to Andi. "He's trying to learn to open up, and I'm trying to learn to ask, pay more attention, and think things through."

"Sounds great."

She nodded. "And trust me, I do know that no one can get everything they want. Every athlete's very aware of that."

"Yes, I suppose that's true," Andi said. "So, everything's good with you two?"

"Great," Tom said. "That fight was the best thing that could have happened to us. We understand each other so much better now." The pair of them stood facing her, arms around each other, very much a couple.

"Should I ask what you've decided about the coach in Utah?"

"We're staying here," Shelley said. "Tom's job is important, and the training program I've set up here is just fine."

Well, how about that? A mature decision. "I'm so glad."

She let them precede her into the dining room for breakfast and hung back, musing. Was she the one who was being immature? And selfish? Expecting Jared to somehow overcome three years of mourning just because he'd met her? She winced.

He was a good man with a proven track record at love. If she'd been his first love and she'd died, of course she'd have wanted him to move on. But not in a huge rush, she had to admit.

He'd left a picture of Beth out. Had that been intentional or inadvertent? If intentional, then it seemed like a step in the right direction. He was talking about his wife, being open and sharing his feelings. That, too, was good.

Glancing into the dining room, she saw the guests grouped at tables, all eating and chatting happily. Tomorrow was the wedding rehearsal, and Saturday was the wedding. She'd be frantically busy.

But today, the guests were going off in several different directions: snowboard lessons, heli-skiing, snowmobiling, skating, and shopping. No way could she keep track of all of them, and there was no particular reason she had to, not until they all gathered again for dinner.

Nervous excitement shivered through her. She could see Jared, apologize, and talk this through with him. Yes, they'd ended the night on a bad note, both snapping at each other, getting hurt feelings. But if they cared for each other, they could get past it the way Tom and Shelley had.

Surely, Jared would give the two of them a second chance. Even though, last night, he'd run to Beth.

She had to think positively. Quickly she turned away from the door and hurried back to her room, where she dialed his home number. No answer. He must have already gone out for the day.

She was about to dial his cell number when her own cell phone, snug in her pants pocket, vibrated. Impatiently she pulled it out and checked the number. Jared!

Flipping it open, she said, "I just tried to call you at home."

"I'm not there, I'm here."

"Here? Where's here?"

"In the parking lot at the Hideaway. Andi, I need to talk to you."

"Me, too." *Please, please let him have the same idea as me: that the two of us stand a chance. Don't let him say he's chosen the memory of Beth over me.* "Wait for me. I'll be out in a few minutes."

Quickly she gathered her jacket and purse and went downstairs. Impatient to be off, she popped into the kitchen to tell Inger. "I have to go out for a while. The guests should be fine on their own. If you need me, call my cell."

The older woman looked up from the muffins she was arranging in a basket. "Problems?"

"No. I, uh, I don't think so. Just something I need to attend to."

"Is that so?" A smile poked dimples in her cheeks. "You might want to put boots on if you're going out."

"Boots?" Andi glanced down and realized she was still wearing house slippers. "Ack. Thanks, Inger."

She flew upstairs and pulled on her boots, then went to the dining room. Conversation barely paused when she announced that she had to go out and wished everyone a lovely day.

And then, finally, she was out the front door.

* * *

JARED was parked in his usual spot, in the back corner of the parking lot.

The moment she opened the door, he started to talk. "I know you're busy, and this won't take long." His face was tense, reserved.

Uh-oh, that wasn't a good omen. She climbed in and closed the door. "No, I—"

He cut her off, starting the engine and pulling away. "I'll just drive over a street or two, and we can park where no one from the chalet will drive past."

"Jared, it's all right. I don't have to be back until late afternoon. Barring emergencies."

"What?" The vehicle gave a tiny skid on the slippery morning snow as he whipped a glance in her direction.

"I'm taking the day off. Let's go to your place and talk."

He shot her another glance, now more puzzled than reserved. "You're taking the day off? Seriously?" When she nodded, he said, "Well then . . ." He took a turn, not in the direction of his house.

"Where are you going?"

"Someplace I hope you'll like."

That was a good sign. He wouldn't do that if he wanted to break up with her. "Okay, but I need to tell you—"

"Andi, I can't concentrate on my driving and have this conversation. Let's just hold off until we get there."

Where? And how quickly would they get there? Nerves fluttered in her stomach, and she was glad she hadn't eaten any breakfast.

His destination proved to be a park, its snow-covered parking lot almost empty. "Jared?" She sent him a questioning look as he turned off the ignition.

He hopped out and came around to open her door. "Let's go for a walk."

"A walk?" Obediently, she stepped down and glanced around. It was a truly lovely morning with a pale sun slanting through snow-clad trees to dapple light on a packed-snow trail. In this beautiful setting, she could tell him the truth. "Okay. And I need to tell you—"

"Me first. Please?"

She took a breath, then nodded.

He clasped her bare hand—a good sign—and tugged her toward the start of the trail. "No gloves?"

"I didn't think to bring them. In fact, if it wasn't for Inger, I'd have run out in my slippers again."

He grinned down at her. "Then I'd have had to rescue you again." He tucked one of her hands in her jacket pocket, then, clasping the other in his, he buried them both in his own pocket. His touch was so comforting it almost made up for the fact that he hadn't kissed her.

She wanted to talk, to spill out everything she'd been thinking. But he'd asked to go first.

They began to follow the trail through the trees, the snow crunching and squeaking under their boots. The air was so fresh it made her nostrils tingle, and the sun held enough warmth that her bare nose and ears didn't feel too chilled.

"It's beautiful here," she said, wondering anxiously when he'd tell her what was on his mind. Whatever he said, she wouldn't let it deter her. She needed to apologize for her insensitivity and tell him how she felt about him. In this crisp new morning, she could believe there was hope for the two of them.

"Yeah." He glanced at her and then away. "Last night I was mad and hurt."

"I'm sorry. I shouldn't have said—"

"Sshh." He squeezed her hand. "I cleaned out the room, Andi. It's empty."

She stopped, pulling him to a halt, too. "Oh, Jared."

"You were right. I sat there for hours in the rocker, looking at the crib, remembering the night we'd put it up. All the hopes and dreams we'd shared in that room."

"I'm sorry. I—"

"A couple of the girls in Beth's quilting circle are going to pick up her stuff later today, and I dropped off the crib and baby things with a cousin who's pregnant."

"Are you sure? I shouldn't have pressured you."

He nodded. "It was time to let go of the things, the room."

"The shrine," she murmured.

"Yeah, I guess it was."

"Nothing will take away the memories. One day I hope you'll share some of them with me." She wanted to know everything about him. Wanted both of them to be comfortable with talking about the past.

"I'd like that," he said softly. "As for those old hopes and dreams"—he gazed down at her, his eyes tender—"now I have new ones."

Her own eyes grew damp as he went on. "Since the moment I plucked you out of the snow, the woman with hair like sunshine and eyes like flowers, you've been worming your way into my heart, whether I liked it or not."

"Worming?" She echoed the word in a teasing tone, but her own heart was turning as gooey as a melted marshmallow, and the tears were threatening to overflow.

"Never said I was a poet. Thing is, I've figured out I do like it. I want it. I want you, Andi. I want you to give me a chance and see if you can fall for me the way I'm falling for you."

"I can." She took her free hand out of her pocket and reached up to touch his chilly cheek. "I am. I have been since I first laid eyes on you." From that first moment, that night of fire and ice, he'd been her white knight. He'd swept her off her feet, and ever since, in his own unique way, he'd been wooing and winning her.

He caught her hand in his, interlaced their fingers, and dropped their joined hands to their sides. "Thank God."

Then he leaned down and brushed her lips with his. His were icy: hers must be, too; but in a moment all that existed was heat. The fiery heat of passion, but also the slower, steadier flame of love.

Andi lost herself in the kiss, in the blissful thought of all the kisses to come.

The chittering of a squirrel's scolding broke the silence, and a shower of crystalline snow drifted down on their heads.

Laughing, she and Jared broke apart, brushing flakes from their hair and faces. "We have a chaperone," Andi said.

"Hey, what was it you wanted to talk about?"

"I almost don't need to now. I was going to say I'd try to be more patient and understanding about Beth. I know your love for her isn't something for me to compete with. It's a part of you, just like . . . your courage, your family, your sexiness." She grinned. "Your oddly charming way with words."

"Oddly charming?" He grinned back.

"I'm counting my blessings that I found a man who has loved so truly and deeply. Because maybe one day, you'll feel that way about me."

His grin had turned into a smile that made his silvery eyes soft and warm.

"I don't want you to forget all those memories, Jared. I just want us to create new, wonderful ones of our own."

"Andi, my lovely Andi." He took her face between his hands. "We already are."

Again, his lips met hers.

And this time, when the squirrel sent a fresh drift of snow tumbling down on their heads, they just kept right on kissing.

Slippery Slope

Slippery Slope Cocktail

INGREDIENTS

1 oz. Godiva Original Liqueur
1 oz. Baileys Irish cream
1 oz. whole milk
Crushed ice

INSTRUCTIONS

Pour all ingredients into a cocktail shaker. Shake well (should be frothy). Pour into a wineglass.

Chapter 1

THE guests around Brianna George in the Alpine Hideaway lounge chatted sleepily, waiting for the all clear that their rooms were habitable again after the fire. Brianna nursed a mug of hot chocolate and was the first to notice when Andi, the wedding planner, stepped in front of the fireplace and called for their attention.

"Okay, folks. Inger and I have checked your rooms," Andi said. "They're aired out, and you can go back to bed, but leave your windows open a crack."

Thank heavens. It had been a couple of hours since the fire alarm had sounded and everyone had evacuated the chalet. That alarm in the middle of the night had been scary, but once she'd jumped in to help Andi ensure everyone got out, her nerves had settled.

As one of her grade ten teachers had said, "Give Brianna a task, and everything else falls away."

It was that focus and sense of purpose that had allowed her to leave her miserable past behind and become the success she was today: the creator and star of *The Scoop*, a soft journalism TV show that aired Canada-wide and was poised for U.S. syndication. Not bad for a Native Canadian girl from a tiny reservation in northern B.C., who'd grown up on a diet of racial slurs.

"Brianna, are you coming?"

She glanced up to see Maddie Daniels, the groom Tom's younger sister, in front of her. Last time Brianna had noticed, she'd been flirting with a rather dangerous but very sexy-looking guy. Logan Carver, one of the guests had whispered. An old friend of Tom's.

Brianna rose, realizing everyone was moving toward the door. "I was lost in thought."

"Planning a story about the idiot smokers who start fires?"

The idea had occurred to her, but it seemed as stale as the faint scent of smoke in the air. Why did her ideas lack originality these days? "Maybe. I'll run it by Tom when he's back from his honeymoon." Tom Daniels was one of Brianna's team on the show, and over the couple of years since she'd hired him, they had become friends.

Together she and Maddie moved toward the door. "Thank God everyone's okay," Brianna said.

"Andi wouldn't have had it any other way. Did you see her, running around in her nightie and slippers without a thought for her own safety?" The younger woman gave a mischievous grin. "Mind you, I might have done the same if it would've gotten me into the arms of a hot firefighter."

They shared a smile, and Brianna thought of how dramatic the firefighter had looked striding through the falling snow with Andi in his arms. "A picture for the cover of a romance novel," she said dryly. Not that she read such things herself or believed in the fairy tale of happily ever after.

In her experience, fairy tales came more in the category of Grimm's.

As she moved through the smoke-damaged downstairs hall, she shivered in the chill air and hugged her fur-lined vest closer to her body as she exchanged good nights with a few other guests. Thankfully, people were loosening up with her. As a child, what she'd most wanted was to blend in and not be noticed. Now, she was torn, loving the status and respect her job brought, yet not entirely comfortable with being a bit of a local celebrity.

Not that she fit with this group anyway. She was the only friend from work that Tom had invited, and everyone knew she was his boss. The other guests were relatives or young friends of Tom or his fiancée Shelley. They were here for a fun holiday, and that concept was foreign to her. They had interests and hobbies, while her life focused on her job.

As she plodded upstairs, she noted that, while she normally never ran out of energy, her legs felt like lead. It took forever to reach the third floor. When she paused to catch her breath, Tom, who was sharing a luxury suite on the fourth floor with Shelley, sent his fiancée on ahead and accompanied Brianna to her door. "Hope you get some sleep," he said.

"You, too."

"I'm sorry about the fire. Are you regretting that you came?"

"Not at all," she said politely, though it wasn't exactly true. She'd been flattered when he invited her to the wedding, but she had said she needed to stay in Vancouver and work. He'd told her to come, that she needed a holiday. She'd pressed, and he'd said too much success could cause problems, and a break would do her good.

Now he said, "I'm sure it didn't help get you in a holiday mood."

"You know me, I'm not exactly a holiday person." She never took—never needed or wanted—holidays, and right now things were heating up with the U.S. syndication. Once, it had seemed an unreachable goal to get on TV, and then to have her own show. When *The Scoop* had gone national, it had taken her months to believe it wasn't a dream. Now she might actually become a fixture on American TV, with her show that was designed to fill a niche between talk/variety and hard news. "I'm hoping I'll find some story ideas here."

"Always working." He shook his head. Then, "Stories with U.S. appeal?"

"Yes." Over the past months, she'd worked hard to find higher-profile topics, ones that would interest American viewers, rather than the local-interest exposés and human interest stories she'd always loved, the kind that had helped her build her reputation. "Whistler, the winter after the 2010 Olympics. There must be stories that will appeal to U.S. viewers as well as Canadian ones." Realizing her temples were throbbing, probably from smoke and tiredness, she raised a hand to massage the ache.

Tom studied her, concern in his hazel eyes. "It's hard to find inspiration when you're stressed out."

"I'm fine, Tom. Don't worry about me or the show." She dropped her hand and forced a smile. "Go on now, it's been a long night, and your fiancée's waiting."

She opened the door to her room and went inside, where she hurried to the open window and closed it but for a tiny crack. Wrapping her arms around herself, she stared out at a dark, snowy night, lit only by a few dim streetlamps. The ghost of her own reflection stared back at her, brown skin unusually pale, tiny lines of strain around her eyes and mouth.

Tom was a perceptive guy. Had he seen something she'd barely been aware of herself? Had she been looking tired and stressed? Had her efficiency been slipping? Was it fear that had made her accept Tom's invitation? She'd worked so freaking hard to get where she was; she couldn't afford even a tiny slip. She was thirty-five, in an industry where a woman's age counted against her. It was crucial that she remained fit, attractive, smart, and on top of her game every single moment if she was to win the U.S. deal.

He said she worked too hard, but her job was her life, her whole reason for being. The respect that went along with it was as essential to her as the air she breathed.

SUNDAY proved to be a washout. Though she spent it tramping around Whistler in search of story ideas, nothing grabbed her. It had been a while since she'd had that *aha* spark when an idea really intrigued her. Surely she wasn't growing stale.

With increasing desperation and a nagging headache she couldn't kick, she popped into shops and galleries and scanned the tourists of all ages who hefted brightly painted snowboards, clomped about in ski boots carrying skis, or sat on outdoor patios where hot coffee and their own breath steamed up the frigid air.

Yes, this was a stunningly lovely place, and people were obviously having fun, but none of that made for a big story appropriate for a U.S.-syndicated show. Surely there were some post-Olympic scandals to dig up.

Frustrated, she went back to the picturesque chalet where the wedding guests were staying. She retreated to her room, signed on remotely to her office computer, and did some work.

THE next morning at breakfast, filling her coffee cup in hopes caffeine would boost her energy and zap her headache, Brianna noticed Andi out in the hallway looking all very cozy with a tall, handsome man who wasn't part of the wedding group.

Though she couldn't see Andi's face, Brianna got the impression the conversation was personal. Even flirtatious? Looked as if the wedding planner might have a boyfriend. There was something familiar about the man's face, but Brianna couldn't place him, which, as a journalist, always irked her.

The guy's steamy gaze reminded her how long it had been since she'd had sex, much less romance. Of course, in her experience, if a man romanced you, it was for his own ends.

There'd been Tony, in high school, the boy from the debate club. He had won her heart and taken her virginity, then told his friends that of course he wasn't taking her to the school dance, that all the little Indian bitch was good for was sinking his prick in.

And then, in her mid-twenties, there was Lionel, a colleague at the station where she'd been working. He'd hidden his ambition, romanced her, told her she was the only woman he'd loved. She'd fallen hard and shared everything with him, including the top secret exposé she was working on—the one she'd hoped would win her the prized special feature spot on the evening news.

Instead, it was Lionel who broke the story and got the job.

Fool me once, shame on you. Fool me twice, shame on me. She'd sworn there wouldn't be a third time, and there hadn't. When men bought her champagne, gave her gifts, and told her how wonderful she was, she always looked for the ulterior motive, and typically she found it. Having her own TV show was like being rich: how could you ever trust that a person loved you for yourself and didn't just want something from you?

No, life without sex—at least man-made sex—was much, much easier and way more productive. For male companionship, she'd stick to the few decent, safe men like Tom Daniels. Men who never flirted or asked for favors. Men she liked but wasn't sexually or romantically attracted to.

She realized that, while she'd been musing, the wedding planner and her companion had said their good-byes, and the man was walking down the hall. Andi turned and caught her watching.

"Hi, Andi. Is that your boyfriend?"

"No!" she said quickly, pink tingeing her cheeks. "He's the firefighter who helped me the other night."

"That's why he looked familiar."

"Turns out he's a friend of the Jacobses, and they invited him for breakfast. He was just asking how I was, and I was thanking him again."

"I see." No, they'd been flirting, whether Andi wanted to acknowledge it or not. Oh well, it wasn't her business, and it certainly wasn't her kind of story. No kickbacks on development deals, no insider trading.

"I'm dying for a cup of coffee and some breakfast," Andi said. "Are you coming for ski lessons this morning, Brianna?"

The wedding planner had scheduled a number of activities throughout the week, and this morning there were ski lessons.

Brianna wrinkled her nose. "I think I'll pass. I've never understood the point of skiing."

Andi's brows rose. "How about fun, exercise, the great outdoors, exhilaration?"

Fun? Work was fun—or at least it had been before she'd become so focused on impressing the Americans, and she knew it would be again once the deal went through. Exercise was for the gym, with a personal trainer. The great outdoors was indeed wonderful, but it didn't make for a story. And exhilaration . . . well, that was when intuition led her to ask just the right interview question and she got a headline-grabbing response.

All the same, perhaps she'd go along and observe. The best stories came from the most unexpected sources.

AN hour later, Brianna stood, warmed by winter sunshine, in the beginners' ski area. Andi had brought her here, along with twenty or so beginners and Tom's eighty-something grandparents, Joan and Walter, who said they, too, had come along to observe.

She gazed around at the solemn, snow-clad evergreens and the grandeur of the peaks rising above them and breathed deeply, savoring the chill purity of the air. Since she'd been a girl, she'd felt a special connection to the environment. "I'm beginning to understand the allure of Whistler," she murmured to Joan.

The elderly woman smiled back at her. "I imagine you don't get many chances to stop and smell the roses."

"True. I'm definitely smelling them now." In fact, the crisp air was even headier than the aroma of a rose in bloom, and her headache was finally easing.

They stood in a snow-packed level area, with a short, gentle bunny hill sloping away below them. Racks of ski equipment stood a short distance away, and the previous students, who'd just finished their lessons, were removing their gear. A half dozen guys crowded around a pretty young redhead in a yellow ski school jacket who, from what Brianna could overhear, was giving them an enthusiastic summary of Whistler's best night spots.

The other group was a bunch of kids, maybe eight to ten years old. As far as Brianna could see, they had no instructor, though several adults—parents?—stood nearby. Then, from the center of the cluster, a man in a yellow jacket rose from where he'd been squatting, apparently helping the children take off their skis.

Oh my. Talk about the allure of Whistler! Now, here was a fine addition to the scenery. A good build was no surprise on a ski instructor, but his strong features, sun-tipped brown hair, and infectious smile made this guy noteworthy.

With a pronounced Aussie drawl, he said, "That's it for today, then, mates. Any last questions?"

A girl with blonde pigtails sticking out from under her pink hat said something in what sounded to Brianna like German. The Australian instructor gave a totally cute grin, tweaked one of her pigtails, and responded fluently in the same language.

An excited female voice interrupted her observations. "Excuse me, but aren't you Brianna George?"

Brianna turned to see a couple of middle-aged women, faces flushed with excitement, and smiled. "Yes, I am."

"We love *The Scoop*," the one who'd spoken continued, while the other nodded enthusiastically.

"Thanks so much. That's great to hear."

"Our husbands do, too. We tape it and watch before we go to bed. You make us see things differently, think about things differently."

"That's a lovely compliment."

"We don't have anything with us but lift tickets, but would you autograph them for us? And could we get a picture with you?" The woman pulled a cell phone from her pocket.

"Of course."

She signed tickets, and one of the guests was co-opted to take a short video clip of Brianna with the two women. Based on past experience, it would end up on YouTube, but that was fine. As always, when she appeared in public, she'd taken pains with her appearance.

When the two women hurried away, jabbering excitedly, Brianna returned her gaze to the cute ski instructor. A dark-haired boy was saying to him in French—a language Brianna did speak, "One day I'll be doing those black diamond runs like you, Zack."

The instructor squatted to look him in the eye. "You bet you will, Pierre," he said in fluent French. "Just practice hard, and take it slowly."

Straightening and switching back to English, he said, "You're all doin' great. Happy skiing."

He waved the parents over and exchanged comments and jokes with several of them, including a few words in Japanese to a young couple. How many languages did he speak?

When all the kids had been claimed, he went over to the perky redhead's group, and she wound things up with her admirers.

The wedding planner joined the instructors, and the three spoke quietly together, then they came over to the group from the Alpine Hideaway. "These are your instructors for the beginner lessons," Andi announced. "How about this half of you," she waved an arm, "go with Tamara, and the others with Zack."

Brianna wasn't at all unhappy to be assigned to Zack's group—as an observer, she figured the viewing would be much more stimulating—and with the others followed him a few feet away.

"G'day, mates. As Andi said, I'm Zack." His smile was utterly engaging, and his eyes were the same deep green as the forest around them. His gaze scanned the guests and paused, eyes dancing, on Brianna's face. "The name of the game is fun."

Chapter 2

A strange jolt of heat tingled through Brianna. Sexual heat? That was a rare feeling. Good God, she'd interviewed George Clooney on her show and barely felt a twinge of sexual awareness. Why would she feel a pull of attraction to a ski instructor who she was pretty sure was several years her junior?

"I'm definitely into fun," Karen, a pretty blonde, said flirtatiously.

"That's what we like to hear," Zack said. He flashed her a grin, but his gaze returned to Brianna.

Had he recognized her? He was an Aussie but lived in B.C., and she wasn't exactly low-profile here. In the last couple of years, *The Scoop* had gone national, she and her show had won a couple of Gemini Awards, she'd been awarded an honorary doctor of laws from UBC, and even her fund-raising efforts for disadvantaged youth had been in the media spotlight.

"Now," he went on, "why don't you introduce yourselves and tell me if you have any experience on skis?"

Karen jumped in, fluttering her eyelashes as she introduced herself, then others spoke up. A couple of people had taken a few lessons before, but most were brand-new. Brianna watched as Zack drew them out, admiring his easy style, outgoing personality, and—let's face it—the eye candy.

When it was Tom's grandmother's turn, Joan said, "Walter and I aren't skiing, Zack, we're just going to watch."

"Yeah?" He tilted his head quizzically. "Why's that?"

Walter crossed his arms over his chest. "We're too old for all that stuff."

"Is that right?" Zack's expression indicated he was assessing the pair.

"I've always wanted to ski," Joan said. "Seems like you must feel like a bird, swooping down those hills."

"It's bloody awesome. There's nothing like it." The enthusiasm on Zack's face made Brianna smile. There was nothing as appealing as someone who loved what they were doing.

Expression wistful, Joan said, "Guess I'll just have to watch and imagine."

"Hmm." The instructor studied her another moment, then said, "Do me a favor, Joan, and walk over toward that rack of skis."

A puzzled expression crossed her face, but she started off. A couple moments later, she glanced back to tease, "You checking out my backside, young man?"

Not that there was much to check out in the bulky pants she wore, but all the same he said cheerfully, "Too right I am. And a mighty fine one it is, too." He caught up with her, put an arm around her shoulders, and bent to say something to her.

Brianna felt an absurd twinge of envy as the pair, chatting together, continued on toward the ski equipment.

A few minutes later, they were back, and Zack was helping a flushed, smiling Joan into ski boots.

"Don't be a damn fool, woman," Walter said gruffly. "You'll break your neck, and then where will I be?"

Brianna loved to see the glow on Joan's face, but she, too, was worried. Even experienced skiers could suffer severe injuries, and she'd hate to see anything happen to such a lovely woman. She stepped over, touched Joan's arm, and said softly, "Are you sure about this? If you fall, you could—"

"No worries," Zack broke in, sharing a reassuring smile between her and Walter. "In addition to having that fine backside, she's fit and coordinated, and she's got a great sense of balance."

Okay, he'd checked out Joan's health and fitness, and the woman was in full possession of her mental faculties. It was her decision to make.

Sometimes a woman had to go after her dream, even if it wasn't the most sensible course of action. If Brianna hadn't believed that, she'd never have made it to where she was today.

She squeezed Joan's arm. "Just come back to Walter in one piece, okay?"

"That's the plan." Joan flashed a smile that took fifty years off her age, then she gazed at her husband. "Stop your fussing now, old man." But her tone was gentle and loving.

Brianna moved over to stand beside Walter, whose jaw was clenched, and put her arm through his.

Zack had put on his own skis, and now he came up behind Joan so his longer skis were on the outside of hers, and he gripped her waist. "That's my girl."

He turned to Walter. "We're going down together. And the last time I fell on a bunny hill . . . well, I'd have been no more than five."

The tension in the old man's jaw had eased a bit. "You keep her safe."

"I will, sir." The two men exchanged a long, steady gaze.

It was the kind of spontaneous, emotional connection that was worth gold when the camera captured it. But this morning, there was no camera, only Brianna's watching eyes, and it brought quick, unexpected moisture to them.

And then Zack and Joan headed down the tiny hill, slowly and easily. Safely. Gliding, the way Joan had imagined.

"She always wanted to do that," Walter said, a sweet smile on his lips. "But I bunged up my hip, we got older, and it just never happened. She never believed it would. That young man has made her dream come true."

Yes, it seemed Zack had more going for him than just good looks, charm, and the ability to speak several languages.

"I'm so glad for Joan," she said. She couldn't help but wonder if, as well as enjoying the thrill of skiing, the older woman was appreciating having a hot young guy's arms around her and his firm body snugged up to hers.

All right, what was happening to her brain? She should be intent on finding killer stories to clinch the U.S. deal. Instead, she was wasting time savoring fresh air, an old lady's dream, and a hottie ski guy's fine looks.

But when the pair returned, walking slowly up the bunny hill in their ski boots with Zack carrying the skis and poles and keeping a firm grip on Joan's arm, Brianna couldn't regret being here. The elderly woman's smile was so wide it almost split her face. Taking off her helmet, she said, "It was just as much fun as I always imagined." When Zack bent to help her out of her boots, she gave him a kiss on the cheek. "Thank you."

He beamed. "My pleasure. You're a natural."

The two of them came to rejoin the group, and Joan hugged her husband. "Walter, that's the most exciting thing I've ever done, except for"—she winked—"you know."

Zack said, "Walter? Gonna give it a go?"

"Not me. Bad hip. I'll stick with getting my thrills from 'you know.'"

They all laughed, then Zack turned to Brianna. "Now, how about you?" His eyes lingered on her face, and she again wondered if he'd recognized her. "Feel like a few thrills this morning?" The twinkle in his forest green eyes gave his words a double entendre.

Despite herself, Brianna's lips curved. "I'll have to pass on the thrills. I'm not here for a lesson, either." She doubted that a ski lesson would lead to a story idea; it would be better to observe and interview some of the students. Besides, if she did something, she wanted to do it well, not make a fool of herself in public. After years of being gossiped about when she was young, image was everything to her.

"Hmm." As he'd done with Joan, he studied her face carefully, but this time he didn't persist, just said, "Right, then, let's get the rest of you set up."

How ridiculous to feel disappointed. As Brianna listened to the skiing granny gush, she watched Zack get the others outfitted. Karen was still flirting. Brianna shifted restlessly. Was she actually feeling twinges of jealousy?

There was no question that the ski instructor could have a different woman in his bed each night if he chose. Did he? And would Karen be one of them? So far, he'd spread his easy charm pretty equally among all the students.

When everyone was outfitted with ski boots and helmets, he said, "Walk around for a bit, carrying your skis and poles, until you get your feet under you."

Then he came over to Brianna, where she stood with the elderly pair. "Come on now, don't be shy." He gave her a sexy wink.

"I'm not shy." Just insecure and afraid of failing, though she would never let a soul know that.

"Got a bum hip like Walter?"

"No, I just don't care to ski."

He moved a few inches closer into her space. "So, you're scared. But you should give it a fair go. It's not that tough. Joan'll tell you." His tone was teasing, but it also held a challenge. "Tell you what, I'll go down with you the first time, too."

As Joan gave a burble of laughter, Brianna found herself imagining the feel of Zack's body behind her, his groin against her butt, nice and snug.

He was cheeky and knew how to push her buttons, as well as to make her thirty-five-year-old body zing with sexual awareness. "I'm not scared. And if I go down—" She broke off, struck by a sudden vision of him, naked, and her going down on him, sucking his erect cock into her mouth.

Quickly she swallowed and resumed, resisting the urge to whip on her sunglasses and hide her eyes. "I'll do it by myself, thanks very much."

He leaned close and said, so softly Tom's grandparents couldn't hear, "Doing it with a friend is more fun."

Oh God, had he really said that? Heat flooded her cheeks, and she gaped at him, flattered and aroused.

He pulled back and said in his normal tone, "By yourself it is, then. Let's get you some skis." He headed toward the racks of ski equipment, not even bothering to look back.

Brianna closed her mouth, which had fallen open. The man had thrown her off balance, and he thought he'd won. Little did he know that Brianna George didn't believe in letting others win. If he thought she'd just fall in with what he wanted . . .

But why did he care if she skied? Why had he spent time flirting with her, when Karen had made it clear she was available? Oh yes, she was drawn. Curious. About Zack, most definitely, and, surprisingly, about skiing itself. Not only did the sport make normally sane people spend small fortunes on risking their necks, but it had put that smile of pure joy on Joan's face.

"Go on, Brianna," Joan said softly, patting her arm. "Don't you want to fly?"

Not long ago, Brianna had touched Joan's arm, hoping to stop her from taking a risk. But Joan had ignored her, and she'd flown.

"Maybe I do," she admitted, putting her gloved hand atop Joan's and squeezing it.

"We're going to head back to the Alpine Hideaway now," Joan said. "You have fun."

Why was everyone so obsessed with fun? All the same, she set out behind Zack, boots crunching the snow.

She was a ground-based person. Solid, grounded, realistic, practical, albeit ambitious. Of course she flew, but only inside the well-engineered shell of an aircraft. Not with the freshness of the wind on her face.

Exhilaration, Andi had said, and that's what Brianna had seen on Joan's face. The older woman had thought it was almost as thrilling as sex. Well, that wasn't saying a lot, in Brianna's experience. So why had her body chosen this morning—this very chilly morning—to heat with arousal?

Zack flashed a grin as she approached.

Yes, here was the reason: pure female appreciation of a gorgeous guy who was showing a flattering interest in her.

"Figure you for a size seven." He hefted a pair of boots.

Had he judged her bra size as accurately? She bent to try to pull off one of her fur-lined boots.

"Here, let me help." He squatted at her feet, taking off his gloves, and tugged off one boot. "Use my shoulder for balance."

"I'm fi—" About to say she was fine, she broke off and grabbed his shoulder as he squeezed her foot through her sock, his sure touch half caress, half massage. Tingly heat spread up her leg. Was he taking an unusually long time fitting her foot into the ski boot? And was he equally skilled at handling other, far more interesting body parts? Heat rose to her face, despite the subzero temperature.

Under the ski school's jacket, his shoulder was hard as a rock, and she clung as he shifted slightly to pull off her other winter boot. Again, sensation tingled up her leg as he caressed her foot. He reached for the other ski boot. "Joan said your name's Brianna?"

She sucked in a breath, really hoping he didn't know who she was. Though this unexpected flirtation was unsettling, it was flattering and exciting—unless he was just schmoozing a celebrity. Was the cute ski instructor a user, like so many of the men she met? "That's my name."

He glanced up, no doubt wondering why it had taken her so long to answer. But his gaze didn't sharpen with the *that's where I know you* expression she knew so well. "People call you Bree?"

"No, they call me Brianna." She wasn't the type of woman people gave nicknames to.

"Ah." He fastened the second boot and rose lithely to his feet. "But I'm not *they*." For a long moment, those dancing eyes stared into hers, mesmerizing her.

The boots forced her to stand oddly, weight forward and knees slightly bent. She felt awkward. This man kept her off balance, both literally and figuratively. Normally, she'd have hated that, but with Zack, it was . . . interesting. This day had turned very, very interesting. From a complete nonwork perspective.

He grinned. "I'll get your skis, Bree."

Bree? She found herself grinning at Zack's back as he walked away.

Speaking of fine backsides . . . His gait was athletic and easy, his body obviously fit and strong. It was impossible not to wonder what he looked like beneath the winter clothes, impossible not to think about that comment he'd whispered, about "doing it" with a friend. No question the man was hitting on her.

The only question was, what did she intend to do about it?

ZACK Michaels whistled under his breath as he chose skis and a helmet for sexy Bree.

The ski school's official policy stated that instructors shouldn't get personally involved with students, but most of the teachers figured a rule so blatantly stupid was asking to be disobeyed. No flirting with minors, of course, but the striking Native Canadian woman was most definitely an adult. A soon-to-be consenting adult, he figured.

Hard to say exactly why she intrigued him so much, but it was clearly mutual. Still, he liked that he'd had to do a little pursuing, that she was making him work for it. Usually, women came on to him, the way that blonde girl Karen had been doing, or at least succumbed easily to what his mum called his "charm-the-birds-off-the-trees personality." The personality his older brother referred to, out of their mum's hearing, as his "charm-the-knickers-off-the-birds line of BS."

But it wasn't BS. He just genuinely loved women. And sex.

Right now, his goal was sex with the woman with the lovely dark-skinned face, full, rosy lips, and sleek body, who needed a lesson in enjoying the moment.

"You here on your own?" he asked as he fastened her helmet,

letting his fingers brush her soft cheek and feeling his groin tighten with arousal. "Or you got a bloke hanging about somewhere?"

She shivered at his touch, and he knew it wasn't because his bare fingers were cold. "If that's your not-so-subtle way of finding out if I'm single, the answer is yes. But don't take that to mean—"

"Mean what?" He gazed into her eyes and sank into pools of bittersweet chocolate. Dark skin, dark eyes. Did she taste like chocolate, too?

She gave a start and blinked. "Uh, that I'm interested in . . . whatever."

"Ah, but you've never tried my brand of whatever," he teased.

Her eyes narrowed. "I've tested enough brands to be skeptical about the overall product."

Aha. The lady'd been burned. She'd been with guys who hadn't appreciated her the way she deserved. Again he touched her cheek, brushing back a lock of black hair that had escaped the helmet. "Then you haven't tried the right one."

"Is there a problem?" Karen called impatiently. "We want to ski."

"Almost ready," he yelled back, not taking his eyes from Bree's face. Softly, so only she could hear, he said, "I think we're getting there just fine."

She snorted, but he saw the gleam of amusement in her eyes.

"Snow check on our discussion of . . . whatever," he told her.

Zack put his gloves and skis on, gathered his group, and began to run through the usual introductory patter and questions. He got his students walking around on one ski, learning how the ski moved and how to turn it, using their other foot to assist. Then he had them change skis and repeat the exercise.

He'd been teaching skiing since his late teens, and he'd done it in almost every country in the world that had mountains high and snowy enough to ski on. He was lucky to make a living doing something he loved, but this morning it was hard to concentrate.

There was something about Bree. An odd combination of assertiveness and uncertainty. Vulnerability, almost, though he'd bet she would reject that term.

After the students had tried walking on both skis, he instructed them on the snowplow position and how to use it to stop themselves.

"Keep your skis in a V," he said. "It's just a bunny hill, but if you put your skis together and point them down it, you'll find it's a slippery slope."

His students took turns going down the very slight downhill slope while he stayed at the top, shouting advice. Finally, only Bree was left, and she seemed more interested in asking questions than in skiing. "Just try it," he said. "Get the feel for it."

"But I want to understand, so I'll do it right."

A perfectionist, afraid of making a fool of herself. "Won't happen on the first try. Just give it a go. It's like anything else worthwhile." He winked suggestively. "Takes practice."

She frowned, not acknowledging his flirting. "Fine, I'll try it." She shuffled her skis a few steps closer to the start of the incline, body stiff with tension.

"Relax. If your muscles are too tight, you won't feel the snow."

"Feel the snow?"

"Sense it. Like being on a motorbike or driving a sports car, when you sense the road through the vehicle. With skiing, your legs, especially your knees, transmit information and adjust to the terrain." He relaxed his knees and simulated the up-and-down, side-to-side, give-and-take motion. "But they can't do that if they're locked up tight."

"That makes sense." Using her poles, she shoved off and snowplowed slowly down the little hill without falling. When she stopped and gazed up at him, her smile was bright.

Feeling a rush of pleasure at her accomplishment and her joy in it, Zack shoved off, swooped the short distance, and executed a sharp stop in front of his group, spraying snow in their faces.

They laughed, and one of the guy students said, "I wanna do that!"

"You'll be doing it sooner than you think, mate. Okay, here we are, bottom of the hill. If you want to go down again, you're going to have to get back to the top. How you figure on doing that?"

"Isn't that why God invented chairlifts?" one woman joked.

They all laughed, then he said, "Seems God neglected the occasional hill. If the snow's not too deep, you can take your skis off and hike, but it's better to climb with your skis on. This technique I'm going to show you, it works for going down, too, if you get yourself into a place where you're nervous about skiing down."

As he spoke, he demonstrated. "Turn so your skis are side by side, horizontally. Weight on the inside edges. Dig them into the hill."

Grinning, he watched as they clumsily began to sidestep their way up the short hill. Bree, he noted, was diligent and mastered the technique quickly. He wished she'd play dumb so he could give her extra coaching, but no, it was Karen who demanded his attention. Couldn't she see that it wasn't her he was attracted to?

For the next hour, he had them doing snowplow stops and turns, moving from the tiny starter hill to one that had a longer run. The group was typical, with a few, including Bree, grasping it quickly and the rest taking their turns falling, laughing, picking themselves up.

He tried to spend equal time with each student, but when he was with Bree, every word, every movement seemed to have a special—sexual—meaning. Enough to keep his dick in a state of semi-arousal. The gleam in her eyes told him she felt it, too, and the rosy flush on her cheeks wasn't just from the chill air.

When the lesson time was running out, he checked in with each student. Karen seemed to have finally gotten the message, thank God, and simply thanked him for the lesson. A few people said they were hooked, which always made him feel good.

Bree was at the bottom of the hill, so he skied down and stopped beside her. "Lesson's almost over," he told her. "How ya goin'?"

She planted her poles for balance and gave a joyous smile. "Terrific. This is so different than working out in a fitness club. The fresh air, this beautiful country—and actually going someplace rather than jogging on a treadmill or pedaling a stationary bike."

"Can't fly on a machine that's going no place."

"True. I can't say I was exactly flying down this little hill, but I can see why people get so buzzed on skiing."

He let his gaze go intimate. "My goal's to get you addicted."

Her eyes sparked. "To skiing?"

"Skiing and . . . " He paused deliberately. "Whatever."

Meaning sex. With him. She pressed her cold-chapped lips inward. "Oh, Zack, I don't think—"

"No thinking. Not if it's going to give you that worried look. Relax and have some fun."

"I don't . . . " She didn't finish the thought, and he had the sense she'd been going to say, "I don't have fun," but that couldn't be true.

Her lips twitched. "Skiing was fun. Thank you for that, Zack."

"Hard to top skiing, but I'll give it a try. Let's get together later."

"I'm not sure that's a good idea."

Did he think she was trying to hustle her straight into bed? He wasn't a total shit. He gave her his best persuasive grin. "Oh come on, we'll have a glass of wine, share a pizza. *Whatever* you're in the mood for."

Her brow furrowed. "A date?"

"Yeah."

Her poles wobbled, and she almost lost her balance, then dug them in more firmly. "Thanks, but I can't go out in public with you."

What the hell? "You told me you're not married."

"I'm not. It's not that. But . . . " She sure was taking her time figuring out what she wanted to say. "I'm pretty sure I'm older than you."

"Yeah?" That wasn't a big surprise. Her face was lovely and unlined, but there was something about it, a maturity and determination, women his age usually lacked. "I'm twenty-seven."

She winced. "I'm definitely older."

And not going to tell him by how much. Not that he cared. Age was a state of mind. "So?"

Chapter 3

BRIANNA stared at Zack, standing there so relaxed and athletic looking on skis, and tried to figure out what to say. He was so appealing, but he was eight years her junior. Almost a decade. If she'd been sixty-five, it wouldn't have mattered, but at their ages, it did. If she hadn't been a celebrity of sorts, it wouldn't have mattered. But she was.

She hated it when celebrities got judged by their personal lives rather than their work. All those detestable stories on the front of grocery store checkout magazines made her stomach ache. In school, she'd suffered so painfully from nasty gossip. The kid of a drunken deadbeat dad and a mom who OD'ed. The Indian bitch who was never good enough.

Now, her image garnered respect. Not only was that crucial for the U.S. deal, she'd become a role model for young women of color. In the last few years she'd dated only rarely, with men who were eminently respectable, and she'd avoided any unseemly public displays of affection. Not that there'd been affection, as it turned out.

Zack wasn't that kind of man. He was a hot young ski instructor, and he was physical and flirtatious, not formal and discreet. The last thing she needed was for some embarrassing cell phone video to be posted on YouTube. She wasn't going to risk the career she'd worked so hard for over a quickie hookup. Because, much as he might dress it up with wine and pizza, she knew that was what they were both talking about.

Feeling her way, not wanting to reveal her identity, she said, "I'm in Whistler with colleagues, and I don't want to seem unprofessional. Having a, um, fling with a, uh . . . "

"Ski bum?" There was a dangerous edge to his voice, the first time she'd seen anything other than his fun, charming side.

"I didn't say that." Being a ski instructor didn't equate to being a ski bum. She hated stereotypes. They'd dogged her life. First the negative ones based on being Native Canadian with a drunk for a dad, and then the affirmative action ones that had made her wonder if she'd won jobs and promotions due to talent or to the fact she was female and aboriginal.

"I don't think of you as a ski bum, Zack. But I know nothing about you except that you teach skiing, have an Australian accent, and speak several languages." And that he was highly competent at his work and equally good with little kids and elderly grandparents. He was pretty impressive, as well as being so hot he'd made her sex-starved body ache with need.

"So let's hook up and get to know each other." The deep green eyes peering into hers were so seductive.

Hook up, being the operative words. Sex. Another surge of arousal heated her. Yes, that was what they both really had in mind. So why not skip the wine and pizza and get to the good stuff?

It was her moment of truth. He hadn't a clue she was Brianna George. Zack didn't want anything from her except sex, and he was being straight about it. He thought she was hot, and he wanted her. More than he wanted pretty, *young* Karen.

Sure, he probably slept with a different ski student each night, but why should she care as long as he used protection? What would it be like to have sex with no complications? No worry about the man fake-romancing her to get something from her?

Skiing had proved to be—yes, she'd use the word—fun. With Zack, sex would be, too. She was sure of it, and her body was clamoring for it with an urgency she hadn't experienced since . . . Had she ever felt this thrill of achy yearning?

"All right," she said softly.

His eyes lit. "Tonight?"

"I can't." She had a conference call with her staff about next week's shows, including their plans for the whistle-blower segment. "Tomorrow night? I could come to your place."

"Great. Only, be warned, I share the place."

"You have a roommate?" If she was actually going to have this fling, no one could know about it. Her image, the respect she'd earned, were critical to her.

"Four. Or five, depending."

She gaped. "Depending?"

"On who's in town. We're mostly from Oz. Seasonal workers. Ski instructors, waiters and waitresses, chambermaids. Most of the accommodation in Whistler goes to the tourists who can pay the big bucks, so the rest of us share whatever we can find."

She'd heard about the overcrowding at Whistler and sympathized, but no way was she going to have sex in an apartment he shared with several roommates. "No, I can't do that."

"Then how about your place?"

The Alpine Hideaway? That would be as bad as going out in public.

One of her fellow students snowplowed to a stop beside them, and she murmured, "Later, Zack," then began to painstakingly climb her way up the hill. She never let obstacles stand in her way. If anything, they made her more determined.

When she reached the top, most of the other students had begun taking off their ski gear. Before joining them, she pulled off her helmet, took out her cell, and dialed information. After exploring Whistler the previous day, she knew the best hotel was the Harrington.

Once she'd made her call, she skied her way over to the other students. As soon as the others were free of their skis, boots, and helmets, they thanked Zack and streamed over to meet up with the second group of students from the chalet.

Bree hung back with Zack. "Tomorrow night, the Harrington," she told him. "Room 714." She'd made sure to get the room number so he wouldn't have to ask at the front desk.

"Harrington?" He whistled. "Nice digs. What time? I get off when the lifts close, so whatever works for you." His face was eager. He was sexy and adorable and eight years younger. What she'd pay for one night at the Harrington was no doubt more than he paid for a month's rent. What the hell was she doing?

And why was she so ridiculously attracted to someone so totally different from her?

Anxiety and arousal made her twitchy. It was really too bad they couldn't do this tonight. "Seven? If we're hungry, we can order room service."

He winked. "I'll be sure to bring my appetite."

BRIANNA felt more energized than she had in a long time when she returned to the Alpine Hideaway. Ready to put in a few hours of work, she got a bowl of soup from the buffet and went to her room. When she checked e-mail, she found a troubling message from her producer about a segment they'd planned for next week and immediately gave her a call.

"Martine, I got your e-mail. You should have called my cell."

"I didn't want to disturb you while you're on holiday."

"It's not a real holiday. I'm working." She felt a twinge of guilt for having goofed off, then suppressed it. Her headache was gone, and she felt refreshed and full of energy.

"Sorry, Brianna."

"No problem. Now, what's happened with our whistle-blower at the power plant? You say he has cold feet?"

"His wife's been diagnosed with a degenerative spinal condition. She'll need specialist treatments like chiropractic and massage therapy, a walker, then a wheelchair, prescription drugs. It's going to be expensive."

How sad for the couple. "Damn. Extended health insurance. He has it at work, and he'll lose his job when the segment airs." The standard universal health insurance for B.C. residents wouldn't cover a number of his wife's expenses.

"Exactly."

"I'll get my team to check into private plans and get some quotes. We can cover his insurance until he finds a new job, right?" They had to. The couple had enough to deal with, without having to worry about medical costs—and *The Scoop* couldn't lose this story.

"I suppose. But how long—"

"I'll phone a headhunter. I have the name of a woman I interviewed last year who's on the ball." As she spoke, she did a quick search of *The Scoop*'s contact file, which was huge but efficiently indexed. "Got it. I'll tell her this is completely confidential, she has to handle it by herself, and get her to line up some interviews for our guy, for right after the segment airs. With ethical employers, obviously, who'll respect what the man's doing rather than think he's disloyal."

She drummed her fingers on the desk. "We could have a story there, too. Good corporate citizens versus bad. How does an employee tell, when they're looking for a job?" On a roll now, she said, "And perhaps a story on health care."

"Health care? From what angle?"

"The Americans talk about Canadian health care like it's some fabulous model. But look at all the things regular health care doesn't cover, unless you're an employee with a good benefits package." She flicked her hair back. "I know, it's not a new story, but there's more U.S. interest now, and more privatization in Canada. I'll ask the team to see if they can dig up some new angles."

"Let me know what you need from me."

"I will."

When she put down her cell, she smiled with satisfaction. The ideas weren't brilliant, and they had nothing to do with Whistler, but you never knew what angles might turn up with a little digging and creativity.

Quickly she dashed off an e-mail to her staff, then she picked up her cell again to dial the headhunter. The whistle-blower was doing a good thing. He and his wife shouldn't suffer for it.

THE next night, as Brianna took the elevator to the seventh floor of the Harrington, she refused to allow herself any second thoughts. For the first time ever, she'd booked an evening off to have sex, and she was going to enjoy herself.

Growing up in poverty with a disabled dad who drank and a mom who, in retrospect, had been clinically depressed, she hadn't been a kid who thought much about fun. Her goal in life had been to escape to something better. The first escape had come when her mom died of an overdose of prescription meds and her dad sent her off reservation to live with Aunt Marie. The second escape had been to Vancouver, to attend university. Every single one of her steps had been upward.

Now look at her, sliding open the door to a luxury suite in Whistler's best hotel. She still felt a sense of achievement at moments like this. With an appreciative eye, she perused the lovely toiletries in the bathroom, noted the pillow menu and boutique chocolates on the pillows, and admired the gas fireplace in the sitting area, all symbols of how far she'd come.

Though the fine trappings were a normal part of her life now, the fact that she wasn't toting a laptop and briefcase was incredibly rare. In the competitive TV business, stopping to smell the roses, as Joan had put it, had little place.

But this week it did. Yesterday, with the skiing, and now, with Zack. In fact, tonight she wasn't even Brianna George, just a tourist named Bree. What an amazingly liberating thought.

Then she frowned. Wait a minute, she'd worked exceedingly hard to become Brianna George, the TV host. Of course she didn't regret a moment of it or yearn for anything different.

Well, maybe a bit more of the flexibility she'd had before she started working toward the U.S. deal. For example, today she'd had a couple of good story ideas, but they weren't ones with U.S. appeal, unfortunately.

Still, it was a good sign. Her freshness and creativity were returning. It seemed Tom had been right, and a little R & R was reinvigorating her. Not, of course, that he would have envisioned her getting her groove back by having a fling with a man his own age.

She let out an uncharacteristic giggle, remembering the movie *How Stella Got Her Groove Back*. An older female executive and a hot young guy she met on holiday. Of course, in Stella's case, meeting that hottie had shaken up her whole life. That certainly wasn't going to happen here. She and Zack were going to "groove" once, and once only.

After ridding herself of coat, boots, and hat, she fluffed up her hair and checked her reflection in the bathroom mirror. Her wardrobe was designed around the principles of class and professionalism, not sexiness, so there hadn't been much to choose from. She'd decided on black jeans topped by a scoop-necked cashmere sweater in an amber color that matched the highlights in her short black hair.

Okay, now what? Should she call room service and get wine? Red or white? Or would Zack prefer beer?

Well, how about that? She, who appeared on TV at noon every weekday, was nervous about impressing an Aussie ski instructor.

A knock sounded on the door, and she checked the peephole, then quickly opened the door. "Hi." Despite all her voice training, that one syllable squeaked.

"Hey, Bree." He came in, bringing cool freshness, a drift of outdoorsy scent. To her surprise, he carried a bulging eco-friendly shopping bag.

Before she could ask about that, he'd put the bag down and let his jacket fall to the floor. As soon as she'd closed the door, he was in front of her. He raised both hands, slid sure fingers through her hair, and tilted her head up to his. "So pretty," he said. "Been thinking about doing this since I met you."

"I, uh . . . " Of course it had been on her mind, too, but she hadn't expected him to do it so soon. Well, maybe she had—and that was why she couldn't go out in public with him.

"Been wondering how you'd taste." He bent his head toward hers and paused a moment. When she didn't say no, his lips brushed hers.

A quiver ran through her. Lust, longing, something primitive and brand-new for her.

His dancing eyes peered into hers, and she let out a soft sigh. An "Oh, yes" sigh.

His lips firmed against hers. Now the quiver inside her was stronger, and it made her kiss him back. His breath smelled of toothpaste, and his sun-tipped hair, when she ran a hand through it, was damp.

The tip of his tongue teased her lips seductively, and she opened to let her own tongue meet it. Nice, so nice, though there was a tentativeness, a sense of exploration, to their thrusts and nibbles. As with skiing, she thought, it was a matter of finding your balance.

They were doing well enough that heat surged through her, tightening her breasts and dampening her thong.

His lips pressed more demandingly against hers, his tongue thrust harder, and she answered back hungrily, feeling a corresponding ache of need in her pussy. His cock had hardened, thrusting rigidly against her belly, and she whimpered with the need to feel him inside her.

Oh God, what was happening? This was too fast. Anxious again, she pulled back in his arms. "Zack, I—"

"Sorry." He shook his head, looking a little dazed. "Didn't mean to come on so strong."

"No, it's . . . I just need to . . . breathe for a moment."

"Yeah. Let's have a drink, get to know each other a bit."

"Good idea." She intended to turn and phone room service, but when she stepped out of his arms, she just had to stare at him in appreciation.

He wore a long-sleeved T-shirt over khaki cargo pants and, oh yes, his build was as fine as any she'd ever seen. The tee showcased broad shoulders and a lean, muscular frame, and the loose pants were distended by his hard-on.

What did he look like naked? What did he feel like? Her pussy, which had felt no stimulation other than her own hand or a vibrator in more than two years, pulsed at the thought.

She followed as he walked into the sitting room carrying the bag he'd brought.

This man—this much younger man—was so different from her work colleagues and the men she occasionally dated. So casual and physical and sexy.

She wet her lips, which were already swollen from kissing. They could just have sex. Get right to it. After all, that's why they'd both come. And yet, it seemed so . . . cold.

Not that she expected or wanted romance, but like he said, it would be nice to get to know each other a bit first. To make to-night's . . . interaction more personal. He was good with personal; she'd seen that in the way he treated people during the ski lessons.

She liked the way that, even though he was obviously turned on, he wasn't pushing her for sex.

He sat on the couch that faced the fireplace, placing the bag on the floor beside him.

She sat, too, leaving a few inches between her thigh and his.

"Nice room," he said offhandedly, as if the luxury was no big deal to him. No doubt he'd been in this hotel before, sleeping with other tourists. Other older women who had the money to stay here.

That was fine, she told herself firmly. This was a one-nighter.

A one-nighter to which he'd brought wine, she realized as he drew a bottle out of the bag. "Took a guess," he said. "Is red okay?"

She glanced at the bottle, reassuring herself it looked like decent wine. "Sure." She didn't drink often, held herself to a one-drink limit, and chose wine that was as different as possible from the rot-gut her dad and uncle used to drink out of gallon jugs.

"It's from Oz. We do pretty good reds Down Under." He began to open it.

"I'll get glasses." She began to rise, but he waved her down.

"Brought those, too." From the bag, he took a striped tea towel, wrapped around what turned out to be two wineglasses.

"I'm impressed," she said.

That charming grin of his flashed. "Yeah, well, that's the general idea."

He must have this down to an art. Bringing wine to women in hotel rooms.

Hopefully, he also had sex down to an art. And hopefully that eco bag of tricks contained a condom. She'd scurried into a drug-store on the way to the hotel and bought a package herself, but it would be nicer if he took care of things.

He poured two glasses, handed her one, then held his out in a toast. "Cheers, Bree. I'm glad you came for that ski lesson."

She clicked her glass to his. "Me, too." And not only because she'd met Zack, but because she'd skied. She had challenged herself, learned something and not done half badly, and she'd had fun.

Cautiously she took a sip, then another. The wine was fruity, rich, and very pleasant. "This is nice. Thank you."

"You haven't had dinner, right?"

"No." She'd been too nervous to contemplate eating.

"Then let's have a snack with our wine."

"I'll get the room service menu." Again, she started to get up.

"Relax." He held up the bag. "I brought a picnic."

He'd brought her a picnic? Men had taken her for dinner in fancy restaurants, picked her up in limos with champagne, and mostly they'd been trying to manipulate her. No man had ever given her a picnic.

"Bree? That okay?"

"It sounds wonderful." Oh yes, Zack was fun and thoughtful. Feeling young, eager, she asked, "What did you bring?"

"A little of this, a little of that."

She leaned forward eagerly as he laid items on the coffee table. A loaf of Italian bread, rosemary ham, smoked turkey breast, pâté, three different cheeses, tapenade, and a container of dark purple olives. Finally, with a flourish he presented a box of strawberries.

"Look okay?" He added paper plates, napkins, and plastic cutlery.

"Perfect." It wasn't pretentious gourmet fare, nor the chips and dip she might have expected from a ski instructor who shared an apartment with four other people. Her stomach rumbled and, embarrassed, she pressed a hand to it. "I hadn't realized I was so hungry."

He shifted closer, nudged his thigh against hers, and caught her other hand, caressing it lightly. "Enjoy. That's what we're here for, right?" His gaze met hers, eyes full of mischief.

She turned her hand palm up, interlocked fingers with him, and gave a squeeze. "Yes, it is. Starting with this delicious picnic." His hand was warm, strong, and almost too good to let go of, but her stomach growled again, so she did. "Will you cut me some bread?"

For a few minutes, they were busy opening little packages and assembling snacks, then she sat back to munch on a slice of bread topped with a thin layer of tapenade, ham, and Camembert.

Curious about the man whose thigh branded hers even through the fabric of their pants, she said, "How did an Australian like you decide to work in Whistler?"

He'd assembled a much thicker open-faced sandwich and demolished half of it. "I've been here before. Three or so years back. Great skiing, interesting place, lots of other Aussies."

"I've noticed a lot of Australian accents among salesclerks and staff in coffee shops and restaurants."

He nodded. "Even got our own pub called Down Under, owned by an Aussie expat who only hires people from home."

Zack's world was an intriguing one. Young, transient workers moving here and there, drawn by skiing and other interests and the urge to travel the world. They were a different generation from her, and few would have grown up with the hardships she had. As a result, they had different values and ambitions.

She and Zack were such opposite people, yet she felt more at ease with him than with anyone she'd met in a long time, likely because he knew her only as Bree, not Brianna George. Tentatively, she asked, "It doesn't bother you that I'm older than you?"

"No worries." He spread pâté on bread, then gave her a quizzical look. "Okay, you got me curious. How old are you?"

Now she wished she hadn't raised the subject. "Several years older."

"Bree, you're hot. No reason to be secretive."

She stared straight into his eyes. If this was going to matter to him, she wanted to know. "Thirty-five."

His lips curved. "An experienced older woman. Very hot."

Sweet. Except if that was what he thought, he was going to be disappointed. She shook her head ruefully. "Sorry to disillusion you, but I'm sure you have more experience than I do. I don't have much time in my life for men."

"Woman says that, it usually means she's a workaholic."

"I'll cop to that." She only hoped he didn't ask what she did.

"Hmm." He picked up an olive and held it to her lips. "A workaholic and a perfectionist."

"Perfectionist? I'm . . . yeah, okay." Brianna sucked the olive into her mouth, letting her lips caress his skin.

"You like to get things right, but you're willing to try something new." His thumb smoothed over her lips as she chewed and swallowed, weather-chapped and sensual. "You like the outdoors, snow country, and you enjoy flying down a hill just as much as you take pride in mastering the skill to do it."

"And you're perceptive. That's probably one reason you're so good with your students. Plus, you love skiing and want to share that with them."

"Now who's perceptive?" He raised his glass to her, drained it, then lifted the bottle. "Hey, you've barely touched your wine."

"I'm making it last. I never have more than one glass."

His quizzical look made her say quickly, "And no, don't add alcoholic to that string of labels."

He filled his own glass and settled back, his hip bumping hers. "More like, control freak."

"I won't deny it." Some impulse—maybe it was the intimacy of picnicking by the fire—led her to share something she rarely spoke of. "If you'd had a dad like mine, and you were Native Canadian, you'd watch your drinking, too. 'Drunken Indian' is a slur I grew up hearing."

Expression serious, he said, "I hear you. Aboriginal Australians get the same shit." He rubbed her knee gently. "Sorry about your dad."

"Thanks." The simple comment and gesture touched her. "Oh well, everyone has some shit in their lives. Because of my family stuff, I developed discipline and made something of myself."

"Good on you." He sliced more bread and built another snack. "So what is it you do, Bree? Lawyer?"

Damn. Given what she'd said, it wasn't surprising he'd asked. Hedging, she said, "No, I work in TV." She leaned forward to slice a piece of Edam and wrap it in turkey.

"TV? Guess that's pretty cool?"

"It can be." She nibbled her snack. "The people I work with are creative and smart. I like my job."

She intended to change the subject, but before she could, he asked, "What d'you do there?"

Everything. She picked something that would sound dull. "Background research."

"Huh. Perfectionism, attention to detail. I guess that fits."

Quickly she asked, "How about you? Do you teach skiing full-time?"

"Pretty much. I've been hooked on skiing since I was a kid. Been working at ski resorts for more than ten years now. Australia and New Zealand at first, then Switzerland and Austria, France and Italy. Aspen and Vail, Banff and Quebec. Even Chile and Argentina."

"My gosh." She'd never had time to travel. Her five- and ten-year plans were all about work. She wondered if Zack had any plans beyond being a transient ski instructor. "Your family's back in Australia?"

"Yeah. I miss them, especially my kid brothers."

"I'm sure they all miss you."

"Yeah." He shrugged. "My parents would've rather I stayed home and went to the uni like my older brother, but they've always said we should follow our bliss. Just never expected that I'd follow it to places like Chile and Quebec. I keep telling them, travel's the best education."

"I'm sure it's a good one." Not the kind that made for an impressive résumé, but he probably didn't care.

Not that his résumé interested her. He'd rolled his sleeves up to reveal strong, tanned forearms dusted with hair that sparkled gold in the firelight. Now he picked up a plump red strawberry and held it toward her lips.

She gazed past the fruit to his face: strong-featured, with a square jaw, slightly crooked nose—broken in a fall?—and those eyes the color of evergreens.

Slowly she took the berry into her mouth, and his thumb lingered to caress her top lip, then her bottom one.

It was such a simple touch, yet so sensual. He made her aware of her body in a way she rarely was. She almost forgot to chew the strawberry, but when she did, the delicious fruity taste burst on her tongue. A sweet surprise, just like the man beside her.

"You have a great mouth," he said.

She swallowed, then parted her lips slightly.

His finger flirted with the crease between them. "Such full, sexy lips. Can't look at them without wanting to kiss them."

She felt the same way about his as he sat half turned toward her, the firelight dancing across the strong planes of his face. "Then what are you waiting for?" Their first kiss had been wonderful, and now she was relaxed from the wine, the delicious snack, and their conversation.

He tipped his head toward hers, and their lips touched gently. Other men had given her tentative kisses and forceful ones. Never had a guy kissed her with this blend of gentleness and confidence. His lips were soft, teasing, seductive, and she had to respond, to open her mouth on a sigh of pleasure.

She'd never felt particularly skilled at kissing, but somehow, with Zack, she knew exactly what to do without thinking about it. Their tongues twined, broke apart, he laughed and darted a kiss on the bow of her top lip, she sucked his bottom lip into her mouth.

This kiss was relaxed and heady, like the first bites of a delicious meal, when you wanted to draw out and savor the pleasure.

Chapter 4

AROUSAL heated Brianna's blood like the lick of flames in the fire-place: slow, thorough, and persistent. Between her legs, a yearning ache built. She freed her mouth, caught a breath. "Mmm, very nice." Darting a glance at his lap, she saw he was erect again under the loose cargo pants. She wanted to see him, touch him, but she'd never been sexually confident.

Zack seemed content to set a slow pace. Did he realize the pow-erful effect of his slow seduction? Of course he did. No question Zack was as expert with women as he was with skiing.

And that was fine with her, she reminded herself. She was having a lovely time.

He held another strawberry to her lips. "You're dessert, Bree. Your eyes are the color of bittersweet chocolate, your skin is brown sugar, and your lips are as ripe and sweet as these berries."

As he spoke, she nibbled the berry from his fingers; then, with the taste of strawberry sweet in her mouth, she leaned forward to kiss him.

His hands gripped her waist, then slid up under her sweater, ex-ploring her back. The clasp of her bra flicked open.

A moment later, he did it back up and broke the kiss. "No, not this way. I want to see you. Undress for me, Bree."

Take her clothes off? Here, in the firelight, while he watched?

Brianna was used to eyes and hands on her body—wardrobe fittings, massages, working with her personal trainer—but undressing for a man who was about to become her lover was a whole different thing.

An incredibly sensual, erotic thing, if she had the courage.

Slowly she got up, put her hands to the waist of her jeans, and undid the button. Fingers trembling, she stopped. "This is embarrassing." Her voice was a breathy whisper.

"You're beautiful. Let me see you." Zack leaned forward, elbows on his knees, his expression one of aroused anticipation.

She took a deep breath, then slid down the zipper and began to ease the slim-fitting pants down her hips and legs. There was no graceful way of doing this, and by the time she'd kicked them off and straightened, she knew she looked as flustered as she felt. Below her sweater, she was naked but for a thong.

"Great legs," Zack said, a husky edge to his voice. "Now your sweater."

Slowly, fingers clumsy with nervousness, she raised the hem, revealing the front of her thong inch by inch. The gleam of appreciation in his eyes gave her courage to carry on, baring her tummy, waist, and rib cage. The skin she revealed tingled and quivered under the intensity of his gaze. She peeled the sweater over her head, struggled to free her arms, and then it was off. She stood in only a champagne lace bra and thong, the fabric light against her dusky skin.

The sound Zack made was somewhere between a sigh and a groan. "Bloody awesome, woman." Then his lips curved into a wicked grin. "Turn around, Bree."

His obvious appreciation sent a sexy glow radiating through her. Her nipples hardened, poking against the lace of her bra, and the crotch of her thong grew damper by the moment.

She might be clumsy about stripping off her outer clothing, but thanks to modeling and acting lessons, she did know how to strut her stuff. In small steps, shifting her weight so her hips swayed, she pivoted, giving him first a side view and then a full-on back view. She knew he'd see a lithe, toned brown back, naked but for the straps of her bra and thong.

"Oh shit, you are so hot."

She felt hot, in all senses of the word. Sexy, flushed, aroused, sassy. A crazy impulse made her spread her feet, bend from the waist, and grasp her ankles. Then she looked back at him from between the V of her legs and said provocatively, "You like?"

"I've got an erection that could pump iron." His words would have been humorous but for the dead-serious tone in which he said them.

Her sex clenched at the thought of that erection pumping into her. Drops of moisture escaped her thong and dampened her inner thighs. He wasn't even touching her, yet he'd got her more aroused than she could remember ever being.

She straightened gracefully and turned to face him. Arching her back, breasts thrusting in his direction, she put both hands behind her back on the clasp of her bra. Flirtatiously, she said, "Want me to take it off?" A sense of power filled her. Maybe in another life she'd been a stripper.

"Oh, yeah."

She flicked the clasp open. Then, before the bra could drop, she clasped her hands over the front of it. For a moment she held it against her skin, teasing him, then in a quick motion she tossed it away, baring her breasts to his gaze.

His very heated gaze.

He surged to his feet. "I have to touch you." Then he was in front of her, hands reaching out to cup her breasts. His thumbs brushed across her nipples, sending darts of aching pleasure through her.

He bent his head and sucked a nipple into his mouth, lips firm but gentle, and she gasped at the delicious sensation. She'd have been happy for him to stay there, but instead, he straightened and pulled her against him. His T-shirt was soft against her skin, but the body beneath it was hard as steel. The fabric of his cargo pants abraded her slightly, and inside them his rigid shaft prodded her belly.

Her breath caught in her throat. Zack was so strong, so physical, so very male.

In the next minute, he proved it by hoisting her into his arms as if she were weightless. He carted her across the room to the bed, where, holding her with one arm, he used the other to fling the bedspread to the floor. He lowered her atop the white sheets.

As he reached for the hem of his T-shirt, she watched in breathless anticipation, and even more so when he unzipped his pants. Then, finally, he was naked.

Oh yes, he lived up to the promise she'd seen and felt when he was clothed. He was lean but powerful, muscles beautifully defined. And his cock was perfect.

"You're gorgeous," she whispered.

She expected him to grab a condom and do her, but he didn't. Instead, he sat on the bed beside her and began to touch her, running his fingers lightly over her shoulders, her chest, her breasts, tummy, and hips. He skimmed the front of her thong and her body thrust up, spontaneously. Oh, his touch felt good. He moved on, though, down her legs to her feet. It was as if he wanted to make sure every cell in her body was totally aware of him.

And he was doing a damn fine job of it.

He lowered his head to her breast and took up where he'd left off, gently sucking her nipple as his fingers stroked the smooth skin of her breast.

"Oh, Zack." She gripped his head, feeling the springiness of his thick hair, and held on as he raised a sweet torment in her body.

When her nipple was tight and aching, he lifted his head and slid up the bed to blanket her body with his. "Can't get enough of you, Bree." His lips took hers hungrily.

She met them with equal hunger, her body pressing eagerly against his, savoring the hard, male feel of him atop her. His tongue plunged in and out of her mouth, mimicking sex, and she caught it and sucked it until his hips pumped against her and he moaned and broke away.

Now he slid down to kiss her other breast, but this time he didn't spend as much time. Perhaps he, like she, was impatient to get to the main event.

Her hips twisted restlessly, and he heeded their message and kissed his way down her body. A finger hooked her thong, and he dragged it down and tossed it away.

His lips brushed across curls of hair, then his fingers teased between her legs, and she spread her thighs to give him access. He made good use of it, gathering her moisture and spreading it across the ultrasensitive skin of her labia, then sliding a finger, and another, inside her.

She gripped him eagerly, whimpering as he slid his fingers out, then in again, creating a delicious, irresistible friction. She was so hot, so ready, so needy, her body couldn't take this much longer without coming apart. Any nervousness or self-consciousness she'd felt earlier had been banished by pure sexual need.

"Please," she murmured desperately. "Oh, please."

His thumb, that weather-roughened thumb, gently brushed her clit, making her gasp. He brushed it again, and she almost screamed at the delicious sensations.

Then he pressed it more firmly and . . . "God!" she cried as the waves of orgasm broke, caught her up, and pulled her under.

After a few minutes, she came to her senses enough to realize her eyes were closed, a deep red glow under her lids. Blinking dazedly, she managed to open them and focus.

The first thing she saw was Zack's face, his smile. "Hey there," he said.

"Hey." She raised a hand, brushed hair back from her damp brow. "Wow." She'd never had such a powerful climax.

"Want to go for a second?" His rigid cock nudged suggestively between her legs.

How could she say no to that? "We need protection. I—"

"It's already on."

She really had zoned out. But she was quickly coming to her senses, her body reawakening to the sexy gleam in his eyes, the tickle of his chest hair against her nipples, and mostly the enticing press of his cock against her pussy. Feeling wonderfully alive, she grinned up at him. "Then what are we waiting for?"

He grinned back, then tilted his hips and in one smooth motion slid inside her.

"Oh," she moaned with pleasure. And "Oh, yes," as he went deeper still, filling her tight and hard.

Slowly he drew back, pulling out almost all the way, making her tingle inside, and then he thrust back in, the crown of his cock stimulating every tingly spot. "So good," he muttered. "Can't believe how bloody good you feel."

"You, too." Bracing herself with her palms on the bed, she locked her legs around him and lifted up to meet his thrusts.

He tilted his hips, sweetening the angle so his cock brushed her sensitized clit, and she whimpered as arousal gathered inside her again.

A thought drifted into her brain. Surely sex had never felt so good before, or she wouldn't have been able to go so long without it. Then her brain shut down, and her body took over in that primal drive to orgasm.

Their bodies pounded together, both of them panting harshly like they were running a race. She felt that physical tightening, that unmistakable intensity of focus when everything centered, built, and . . .

She shattered again, consumed with pleasure, barely aware of Zack giving a groan of release as his own climax hit him.

Clinging to him, she rode out the aftershocks that rocked both of them. Then, as the tension slowly eased from her body, she lowered her trembling legs. On no, sex had never been anywhere near this good before.

Zack took his weight on his hands, withdrew from her and dealt with the condom, then flopped down beside her.

He worked one arm under her shoulders and tipped her toward him so she lay curved against his body, her head on his shoulder. With his free hand, he stroked her hair. "You're really something."

In her work life, she was. Never had she thought of herself as "really something" in bed. "Thanks. So are you." In his case, it was the truth.

How many women had he lain with like this, so gentle and considerate after sex? As well as being a terrific lover, he really was a sweet man, with the picnic and wine, the cuddling in bed.

"Want anything?" he asked lazily. "Wine? Snack?"

She shook her head and pressed her lips against his chest. "No." What she really wanted was to lie like this until they both fell asleep.

For a moment, she explored that possibility. If she stayed at the Harrington until morning, she could return to the Alpine Hideaway later and pretend she'd gone out at dawn on some research trip. But she and Zack were about sex, not a sleepover. Waking up together . . . Well, that was serious. The last time she'd done that she'd been Zack's age. With Lionel, the man who had betrayed her.

A smart journalist knew exactly when to end the story without letting it drag on too long. With more than a little regret, she said, "I should get going."

ZACK, who'd been lying there in a state of drowsy contentment, a lovely woman curled up against him, stared at Bree as she started to get up. "Going? Where?"

"Back to the chalet where I'm staying."

"Huh?" He shoved himself up to a sitting position. "You're not staying here?"

"No. My group is at the Alpine Hideaway. But it would have been impossible to get together there, so I booked this room." As she spoke, she walked away from the bed to gather her scattered clothing.

He climbed out of bed, admiring her naked body as he tried to figure out what was going on. "You got this room just for tonight?"

He'd noticed there were no personal items beside the bed or on the dresser but figured Bree was a neat freak.

"Yes."

He caught her by the shoulders. "But why go? It's early. Come back to bed." He lowered his head until his forehead touched hers, and he gazed into her eyes. "We Aussies have a lot of stamina."

"I'm not questioning your stamina." She gazed at him almost wistfully, then shook her head. "I need to get back."

Sighing, he bent down, picked up his boxers, and began to pull them on. "Okay, I hear you. I'll pay for the room, drive you back." Pity she'd picked one of the priciest hotels, but the fireplace had been great for their picnic.

"The room's already paid for." She pulled on her thong. "My treat."

"That's not—"

"You brought the food and wine. Tonight was special for me. An unusual treat."

He scowled. It sounded like a token, thrown out to salve his male pride. She made good money and obviously knew he didn't. Not that he was hard up, what with sharing rent and getting good tips. Maybe he was just sensitive because his parents had been on his case lately, asking him when he was going to grow up and get a real job.

She'd put on her bra and scowled back. "You weren't worried when you thought I was staying in this hotel. And I know you've gone back to other women's rooms."

Sure, he had, but all the same . . . "Seems different, you going and getting a room just for . . . " Just for sex. He pulled on his cargo pants as she put on her jeans. Last year there'd been a woman, forty-ish, who'd basically wanted to hire him to be her boy toy. She'd carted around a designer dog in her Coach bag and wanted a matching man to flaunt, and it had pissed him right off.

Not that Bree was like that, of course. Flaunting him was the last thing on her mind. "You're spending a lot of money to keep people from knowing you're getting it on," he commented as she pulled her sweater over her head.

She ran her fingers through her hair. "I have a professional reputation. If people knew I'd had a one-nighter with a much younger
guy . . . " She grimaced.

Why did women get so hung up about age? And what was this
bullshit about a one-nighter? They were good together, and not just
in bed. She was the most intriguing woman he'd met in a long time.
A woman from a crappy background who had, to use his mum's
expression, pulled herself up by her bootstraps. A control freak who
worried about elderly Joan skiing yet stepped back when she saw
how much it meant to her and instead offered comfort to poor old
Walter.

"I want to see you again," he said.

"What?" Her eyes widened. "But, we . . . I mean . . . "

He rested his hands on her shoulders and dipped his head until
their foreheads touched. With as much of his famed charm as he
could summon, he said, "We're nowhere near done."

"We aren't?" Her voice, normally so well modulated, squeaked.

That squeak put a grin on his face. He shook his head slowly.
"You know I'm right. Just think of all the things we've yet to do."
Gently he rotated her until her back was to him, then he brushed
featherlight kisses across the nape of her neck below her short hair.

She shivered. "What kind of things?"

He licked her soft skin, then nudged his swelling cock suggestively against her arse. "Anything you want." He imagined all the
things he'd like to do with Bree. To his surprise, the words that
came out of his mouth were, "Let's go skiing."

An image popped into his mind. Somewhere remote enough to
offer privacy, yet where the skiing was easy enough she'd be okay.
They'd enjoy the outdoors and the exercise, sip something out of a
thermos, fool around. He'd bet she'd never had sex on the slopes, but
he'd also bet he could keep her warm.

She'd swung around to eye him skeptically. "You want to ski with
me."

"Among other things."

Her brows pulled together, and she studied him for a long

moment, as if puzzled he'd suggest skiing rather than sex, then asked warily, "Where?"

"Shit, Bree." Much as he'd hated the idea of being flaunted, being hidden away like he embarrassed her was crappy, too. "I don't get what's so wrong with us being together."

"Skiing, eh? I guess there's nothing wrong with going skiing."

He rolled his eyes. Much as he loved women, they could drive a guy crazy. "Good. Tomorrow morning?"

"Aren't you teaching?"

He shrugged and dropped a kiss on her nose. "I'll trade off with someone. No worries."

"Well, all right."

"Good." This time he kissed her lips quickly and firmly. Then he went to the sitting room to collect the picnic stuff. "You want any of this? A midnight snack?"

She'd followed him, and she picked up her glass, which still had a mouthful in it. "No, but it was delicious. Thank you, Zack. It was much more fun than a room service meal." She took a sip and glanced at him over the rim. "Are you going to tell your friends about us getting together?"

He gave an exasperated sigh. "I might've said I'd met a great woman, but I won't if it's such a big secret."

"Don't mention my name."

Annoyance mounting, he said, "Bree, I don't even know your last name."

"Right. Okay then." She walked toward the closet.

Without telling him her name. He gaped after her. She'd have sex with him, but she wouldn't tell him her name. Insulted, he was halfway tempted to tell her to forget the skiing. But he thought of another of his mum's expressions: don't throw the baby out with the bathwater. Meaning, don't throw out something great just because there's a little bad mixed in. When it came to Bree, so far the good definitely outweighed the bad.

Picking up his jacket, he said, "Ready to go?"

"You go first. I'll call a cab."

"I'll give you a—" No, of course she didn't want a ride. Someone might see them together.

"Where shall we meet tomorrow?"

"I get that you don't want anyone to know about us. But don't take it to extremes." Jeez, the woman behaved like she was a princess in disguise. "Walk down the street the Alpine Hideaway's on, out to the main road, and I'll pick you up there. Ten o'clock." He stared at her through narrowed eyes. If she objected to this, he was pulling the plug.

She studied his face, then said, "I'll be there."

"Good." He dropped a quick, hard kiss on her mouth and let himself out the door before one of them changed their mind.

Chapter 5

BRIANNA woke the next morning with an amazing sense of well-being that lasted until breakfast, when Shelley started acting like a self-centered brat. It wasn't the first time.

Brianna well understood the cult of celebrity and what it felt like to be the center of attention. And yes, Shelley deserved kudos when it came to her skiing, but that didn't give her the right to boss Tom around.

Tom was a good guy, bright and creative and a valued member of Brianna's team as well as a friend, but he had one flaw. He needed to grow a spine—both to get ahead in the world and to survive his marriage to Shelley.

This morning, Shelley announced that, rather than living in Vancouver and Whistler as they'd planned, the two of them ought to move to Utah because some incredible coach had just relocated there.

"But we agreed you'd work with a coach in Whistler," Tom said, for once sounding less than even-tempered. "We've got a mortgage on a condo in Vancouver and a lease on one up here."

Shelley waved a hand dismissively. "Things change. You know my skiing always comes first."

Brianna gaped at her. What a terrible thing to say! She glanced around and saw that the others at the table—Tom, his sister Maddie, and Andi—looked equally stunned.

This must have gotten through to Shelley, because she said, "Oh man, sorry. That came out wrong. I mean, after you and me, of course. But, Tom, this is a great opportunity. I can't afford to pass it up. The next Olympics are only three years off."

Brianna frowned, understanding Shelley's point. But Tom's career, even if less prestigious, was important, too.

"And what about the next great opportunity?" he demanded. "Where the hell's that one going to be, Shelley? And when? Next year, or a couple months from now? Are you going to want to pack up and move to France? Switzerland?"

"Well, I . . . Who can look that far ahead?"

When Tom didn't respond, Brianna couldn't remain silent. "Shelley, Tom has a career, too. A good career with lots of potential. And it's in Vancouver."

"You're being selfish. You just don't want to lose him."

This girl was enough to try anyone's patience. "No, I don't," Brianna said evenly. Not as a colleague nor as a friend. "Because I value him. Maybe I value him more than you do."

"Ooh! You just keep your cougar paws off my man!"

Cougar? Did Shelley actually believe Brianna had a *thing* for Tom? "That's not what I meant."

"It's disgusting when a middle-aged woman goes after a younger guy."

Middle-aged? Disgusting? Stunned, she stared at Shelley, feeling every one of her thirty-five years. Tom was Zack's age. And no, she wasn't *going after* Zack; he'd done the pursuing. But from the outside, would their relationship look disgusting?

Nausea cramped her stomach. She hated that word. Too many times, as a kid, she'd heard it applied to her dad, her mom, herself.

She'd worked so hard to reach the point where she'd thought she would never, ever, hear that word applied to her again.

Echoes of past taunts ringing painfully in her head, she rose without saying another word and hurried out of the dining room to the sanctuary of her own room.

There, she reached for the phone. And put it down abruptly when she realized she'd never gotten Zack's phone number. Nor did she know his last name.

And she deliberately hadn't given him hers. Oh yeah, from the outside their relationship would look pretty freaking tawdry. Because it was. She sank into a chair. An hour ago she'd been on top of the world and now . . .

Wait a minute. She sucked in a deep breath and let it out slowly. What was she doing, letting an immature girl get to her this way? It was confirmation that she needed to keep her affair private so as not to risk her career, but that's all it was. Zack was fun, this holiday thing was mutual, and there was nothing wrong with her going skiing with him. She could look at it as a private lesson.

And after, she guessed Zack would give her an even more private lesson in something he excelled at even more than skiing.

BRIANNA didn't own ski clothing, but yesterday she'd found that stretchy woolen pants with silk leggings underneath, thick socks, a turtleneck sweater, and a warm jacket had kept her plenty warm. So, dressed in a similar outfit, she headed for the front door of the Alpine Hideaway, excited anticipation putting a bounce in her step.

She hadn't glanced at the activity schedule Andi painstakingly drew up for each day, and so she was surprised when she found most of the guests hanging around the lobby and spilling out the front door.

Andi hurried up behind her. "Is everyone set?" the wedding planner said to the group. "The shuttle buses are outside." To Brianna, she said, "You're coming skating with us? That's great."

"Sorry, I have other plans." Andi's face bore signs of strain. Voice low, Brianna said, "Did everything work out with Tom and Shelley?" She hoped Tom hadn't knuckled under; if his marriage was to work, he needed to be assertive.

Andi shook her head. "They fought. Shelley stomped off in a huff. Tom's sister said she'd try to talk to Shelley, but I haven't seen a sign of any of them." She paused. "She was a bitch to you, and Tom set her straight."

"I'm glad, though I'd hate to be the reason they fought."

"That was just the icing on the cake." She grimaced. "Wedding planner humor." The woman looked exhausted, and Brianna could empathize. The wedding she'd worked so hard on might fall apart. It wasn't like the whistle-blower situation, where Brianna'd been able to come up with concrete solutions to the problem. The wedding planner was more or less helpless and could only wait.

"Andi, let me know if there's anything I can do to help."

"Thanks, I appreciate that. For now, just don't say anything to the others, okay?"

"My lips are sealed." She blew out air in frustration. "Tom's a great guy, and he deserves someone special."

"Every one of us does, and we shouldn't get married until we find them."

"Right." Not that Brianna harbored any romantic fantasies about finding true love. Tony, then Lionel, had disabused her of that notion.

"Want a lift in our shuttle bus?" Andi asked. "Where are you going?"

"Thanks, but I'm okay." Deliberately, she avoided answering the second question, and Andi, realizing everyone was waiting for her, hurried away without seeming to notice.

As soon as the bus left, Brianna walked down the snow-covered street of the housing development. Her sense of anticipation returned, and her stride lengthened. What a lovely morning: the soft fresh snow underfoot, the crispness of the air, the chatter of chickadees in a tree above her. Sunshine glinted brightly off all the snowy surfaces, making her sunglasses a necessity.

When she reached the main road, Zack was waiting for her in a battered red Jeep with skis and poles in a rack.

She hopped in, feeling very far away from Vancouver and the TV studio, and glad of it. A few days ago, she'd never have believed she could feel this way. She beamed at Zack, who looked as fresh and outdoorsy as Whistler itself, as attractive and sexy as she remembered. "Good morning."

He grinned back. "Mornin', Bree." She didn't even think about resisting when he tugged her toward him, removed her sunglasses, and kissed her. He tasted of mint toothpaste rather than morning coffee, and his kiss was warmer than the sun that beamed through the window.

Her body throbbed to aroused life as she answered him eagerly, losing herself in the kiss until a cheeky horn toot made them break apart.

"Here." He handed her back her glasses. "Put your sunnies on and buckle up."

She obeyed. "Where are we going?" Though he'd been right about her being a control freak, it was fun, for once, to relax and put herself in someone else's hands. So far, Zack's had seemed eminently capable.

"I'm mostly a downhill skier," he said as the Jeep bounced down the road, "but I figured you might like cross country."

This really was a date. One that wasn't about business or favors or even sex, just about hanging out. How wonderfully refreshing. It seemed she'd met one of those rare good guys, the kind she could trust. A good guy, great sexual chemistry. Now, if only she were closer to his age, and they weren't complete opposites . . .

She caught herself. What was she doing, thinking like a romantic? This was holiday sex, holiday fun. Period. She and Zack would never have a *relationship*.

"And the scenery's beautiful," he was saying. "Got a feeling yesterday you're into the scenery, right? Into snow country?"

"I do think it's lovely here." Reflecting, she added, "It's not just snow country, it's the outdoors. I love beaches, meadows, anything that hasn't been too spoiled by man."

"Where do you live?"

"Vancouver." Because of her job. "I know it's a big city, but Zack, it's one of the most nature-oriented cities I've ever been in. The mountains and ocean are right there, and even in the heart of the city there are flowering trees." As she bustled around town, she'd catch glimpses of mountain peaks and see magnolia and cherry blossoms unfurl in spring.

The Jeep rattled into a snow-rutted parking lot that held only a few cars. She climbed out and gazed around while Zack unstrapped the skis and poles. Ice on tree branches glittered like diamonds in the sun, and the chill air was so pure she could taste it on her tongue. "What an incredible day."

"Nothing like it," he agreed. "I've loved snow since I was a little tyke. Grew up in Cairns, and the first time the family took summer hols at Mt. Buller, I was hooked."

Summer? Oh yes, seasons were reversed Down Under. "Mt. Buller?"

"An Aussie ski hill. Not so grand as Whistler Blackcomb, but good enough for a kid to cut his teeth on."

As he helped her into skis that were skinnier than the ones she'd worn yesterday, he said, "How come you've never gone skiing before? Whistler's so close to Vancouver, and like you said, you're an outdoors girl."

"Not an outdoors girl," she corrected. "Only one who loves the outdoors. That doesn't mean I get many opportunities to enjoy it. As a kid, my family didn't have the money for fancy things like skiing." Much less proper food, half the time.

He nodded, eyes narrowed as if he'd heard her unspoken words.

"As I got older," she said, "my focus was on my education, my career."

"There's more to life than that."

Like teaching skiing at a different resort each season, and

seducing a different woman each week? Yes, she was career-driven and he was . . . fun-driven.

"Anyhow," she said, "I enjoy the city and all the amenities." Having grown up on a reservation in northern B.C., in a house where heat and power were cut off as frequently as they were on, she thoroughly appreciated a comfortable—even semi-luxurious—lifestyle.

"Don't get scenery like this in the city." He gestured to a frozen creek, trees decorated with sparkling snow, the spectacular panorama of mountains in the background.

"True." Fine hotels, restaurants, and shops were appealing, too, but they didn't resonate deep in her soul the way nature always had. Excitement filled her. "Okay, let's get going and explore." Experimentally she slid the skis back and forth. Weird. Only the fronts of her feet were fastened to the ski.

He'd put his own equipment on, together with a small pack on his back. Now he bent over to press a quick, hard kiss on her lips, then broke away, beaming. "You're on."

He headed off, calling over his shoulder as she followed clumsily. "We'll be skiing in pistes. Cut tracks." Gesturing, he showed her two sets of narrow parallel tracks carved into the snow. "Fit each ski into each track and shove yourself along with the poles. Easy."

"Like walking on skis?"

"Yeah, but you can also glide, especially when you get a slope. Both skis at the same time, knees bent like yesterday, shoving off with both poles at the same time. Or you can kind of run-glide, one ski at a time, with a kick-forward motion. I'll show you once you get your feet under you."

Her fear of appearing incompetent surfaced. "Go ahead, and I'll learn from watching you."

"As our friend Joan said, you just want to check out my arse."

She chuckled. "You got that right." Oh yes, being with Zack was an adventure. He was sexy and flirtatious, physical and confident, and he was teaching her how to have fun in ways she hadn't experienced before.

"Nope," he said cheerfully. "We'll ski side by side so I can keep an eye on you." He tossed her a wink, letting her know he intended a double meaning.

Resignedly she slotted her skis into the tracks alongside the ones he'd claimed. This walking on skis business took some effort, but she'd often used a ski machine at the fitness club so got the feel of it quickly.

He grinned. "See? No worries, Bree, you're good at this stuff."

She grinned back. Sliding along, she felt carefree and young. Younger than she'd felt . . . ever? At least ever since she could remember.

Zack set an easy pace, and for once she felt no need to be the superachiever and push herself. The snowy countryside was peaceful and easy on the eyes. She should be thinking of work, planning stories or plotting strategies for winning the U.S. deal, but her brain didn't want to go there. When she'd been a kid, nature had been her sanctuary, a place to escape the nastiness of home and the hurtful comments at school. It still had the power to soothe her soul.

"Zack, stop a minute." She pulled off her sunglasses to enjoy the way a scattering of frost-rimmed dead leaves caught the sun. "Look."

He took off his glasses, too, studied the leaves for a minute or two, then leaned over to kiss her. "Thanks."

They skied off again, moving through patches of forest and across smooth open areas, gliding down little slopes, and from time to time traveling alongside the frozen creek.

"Beaver lodge," he said, and they both stopped to look. "They don't hibernate, you know. They're awake in there."

"I know." She pointed to a break in the ice. "That's one of their exits. They'll have branches stored somewhere nearby." There'd been beaver where she grew up.

"Outdoors girl."

She chuckled, and they moved on, side by side.

A group of four skiers caught up and passed them, everyone calling cheerful greetings, but other than that, it was them, chirping birds, and an occasional squirrel.

"You're not gabby," he said. "I like that."

"You don't like women who talk?" she teased.

"Not out here. At least not talk that's just to fill up the silence."

She nodded. "The silence is good."

Normally, her life was a bustle of people to talk to and work to organize. Now, she simply enjoyed the sheer beauty around her, the crisp pureness of the air, the repetitive motion, the burn in her muscles. And, yes, the sight of Zack's body moving with fluid grace beside her and the engaging flash of his grin.

After an exhilarating swoop down a small hill, he pulled to a stop, and she did the same. "Thank you for bringing me," she told him. "This is perfect."

He took off his sunglasses—sunnies, as he called them—and his eyes twinkled. "Hey, you didn't give last night a 'perfect.'" Poles in one hand, he stripped off a glove and reached over to caress her cheek, then took off her glasses.

"Last night was pretty amazing, too," she told him.

He stared down at her, the twinkle replaced by a deeper kind of heat. "Look at you, Bree. Your cheeks are rosy, your eyes are sparkling as bright as the sun on the snow, and your lips . . . " He shook his head, then he leaned over.

At first her chilled lips barely felt the pressure. Then heat surged, her lips tingled as they came to life under his, and she answered back eagerly. It was impossible to kiss Zack and not want more.

His arms came around her, and she realized he'd dropped his ski poles and their sunglasses. This was so awkward, kissing sideways as they stood in their skis, both of them fully clothed. She groaned with frustration.

"There's a warming hut over there," he said.

"A what?"

He grinned. "Come on." After gathering the things he'd dropped, he led her to a wooden shack tucked back from the path. Rustic and cute, it had smoke rising from the chimney. Inside, she saw a couple of plain wooden benches and a black Franklin stove. Cut wood was stacked beside the stove, and inside its firebox flames crackled.

"It's a place to have a rest, warm up, and get out of the weather if it's storming," he explained.

"You already warmed me up," she teased, but she sank gratefully to a bench. Her legs appreciated the break.

Zack put his backpack on the other bench and unzipped it. "Trail mix or chocolate?"

"Chocolate," she answered promptly, smiling up at him as he handed her a bar of honey-almond Toblerone.

She ripped open the wrapper and took a bite, then closed her eyes and, around the mouthful of candy, said, "Mmm." It wasn't sex, but it came a close second.

He shook a thermos then unscrewed the cap. "You warm enough? I thought of bringing hot chocolate, but I usually find cross country skiing keeps me plenty warm."

"It did. And that kiss didn't hurt, either."

"Then try this." He poured a frothy pale brown cream into the thermos cap and handed it to her.

The contents smelled rich, a little chocolaty, and . . . She sniffed again. "Is there alcohol in this?"

His grin flashed. "One glass. Cut loose, Bree."

"It isn't even noon."

When he rolled his eyes, she took a cautious sip. Icy cold, rich and creamy, there was definitely chocolate in it. "That's delicious. What is it?"

"Chocolate liqueur, Baileys, and milk. It's called a Slippery Slope."

"Seriously?" She laughed and sipped again. "What better drink for a ski instructor?"

When she handed him the cap, he took a drink. "You know the thing about Slippery Slopes? Once you get going, it's hard to stop."

"Sounds kind of like kissing," she teased. Or at least, kissing him. She took another sip, letting the delicious liquid coat the inside of her mouth and trickle down the back of her throat. "Though you'll have to be some kisser to top this drink."

"Happens I am." He took the cap from her hand and put it down on the bench, then he caught her hands in his and tugged her to her feet. Hands clasped at their sides, he bent down and leaned into her, tilting his head down as she tilted hers up.

Oh my, Brianna thought. The kiss was chocolate and cream, with the heady underlying burn of alcohol. Sweet but dangerous—dangerously seductive.

He'd called the drink a Slippery Slope. For a moment, she thought that this *thing* with Zack might be a slippery slope of its own. And who knew what was at the bottom of that particular hill? But then the kiss made second thoughts—any thoughts—impossible.

There was only Zack and her, and she needed to touch him. His back, his hair, his butt. Anywhere. She whimpered, trying to free her hands.

But he held her tight, so that the only parts of their bodies to touch were their mouths.

Everything focused there, on the thrust of slick tongues, the suck of soft lips, the gentle nip of sharp teeth.

She gave herself up to the kiss, to the crisp scent and heady taste of him, to the confidence and passion of his mouth. To the sensations that tingled and pulsed from her mouth and heated her blood, tightened her nipples, and made her pussy clench with the need to feel him inside her.

What was it about this man? In no rational way was he her type, and she knew she was just another tourist to him, yet he'd given her so much in such a short time. Things that were brand-new to her: a picnic by the fire, a sunshine-on-snow winter morning, sex that was off the charts, and a feeling of freshness and exhilaration that was almost like being reborn.

God, she wanted him. Her body strained to get closer, and finally he released her hands. Hurriedly he stripped off his jacket and let it drop, then he attacked the zipper on hers. His hands were inside her sweater, chilly at first but rapidly heating, branding her skin as he caressed her back. She'd worn a sports bra today—no clasp—but that didn't stop him. He pulled it up at the front so he could fondle her breasts.

"Beautiful breasts," he murmured.

When he squeezed her aching nipples, she moaned with plea-sure, and his mouth again took hers. She pressed closer, feeling his rigid erection through the layers of their clothing. She wanted him now, not when they eventually made it back to Whistler and found a room.

His hand brushed her ribs, her waist, and then he was undoing her pants.

Despite how good it felt, she said, "Zack! Stop. We can't make out here like horny teenagers."

"Sure we can." His eyes telegraphed a message of intense sexual need that mirrored her own.

"Someone might come."

"Haven't seen many people on the trail this morning."

"No, but—"

His mouth closed on hers, silencing her protest. And now he'd undone her zipper and his hand was wriggling its way inside the silky leggings that were all she wore for underwear, and then—oh, yes!—his fingers stroked between her legs where she was damp and aching.

"Since you're so shy and all," he drawled against her mouth, "we won't take our clothes off. But Bree, you know you want this."

Orgasm. Zack. Oh yes, she wanted it. "Keep watch out the win-dow," she said, then she gave in to the need, grinding herself against him.

When he used his free hand to pull her pants down her hips to give himself better access, she helped out. Common sense had flown, and she was pure sensation, pure need, as his fingers slipped inside her, pumped in and out, spread moisture over her swollen clit in swirling strokes.

Her legs trembled so she could barely stay upright, but the cli-max was there . . . just, almost, there, and she reached for it with ev-erything inside her as he again stroked her clit in a firm, slick caress.

Her body broke in surging spasms of release, and she cried out, clinging to Zack so she didn't melt into a puddle on the floor.

Chapter 6

ZACK struggled for control as Bree shuddered with orgasm in his arms. She was so hot, so responsive. His dick strained against his winter clothing, aching to be where his fingers were.

Gently he freed his hand from between her legs. He sucked in a breath, held it, let it out slowly. And remembered to look out the window. Maybe the snowy winter scene would cool him down.

Instead, "Shit, Bree, someone's coming."

She jerked out of his arms and struggled to pull up her clothing. "You saw someone?"

"It's the trail patrol guy. He'll be checking the hut."

Her fingers fumbled with the zip of her pants, then she gave up and plunked down on the bench, bundling her jacket in her lap. She was just in time, because the door was opening.

Zack faced the fire, back to the door, willing his hard-on to subside.

"Hey, folks," a male voice said easily. "Having a good day?"

"Very good." Bree's voice was breathy.

"Fire's okay? There's enough wood?"

Zack glanced over his shoulder. "Yeah, it's good." Fortunately, the patrol guy, a man about his own age, wasn't someone he knew. "We'll put more wood on before we leave."

"Great. Have fun." The smirk in his voice said he'd guessed what they'd been up to. The guy glanced again at Brianna, and his gaze sharpened. "Do I know you?"

She slipped on her sunnies and shook her head. "Maybe you've seen me around the Village."

"Sure. Maybe."

After he closed the door, she said, "That was close."

Zack turned toward her, still erect, hopeful. "Good news is, he'll ski the loop and won't be back here for another hour or so."

"Other people could come along." Still, she pulled her glasses off again, thrust her jacket aside, and did up her pants zipper, then came into his arms, rubbing against him like a cat. She reached between them and gripped his dick through his pants.

He groaned. "Jeez, Bree, don't do that unless you mean it."

Her fingers worked his zipper, and he couldn't stop himself from thrusting against the welcome pressure of her hand.

"Doesn't this feel like I mean it?"

Shit, yeah. She was holding his naked dick between soft, warm palms. He didn't know exactly what she had in mind, but it was going to be good. Hurriedly, he shoved his pants down his hips.

She sank to her knees in front of him, and he waited, muscles trembling with need, while she studied him. Then, wrapping his shaft firmly with one hand—did she think for a single moment he'd try to escape?—she turned away and picked up the thermos cap she'd set on the bench. The woman was thirsty *now*?

Taking her time, she rolled a slug of the cool, chocolate cream in her mouth, then swallowed. Then she closed her mouth over the head of his shaft, and coolness enveloped him.

"God, that feels good."

Her mouth heated up quickly against his throbbing flesh. Her touch seemed tentative as she licked the crown and down the shaft, then again took him in as deeply as she could.

He gasped as wet heat enveloped him.

Her tentativeness vanished. She clasped the base of his cock in one hand, and his hip with the other, for balance, and devoured him as if she couldn't get enough. Each stroke, lick, and suck stimulated flesh that already throbbed with need.

This was heaven. And hell, because he wanted it to go on forever, yet the need to climax was becoming urgent. He stared down, finding it unbearably sexy to see his cock between her lips as she worked him to the breaking point. His hands threaded through her springy hair, fingers taut as he forced himself not to grip too hard.

She freed him to say, "You're keeping watch?"

Watch? Oh, yeah. Out the window. He groaned. "Yeah." He forced his gaze away from her and to the scene outside, which, thankfully, was empty of human life.

She sucked him in again, and one hand toyed with his balls.

They hardened, and his hips jerked. "I'm gonna come. If you don't want—" He broke off as she squeezed his balls gently.

No way could he hold back now. He cried out, jerked again, and his come jetted into her mouth. So good, so bloody awesome.

She didn't let go. He felt the ripple of her throat as she swallowed.

He thrust again, then more slowly, weakly, not wanting this to end.

The sun-dazzled snowscape outside, the crackling fire at his back, the warm heat of Bree's mouth wrapped around him . . . it was one of life's perfect moments.

Finally, she released him and sat back on her heels.

Struggling for breath, he gazed down at her lovely, flushed face. "Man, Bree." He smiled and held out a hand to help her rise. "You blew the top of my head off."

"Oh?" Mischief lit her face. "Is that what I blew?"

He laughed and pulled her to him. "Aren't you the dirty girl."

"Woman," she said, and it sounded like an automatic correction she'd made many times. Then she laughed. "No, you're right. Today I'm a girl."

"My girl," he said smugly, knowing full well she was a woman, too. A complex, fascinating woman whose company he enjoyed more than anyone's he could remember.

He loved women, and any time he wanted female companionship—be it for skiing, sex, or to share a pizza—it was readily available. Yet there was something different, something special, about Bree.

BY the time they'd skied back to the Jeep, Zack had worked up a real appetite: for food and also for his sexy companion. "I have the leftovers from last night back at my place."

"I don't want to run into your roommates. We can get a hotel room again."

He tamped down annoyance. So, the woman had a hang-up or two. Who didn't? "A hotel's expensive." And no way was he letting her pay again. Besides, he had some weird desire to be with her in his own space. "My roommates will all be gone."

"Are you sure?"

"It's noon on a sunny day. Half will be working, the other half out snowboarding or skiing."

"Well, all right."

As he drove, she rested her hand on his thigh, which went a long way to restoring his good mood.

When he parked in front of a rambling ranch-style home, he said, "We're in the basement. There's a shared living room and kitchen, couple of baths, four bedrooms." He climbed out and went around to open her door.

She hopped down, pushed her sunnies up her nose, then followed him to the side door. Inside, the entrance area was the usual jumble of outdoor clothing and gear, and the living room was a mess, too. Usually, he didn't notice, but today he felt embarrassed. It looked like a bunch of immature kids lived here.

Quickly he led her to his bedroom. The furniture that came with the house was basic, but at least he'd tidied up.

After casting a quick glance around, she went straight to the framed photo on the desk and picked it up. "Your family?"

"Yeah. My parents, older brother Ty, his wife Brennie, and my kid brothers Eddy and Sam. They're ten."

"Identical twins?"

"Identical nuisances," he said fondly, missing them as he always did when he was away from home for months on end.

She stared at the photo in silence, and he wondered if she was comparing his family to hers. Her dad had been a drinker, but she'd said nothing about her mother nor mentioned siblings. "How 'bout you?" he asked. "Any brothers or sisters?"

She shook her head, still hanging on to the picture. "I'm an only."

"Tell me more about your family."

She glanced up, expression flat. "Long story short, a drunk for a dad, a mom who was clinically depressed, a no-good uncle. That was on the reservation. After Mom died—maybe suicide, maybe an accidental overdose on meds—Dad sent me to her sister. There, I had seven cousins, most by different dads, and Aunt Marie took in other stray kids who needed a home."

"Man, Bree, I'm sorry. That's rough." He reached out to her, but she turned away, body language saying she didn't want sympathy.

When she put the picture back on the desk, her hand knocked against his open laptop, and the screen saver flicked off to reveal the story he'd been working on.

She glanced at the screen, then peered more closely. "What's this?"

"The latest adventure of Eddy and Sam, twins from Oz who travel the world with their pet roo. They solve mysteries and get themselves involved in all sorts of adventures."

She stared up at him. "Can I look?"

"Sure."

She scrolled through a few pages. "You did all this yourself? The writing and the graphics?"

He nodded. "I send stories home to the twins."

"It looks like a cross between manga and a graphic novel."

"Yeah, kind of. But those are for print format, right? With comic-type illustrations and text. This is interactive, see?" He clicked a link to show how a reader could jump out of the story to see pictures of a location, then showed her how the reader could select between possible actions and get a different outcome. "So, they're kind of like video games, too."

Her eyes were wide with interest and admiration. "You do all this just for your brothers?"

"Yeah, I've been doing these for years. Started out with simple comics. As the real Eddy and Sam got older, so did the twins in the stories. And the words, illustrations, concepts, and technology all get more complex."

"How did you learn all this?"

"Taught myself. Doing the stories makes me feel closer to the twins."

"You're a man of many talents." She reached for the mouse again.

"Hey, I didn't bring you here to read stories. And on the subject of talents, I have way better ones than writing kids' stories."

Her deep brown eyes sparkled up at him. "I've heard that rumor. And I know you put together a mean picnic. I'm starving."

"Food it is." He tugged on her jacket collar. "How about you pull off some clothes, and I'll get us a snack."

"Could we start with dessert? I'm usually so disciplined, but today I'm throwing the rules out the window."

"I'm all for that. Okay, what do you like for dessert?" He wiggled his eyebrows. "Me?"

She chuckled. "Well, you're certainly *filling* . . . "

He laughed, too. "But you're hungry. Let me see what I can find in the kitchen. I'm guessing your first pick would be chocolate?"

She nodded. "Everything goes better with chocolate."

Smiling, he went into the kitchen and opened the fridge. The sight of leftover pizza and Chinese take-out boxes made him wince. A chocolate cake didn't magically materialize, but his gaze lit on a container.

Everything went better with chocolate, she'd said.

Chapter 7

IN Zack's room, Brianna stood up from the computer and hung her jacket on the back of his desk chair. The basement apartment wasn't awful, but it was shabby and messy. It reminded her of Aunt Marie's house, where she'd lived as a teen. Impossible to keep the place clean and tidy with all those kids, and everything in it had come either from the thrift shop or garage sales.

Zack's room was basic but kind of cozy. The family photo, the open computer with that amazing story, and a jar of nuts and a paperback lying facedown on a small dresser that doubled as a bedside table made it personal. Like Aunt Marie's, it felt comfortable and lived-in.

Brianna's own condo was sleek and modern, decorated by a Yaletown firm and kept spick-and-span by the housekeeper who came in every two weeks. Returning home at the end of each day's work, she always felt a sense of achievement and security. And yet her place didn't feel homey.

Brushing that thought away, she wondered where she and Zack would eat. Aside from the dresser and desk, the only furniture was a double bed. Hmm. Dessert in bed.

Ooh, she had a fun idea, a very un-Brianna idea.

She stripped off her clothing, flinging it all on the chair, then dashed over to the bed and slid between the sheets.

A moment later, the door opened. Zack's expression was priceless as he saw her in the bed and then glanced at the heap of clothing on the chair. A grin widened on his face, and he quickly closed and locked the door and set something on the desk.

Dessert. She'd been too busy watching his face to see what he'd brought, and now his body concealed it as he began to undress.

As his pants went down, she saw a growing erection that made her mouth water, remembering the salty male taste of him. Mesmerized, she stared at his jutting cock as he strode toward her. Okay, there was one thing in the world that beat chocolate.

When he reached the bed, he yanked the covers off her. "Dessert time," he said. He lifted a bottle, and she jerked upright as something dark brown spurted onto her chest.

Cold, gooey, and smelling like— "Chocolate syrup?" She swirled a finger through it and tasted cautiously. Yum. That's exactly what it was. "What about the sheets?"

"They'll wash, and so will we." Chuckling, he squirted more, so it dripped down her breasts, onto her belly, into her navel, and now between her legs in a tantalizing trickle. "Loosen up, Bree."

Loosen up? He thought she was inhibited? After what they'd done in that ski hut? Ooh, he wasn't going to get away with that. Deliberately, she dipped her index finger into her navel, scooped up some syrup, then popped her finger into her mouth and sucked. Slowly, sensually, finally letting her lips release her finger with a soft pop.

He'd stopped pouring and was standing beside the bed, cock erect, staring at her mouth.

She grabbed the bottle out of his hand and tackled him, tumbling him to the bed. Then she squirted syrup onto his chest and down the center of his body.

"Where you going with that, lady?"

"As if you didn't know." She dripped chocolate onto his cock then bent to slurp up the syrup. "Mmm," she said between licks, "you taste even better coated in chocolate."

His hips jerked, and he threaded his fingers through her hair and pulled her away. "Okay, enough, give that to me."

She chuckled. "I don't think so."

He gave her a wicked grin, then caught her around the waist and tried to heave her flat on the bed, but she dropped the bottle and grabbed him by the shoulders, doing her best to hold him down. Both laughing, they wrestled for control, chocolate syrup spreading and heating between them. Her hands slipped, and the two of them thumped down on the bed, her sprawled on top of him. His arms locked around her, and she squirmed and wriggled, giggling helplessly, trying to free herself.

"You're as slippery as an eel," he said.

"Chocolate-covered eel," she got out between giggles.

"A new treat. Can't wait to eat you up."

That definitely sounded appealing. And so did licking all the chocolate off his yummy body. Changing tactics, she stopped struggling and reached between their bodies, coating her hand in chocolate. Then she raised it and plastered it across his face, giving him a chocolate handprint.

Bracing herself with both hands on the mattress, Brianna leaned over him and began to lick off the chocolate, starting with his forehead. Mmm, so sweet and rich and delicious. Then from his cheeks, down that charmingly crooked nose, and finally she lapped his chocolate-coated lips.

His mouth opened, and he mumbled, "How's it taste?" against her lips.

"Try it." She slipped her tongue inside his mouth.

He kissed her greedily, then he held his hand up between their mouths. His fingers dripped with a fresh coat of syrup. They both attacked, two mouths licking and sucking at his chocolate fingers and at each other. Kissing, giggling, humming with pleasure.

She lifted her body off his and went to work on his chest, taking long swipes with her tongue, then smaller, sucking ones as she reached his nipples.

When she sat up, he grinned at her. "Look at you, Bree."

Glancing down, she saw a body streaked in chocolate and grinned happily. "I'm a mess." She'd never played like this. She barely knew Zack, yet he'd shown her so much about herself she'd never known.

"Lovely mess. Delicious mess."

He grabbed her hips and rolled her beneath him, then began to lick her breasts. "When I met you," he said between licks, "I wondered if you tasted of chocolate." He cleaned the syrup off everything but the areolas, and then sucked one into his mouth as if it were a lollipop.

Her eyes closed, her body twisted, and she gave a whimper of pleasure as his tongue sent darts of arousal straight to her core. Turning to her other breast, he repeated the process, then he licked his way over her tummy.

Her sex pulsed, and she knew the moisture between her legs was more than just chocolate. Impatiently, her hips lifted and she thrust against him, urging him to where she really wanted him.

Finally he reached her pussy, that masterful tongue making her body dance with delight. He was doing a thorough job of laving the stickiness from her labia, sending hot, pulsing tingles through her and making her whimper. But he was avoiding her clit.

"Mmm, now that's a flavor they should bottle," he murmured.

The tension and the need in her body made her writhe demandingly against him. His every lick was erotic, but it wasn't enough; she wanted more. "Zack, please."

When finally he swirled his tongue over her clit, she almost came off the bed. A suck, another swirl, and a quick shock of orgasm burst through her, catching her by surprise and making her cry out.

Waves of pleasure rippled through her, and she rode them until they ebbed. "So nice, Zack." A sweet relief from the sweet torture he'd inflicted on her.

Now, she'd be the one to do some torturing. She slipped away from him. "Lie down."

When he did, she went straight for the giant chocolate treat that jutted up from his groin. Starting at the base, she licked her way around, up, flicking against the bulging vein, then the ridge beneath the head.

Zack squirmed and gasped, "Holy shit, that feels good."

She took the head of his cock in her mouth, holding it firmly with her lips while she tongued it clean. He groaned. "God, I want to be in you."

"Yes." Her pussy was drenched and aching for him, for this man who made her feel alive, playful, and sexy, and whose passion for life was contagious.

When he reached over to get a condom package from the dresser by the bed, she took it from him and ripped it open. Then, fingers trembling in haste, she sheathed him.

He arranged her on the bed so she was on her hands and knees, butt toward him, her sex exposed and juicy between her legs. With one hand, he guided himself into her pussy.

She braced herself, thrusting back against him until he'd filled her all the way.

Putting both hands on her hips for leverage, he began to pump into her, deep and hard.

It felt fantastic, each stroke driving to her core and making her pulse around him, yet she missed being able to touch him, missed seeing his face. She lowered herself to balance on one forearm, freeing her other hand. Reaching back, she caressed the inside of his thigh.

After another few thrusts, suddenly he pulled out.

"What—" she started to say, but then he was tugging her around to face him. He pressed her down so she was lying on her back.

She spread her legs, and Zack lay between them, his sticky body pressed against hers.

He just lay there, not entering her, then leaned forward to give her a kiss that tasted of chocolate and sex. Oh yes, this was better.

Circling his torso with her arms, gazing into his eyes, she felt the strangest feeling, rather like when she'd been out in the snowy wilderness, of something that resonated deep inside.

She'd actually found a man who liked her for who she was, not what she was, a man who didn't want a single thing from her but her company. Their relationship might be short-lived, but it was special, a treasure she'd always hold close to her heart.

He was tender at first, licking her lips and tasting her mouth, flirting with her tongue. Then he kissed her with a rising passion that made her whimper with the need to join with him. "Zack, I want you."

Her knees came up, he raised his body, and then he slid inside her again. She wrapped her legs high around his waist. Her fingers wove through his hair, down his neck, gripped his strong shoulders, then found their way to his firm butt. Under her hands, his muscles clenched as he plunged into her.

They kept kissing, swallowing each other's gasps and moans as he thrust into her faster, ever faster.

Inside her, the sensations were so intense and wonderful, it was almost like a continuous orgasm, yet she also felt that sense of reaching, spiraling, aiming for something even better.

Zack's movements became frenzied, and the tension inside her mounted impossibly higher. Then he gasped out, "God, Bree," and exploded inside her.

His spasms triggered her own. Sensations crescendoed, peaked, crashed through her in dazzling waves of pleasure that went on and on.

Finally, she and Zack collapsed, hot and sticky and pretty much glued together as they both struggled to get their breath.

"Best food fight I've ever had," he murmured.

"Only one I've ever had." She felt a strange urge to say something mushy and sentimental but suppressed it. That wasn't what she and Zack were about. "Speaking of food, I'm still hungry."

"Can't have you starving on me," he said, unsticking his body from hers. "I'll get some real food."

When he slipped off the bed, she sat up. "I don't want to put my clothes on over this sticky skin."

He opened a drawer and pulled out a T-shirt and a pair of sweat-pants. Tossing the shirt to her, he said, "Make yourself comfy. We'll shower later."

He pulled the pants over his naked skin and, bare-chested, left the room.

Brianna pulled the tee, soft and fresh-smelling, over her head and savored the moment. A girl wearing her guy's tee after they'd had incredible sex. She stretched luxuriously. He was fixing another picnic, treating her as if she were special. What an amazing man he was.

Across the small room, the open computer caught her attention. That story had been fascinating. He'd told her she could read it, so she wouldn't be invading his privacy. Unable to resist, she hopped out of bed.

In the kitchen, Zack hummed as he piled the leftovers from last night onto a tray and added a couple of bottles of water.

When he went back to the bedroom, Bree was sitting on his desk chair, one leg curled under her, his T-shirt sliding enticingly off one shoulder, and smears of chocolate on her cheek and forehead. Oh yeah, this woman was special, whether they were sharing the great outdoors or squirting chocolate all over each other. This wasn't just his usual sexy fun. He was actually falling for her. He dropped a kiss on her bare shoulder.

Her attention had been focused on his computer screen, but she lifted her head to stare up at him. "Zack, this is good. Really good."

"What?" He glanced at the screen. "Oh, you read the rest of the story? You liked it? No shit?" Her praise meant a lot.

"Very much. You said you have more?"

He put the tray on the desk. "Here, help yourself to food. Yeah, I've probably done ten stories a year for the last five, six years."

"Have you tried to sell them?"

"Sell them? You're kidding." He parked his hip on the edge of the desk and spread pâté on a slice of bread. "They're just family stuff." In two chomps, he ate the bread.

She shoved the chair back from the desk and turned to face him. "I'm no expert, but I'm guessing there's a market for these. Kids other than your brothers would enjoy them."

"Seriously?" That was flattering and kind of exciting. She thought that he, Zack Michaels, could be a published writer?

"Absolutely." Eyes bright with excitement, she said, "Format would be interesting. Your stories would work as books, without the interactive links, but they'd also be great in electronic format with all the bells and whistles, maybe even animation."

"Whoa! Animation? That's big-time."

She smiled.

"Huh. Okay, this is sounding pretty cool." And maybe the coolest thing was her approval.

"Isn't it? Zack, this could be a real career for you."

A real career? Now there was a slap in the face. So much for her approval. "Real? Like, being a ski instructor counts for nothing?"

Her brows drew together. "No, but . . . Is that where you see yourself in five years? Ten years?"

"Shit." He pushed away from the desk. Now Bree was giving him this crap? "You sound like my mother."

"Oh!"

"It pisses me off when she and Dad tell me to grow up and get a real job." He paced the small space in the bedroom. "I'm twenty-seven, for Christ's sake. I've been financially independent since I was nineteen, and I'm doing something I love."

"That's great," she said in that adult-humoring-a-child tone he hated. "But it's kind of a marginal life, isn't it? Always being the transient worker, living in an apartment you share with a half dozen other people. Is that really where you want to be when you're—"

"Your age?" He stopped pacing and stood, fists on his hips, glaring down at her where she still sat in his desk chair. "The ripe old *grown-up* age of thirty-five? Oh yeah, by the time I'm that old, I'll definitely want a five-year plan, because I'll be heading into middle age."

"Zack!"

The hurt in her eyes brought him to his senses. "Sorry, sorry. You know I didn't mean that."

"No, I don't," she snapped, wrapping her arms tightly around her chest.

He took a deep breath, then let it out slowly. "Bree, I really am sorry. You pushed a hot button, and I said something I didn't mean." Because he was coming to care for her, to want her approval, that hot button had a hair-trigger release.

She nodded warily. "Okay. It happens. And I didn't mean to criticize the way you live. It's just that I've always had a plan, so it's hard to relate to someone who doesn't."

He sat down on the end of the bed, across from her, wanting to understand. "So, what's your plan?"

Her face shuttered, and for a moment she didn't speak. "A bigger and better career in TV."

Given her workaholism, that didn't surprise him, but she'd said so little about her job that he still didn't get it. "Why?"

"What do you mean, why?" There was annoyance in her voice again. "I told you about my past. I want to get as far away from it as I can."

"And that'll make you happy?" Seemed to him like she was running away rather than running toward, and that didn't sound like the route to happiness.

Her eyes flared wide, then narrowed. "Yes. Yes, it will."

He shrugged. She was the expert on planning the future, so he guessed she must know what she was doing.

She rubbed her hands over her cheeks, further smearing the chocolate. The simple gesture made him wonder how the hell they'd gone from tender, passionate lovemaking to squabbling.

"Look, Bree, I'm sorry I went off on you like that." He reached for her hands, and she let him take them and returned the pressure when he squeezed them.

"I'm sorry, too. I understand that you love skiing, you love snow country, and you're a great teacher. All I meant to say is that, if you wanted to, I think you could add a writing career. It's obvious you enjoy creating these stories. They're full of energy and fun." Her lips trembled in a tentative smile.

Why hadn't she said it that way the first time? "Thanks. I do have fun with the stories, and getting paid for that would be cool." She'd come up with a great idea, so he'd follow up on it. "Cool, but I have no idea about this stuff. I mean, how would a ski instructor in Whistler find a publisher? Or is it even a conventional publisher I'd be selling to?"

Bree was the one with all the ideas. Perhaps she'd learned about all this through her research job. "Hey," he said, "with your job, maybe you—" He broke off when he saw the expression on her face.

She paled, her eyes narrowed, and for the first time she looked her age—despite the smears of chocolate on her face. She glanced at the open computer, the bed, then back to his face.

"Bree?"

No response.

"Brianna? What's wrong?"

"My job. *Brianna's* job." Her voice was brittle, and she spoke each word with deliberation. "You want me to use my job to help you get published."

Oh, Jesus. "No, I didn't mean it that way." Hell, he was an independent guy. All he'd been going to do was ask if, in her research, she'd come across any information that might help him get started.

"Yeah, right. I bet you set this whole thing up from the time you met me."

Zack gaped at her. Had she gone completely bonkers?

BRIANNA stared at Zack, her heart aching. He'd never really liked her; all he wanted was to go on her show and promote his stories.

He scowled. "Talk about overreacting."

"Overreacting? You think I'm overreacting?" That was exactly what Lionel had said when she'd challenged him about scooping her exposé. Oh no, she wasn't overreacting. She knew betrayal. Zack was another Lionel, another Tony. A total user. He must have recognized her from the beginning. He'd written those stories, wanted to sell them, and had seen his opportunity. A guest spot on her show would be the perfect platform to launch his writing career, so he'd set out to seduce her, to set her up so the whole thing would look like her idea, and she'd be just dying to help her hot young lover.

She was so freaking pathetic. She'd sworn this wouldn't happen a third time, yet somehow Zack had made her trust him. Angry tears filled her eyes, and she forced them back as she rose, found her pants, and began to drag them on under his T-shirt.

"Yeah, I think you're overreacting. Get a grip, Brianna." He grabbed her shoulder. "Let's talk about this."

She pulled away. "Oh no, your charm isn't going to work this time." Turning her back to him, she yanked off his stupid shirt and put on her sweater and jacket. She grabbed up her leggings and bra and stuffed them in her jacket pockets.

About to stalk out, she realized something. "What's the address? I need to call a cab." She took her cell from her waist pack. Her cell, which she'd had turned off all day because she hadn't wanted work to disturb her special time with Zack.

Freaking pathetic.

When he told her the address, she headed outside without another word. She'd rather wait in the snow than spend another minute with Zack.

Chapter 8

FORTUNATELY, the taxi arrived promptly.

She was shaking from cold and emotion when she climbed into the backseat. Behind her sunglasses, tears of anger and hurt threatened, but she forced them back. Why, after being so careful about men, had she let down her defenses with this particular one?

Because he'd seemed so genuine. He'd shared the snowy wilderness with her, he'd touched her face with tenderness, he'd brought her a picnic. He'd wrestled in chocolate syrup with her, and he'd made love as if—

No. She blinked rapidly, refusing to cry. They hadn't been making love. They'd been screwing. In fact, he'd been screwing her over from the moment they met. Would she ever learn? When it came to men, if she trusted her heart, it would lead her to disaster.

When the taxi turned into the development that housed the Alpine Hideaway, she had enough presence of mind to hunt in her waist pack for a comb and lipstick. All the same, she felt sticky and disheveled and hoped she could make it to her room without running into anyone.

No such luck. Tom's sister Maddie was walking toward the lounge as Brianna came in the front door, and she paused to greet her. The younger woman peered at her face. "Is that . . . chocolate?" Her finger hovered near Brianna's cheek.

Quickly Brianna swiped a hand across her cheek. "I was, uh, eating a chocolate croissant. Guess I got a smudge."

Maddie raised her brows. "There's some on your forehead, too."

Heat rose to her cheeks. "I must have got chocolate on my fingers, then scratched my forehead. How embarrassing. I'll go wash my face."

"Are you coming for the sleigh ride excursion?" Maddie asked as Brianna turned away.

Best to blend into the group and not call attention to herself. "Wouldn't miss it for the world," she said, hoping Maddie didn't hear the flatness in her voice.

Only after she'd reached her room did she realize she'd never asked Maddie how her brother and Shelley were doing. If the sleigh ride expedition was going ahead, the couple must have made up, but was that a good or a bad thing?

She went into the bathroom, stared at her face in the mirror, and grimaced. The smudges on her face looked like exactly what they were: chocolate syrup smeared by a tongue. There was one good thing about her public image, though. Likely, Maddie would never for a moment imagine Brianna George sex-wrestling in chocolate.

Damn. It had been fun. Zack had been fun. She'd actually believed a man had liked her for who she was. The chocolate-smudged face staring back at her wore a tragic expression.

"Oh, get a grip," she muttered, "enough with the self-pity. You've only known the man for three days, and you've known all along it was just a quickie affair."

Briskly, she stripped off her clothes and climbed into the shower where she absolutely refused to cry.

Half an hour later, hair blow-dried to perfection, makeup subtly elegant, dressed in her most stylish winter wear, Brianna went down the stairs to join the guests who were heading out for sleigh rides.

Tom and Shelley joined them, smiling and holding hands. Brianna wished she could take her friend aside and make sure he knew what he was doing. She so wanted him to be happy.

Two vans transported the group to the base for the sleigh rides where, as usual, Andi got everyone organized efficiently. Brianna piled into a large sleigh along with Tom's parents, Maddie and a girlfriend, and a bunch of other guests.

She glanced at Maddie, hoping Tom's sister wouldn't mention the chocolate incident, and saw she was gazing toward where Tom and Shelley and a few other couples were getting settled in tiny sleighs that held only two people.

The wistful expression on the girl's face told Brianna she wished she was in one of those sleighs, snuggling under the warm blankets. Young Maddie was a romantic. And, clearly, she wasn't feeling romantic about that nice friend of Tom's, Michael, who'd been making no bones about being interested in her. Michael was in a different sleigh.

Logan Carver, predictably, wasn't there at all. Was he the man Maddie was longing for? If so, the girl had as poor judgment as Brianna herself. Logan, sexy as he might be, was a loser who would only hurt her. Even Tom was clearly upset with him and regretting that he'd invited the man. It turned out they'd been friends eons ago, then not seen each other again until recently. Again, she wished Tom had more backbone. He should simply tell Logan to leave.

Right now, Tom looked happy as he tucked a warm rug around Shelley and himself and they snuggled side by side in that cute little sleigh. Okay, Maddie wasn't alone in thinking it was romantic. Brianna, too, felt the appeal. Romance wasn't about expensive candlelit dinners with men who wanted something from you. It was about skiing across a fresh expanse of snow on a crisp, sunny morning, sharing a decadent drink in a ski hut, and splashing each other with chocolate syrup and licking it all off.

Or it would be, if the man in question didn't have an ulterior motive.

As her sleigh got under way with a jingle, she settled back.

Despite the chill on her face, the blanket kept her warm. Unfortunately, there was nothing to do but stare at the scenery—which at the moment had lost its power to enchant her—and think. And the only thing on her mind was Zack.

When they'd met, he'd hit on her and tried to get her back to his room, no doubt so she'd see his stories. Poor guy, it had taken him an extra day of seduction. What had he figured? She'd be so grateful for the sex that she'd give him whatever he wanted? Oh please, he wasn't that good in bed.

Well, okay, he was. No other lover had come close.

But she wasn't pathetic or disgusting. She was Brianna George.

Ooh, why did she keep obsessing over the man? He wasn't worth another thought. She turned to the woman seated next to her. "How are you enjoying your stay in Whistler?"

There was a reason she made a good interviewer: she was genuinely interested in people and their stories, and she had a talent for drawing them out. It had always been easier to talk about others than about herself. Now she put that to good use, distracting herself from her worries.

She was feeling a bit better by the time the sleighs deposited the group at a charming log restaurant for a fondue dinner. Snow had fallen gently during the ride, and as she entered the rustic restaurant, she took off her hat, shook it, and smoothed a hand through the damp fringes of her hair.

A middle-aged hostess had been greeting the guests and broke off in mid-flow, gaping. "Brianna George?"

She smiled. "Yes. Hello."

"It's so great to meet you," the woman gushed. "I love your show! That interview with George Clooney, oh wow, he's so hot! And the story about the pregnant teens, I was laughing and crying at the same time. And then—"

"Thanks so much," Brianna broke in, since the woman showed no signs of stopping.

Andi stepped up. "Why don't we get everyone seated, then I'm sure Brianna will give you an autograph."

As usual, the wedding planner had mixed and matched the guests so people got a chance to meet each other and no one was left out. Tonight, Brianna was seated with Tom's grandparents and Shelley's parents.

Joan, Tom's grandmother, sat across from her. "I heard that woman gushing, Brianna. Just the same as on the ski slope the other morning."

She remembered the two women who'd recognized her. Zack might well have overheard.

"Is it flattering or kind of a nuisance?" Joan asked.

"Both. I'm grateful viewers like my show, but sometimes anonymity and privacy would be nice." Anonymity, so she'd know whether people liked her for herself or were just using her.

"It can go to a girl's head, that kind of attention," Shelley's mom put in. "It's flattering, but it puts pressure on you, too."

"Yes."

"And of course," the other woman went on, "fame is such a fleeting thing."

"Tell that to George Clooney," Joan put in, and they all laughed.

"Okay, there are always exceptions," Shelley's mother admitted. "But look at our daughter. If there's one year where, for whatever reason, even injury, she's not on the podium, the world will forget about her."

A has-been at the age of twenty, twenty-one. In some ways, Shelley had it even tougher than Brianna. And Brianna had been more judgmental than understanding. "That must be hard," she said softly. "She's so young to have that kind of pressure."

The woman gave a rueful smile. "Age. When you're a woman, you're never the right age. Too young, too old. I guess it's the latter for you, isn't it? It's hard for a woman to maintain a career on TV as she gets older."

"The situation is better than it used to be." All the same, she felt constant pressure to keep looking and acting young, attractive, and vital. Especially if she wanted to make it in the appearance-oriented U.S.

"I watch your show all the time," Joan said. "It's not about your age. You're smart as a whip, and you draw people out. We—your viewers— trust you. You're sympathetic when you should be, and you call people on it if they're talking bullshit. Pardon the expression."

"Thanks."

"You're a lovely role model for young women," Joan said.

Embarrassed, Brianna murmured another thank-you.

"Tom told me *The Scoop* may be picked up in the States," his grandmother said. "That's a big step."

"Yes."

"I'll be kind of sorry, myself," she went on. "Have to admit, I liked it in the old days. The stories seemed to hit closer to home. But I guess that doesn't work so well for a U.S. audience."

Beside her, her husband snorted something about the damn Yankees.

Brianna ignored him and answered Joan. "Yes, we've been changing the focus of the show, doing what it takes to appeal to the U.S." In some ways, she, too, had preferred her show's original focus. But it had been kind of folksy, and now she was going for a slicker, more international image.

Yes, it was all about image. And the image of the show was all about the image of Brianna George: female, Native Canadian, awards of distinction in journalism, supporter of kids from disadvantaged backgrounds. Of course, it wasn't hard to maintain a dignified image when you had no personal life.

Until this week.

What had she been thinking, messing around with Zack? She could just imagine the spin the media would put on that one. Either she'd be the pathetic, disgusting middle-aged woman, or she'd be the trendy cougar with the hot young boy toy.

Thank God she'd at least had the sense to keep the affair secret. If photos had shown up on YouTube . . .

A waitress came to take drink orders, and as the others debated their choices, a horrible thought struck Brianna. What if Zack went to the media? He could damage her credibility, maybe cost her the

U.S. deal. Or he might try to blackmail her into putting him on the show.

Panic fluttered in her belly, but the emotion that throbbed in her heart was pain. Zack? Surely not. He'd never do anything like that. She was being paranoid.

And yet she hadn't believed Lionel would betray her, nor Tony, the boy in high school. When it came to lovers, when her heart got involved, her judgment sucked.

She needed a few moments alone to control her panic and think this through rationally. "Just water, please," she told the waitress, then she excused herself and fled toward the ladies' room.

As she hurried past the bar, she almost bumped into Tom, who'd turned from talking to the bartender.

"Hey, Brianna, you're in a hurry." He reached out to steady her, then took a second look at her face. "Are you all right?"

"I'm fine." She took a breath and collected herself. "How about you?" she asked quietly. "Did you and Shelley get things resolved?"

"We're on the right path." He looked tired but satisfied.

"Tom"—she touched his arm—"you know I think you're terrific, but, uh, sometimes you need to be more forceful. Don't let Shelley push you around."

A wry grin flickered. "I hear you. I was brought up to make nice, so I keep quiet about my feelings and avoid confrontation. Doesn't work so well with a woman like Shelley who blurts out whatever she's thinking."

"A habit she might learn to temper. Doesn't she realize words can hurt?"

"She's starting to. She's young and impulsive, but honestly, she has a good heart."

She hoped he was right. "So, what about the move to Utah?"

"Not happening. Though she might go down a few times to supplement the coaching she'll get here."

"I'm glad." Glad for the two of them and for herself. "I'd miss you."

"The show'd survive okay without me."

She smiled. "That's not what I meant, and you know it."

"Yeah, I do. I'd miss you, too."

"Oh jeez, you two," a teasing female voice said. "Talk about a mutual admiration society." Shelley came up behind Tom, hooking an arm around his waist and snuggling against him.

"We weren't—" Brianna started, but Shelley was waving a hand. "I know, I know," Tom's fiancée said. "Sorry, I was a bitch this morning. I said stuff I shouldn't have. *Lots* of stuff. Chalk it up to pre-wedding jitters or just general stupidity. My bad, and I'll try not to do it again."

Easy to say. All the same, the girl had been big enough to apologize. "Apology accepted. I'm glad you two worked things out."

Tom hugged Shelley close. "It was good for us. Made us face some things that could've caused problems in the future."

His fiancée grinned up at him. "Yeah, like how I can't read your mind." Then her expression went serious. "And how I need to be more sensitive about people's feelings."

And that was an excellent bit of self-knowledge. It did seem as if Shelley was growing up. Maybe there was a tiny bit of a romantic inside of Brianna after all, because she found herself wishing things would work out for the pair.

An idea struck her. "You know the clip we talked about, featuring your wedding?"

Shelley wrinkled her nose. "You've decided to cancel it? Yeah, I deserve that."

"No. No, you don't, and I'm not canceling. But the idea we were working with was straightforward: a happy ending to an Olympics romance between one of *The Scoop*'s staff and a gold medalist. But we could add depth. Shelley, think of how hard you need to work to achieve gold."

"You can say that again."

"And there can be setbacks and lessons to learn. Maybe we could do a parallel to the, uh, course of true love." Had those words really come out of her own unromantic mouth?

"That's a good angle," Tom said. Then, to Shelley, "Good from a story point of view, that is. What do you think, sweetheart? If we shared some of our problems, it might help other couples."

"Sure, why not? Everyone wants to know the personal stories behind celebrities' lives. Right, Brianna?"

"Right," she said grimly.

When Tom and Shelley returned to the dining room, Brianna continued on to the ladies' room. There, she went into a cubicle, locked the door, and tried to think.

Zack had the power to jeopardize her career. Lionel had done exactly that. She buried her face in her hands. It wasn't fair to judge based on previous men and her own crappy judgment. She had to focus on what he'd done, what he'd said.

Maybe he hadn't set her up from the beginning. Even if he'd just seen an opportunity when she started raving about his stories, it was inappropriate to use their relationship to try to get on her show. And that's what he'd done. He'd said, "With your job, maybe you . . . "

Wait. She raised her head. Had he finished that sentence? In her head, she'd heard, "maybe you could have me on the show." But had he actually said that? If not, was that what he'd been going to say? She was so freaking confused.

If he intended to threaten her, he'd be in touch soon, and then she'd know what she had to deal with. And if he didn't get in touch . . . Then she'd misjudged him horribly and owed him a huge apology.

THE next morning, Zack was still pissed off, but he was also baffled. Yeah, women were unpredictable, but he'd thought he was getting to know Bree. The woman who'd shared cross-country skiing and chocolate syrup sex with him, the woman he'd begun to fall for, wouldn't have irrationally gone postal on him. So something had happened. He wasn't going to let her walk out of his life without finding out what the hell had gone wrong.

He phoned the Alpine Hideaway and asked for Brianna. No last name, because she'd never deigned to share it. Okay, there'd been something weird going on from the beginning, and he needed answers.

A couple of minutes later, she said a cautious hello.

"Bree, it's Zack," he said, trying to sound rational rather than angry.

A pause. "Zack."

"I need to talk to you. About your job and our relationship."

A pause. Then, "It seems I need to talk to you, too." She sounded hard, almost bitter. A stranger. "In person."

"I'll pick you up. Same place as yesterday. Half an hour."

"Right."

He took a quick shower, threw on some clothes, and headed out, anxious but determined.

A few minutes after he'd parked the Jeep, Bree strode down the road.

She opened the door, pulled herself in, and gave him a stony look. "Drive somewhere. I don't want to talk here."

Without a word, he started the Jeep and drove, while tension filled the air between them. He chose the lot where they'd parked when they went cross-country skiing. Yesterday, they'd felt so connected, and now he didn't even know her. He clicked off the engine and turned to her.

"I'll go first," she said coolly. Her face was perfectly made up and looked like an expressionless mask. "I won't let you jeopardize my career." She spoke the words defiantly, but muscles quivered beside her eyes as if she was uncertain or even scared.

"Your career? Your research job? Jesus, Bree, no way would I ask you to jeopardize that."

Doubt flickered in her eyes. "Oh come on, you know who I am. I bet you knew that first day when you saw those women speak to me."

When he'd first noticed her, she'd been with a couple of other women, with someone taking their picture. A holiday snap, he'd assumed. "Who you are?" Oh, man, maybe she really was a princess in disguise. "Uh, I guess all I know is your name's Brianna. If that's even true." She hadn't given her last name, and it seemed she'd lied about her job. Had anything been the truth? He glared at her.

"I'm Brianna George."

He shook his head. "Means nothing to me."

"How about *The Scoop*?" Those bittersweet chocolate eyes were piercing.

That name was familiar. "That's a TV show, right? I've heard a couple of my roommates mention it. So you really do work on a TV show?"

She blew out air. "It's my show, my concept. I develop the stories and I'm the host."

"Seriously?" His eyes widened, surprise temporarily overruling anger.

Expression guarded, she nodded. "The show started out locally, but now it's national, and we're in talks to have a major U.S. network pick it up. But you already knew that."

"I didn't." He shook his head, still confused. "And what are you talking about, that I'm trying to jeopardize your career? Shit, Bree."

"Being on the show would give you a platform that could help you get published."

His jaw dropped as he processed that. "You thought I wanted to be on your show? I didn't even know about your show. 'Sides, even if I'd asked, you could've just said no. End of story."

"Yeah, right. And you wouldn't have threatened to go to the media?"

"What? Go to the media about what?"

"Our affair."

He was so stunned, he couldn't even respond. Here he'd actually thought they had something special going. He scrubbed his hands over his face. "You sure don't think much of me."

"I just met you. In the past I've been manipulated and betrayed." Those bittersweet chocolate eyes were all bitter today. "Why would you be any different?"

"Because . . . " Clearly, what he'd been feeling was one-sided.

"Shit. Fine, I'm just some loser ski bum who's not even fit to be seen with you. I get it. But *you* get this, woman." He thumped a fist against the dashboard. "I would never threaten you. You're safe. You and your fucking job. It's clear that's all that matters to you."

He jerked the key in the ignition, and the Jeep's engine rumbled. He was about to shift into gear when she said, "Zack, I . . . Wait. Stop the engine."

He eased his foot off the clutch but didn't turn off the ignition. "What?"

"I . . . I'm sorry. Maybe I jumped to a conclusion." She sounded tentative, still not believing him.

"You sure as hell did."

"I've been used by men before. Men who seduced me to get what they wanted."

His jaw clenched. Tough for her, but shit, he wasn't like that.

Before he could speak, she went on. "That first day, I said they call me Brianna, and you said you weren't 'they.'"

He glared at her. "I'm not, damn it."

"I wanted to believe that. I did believe it. Then, when we were talking about your story, you said you had no idea how to get published and you started to ask me about the show—"

"To ask if, in your *research* job, you'd come across any info to get me started."

"And I leaped to the wrong conclusion. I didn't see you, Zack, I saw those other guys. The ones who'd betrayed me. I'm so sorry I was so mean to you."

Finally, he clicked off the ignition and turned to her. Her face was open, vulnerable, and her apology, her explanation, were penetrating his anger.

"Men betrayed you?" he asked.

"One romanced and seduced me, he got me to share all my ideas, then he stole the best and got the promotion I'd been working so hard for."

"And you thought I was like that?" How could she?

"That was eight years ago, and I never trusted a lover after that. Until you." She bit her lip. "Yesterday, you said I sounded like your mother, and you made a nasty comment about heading into middle age. Then you apologized and said I'd pushed a hot button. Well, that's what you did with me. A really hot one."

Hot buttons with hair-trigger releases. Yeah. People had them. The last of his anger faded. Holding a grudge wasn't his style. Slowly, he nodded. "Okay. I get it. Apology accepted. And for the record, Bree, you can trust me."

But, even if she did, she was still obsessed about her job and image and the whole crazy age thing. Did he want to see her again? What could possibly come of it?

More mornings like yesterday. Sharing the wilderness, laughter, fiery sex, tender intimacy. Hell, she was special to him, and even though she was plenty mixed up, she was making an effort. In fact, her emotional reaction yesterday, and the effort she was making today, told him she had feelings for him, too.

He'd seen, that first morning when she hadn't been going to ski, that she could change her mind. Maybe her views about age and her priorities in life could change if the two of them grew closer.

If he quit now, he'd never know what they might have together. And that was unacceptable.

BRIANNA gazed into his eyes, so green it was as if they'd absorbed the color of the forest he loved. "Zack, I want so badly to believe in you. Except, it isn't really you I have to believe in. It's me. My own judgment. And it sucks so badly when it comes to lovers." She took a breath. "If you never want to see me again, I'll understand. But I'll hate it. Hate things to end this way."

His lips twitched the tiniest bit, giving her hope. "I could live without seeing that cold, snarky woman."

"Me, too. She's a bitch. That's not the real me." She swallowed and confessed, "Well, she's the insecure me. Sorry, but I guess she's a part of the real me."

"Insecure," he echoed, expression thoughtful. "About me, or in general?"

"In general," she admitted softly. "I'm always afraid I won't be good enough."

He nodded. "Yeah, that fits with the other things. Perfectionist, workaholic, control freak."

Oh yes, Zack really saw her, warts and all. "I like to think I'm strong and capable, but I guess I'm kind of a mess."

His lips quirked up. "Hey, I feel like I'm finally coming to understand you. Being a mess is okay. It's human."

"That's reassuring," she said dryly.

"It allows room for growth and change."

Before she could dwell on that comment, he leaned forward to place a kiss on her forehead. Right about where that smudge of chocolate had been.

"You let me go back to the chalet with chocolate on my face," she accused.

He kissed her nose. "I'm a vengeful bugger, aren't I? Remember that, next time you think of crossing me."

Before she could respond, his lips were on hers. She gave a sigh of relief, of pleasure, and answered his tender kiss.

He was always so fresh, like mint and mountain air. So warm, like a cozy fire. And so very, very hot, like . . . like Zack. Only Zack.

When the kiss turned passionate, he eased away. "I have lessons all day. I guess I could swap with someone, but it's late to set that up. And a couple of the lessons are private ones with students I've been working with."

"You have responsibilities. I understand."

"Can you get away tonight?"

"Yes."

"Let me take you out for dinner."

Holding hands with this handsome guy across a candlelit table . . . Then seeing photos show up on YouTube. "Zack, our age difference may not matter to you. And maybe it doesn't to me, either. But there are people who'd see me as a cougar." Shelley's words still rang in her head. Yes, the girl had apologized, but that didn't erase her gut-level initial reaction. "People who'd think I'm disgusting for fooling around with a man who's eight years younger. And there are others who'd joke that you were my trophy boy toy."

He winced. "Yeah, I get that. But our relationship is our business. Not anyone else's."

"People take pictures of me and post them on YouTube. The media, the tabloids have pictures."

"Shit. Okay, I'm getting it. You're a celebrity."

"In a small way. I've worked very hard to gain the respect I never had as a child. Having a holiday fling with a younger man . . . No, there's nothing wrong with it. But it's not exactly dignified."

He gazed at her, not speaking.

Yes, she was a mess and her life was complicated, but she didn't want to lose him now. "Zack, I'm only here for three more days. Can't we put all this aside and just enjoy being together?"

"Three more days." He studied her, and she wondered what her perceptive lover was seeing this time. "Okay. We can do that."

Chapter 9

FRIDAY, for the second night in a row, Brianna headed off to the town house Zack had booked for them. Far more cozy and personal than a hotel room, it was one of several dozen in this housing development. He'd reserved it for three nights, and she hadn't argued when he insisted on paying.

Yesterday evening had started out a little rocky. They'd both still been sensitive over their hot-button issues. Rebuilding trust had taken some time, but, over an artichoke heart pizza delivered to the door, they'd gotten there, ending up talking for hours about everything under the sun and making sweet, passionate love.

Tonight, she paid off the cab and climbed out. There was definite appeal to walking up a freshly swept walk to a cute little house where lights glowed in the window.

Glancing in, she saw Zack's head as he moved about in the kitchen, and she smiled with pleasure. She'd definitely gotten her groove back. She felt younger and reenergized. Story ideas were coming to her left, right, and center. Not ones that would play well in the U.S. market, unfortunately, but those would come, too.

Though part of her was eager to get back to work, the other part knew she'd miss Zack like crazy. Since she'd made that comment about only having three more days, neither of them had mentioned the future. And her foolish heart was starting to wish for a future. Yet she knew that was impossible. Much as Zack might enjoy her company, even care for her, she was just one in a long string of women. Next week, he'd find another one.

The thought made her heart ache. But the reality was, in a few months, he'd be off to another ski resort anyhow. And she, hopefully, would be debuting on American TV. Even if their age difference hadn't been a factor, their lives were going in such different directions, literally as well as figuratively.

Zack would soon be a fond, very fond memory. For now, she refused to be depressed. She was going to live in the moment and enjoy every minute of time with him.

The front door was unlocked. She removed her outerwear in the mudroom, then entered the attractive open-plan downstairs.

"Bree." Zack looked up from what he'd been doing at the kitchen counter, wiped his hands on a towel, and came toward her.

"Wow." She took him in. Until now, she'd seen him only in ski clothing or cargo pants, usually with tousled hair. Tonight, he wore black pants and a gray green shirt that complemented his eyes, and his golden-tipped hair was neatly combed. He looked older, more sophisticated, and as sexy as ever.

"What d'you think?" He gave her a teasing grin. "Do I clean up okay?"

"You look wonderful. Good enough to . . . " She reached out and tugged him closer.

"Yeah? We'll see about that." His arms went around her back and he bent to kiss her, snugging her body tight against his own.

"Mmm." His lips were familiar now, and even the nicer for that. Walking into this town house, to Zack's arms and to the smell of something delicious cooking all felt oddly like coming home. Strange, since she'd never before had such a delightful homecoming experience. Maybe this was what home was *supposed* to feel like.

"What do I smell?" she murmured against his lips.

"Coq au vin."

"I love that. Where did you get it?"

"Made it."

She pulled back to stare at him. "You made coq au vin?"

"Wanted us to have a real meal for once."

"Thank you. It smells wonderful." She wriggled her pelvis against his growing erection, feeling a surge of hunger deep in her core, one that had nothing to do with French food. "How long before it's ready?"

He thrust suggestively against her. "Long enough." Then he grabbed her hand and tugged her upstairs to the master bedroom. The electric fire was already glowing, the bed was turned down, and candles burned on the bedside tables.

She laughed. "Am I that predictable?"

"I was that hopeful."

Then he was pulling her sweater over her head, and a few minutes later they were under the covers in a tangle of limbs. The sex was fast and sweet, their bodies learning more of each other's secrets each time they were together.

They mock-wrestled for top until finally she rode him triumphantly to orgasms that rocked both their bodies.

Sighing with satisfaction, he pulled her down and rolled her again, so his body blanketed hers.

She kissed the hollow of his throat where his pulse thrummed against her lips. Oh, how she'd miss him.

"Dinner'll be done," he said regretfully, lifting himself off her. He pulled on his clothes and headed downstairs.

A few minutes later, she followed. He greeted her with a kiss and led her into the living room. A small table in front of the fire was set with a tablecloth and silver. Empty wineglasses sat at each place, and on the table was an opened bottle of Australian zinfandel. "Have a seat." He pulled out a chair. "Dinner will be served momentarily."

"This looks wonderful." She settled into the chair. When Zack took charge, she felt feminine and pampered.

A few minutes later, he presented her with a plate containing fettuccine topped with chicken, tiny onions, and mushrooms.

"I'm seriously impressed."

He gave her an easy smile. "That's the plan."

When he'd poured wine, she raised her glass. "To you, Zack. For tonight, and for giving me a wonderful week."

"To you, Bree. For being you." And she knew, when he said that, he didn't for a moment mean the successful TV personality, the public persona. He meant her, the woman. Mess that she was.

They clicked glasses and she tasted the wine. "This is excellent." Then she tasted the food. "Oh my, you can cook for me any day." Realizing what she'd said, she quickly amended, "I mean . . . this is really good."

He caught her gaze and held it. "I liked the way you said it first."

Her heart raced, though she told herself it was just another of his charming compliments.

They ate quietly for a few minutes to the accompaniment of instrumental music she didn't recognize but enjoyed. Zack's choice, like this town house, the meal, the wine. He had great judgment.

She, however, had misjudged him time and again. But maybe she could make it up to him. There was one way to show she trusted him and help him out. "Zack, I've been thinking about your stories. I really think you should pursue publication."

His mouth kicked up on one side. "I've been doing some research in the local bookstore and on the Internet. Believe it or not, I'm working out a plan."

"A plan?" Zack, who'd scoffed at the notion a couple of nights ago? "That's great. I had a couple of kids' book writers on my show when I did a segment on censorship. They mentioned an association they belong to. I'll look it up and let you know. You'd probably get a lot of help there."

"Thanks."

She reached across the table and squeezed his hand. "Appearing on my show would give you the kind of platform that would help you sell."

*   *   *

ZACK gaped at Bree. That was the last thing he'd expected her to say. "No way," he said firmly.

"I'm sorry for what I said before. It was my insecurity speaking. It wasn't about you." The warmth of her hand on his and the concerned expression in her eyes told him this wasn't a test. She meant it.

He intertwined his fingers with hers. "I get that. And thanks. But if I do this, I want to do it on my own."

Last night, he'd known he was falling hard for Bree—harder than he'd ever fallen for a woman—and been confused as hell. Then, this morning, his first student had canceled and he'd skied alone, swooping down a virgin slope on a crystal-pure morning. And things had come clear in his mind. He'd realized the truth of what Bree and his parents had been saying. It was time to think about the future, to think about what he wanted.

Not just about selling his stories, but about his lifestyle and about Bree. Without her, the future looked as flat as the bottom of a bunny hill. With her . . . yeah, things would be complicated, but the most challenging runs were the most exciting, worthwhile ones.

A man needed to go after what he wanted. And to do that, he did need a plan. Tonight, Zack was executing that plan. He had to prove to Bree that, even if he was a few years younger and didn't have as high-powered a career as she did, she shouldn't be embarrassed to date him.

It would've been so much easier if her career wasn't so bloody impressive. He let go of her hand and reached for his flute glass. "*The Scoop* is on TV, even though you're here this week."

"We taped segments ahead of time. Are you saying . . . ?"

"I set the machine to tape and watched the show." Her show was his competition. Almost grudgingly, he said, "It was good." Scarily good. How could a mere man—even one her age or older—compete with that kind of power and success?

"That was the show with the segment where we traced those adorable puppies in the high-end pet store back to a puppy mill?"

"Yeah. And the one on the American figure skater with bulimia."
He had to tell her the truth. "You blew me away, Bree. You've got
the heartwarming human interest stuff and the exposé element, and
you handle both well." He gave a self-conscious chuckle. "Not that
you need me to tell you that."

"I appreciate hearing it. Thanks, Zack."

"I can see why your show's such a success. Why the U.S. wants to
pick it up." The U.S. deal would likely mean even more work for her,
less time for a social life, and even greater concern about her public
image—none of which would help his cause. He really wondered if,
as she'd said, syndication would make her happy.

He took a slug of wine for courage. "Why does your career always take top priority? It has to do with the way you grew up?"

She nodded. "I imagine it's hard for you to relate to."

"Kind of. Things have always been easy for me." So easy, he'd
never had a goal he'd had to plan for, to work for.

"You're a golden boy," she teased. "I'll try not to hold it against
you. For me, it was the opposite. All I wanted was to get away, and I
worked hard to do it."

"Get away to . . . "

"Independence and security. Good food, clothes that didn't
come from thrift shops. Respect."

And she'd done it, all on her own. But she'd gone further. "And
then?"

"Increasing success. Status. And believe me, when you've—" She
broke off.

"What?"

She gazed down at her plate. "When you've been treated like
trash, status is important."

He winced and felt a crazy urge to protect her, but of course she
no longer needed that. "Yeah. And now look at you. I Googled you,
Bree. Read about your Gemini Awards, the honorary degree, the
award for philanthropy. You achieved that all on your own."

"Yes and no." She looked up. "In my career, being female and
Native probably helped. Networks had an old-fashioned image and

needed female, multicultural faces. An intelligent, articulate, presentable woman of color had a leg up."

"Maybe a leg. But," he said with certainty, "you've succeeded because of *who* you are, not *what* you are."

"Thank you." She gave him a warm smile, and their gazes held for a moment before they went back to their meals.

After a few more bites, he said, "So, what will U.S. syndication mean for you?"

"It's . . . " She paused, fork in midair. "A big step. Away from where I started out."

Away from him. "Bree, you can't escape the past. It's part of who you are. You don't just do fluffy chat stuff, you do exposés because you care about justice. You raise funds for disadvantaged kids."

"Yes, okay. But I'm still proving myself."

"Proving yourself? To who?"

"Everyone who ever belittled me," she said, an edge in her voice. "Everyone who ever used or tried to use me."

She'd confessed that she was insecure, and now he understood how powerfully that motivated everything she did. The person she really had to prove herself to was Brianna George. "How far do you have to go?" he asked softly. "When will it be enough?"

"Uh . . . I guess I'll know when I get there."

That sounded pretty vague for someone with five- and ten-year plans. Did she just keep setting bigger and bigger goals, without considering what would make her happy inside? "I hope so, Bree." He did things because he wanted to. Not for status, not to prove anything. He'd always known who he was and been content. He wondered if, soul deep, Bree would ever be content with who she was. He was damned sure the U.S. deal wouldn't fix things for her.

He couldn't say that, though. It'd just piss her off, and it was something she'd have to figure out for herself. So he'd approach from another angle. "The wedding rehearsal was today? How did it go?"

"A minor glitch or two, but Andi will iron them out."

"It's a big thing, committing your heart, your life, to someone else." He'd seen his parents' happy marriage, watched his brother fall in love and marry, and always figured it would happen one day for him, when the time was right. There were times, lots of times with Bree, when he wondered if she was the one. He'd never felt this kind of emotion before.

She focused too much on the differences between them. He saw the similarities, and the ways they complemented each other. "How do you feel about marriage?" he asked, straight out.

"Oh . . . " She toyed with her glass, looking at it rather than him. "My experience with men made me cynical. But there are good guys in the world." She darted him a quick smile that touched his heart.

"My friend Tom's another," she said. "Seeing him and Shelley . . . I believe they love each other, and they're going to be good for each other. She's pulling him out of his shell, and he's helping her be more sensitive. They're quite different people, but they kind of . . . fit together." She tilted her head. "Does that make sense?"

"Yeah." The way he and Bree could, if she'd give them a chance. "Like they say, opposites attract."

"I suppose." Her eyes, pools of melted chocolate, rested on his face.

It was progress. With Bree, he'd learned to measure progress in small steps. And now he really wanted to make love to her. "Ready for dessert?"

"You made dessert?"

Her hopeful expression made him laugh. "Sorry, I'm a chef, not a baker." He went around and tugged her to her feet. "But I did buy a bar of Toblerone." He dropped a kiss on those full, soft lips. "Now, where did I put it? Oh yeah, the drawer of the bedside table."

"Sounds like a ploy to get me into the bedroom."

"Bet on it. Any objection?" He took her hand and pulled her toward the stairs.

"Not a one." She freed her hand and cupped his arse.

The bedroom was dark but for the flickering light of the gas fire. With the light from the flames dancing across her striking face,

Bree was so beautiful. He stroked his fingers through the short, shiny hair at her temples then left his hands there, cradling her head.

She came up on her toes as he bent down, and their lips met in a kiss that was sweeter than any chocolate.

When they broke, he said, "Let's do this slowly this time."

"No chocolate syrup?" she teased.

"No, but I'll lick you all over, if you'd like."

She smiled up at him. "So long as you concentrate on the best places."

"With you, they're all the best places."

He led her to the bed, messy from their earlier lovemaking. Slowly, he removed the soft golden sweater, a shade or two lighter than her pretty skin, then the cream-colored pants that hugged her long, shapely legs.

Gently, he traced the lacy top edge of her ivory-colored bra where it lay against her silky skin. Her nipples were beaded, and he rubbed his thumb across first one, then the other. Then he removed her bra, leaving her in only a matching thong.

She stood, not saying a word. But the taut nipples and the quick rise and fall of her chest told him she was aroused. So did the damp heat between her legs when he stroked her gently there, then tugged the thong down her long legs.

His own body ached with desire, but there'd be no down-and-dirty sex this time. He wanted to show her how special she was to him. "Lie down."

When she did, he lit the candles and quickly undressed, freeing his hard-on. He bent to kiss her, smiling at the welcoming sparkle in her eyes. Feasting on her mouth, he loved the way she responded so totally, not holding anything back. She was generous with her body yet too afraid, too career-driven, to open up emotionally.

He'd have to teach her.

From her mouth, he made his way down, kissing the elegant line of her neck, the sweet hollow at the base of her throat, the silky skin of her chest, then the top curve of her breast. His tongue circled her areola, swished across the tight bud of her nipple.

"Mmm, nice," she said, her fingers in his hair.

"Yeah, very nice." He sucked her nipple into his mouth, the sweetest of candies, applying gentle pressure with his lips and tongue. Holding it between his lips, he flicked the tip of his tongue back and forth.

She whimpered, arching up, fingers gripping him more tightly.

He moved to her other breast, then made his way down her stomach. His tongue swirled into her navel; his lips charted her smooth belly with damp kisses. As he moved lower, crisp curls of black hair tickled him.

Her legs parted, inviting him between them. His fingers found her center, slick and hot. He grabbed a pillow and thrust it under her, raising her lower body.

What a beautiful sight: firelight on the folds of her most intimate flesh, rosy and gleaming with arousal. He stroked her, spreading moisture, feeling her shift, press, squeeze against him in a silent plea for more.

He bent and followed the same path with his tongue. His dick, hard and aching, pressed against her leg. He wanted to thrust but forced himself not to. This was about Bree. When she was whimpering with need, he eased two fingers inside her and began to pump slowly.

"Oh yes, Zack," she whispered. "So good. You make me feel so good."

Taking his cues from the way she responded, he stroked faster, then licked her clit with the flat of his tongue. Faster, firmer, as he could feel her body tremble, tighten, gather every sensation.

When he sucked her clit gently, she cried out, and her body surged in climax, pulsing against his fingers and mouth.

As the spasms faded, he sheathed himself, straddled her, then eased inside that fiery moist world with a groan of relief and pleasure.

She reached up to circle his shoulders with her arms and pulled his head down to hers. Eyes glowing in the light from the candles by the bed, she didn't say a word, just kissed him with a passion that made it impossible not to pump harder.

He wanted to control himself, to take things slow and give her another climax before he let himself come, but all his good intentions got lost when he was in this woman's arms.

Answering her kiss hungrily, he slammed into her as her hips rose to meet him. Her hands were on his arse now, fingernails digging in, urging him on.

They broke for breath, captured each other's mouths again, muttered "Yes" and "Oh, God," and all the time their bodies drove each other closer to the peak.

Then she froze, holding absolutely still as he thrust hard and deep. A moment later her body shuddered around him, coming apart in waves that rocked him, while she cried out, "Oh, Zack!"

Now, now he could let go, and he did. Everything—his uncertainty and fear as well as his passion and growing love—poured out of him and into her. "Bree." His Bree.

Together, they clung for long minutes as waves of sensation pounded through them, then faded to ripples. And finally, there was nothing but soft pants for breath, the gentle heaving of their sweat-slicked chests against each other, and the warm weight of her hands, relaxed now on his back.

He could have lain there forever, but he forced himself to shift off her. He flopped onto his back beside her and curled an arm around her shoulders. She tucked her body around his, head on his shoulder, arm across his chest, leg over his thighs.

There was something he needed to ask her. Would he meet with a different response than he had last night?

He kissed the top of her hair. "Stay, Bree. Stay the night."

Chapter 10

AT the moment, Brianna wanted to stay in this bed with this man and never get up. "I shouldn't," she murmured.

"It's better sneaking in at midnight than walking through the front door in the morning? Say you went out early for a walk."

She'd thought the same thing herself. The true danger in staying wasn't the risk of having her affair discovered. It was the danger to her heart. She already cared so much. If she slept with Zack, woke up with him, how could she bear it when they parted?

She was coming to understand how Tom and Shelly felt about each other, and why they were willing to put so much emotion and effort into working things out. But she and Zack . . . they weren't like Tom and Shelley. Were they?

His arm tightened around her shoulders and squeezed. "Bree?"

No, of course they weren't. Zack traveled where the snow was, and she had her brilliant career. Brilliant, even though he'd said some things that troubled her. Just who was she trying to please, with U.S. syndication? Honestly, she'd been happier doing local interest stories than always hunting for an American hook. As a girl, she'd had a dream, a dream of getting away and succeeding, and she'd gone after it with every ounce of energy.

How would she know when she finally arrived? And why did her heart yearn for a new, completely different dream? A romantic one?

Yes, being with Zack was dangerous, and yet she couldn't resist. "I'll stay."

"That's my girl," he said with satisfaction.

A woman could get very, very used to this. To everything about this man. She inhaled the sexy, outdoorsy scent of his skin—why did Zack always smell so good?—and pressed her lips against his shoulder. If she focused on the wonderful sensations, maybe she could turn off the turmoil in her brain.

Her arm lay across his body, and he stroked it in a gentle caress, up and down. Repetitive. Soothing. Gradually, a sense of peace, of security, stole through her. She sighed contentedly, her whole body relaxing into his, and her eyes drifted shut.

BRIANNA woke slowly, feeling disoriented. When she opened her eyes, a flickering gas fire reminded her she was in the bedroom of the town house. But Zack wasn't in bed beside her.

From downstairs she heard noises: humming, the soft clatter of dishes, a swish of running water. She should go and help.

But it felt so good to lie here, in her cocoon under the duvet, and listen to the sounds of a man moving around the house, humming. She loved that he was humming. If she'd been able to carry a tune, she'd have done it herself.

As a child, when she'd woken at night, often it was to the sound of voices shouting, things being thrown. Threats, tears, sometimes the thud of fists against flesh.

Not tonight. She was safe and secure. Almost, she felt . . . loved. For the first time in her life.

His footsteps sounded on the stairs, then he stepped into the room, clad only in his black pants, his chest buff and golden in the firelight. "Hi there," she said.

"Hey, Bree. Sorry. Didn't mean to wake you."

"I should have come down and helped, but I was too lazy."

"No worries. I liked knowing you were up here in bed." He stripped off his pants. Oh, very nice, all rippling muscles.

"It's not like me to sit back and let someone else do the work."

"You gotta learn to let someone take care of you now and then." He tossed back the covers and climbed in beside her.

About to say that he took care of her exceedingly well, she instead protested when his cool flesh brushed hers. "Ooh, you're cold!" Giggling, she moved away as he came after her, then surrendered and let him wrap himself around her heated body. She loved his strength and agility and the fact that he never, except teasingly, tried to overpower her.

ZACK held her for a long moment, letting himself savor her warm curves. Bree, in his arms.

He couldn't wait any longer. If he didn't speak now, they'd either have sex or she'd fall asleep, and the moment would be lost.

He took a deep breath and let it out slowly, then gazed into her eyes, sparkling and almost black in the flickering light. "Bree, I don't want this to end when you leave Whistler."

"Oh!" Her face lit, then went guarded. "Being with you is wonderful. But I'm not sure if it's wise. I mean, where is this going?"

"Opposites attract, Bree, and I'm falling for you."

Her eyes grew luminous. "Oh, Zack, I feel the same."

He'd known it, just not been sure she'd admit it to herself or to him. He touched her cheek. "I want to date you. Out in public. I'm sick of sneaking around."

She worried her lips together. "Zack, you'll be gone in a month or two. You follow the snow."

"Only because I've had nothing more important. You could be

more important." It was too early for guarantees, yet he felt a sense of certainty—in his heart, maybe even his soul—he'd never experienced with another woman. Crazy, what with her high-powered career and all her hang-ups, but there it was.

"Really? More important than skiing?"

"Jesus. Yeah, than skiing." Had she been thinking their affair could never be anything more than temporary because he'd be off to some other ski resort? Well, of course she had, because that's how he'd lived his life until now. "Bree, I've been thinking about the future. Where I want to be in five years, like you said. I love skiing and teaching, but I don't have to do it year round. Don't have to travel. You know, if things worked out with us."

Her expression was a little stunned, as if it was all too much to take in. Then she frowned. "But you're still . . . There's the age thing. The gossip."

And in the end, it came back to that. "That's bullshit," he said harshly. So much for a home-cooked meal and dressing up to impress her. "You don't think I'm good enough for you."

"No! No, of course not. You're great, Zack."

"Great to fuck, but not good enough to be seen in public with, much less to meet your colleagues."

Her face froze, and her eyes focused somewhere else—in the distance, or maybe inward. She didn't speak for an achingly long couple of minutes, but there was revelation, pain, and confusion in the depths of those brown eyes. Had he destroyed his chance with her? Or had he even ever had one?

When she still didn't speak, he said, "Bree?"

"Give me a minute," she muttered in a preoccupied tone.

Clenching his jaw, he continued to wait.

Finally, she shoved herself up to a sitting position, the duvet hugged around her shoulders so only her head stuck out. "Let me tell you a story."

"Okay," he said warily. He sat, too, his share of the duvet pooled around his hips.

"There's a girl, a teenager," she said, speaking slowly, as if she were searching for words. "A girl who's mostly been treated like trash."

A story about herself. A painful one, or she wouldn't be telling it in this distanced way.

"In high school," she said, "this boy who's way out of her league, he pays attention to her, takes her driving and parking. She believes he cares for her, and she falls for him. Lets him take her virginity. There's a school dance coming up, and she's sure he'll invite her to go with him."

"But he doesn't." He wanted to touch her, but the way she was huddled inside the duvet wasn't encouraging.

She shook her head. "She's leaving the girls' restroom one day when she hears him, out in the hallway with his friends. They're talking about who they're taking to the dance. One of them asks him if he's taking the"—she swallowed audibly—"that little slut he's been nailing."

"Oh, Bree."

"He says, 'No fucking way. The Indian bitch is good enough to sink my prick in, but I'm sure the fuck not going out in public with her.'"

Now it was Zack's turn to swallow. He wished he could go back in time and whip that bastard's arse.

"I'm sorry," she said, gazing into his eyes, her own sheened with tears. "It was people like him who motivated me to get ahead. And I thought I had. But look at where I've gotten." Her mouth twisted. "I've turned into someone who's just as bad as him."

He reached out to touch her face and smooth her hair behind her ear. "You're not—"

"I am. That boy treated me like trash, and I was a nice girl. Well, you're a fine man, and look how I've been treating you. Oh, Zack, I'm so sorry."

"I've tried to understand your side," he said, "but yeah, it hurt."

"I should be proud to be with you. Any woman would be."

"I get it about your job, your image. But I want to be as important to you as they are."

"Oh, Zack, you are." The duvet dropped, and there she was, all gorgeous brown skin, sweet curves, and earnest expression. She rested her hands on either side of his face. "A job should never be that important. It's people that truly matter. I don't know how I could have lost sight of that."

She touched her lips to his. "Thank you."

"For . . . ?"

"For putting up with me. For talking to me so openly. For c-caring for me."

He rested his forehead against hers. "Can't help caring for you, Bree."

A smile curved her lips. "I can't help caring for you, either. But I'm not used to caring. Or being cared for. I couldn't let myself believe this was anything more for than a holiday fling. But now I do, and it feels so good."

Warmth flooded him at those words. Yet he was wary. Had anything really changed? A couple of days ago, when he'd realized that insecurity was at the root of so much she did, he'd said it was okay to be a mess because you could grow and change. Had she?

She pulled back and studied him for a long time, then a sparkle lit in her eyes. "Can you find someone to cover your lessons tomorrow afternoon?"

"Saturday?" The wedding was Saturday afternoon. What was she saying?

"I know it's late notice," she said, "but if you can, I'd love it if you'd come to the wedding. As my date."

Relief surged through him so strongly that for a moment he couldn't catch his breath. When he did, he hugged her tight. "I'll be there."

About to kiss her, a remaining trace of uncertainty made him say, "Maybe after, we could go to Down Under, the Aussie pub I told you about. You could meet some of my mates."

"I'd love to meet your friends." Then she kissed him, and that kiss told him everything he needed to know. The successful TV host might get tongue-tied when it came to her personal feelings, but when her mouth touched his, she spoke a brand-new language.

She was no longer avoiding or denying what they felt for each other. The caress of her lips against his, the dart of her flirtatious tongue, and the way their mouths melded in the slow simmer of passion all validated the emotions that had been growing between them this week.

So far, their romance had been quite the slippery slope, with more than one mogul and spill along the way, but now they were flying.

In *Hot* Pursuit
of a *Bad* Boy

Bad-Boy Cocktail

INGREDIENTS

1 oz. Alizé Gold
1 oz. peach schnapps
1 oz. raspberry schnapps
3 oz. peach or passion fruit juice

INSTRUCTIONS

Pour all ingredients into a cocktail shaker. Shake well, and pour over ice cubes into a highball glass.

Chapter 1

"GOOD game," Logan Carver said, clicking the remote to the luxury Hummer SUV. At this hour, the parking lot under the ritzy hotel was empty but for him and his companion, Joe Lee. "Hope I can do it again." He kept his tone casual, slurring his words slightly.

Lee was checking out the vehicle, no doubt making mental note of the license plate. That's why his boss, Eddie Tran, had sent him down with Logan.

"Maybe the boss'll give you a call," Lee said noncommittally.

If Tran was a drug dealer—maybe even if he wasn't—he'd likely have his henchman Lee check Logan out before an invitation was issued to another high-stakes poker game. Tonight, Logan's entrée had been through an occasional player, a lawyer he'd supposedly bumped into by coincidence at a bar in Whistler today. A lawyer with a fondness for cocaine, who happened to be a police informant. The lawyer, Harvey Binder, had been invited to the game and had taken Logan along as a pal with money to burn.

Logan climbed into the Hummer, a vehicle chosen to fit his cover: a guy who liked expensive toys and didn't care how he got the money to buy them.

He pulled away with a lurch, playing half drunk. Over years of undercover work, he'd built up a high tolerance for booze, and tonight he'd managed to discreetly dump a good portion of the Glenfiddich that had been poured for him.

When he pulled out of the hotel's underground lot, he found a peaceful Whistler night with gently falling snow. From one world to another. Ten minutes ago he'd been in a penthouse suite, drinking scotch and smoking a cigar while he played poker with a man he suspected was a kingpin in an international drug ring. Now, throat and eyes burning, he was heading to a Swiss-style chalet where a wedding party of fifty snuggled cozily under duvets.

Neither world was a good fit for Logan, but then no world ever had been.

Looking forward to showering away the foul cling of cigar smoke, he turned into the White Gold subdivision. His foot jerked on the gas pedal at the sight of flashing lights strobing the night. What the hell? Was it cops, ambulance, or—fire. An engine and a chief's car, right outside the chalet. And a few minutes earlier, an ambulance had passed him on the main road, coming from this direction.

Shit. What had happened? Were Tom and Maddie okay? Worry sent a charge of adrenaline through him.

Hurriedly, he parked and jumped out of the Hummer. No flames, thank God, though the acrid scent of smoke tainted the crisp, snowy air. As he strode toward the scene, he saw firefighters moving about purposefully and clusters of people in hastily thrown-on clothing dotting the yard and street.

He scanned the groups, located Tom's parents and grandparents, and over there were Tom and his fiancée Shelley, arms around each other.

Maddie—where was Maddie? Little Maddie Daniels, as he'd tried to think of her. Two and a half years younger, at first she'd been the typical kid sister, always wanting to hang around and butt into his and Tom's business, annoying and cute at the same time. Then she'd started growing up, and she'd been annoying and cute in a whole different way.

He scanned the clusters of guests impatiently. Maddie might have had her head in the clouds sometimes—like when she'd got that crush on him—but at her core she'd been practical. She'd have gotten out safely, no question. The firefighters were rolling up the hose; the drama was over.

Still, he had to know for sure. And he had to see her, for the first time in ten years.

Ever since he'd been given this assignment and had won Tom's agreement to invite him to the wedding, he'd been wondering about Maddie. He'd Googled her and found out she was a massage thera-pist, but there'd been no photo. According to Tom, she wasn't mar-ried, but she was dating someone seriously. It was the same story he'd gotten on the few occasions over the years that he and Tom had been in touch. Always dating seriously yet never married. That surprised him. She'd been the white-picket-fence kind of girl. Of course, she was only twenty-five; likely, she was being selective about finding the right man.

His gaze scanned the ever-shifting groups and then—yes, there she was, talking to several others. Maddie. Something in his chest eased.

For a moment, he thought her gaze met his, but likely she wouldn't recognize him. And now she was moving away, heading for the chalet, and then she was hidden behind a couple of firefighters.

Still, he'd got enough of a look to freeze a picture in his mind. He didn't know whether to be glad or disappointed, but she hadn't changed much. Her brown hair was pulled into a haphazard pony-tail; her pretty face was fresh despite the hour, and clear of makeup. She was bundled in a big, fluffy pink bathrobe and red gumboots.

When he'd last seen her, just after he'd finished grade twelve, she'd almost looked older in the figure-hugging jeans and tank tops she'd taken up wearing. She'd been fifteen. Going on sixteen, she'd told him defiantly that last night. And he'd been eighteen. Tempted, seriously tempted, but not a fool. Despite her flirting, she was a good girl; he most definitely was a bad boy, but not bad enough to ruin her life.

Logan realized all the guests were heading inside. There was a shower calling his name, so he followed, only to find that the fire had originated in a room two down from his, and his room stank of smoke. Inger Jacobs, who with her husband Gord owned the Alpine Hideaway, was directing traffic. "Leave your windows open to air your rooms," she told everyone, "then come along to the lounge for hot chocolate."

He sighed. The night wasn't over yet. He flung the windows wide, splashed water on his face and brushed his teeth to get rid of the taste of cigars, then headed for the lounge. Stopping in the doorway, he surveyed the room. People were in clusters, as they'd been outside. They looked tired but relaxed and chatty, comfortable with each other.

It wasn't in his character to join in, nor did it fit his cover story. Essentially, he was supposed to be an older, badder version of his teenage self.

This week, his job was to do recon on Eddie Tran. It was an initial step in the joint RCMP/Vancouver Police Department's Project Takedown, which had been created to bust an international drug trafficking ring. Logan had recently returned to B.C. as part of the team.

Intelligence told them Tran might be a kingpin. Their informant Binder's occasional participation in Tran's poker games in Whistler provided a possible in. Then research turned up the fact that Logan's old friend Tom was getting married in the Village.

Logan had approached Tom, who'd agreed to give him a reason for being in Whistler. They'd settled on a story: old friends who'd been out of touch, meeting accidentally and reconnecting; Tom inviting Logan to the wedding; both of them realizing they no longer had anything in common; Logan, a restless loner, finding the wedding stuff too tame and blowing it off, looking for excitement.

Showing Tran, with his disdain, that he had no real connection to any of the people at the Alpine Hideaway. Even though this was just recon, Logan had to ensure that Tom, Maddie, and their family and friends were safe.

A couple of guests came up behind him and brushed past, into the room. He followed, intent on finding a quiet corner. A laugh burbled, and he froze, then turned. His gaze locked on a woman sitting with half a dozen other people: glossy chestnut hair curling to her shoulders, a vivid red sweater that hugged curves so sweet they made his fingers itch, and shapely legs in tight black leggings . . .

Maddie. And—Jesus Christ!—had she ever grown up.

As if she felt his gaze on her, her head turned, and then she was staring at him. A bright smile lit her face.

Her smile touched a chord in his heart that hadn't been strummed since that last night he'd been with her.

But back then, he'd been the wrong guy for Maddie, and nothing had changed. She'd have recovered from her childish crush long ago, but buddying up with her or any of the wedding guests didn't fit his cover. So he gave her a curt nod, turned his back, and found a seat on the opposite side of the room, one that just happened to keep her in his line of sight.

The hurt on her face made him wince.

A fair-haired young woman who looked rather like Inger—a daughter or niece?—came in with a tray of mugs and began distributing them. When she came to him, she said, "Hot chocolate or sex on the slopes?"

He blinked. "What?"

She chuckled. "Oh, you haven't heard about it? It's Uncle Gord's specialty drink."

Tough guys drank hard liquor. "Got any scotch?"

"I can get you some as soon as I've passed out these drinks."

Seizing the excuse, he said, "Forget it. Give me one of those." He reached for a mug of hot chocolate with a disdainful grimace. But when she was gone, he cradled the mug between both hands, enjoying the warmth, the old-fashioned smell, and the sight of two fat marshmallows melting. A wholesome drink, in the hands of a man who was—had always been—anything but.

Instinct told him he was being watched. Head still bent, he raised his eyes slowly. Maddie. When she caught him looking, she quickly glanced away, back to the person beside her.

Tom and Maddie's mom used to serve hot chocolate in winter, lemonade in summer. Out of Ms. Daniels's earshot, he'd scoffed, saying they were little-kid drinks and he'd rather have beer or hard liquor. Yet they'd slid down his throat like the taste of everything he'd never had: home, tradition, security . . . family.

Now he sipped his drink. Was Maddie drinking hot chocolate, too, or was that grown-up woman with the dynamite curves into Sex on the Slopes?

His groin tightened at the thought. Sex. Maddie. He glanced over again. She was absorbed in a conversation with a fair-haired guy about his own age. Must be the serious boyfriend, the way he was hanging on her every word. Logan felt a ridiculous twinge of jealousy.

He let his gaze linger on Maddie, rather than her date. She'd been fresh and pretty as a girl, and she was fresh still, but with a woman's beauty, a beauty that grew more seductive the longer he looked.

His cock throbbed and swelled. He stared down at his mug, trying to replace the image of her in that figure-hugging outfit with the one of her in the bulky, girlish bathrobe, but now even that one was a turn-on. What had been under the robe? A see-through nightie, flannel pj's, or a tank top and boxers? Didn't matter, because underneath was Maddie, all sweet flesh and womanly curves.

And a tender heart. A heart that had wanted to see things in him that didn't exist—or couldn't exist.

Overheated now, he shrugged out of his jacket and tossed it to the floor. When he looked up next, he carefully avoided glancing in her direction. Instead, he gazed at Tom, holding hands with Shelley as the animated blonde told a story to their friends. Then he looked over to see Mr. and Ms. Daniels talking to Tom's grandparents.

He'd only met the grandparents two or three times but, to his surprise, Gram Daniels had been rather kind to him. Another soft heart like Maddie, he figured. Gramps Daniels and Tom's parents, on the other hand, had always been wary of him, and rightfully so.

It was weird that he—the troublemaker who couldn't last in a foster home for more than a few months—had become friends with the squeaky-clean boy from the squeaky-clean family. In grade nine, they'd been assigned to work together on a history project, and to both their surprise, something had clicked.

Mostly, he figured, it was a fascination with each other's "otherness." For Tom, hanging out with Logan added an edge to his life. For Logan, Tom was . . . Hell, he and his family were straight out of that old TV show, *Growing Pains*. Logan had loved that stupid show, although—as with the hot chocolate—he'd pretended not to. The Seaver family and home were everything he didn't have, could never have, and had secretly longed for.

And he'd been the Leo DiCaprio character, Luke Brower.

His and Tom's was an on-again off-again friendship, but somehow it lasted through grade twelve. How many times had Logan sat at the Daniels's kitchen table or hung out in the rec room, more often watching than participating? He'd felt like the kid outside the playground fence, always looking in at the game.

Fuck. Here he was, traveling memory lane like some loser.

Yeah, he was an outsider then, now, and always. And he didn't give a shit. He was here to do a job. Period.

Feeling someone watching him again, he glanced over to see the wedding planner perched on the edge of her seat as if she was about to come over. The last thing he needed was some perky activities director trying to make him socialize. He scowled to discourage her.

Her face tightened, and she gazed down into her mug.

Chapter 2

ACROSS the room, Maddie Daniels surreptitiously watched Logan.

She'd glimpsed him earlier, when everyone was out in the snow. Even across the yard, in dim light, not having seen him for ten years, she'd recognized him immediately. Her heart had, quite literally, leaped into her throat.

Her first instinct had been to run over. Thankfully, before she'd done that, she'd realized what she was wearing. How totally embarrassing. Hoping he hadn't seen her, she'd rushed inside to dress.

To dress like a woman. A confident woman, who'd greet her long-ago crush with a warm smile and perhaps a hug and a kiss on the cheek. No need for him to know she was all nerves, wondering if he still made her heart lurch and her hormones zing the way no other man ever had.

Then, blast him, he'd walked into the lounge and blown her off. Just as he had ten years ago, when he'd left town without a word.

Ten years ago, she'd thought they were friends. Of course, she'd wanted more—in her mind, he was the one, and she'd dreamed of a future with him—but he'd always pulled back. Until that last night, when he'd kissed her in the starlight. Well, okay, she'd kissed him, but he'd kissed back. Two days later, her brother told her Logan had left Vancouver.

In a few years, she'd gained some perspective and realized she'd been too young for a sexy, exciting older boy like Logan. But still, she'd thought they had something special. She'd believed she was the only person who really *got* him. Who saw past that bad-boy image, sexy as it was.

Now, while she sipped Sex on the Slopes and chatted with a few guests, including a really nice single friend of Tom's named Michael, she studied Logan from under downcast lashes. The boy had certainly turned into one very hot man. One who still looked rough around the edges but in a far more expensive way than he used to.

His dark brown hair was still overlong, he still had a small gold hoop in his left ear, and the stubble on his face was heavier. He'd added a flashy diamond ring, and there was that indefinable something about his jeans and black sweater, the leather jacket tossed casually to the floor beside his chair, that told her their labels were pricey.

The years had added height and muscle, and he looked powerful, tough, despite the nice clothes. If she'd seen him on the street in Vancouver, she wouldn't have known if he was an actor or a professional gambler. He still had that sexy aura of . . . mystery? Danger?

Once, in one of those precious moments she'd treasured, he'd confessed that he wanted to right wrongs and see bad guys punished. Romantically, she'd envisioned him as a knight; more practically, she'd thought he might become a lawyer. Was the good guy still there inside that sexy, edgy exterior? Had he ever been?

She'd been startled when, out of the blue two weeks ago, Tom had said he'd run into Logan and invited him to the wedding. She'd demanded details, but her brother had frustratingly not obliged. He'd been just as closemouthed all those years ago when he'd told her Logan had left town. Then and now, all he'd said was that she should forget about him. As if. Just hearing his name had reawakened those old dreams.

Now, glancing down at her fingernails, she thought that the mani-pedi and haircut, not to mention the Brazilian wax and sexy new lingerie, had been totally wasted.

Unless, of course, things heated up with Michael. She'd met him a couple times before, with Tom, and they'd hit it off. He was handsome, with his dirty blond hair and blue eyes, he was intelligent, and he was a healer, too. A chiropractor. Chiropractor and massage therapist; they were a perfect pair.

Michael was interesting, even though right now she was having trouble concentrating on the conversation. Damn, Logan was just plain rude. Ten years ago, she'd had no choice but to let him get away with it because she'd had no way of tracing him. Now he was right in front of her.

If he feared she still had a puppy-dog crush on him, she'd show him differently.

Annoyed, she refocused on his face. What she saw made her catch her breath. He had that same wistful air she'd seen occasionally when he was young and let his guard slip, as if he was the only kid in the class who hadn't been invited to the party, and he was standing outside the window staring in.

She let her breath out in a sigh. *This* was what she'd seen in Logan that no one else seemed to. Much as he played the tough guy, the loner, he secretly yearned to belong. The combination of edgy bad boy and secret yearning had been impossible to resist.

It still was.

"Would you excuse me?" she murmured to Michael and the others she was sitting with. "I need to say hi to an old friend." Carrying her mug of Sex on the Slopes, she walked straight to Logan.

He'd been watching her parents and grandparents, but now he focused on her, face stripped of expression.

She stopped in front of him so he had to look up. "Hello, stranger," she said, trying to sound calm and wishing her heart wasn't jerking like a jackhammer.

"Madeleine Daniels," he drawled.

"You know I hate that name."

"You used to. It's been a while. Things change."

"They do. But not that particular one." Nor the fact that, even two or three feet away from him, she could feel the energy he gave off. It was like a magnetic force, making her want to draw close, and closer still, until the two of them—

She realized she had actually moved toward him, unwittingly, and now pretended that she'd meant all along to perch on the arm of his overstuffed chair. There were no empty seats nearby, so it was a reasonable thing to do. "You don't mind if I sit here?" As if she was giving him any choice.

He shrugged, a movement of broad shoulders under close-fitting black wool that was so purely male it robbed her of breath. Then he turned toward her, the movement brushing his leg against hers, and she barely suppressed a gasp of awareness at the tingle that radiated from the spot.

Breathe, she told herself. Okay, she was here, talking to Logan. Except he wasn't talking. He was leaving it to her, and she didn't have a clue what to say next.

Wait. Yes, she did. She glared at him. "You left town without saying good-bye. And you weren't in touch, not once in ten years."

He sucked in a breath. "You needed to grow up."

"Maybe so, but you were rude. And I see you haven't changed, coming in here tonight and not even saying hello."

He cocked an eyebrow. "You expected politeness? From me?"

She huffed. "You run into Tom after all these years, he invites you to the wedding, and you come. Why?" Clearly not, as she'd secretly hoped, to see her again. After all, if he'd wanted to do that, all he'd have had to do was phone.

Another negligent shrug. "Seemed like a good idea at the time."

"And yet you sit alone in a corner rather than mixing and mingling."

"Yeah. So maybe it wasn't such a good idea."

Was he still the guy who watched from the outside, wishing he could join in but not knowing how? "You missed the welcome dinner."

His eyes, a golden brown that had always reminded her of a lion, glittered. "Poker game."

He'd socialize with poker players but not wedding guests?

Perhaps he guessed what she was thinking, because he shook his head impatiently. "Since when was I known for social graces, Maddie?"

Hearing his voice shape her name sent a pang through her, and so did the reminder. This was Logan. She was really with Logan again. And he was familiar and unfamiliar, and—blast him—as sexy as ever.

More sexy. Off-the-chart sexy. Enough to send pulses of hot arousal, tiny electrical charges, rushing through her. She felt more alive than she had in . . . maybe ten years.

She shifted restlessly. "Okay, much as it might have been nice if you'd spent the last decade developing some social graces, you haven't. So, what have you been doing with your time?"

His lips twitched, then straightened. "This and that."

The twitch of humor warmed her; his refusal to give a proper answer frustrated her. But Logan had always been hard to get to know, and she wouldn't give up so easily. She went for a more direct challenge. "How's it going with righting wrongs and getting bad guys punished?"

Shock flashed across his features before he controlled them. "You remember that?"

She remembered every word he'd ever spoken to her. How pathetic was that? She shrugged. "It stuck in my mind. Made me wonder if you'd become a lawyer." Most people had predicted he was headed for serious trouble, but not her. "Did you?"

He snorted. "A lawyer? Too many rules." Something wickedly suggestive gleamed golden in his eyes. "I've never been much of a one for following the rules."

She was a rule-follower, but she'd happily throw the rule book out the window if he kept looking at her that way. Striving for composure, she said, "So what do you do, Logan?"

Gaze holding hers, he said, "Found I had a knack for investments."

Now, that was a surprise. "You mean, like the stock market?"

"Like that."

He was hedging. Did he think she'd pump him for investment advice? It must be an occupational hazard. "That's impressive." Though she was sorry he hadn't stuck with his teenage dreams.

"That's me, Maddie." There was a teasing note in his voice. "Impressive."

Out of old habit, she made a fist and socked his shoulder lightly. "Full of yourself."

In the old days, he'd have grabbed her hand and twisted her arm until she giggled and cried uncle. Tonight, he did catch her hand, but he held on to it and held that balled-up fist inside his much bigger hand.

And oh my, did she want to cry uncle. Heat surged up her arm, zinged through her body, and settled thick and moist between her thighs. "Logan?" she breathed. This man was the reason she'd never been able to see another man's face in her dreams of the future.

Staring into her eyes, his own flared with heat—pure male heat. Then he gave a sudden jerk, looked away, and released her hand. "Shit. Sorry."

When they were kids, she'd sometimes caught him gazing intently at her or noticed him turn away abruptly, and she had wondered if he was attracted to her. Aroused. But she'd been too young to be sure. That was then. This was now. And she knew. Her own feelings must be equally apparent on her face, so why had he backed off?

There was something between them—sexual, yes, but maybe more—and she needed to explore it. Maybe Logan truly was the man she'd been waiting for.

"You're attracted to me," she said, glad he'd picked a chair that sat at a distance from any other guests. "What's wrong with that?"

"Christ, Maddie, you're dating someone else, and he's right across the room." He stared past her, his expression grim. "Watching."

"What are you talking about?" She glanced over her shoulder and saw blue eyes fixed on them. Oh yeah, Michael. Giving him a quick smile, she turned back to Logan. "I'm not dating him. I'm not dating anyone right now."

He frowned. "Tom said you were seriously involved with someone."

Baffled, she shook her head. "I haven't dated anyone seriously for almost a year." Then realization dawned. "Damn it, my brother's still interfering." He'd always warned her off Logan.

"Yeah, well, he's right. I'm no good for you."

She fisted her hands on her hips. "So you and Tom are going to protect me from myself? Get a grip, Logan, I'm a grown-up."

"Yeah, I noticed." He didn't sound happy about it. "Shit, Maddie, I figured you'd have been married by now, with maybe a kid on the way."

"Still waiting for the right man. I take it you don't want to audition?"

He chuckled, then sobered. "I'm not him."

Was he really that sure? "Did I say you were? But there's a mutual attraction, and we're both grown-ups, so what's wrong with getting to know each other again?"

"You'd only get hurt again."

Maybe, but that was only one of the many possible outcomes. "Get over yourself, Logan Carver."

He shook his head. "It's not ego. I'm just saying we're different. You're . . ." He trailed off, and she held her breath, waiting to see how he'd finish. "You're nice, sweet," he finally said. "Wholesome. Everything I'm not."

"Wholesome?" Her voice squeaked in outrage. Boring was what he meant. A good girl, not a sexy, fun one. "I'm not so—"

Her protest was interrupted by the sound of a female voice calling for attention. Maddie looked up to see Andi, the wedding planner, standing in front of the fireplace. "Inger and I have checked your rooms," she told the assembled guests. "They're aired out, and you can go back to bed, but leave your windows open a crack."

People began to rise, and Maddie hopped off the arm of Logan's chair. "Where's your room?"

"Two down from where the fire started. It was pretty smoky." He got to his feet.

Teasingly, she said, "Do let me know if you need a bed for the night . . ."

For a long moment he didn't answer, just stared into her eyes. She could actually feel sparks of energy darting between their bodies. This time, when she felt the impulse to sway toward him, she didn't resist it.

Before her body could touch his, he stopped her by placing his hands on her shoulders. "Maddie, it's not a good idea."

Because he thought she was boring and wholesome. Miffed, she stepped back to free herself from the warm hands that felt so very good.

He bent to pick up his leather jacket, clasping it casually in front of him. But not before she'd seen the erection that pressed against the fly of his jeans.

"Not a good idea?" she drawled, glancing up. "Well, how about that? A man who thinks with his big head rather than"—she flicked her gaze down—"his little one."

Then she forced herself to turn away. The others were trailing out of the lounge, except for Michael, who'd paused in the doorway, probably waiting for her, and Brianna George, Tom's boss and friend, who was sitting alone, seemingly lost in thought.

Maddie didn't want to deal with Michael now. He was a nice guy, but her senses were overloaded on Logan, so she stopped to chat for a minute with Brianna. By the time the two of them joined the tail end of the straggly line of guests, Michael had gone.

In the hallway, Logan was opening the door to his room. Maddie paused to murmur teasingly, "Bet I know what you'll be dreaming about." Before he could reply, she headed toward the stairs.

When she reached her own room, it was smoke-free but freezing cold. Heat was pumping out, though. Once she'd narrowed the window opening to only a crack, the room would soon warm up. If Logan had taken her up on her offer, it would have heated even faster.

Of course, she hadn't really meant it when she offered him a bed for the night.

"Oh no," she muttered, "you're too *wholesome* to leap into bed with a man you haven't seen in ten years."

Wanting to shower before bed, she carried her jammies into the bathroom and piled them beside the sink. They were warm flannel, blue, printed with whimsical sheep. She began to pull off her sweater, then stopped. Flannel pajamas with sheep? Oh God, she really was hopeless.

But the jammies were cozy, and she was alone. She continued to take off her sweater, then let her fingers graze the front of her bra. Her nipples were sensitive and achy.

Yeah, she was alone. Alone and burning with unsatisfied need for Logan. A need that was much more powerful and specific than the diffuse longing she'd felt in her teens. *Specifically*, she wanted sex with Logan Carver. Sex, and the chance to find out who he was now. To find out how she felt about him—and how he might feel about her, now she was all grown-up.

How could she ever talk him out of that stupid idea that they were wrong for each other because she was so wholesome?

Hmm, maybe talk wasn't the answer . . .

LOGAN paced his room, uncaring that the air was chill and held a faint scent of smoke.

His body was plenty fucking hot, thanks to Maddie Daniels, and the aroma that lingered in his nostrils was vanilla, her scent.

If he'd played his cards right, he could've been in her bed right now, using his rigid boner for something much more satisfying than holding up his jeans.

But hell, it was Maddie, not a sleazy one-night fling.

Yeah, she was grown-up and knew how to flirt, but he doubted she'd changed all that much. He'd bet she still wanted a home like the one she'd grown up in. She deserved that, and a husband who was a good guy like her brother and dad.

A husband, not a loner who didn't even know what love was. An undercover cop who disappeared into the criminal world for months on end.

She'd thrown him, asking if he was righting wrongs and seeing bad guys punished. Who'd have imagined she would remember the boyhood dream he'd once, in a vulnerable moment, confessed to her.

Maddie. Oh hell, Maddie. There'd always been something about her that cut straight through his defenses.

A tap on the door interrupted his thoughts.

Figuring it would be one of the Jacobses checking that his room was okay, he checked the peephole. Maddie? Had she come to argue some more? Or to try to seduce him? His cock surged at the idea.

She tapped again. If she kept it up, guests would stick their heads out to see what was going on.

He opened the door. "What are you—"

A cop was supposed to react quickly, and he did, but she was quicker still. In a split second, she was pushing past him into the room. "Close the door," she said.

"Maddie?" He eyed her warily. She was dressed exactly as she had been earlier.

"I need to borrow your shower." She stared at him almost defiantly, but there was a quaver in her voice. "My hair and skin smell of smoke."

"There's something wrong with your shower?"

"Yes, there is." She went into his bathroom and closed the door.

Okay. She hadn't come to argue or to seduce. He should be glad. Instead, he was horny. When he heard the water begin to run, he imagined Maddie, naked under the spray. He groaned and began to pace again. When she left, he was sure going to need one very long, icy-cold shower of his own.

After only a minute or two, the water shut off. The bathroom door opened, and she stuck her head out. "Logan?"

"What?" he snapped. "There's no soap?"

"There's soap. But your shower has the same problem mine did." The door widened, and she stepped out, wreathed in tendrils of steam. Her skin was still dry. He could tell because she wore only a towel. "You're not in it."

He barely heard the words, and he sure as hell didn't process them. His entire focus was on the creamy skin so erotically revealed by the fluffy white towel: arms and shoulders, the top curve of her breasts, and long legs that weren't even covered to mid-thigh. Oh yeah, Maddie Daniels had definitely grown up.

And his erection was going to split his jeans.

"Logan?" Her voice was pure teasing seduction, and her blue eyes gleamed.

"What?" he asked hoarsely.

"You need a shower, too."

"Yeah."

"So, get in here." She hooked one hand into the top of her towel, twisted it, and—

There she stood, totally naked. Breasts full and perky, hips and thighs curving softly, and a completely waxed mound. Jesus Christ, Maddie Daniels waxed her pussy?

"If you like what you see, would you move it?" she said impatiently. "It's cold in here."

"Maddie, I . . . " Words jumbled in his skull. He wanted her, but he couldn't have her. There was some reason he couldn't have her. Why couldn't he remember?

Her eyes narrowed. "I'm grown-up, I want you, you want me. I am *not* wholesome. Does a wholesome woman do this?" She ran a caressing hand over the curve of one taut-nippled breast, across her sleek tummy, and down over the smooth flesh at the apex of her thighs.

His gaze followed the motion of that hand. He could touch her that way. That's what she was offering. Somehow he forced words out. "You're the kind of woman who wants a relationship. I'm not that kind of guy. Most I'd ever be for you is a quickie fling."

Her chin went up, and she stared at him for a long moment. "Like I said before, get over yourself, Logan. What I want is a fuck buddy."

That term, even more than her wax job, jolted him. The old Maddie would never have thought that way, much less used language like that.

"You're Tom's sister." Ten years ago, when Tom had seen him kiss Maddie, he'd punched Logan. Logan hadn't defended himself, because he'd known he was in the wrong, and he'd let Tom convince him to leave town.

She scowled. "Good God, Logan, I'm an adult. Tom has nothing to do with this. It's between you and me."

One night. Their secret. Hell, he wanted her so badly his entire body ached.

She sauntered toward him, hips swaying, nipples hard as pebbles. "I want a fuck buddy, and I choose you."

In one move, he could have all that sweet, naked flesh in his arms. He could have Maddie, the only girl who'd touched his heart.

A tiny part of him grieved the loss of the old Maddie, the sweet, innocent one. But the rest of him celebrated the birth of this fascinating new one.

"I choose you," she repeated. "And you want me. You can't hide that." She reached out and gripped his erection through his jeans. "Fuck me, Logan."

Logan's cock pulsed, and he sucked in a breath. Shocked, aroused beyond belief, he gaped at this new Maddie.

Chapter 3

MADDIE tried not to let her hand tremble as his heat pulsed through the denim of his jeans. She was actually gripping Logan Carver's penis, rigid and hot and so sexy she wanted to whimper with the need to feel that thick, throbbing length buried deep inside her.

Was this really her, being so bold? She'd never before tried to seduce a man, but if the size of his erection was any indication, it was working.

"Hell, Maddie." The words grated out. "You sure about this?" His eyes, gleaming like a lion's, searched hers.

She forced herself to meet his gaze without blinking. He'd made it clear the only way he'd let her into his life, into his bed, was through no-strings sex. So here she was, pretending that all she wanted was a . . . fuck buddy. Even now, she had trouble believing she'd said those words aloud.

"What does it take to convince you, Logan?" Before she lost her nerve, she shoved up his sweater, flipped open the button of his jeans, yanked down the zipper, and reached inside. A moment later, his penis sprang free, thrusting firm and proud up his belly, only inches from her own naked body.

It was all she could do not to moan as her pussy clenched with need, and the dew of arousal tracked down her thighs. Boldly she reached out and grasped him in one hand, curling her fingers around his shaft, feeling his heat sear her palm. "What does it take?"

"That." His voice was gravel. "It took that."

He pulled away from her, and in two seconds flat stripped off his clothes. She barely had a chance to gaze in wonder at his muscular body, to notice a dragon tattoo covering one shoulder and upper arm, to glimpse—was that a scar below his rib cage?—when he scooped her up unceremoniously and strode toward the bathroom. "You want a shower? We'll have a shower."

When he reached the middle of the bathroom, he released her slowly, so she slid down his body. Legs trembling, she put her arms around him and clung, and he hugged her close. Nothing in her life had ever felt this good. Logan's arms around her. His chest, thighs, penis, all so hard. And so warm, pulsing with life.

Still, she knew a thing or two that would top even this. Slowly, she rose on the balls of her feet, belly rubbing his erection. Holding his gaze, she said, "I kissed you once."

"I remember."

"You kissed me back."

One corner of his mouth curved up. "Remember that, too."

"Then you stopped." He'd stalked out of the backyard and out of her life.

"Your mother was calling."

"She was?" They'd been at the bottom of the garden, hidden from the house by her mom's wisteria trellis. "I didn't hear her."

"She said it was past curfew. Curfew, Maddie." His voice went rough. "It reminded me you were just a kid."

"You left town—you left *me*—without a word."

"Vancouver was a bad place for me."

Pain made her shiver and tighten her grip around his waist. "But I was there. I was your friend. I wasn't bad for you."

He touched her face then, stroking her cheek with a single finger. The tip was a little rough, but his touch was gentle. "I was bad for you."

"You weren't."

"I was. You just didn't want to see it." His mouth twisted. "I'm still bad for you."

Maybe; maybe not. She wanted the chance to find out. She scowled. "I didn't want to be protected then, and I don't now." She lowered her hands and squeezed his butt—deliciously firm and taut—roughly. "Just what part of *fuck buddy* don't you get?"

Humor lit his face. It was a rare sight—at least as rare now as it had been then, she guessed. It transformed him from the brooding bad boy to a vibrant, charming, irresistible one. "I think you've made your point, Maddie." Then he grabbed her head firmly between his hands, bent toward her, and touched his lips to hers.

Oh. My. God.

When Logan made up his mind, he really made up his mind. The kiss was explosive, the opposite of the tentative one she'd given him all those years ago. He didn't bother teasing her lips with his tongue, he simply took her mouth as if it belonged to him.

Which, in truth, it always had.

No kiss had ever felt quite right, not since that very first one. Yet this one, so totally different, was perfect.

She surrendered thought as pure pleasure seared through her, and she answered Logan's kiss with years of stored-up need. Her tongue twined around his, thrust and parried with it, as little moans rose from the back of her throat.

His stubble was that fashionably scruffy length, long enough that its abrasion against her skin was soft and erotic, not painful.

His hips pumped, driving his rigid penis against her soft stomach so hard it hurt, but it was the right kind of hurt, and she ground herself against it. If only she were a few inches taller, so she could impale herself on it and take him.

Her whole body quivered with arousal, with need, the desperate need to merge totally with Logan. Panting, she ripped her mouth from his. "Fuck me, Logan." She had a new favorite word and had never suspected how good it would feel on her tongue.

His eyes, glazed with passion, stared into hers. "Hell, yeah." Again, he scooped her up in his arms.

She expected him to cart her off to bed. Instead, he held her in one arm, flipped the fluffy bath mat onto the floor, then bent to deposit her on it.

From a black bag on the bathroom counter, he grabbed a condom, and in a moment he was sheathed and sliding between the legs she opened for him.

"Maddie." His golden gaze searched her face as if to confirm it really was her, and she really wanted this.

She nodded, smiling. "Logan."

Again he kissed her, hard and intense, and a deep hum began in her blood, an earthy throb of anticipation, need, of passion and desire gathering and waiting.

His hand slid between their bodies, stroked between her legs where she was soaking wet, then the head of his penis nudged her in just the right place.

Pure awareness, arousal, shot through her. "Yes," she gasped against his lips. "Yes, Logan. Now."

He seemed to hold his breath, gather himself, and then he surged into her in one long, hard slide that took him deep, deep, exactly where she needed him.

Never, with another lover, had she experienced anything so raw, so amazing. And with that, just that, she shattered with a cry.

He shuddered, groaned, then he slid out, almost all the way out. Then, on another groan, he plunged deep into her again, hips bucking as he came.

And she came again, with him, so strongly her vision dazzled and she saw stars. Heaven. He'd taken her to heaven.

*   *   *

LOGAN had no idea how long it was before he realized his knees hurt like hell, grinding against hard ceramic tiles. The rest of him, buried in soft curves, felt incredible, though.

Maddie's eyes, a sky blue he'd never seen on another woman, blinked open, and she said, "Wow."

"Yeah." He'd never come so fast in his life. He levered himself off her, threw away the condom, and sat on the closed toilet seat. Cautiously he touched his head. "Still there. Felt like I blew the top off."

"I know the feeling," she said as she pulled herself up to sit on the bath mat. She was flushed, tousled, gorgeous, and looked as stunned as he felt.

Shaking his head in wonder, he said, "Maddie Daniels. Who knew?" He'd never have guessed that the sweet girl from his childhood would have turned into a woman who'd brazenly seduce him.

A twinkle in her eyes, she said, "*Wholesome* is no longer the word that comes to mind?"

"Words? Who has words?"

He rose and held out a hand to pull her up. "We were on our way to the shower."

She took his hand, a simple connection that felt awfully good. Slowly she got to her feet, her gaze taking him in from top to bottom. "You've filled out pretty nicely, I must say. And your dragon's sexy." Then a gentle finger traced the scar that ran down his side. "How did you get this?"

Her soft touch, combined with the sight of all that beautiful naked skin, was enough to make his cock swell again. "Had a little disagreement."

"With someone carrying a knife?"

He nodded. "No big deal." It would've been, though, if he hadn't turned in time to deflect the blow. No one had ever said going undercover was a risk-free job, and he'd gotten off lightly. So far.

Her fingers drifted down and grazed his cock. "You're not circumcised. How come?"

Her touch, warm and soft, made him harden further. "Wasn't born in a hospital, and my mother wasn't into seeing doctors."

"She was an addict." She said it matter-of-factly, thank God. As a teen, he'd hated it when people gave him pity, and he'd gotten that message across to Maddie.

"Yeah. Now, you want that shower, or are you ready for round two on the bath mat?"

She gave a soft chuckle and released his cock. "The shower. I must smell of smoke from the fire."

"Vanilla."

"Hmm?"

"You smell like vanilla." With a hint of smoke as well, but no need to mention that.

"Body lotion. Is it too, uh, wholesome for you?"

It was a scent he associated with her family's kitchen. "It's nice. It's like you have two sides. You show the world the good girl." He thought of that fluffy pink bathrobe. "The one who probably bakes cookies. But hidden inside is this down-and-dirty sexy woman who I'm guessing would do pretty much anything."

"I love cookies." Gazing up at him, she said it slowly, seductively, drawing the word out as if cookies were the last thing she was really talking about. "And as for doing anything . . . try me, Logan. Just try me."

"You got a deal." His cock was rigid again, his mind flooding with images of all the ways he wanted to have sex with Maddie. Weirdly—well, maybe not so weirdly, given their history—he also imagined them sitting by a fire, mugs of hot chocolate in their hands, eating cookies and talking.

In his life, she'd been the only person he could really talk to. Though she'd changed in more ways than he could count, he somehow knew he'd still be able to do that.

"I missed you," he found himself saying. Standing in the middle of the bathroom, both of them naked, the words just slipped out, and her eyes widened with surprise. Gruffly, he went on. "You're right that we were friends." He didn't have many of those in his life. Like, none, except for his casual relationship with her brother. The only people he spent any length of time with were criminals.

She nodded. "You shouldn't have left."

"I had to."

Her lips pressed together. "Maybe you felt that way. But you should have stayed in touch. And you should have come back."

Maybe I have. The words sprang to his lips, but this time he managed to hold them back. Hell, he was crazy to even think them. No way could he start up with Maddie for real. Right now she only wanted sex, probably to see what it was like with her high school crush. But long term, she wanted and deserved a different man, a different life. So he said offhandedly, "Water down the drain. Speaking of which, you want that shower?"

She studied his face for a long moment, then glanced down at his cock, and her lips curved. "Yeah, I want that." Turning away—what a curvy, sexy ass she had—she reached behind the shower curtain and turned on the tap.

After adjusting the temperature to her liking, she stepped in, and he promptly followed.

She stood under the shower, facing away from the spray, eyes closed, and he studied her hungrily. She tilted her head back, raising her hands to guide the water through her hair. Chestnut locks darkened; slick to her head, her hair was dramatic against her creamy skin. Water cascaded over beautifully shaped shoulders, across full breasts with pale pink nipples, down her gently curved stomach and full hips. His gaze fixed on her waxed mound, so smooth and silky. It made her seem even more naked.

"Hand me the shampoo?" she requested.

He picked up the small bottle of hotel shampoo, opened it, and squeezed liquid onto his palm. "Turn around."

Surprise flickered on her face, but she obeyed, turning her back to him.

More pale, silky skin and sweet curves, especially the dip of her waist, the flare of her hips, and the lush rounds of her ass.

"Logan?"

"Sorry. Admiring the view."

"Don't be sorry for that," she teased.

He moved closer, rubbing his palms together to spread the shampoo, releasing the scent of pine into the air. Then he touched her head gently and began to work the shampoo through her hair, stroking through the soaking-wet strands to massage her scalp.

"Mmm, nice," she purred. "You're good at that, Logan."

Odd, because he'd never done this before. "Glad it feels good." It did for him, too. It was like subtle foreplay. But now he wanted to touch more than her head. This time he lathered his hands with soap and stroked down her neck under her hair, around the curve of her shoulders, across her back. She was toned, well muscled. A massage therapist, he recalled. She was a strong woman, as well as beautiful.

He dipped down to that curvy ass, where his fingers lingered in the crease between her butt cheeks, then trailed down between them.

Maddie squirmed against his fingers. "Now that feels *really* good."

He took a step closer and bent his knees so he'd be at the right height, then, holding her hips to steady her, he slid his erect cock between her legs. Without entering her, he rode the soapy slick forward and back between her thighs.

She put her hands against the shower wall, bracing herself, and arched back to give him even better access, or maybe to ensure his cock stroked her just right. Foamy, slippery, steaming hot, it was damned erotic.

Now her hand came down, fingers curling around the underside of his shaft. Loose enough so he could keep pumping, but holding him so he pressed harder against her with each stroke. "Keep doing that," she sighed, hips giving a wriggle. "Just like that."

If he kept up much longer, he'd come, but he sensed she was close to orgasm. Struggling for control, he kept thrusting, her whimpers and sighs a sweet music that made it even harder to hold back his own climax.

She cried out, her body clutching as she came.

He held her through it, then slid cautiously away from her, keeping his hands at her waist until she straightened, arched, and said, "I like the way you shower, Logan."

She turned and stretched up to kiss him, but when he tried to pull her into an embrace, she stepped away. "Better rinse out the shampoo." Her teeth flashed in a mischievous smile. "Then it's my turn to wash you."

If she soaped him down, he'd explode. So he quickly lathered shampoo into his own hair, and when she'd rinsed, he moved her aside and took her place under the spray.

When he emerged, she pouted. "You're ruining my fun."

"I'll make sure you have plenty."

Logan grabbed the soap and hurriedly washed himself, not even daring to touch his cock. The way Maddie watched every move and the arousal in her eyes didn't do anything to cool his own.

When he was done, he said, "I never washed your front."

"Make yourself at home," she purred.

He lathered up, wanting to explore every inch of her, to tease those pink nipples and suck on them. But pressure pounded inside him, urging him to bury himself in her and find release. Sketchily, he ran his hands over her. Too quick, too rough, but his hands were almost shaking with need.

When he slid soapy fingers over her bare mound, then between her legs, she trapped his hand in hers. "Fuck me, Logan. Now. With your penis, not your fingers."

He groaned. Those words, spoken by Maddie, almost tipped him over the edge. He turned away from her, sucking air into his lungs, and shoved the shower curtain back so he could pull a condom from his bathroom bag.

When he'd put it on, he tugged her into his arms, their fronts slick and slippery against each other, and kissed her wet face. The kiss was fast and hard, and her blue eyes glittered with the same need that he felt.

Breaking the kiss, he reached down and hoisted her, hands under her butt and thighs. She grabbed onto his shoulders and twined her legs around him, and his rigid cock brushed the folds between her thighs.

She wriggled, adjusting her position and driving him wild, and then—God, yes!—he slid inside her.

He braced his legs, arms full of hot, wet Maddie, cock surrounded by steam heat and friction. And then he began to pump, in long, hard strokes. He started out slowly, but after three or four strokes, his need drove him to speed his pace.

Faster, almost desperately, he plunged into her, and she squeezed around him, whimpering, gasping, "Oh, yes, yes."

He had to come. Come inside Maddie. Now.

He shuddered, jerked, groaned, and exploded inside her.

She cried, "Logan!" and broke around him in waves of sultry heat.

Somehow, he managed to hold on to her until the aftershocks had faded. Then he let her down slowly. They leaned together, clinging, slick, and panting.

Finally, he reached over to turn off the shower. Before, he'd been only subliminally aware of its pounding, but now the silence was a throbbing presence, one that waited to be filled.

"Man," he said, "you're hot, Maddie." The words were honest but sounded hollow and insufficient. What could he say? If he told her the rest of the truth—that this was the best thing that had ever happened to him—she'd get the wrong idea. He couldn't have her getting romantic notions again, the way she'd done as a teen.

She didn't seem to notice, though, as she shoved the shower curtain back and reached for a towel. "You, too," she said casually, tossing him the first towel then grabbing another for herself. She bent from the waist and began to dry her hair, her face hidden from him.

Logan stepped out onto the bath mat—*that* bath mat—to give her space, and dried himself. He was running a comb through his hair when Maddie climbed out of the tub. "Can I borrow that?" she asked, reaching for the comb.

He watched as she tidied the damp waves of chestnut hair, and he wanted her again. Slowly, this time. Sensually. "Let's go to bed."

She paused in the act of putting the comb down, then set it on the counter and gazed up at him. "Mmm, very tempting. But it's late. Early. You know what I mean. We both need to get some sleep."

What the hell? Maddie, who'd once worshipped him, had turned him down? He should be relieved, but instead he felt . . . hurt? Nah, it was just his male ego taking a hit. "It'll be better this time," he promised.

She gave a soft laugh and touched his chest right over his heart, either by coincidence or design. "Logan, it was perfect. Just what I needed. And maybe we'll do it again if we're both in the mood. But not now. I need sleep." She turned away, picked up the clothes that lay folded on the counter, and left the bathroom.

He stood alone on the bath mat where they'd come together with such fierce passion.

She was treating him like a fuck buddy, which was exactly what he'd wanted. So why did he feel such a sense of letdown? He wasn't the kind of guy who cuddled and talked after sex. And yet, with her, maybe that would have been nice.

He followed her out of the bathroom. She'd almost finished dressing. It seemed she was eager to leave him and curl up alone in her own bed. Smoothing her sweater over her curvy hips, she headed for the door. "See you around, Logan." She gave him a cheery finger wave, and then she was gone.

"See you around," he echoed flatly as the door closed.

MADDIE closed her bedroom door and leaned against it. It had been all she could do to force her legs to carry her down the hall and upstairs to her room. As a girl, she'd dreamed of spending the night in Logan Carver's arms. Tonight, leaving him had been the hardest thing she'd ever done.

But staying would have not only meant a third round of sex—oh

God, she'd actually turned that down—but quite likely falling asleep in each other's arms. Waking up together. A sleepover.

Logan likely hadn't thought that far ahead. In the shower, after the second round, he'd said she was hot, implying that, as far as he was concerned, it was sex, plain and simple. Waking up with Maddie Daniels in his arms would make him feel both trapped and protective. He might well run, as he had ten years ago. For her own good, he'd figure.

No, tonight it had been better to walk away, leaving him wanting more.

For once, she had the upper hand. Or at least she hoped she did. Her plan could well backfire. He might decide that quickie sex had been enough.

She doubted that, though. She had a secret weapon. She'd seen the way the man's eyes widened and his penis surged when she said those three magic words: *Fuck me, Logan.*

Admittedly, they weren't the three magic words she'd once dreamed of speaking to him. But they were liberating and arousing, and she was pretty sure she'd picked the right approach.

If she and Logan spent time together, she'd find out if the boy she'd loved was still inside him and if he'd grown into a man she'd feel equally passionate about. If she did, surely he'd love her back. He'd always been the man in her dreams of the future, and she knew he had a dream, too. Of belonging. She could give him that.

She changed into her sheep jammies and tumbled into bed, hugging the wonderful possibilities close to her heart.

Chapter 4

MADDIE slept in, as their group had agreed to do after the fire. When she rose, her body felt alive and glowing, and the twinge of stiffness between her legs made her smile.

Hoping to see Logan, she put on another clingy top and figure-hugging pants, then went down for breakfast. Glancing into the lounge, she saw a few people with coffee mugs, some reading the paper, four playing a board game, and a couple chatting by the fire. No Logan.

Nor was he in the dining room. Disappointed, she poured herself coffee and took a sip of the rich, dark brew, then dished out scrambled eggs and French toast from the breakfast buffet. Kim, a friend of hers and Tom's, beckoned her over to where she was sitting with a couple of Shelley's friends.

"We're talking about going skiing this afternoon," Kim said. "Interested?"

That depended on Logan. "Give me a break, I just woke up." Pouring dark maple syrup on her French toast and trying to sound casual, she said, "Have you seen Logan Carver this morning?"

"That's the hot bad boy with the earring?" one of Shelley's friends, Samantha, asked.

"Yeah, that'd be him." She took a bite of French toast and sighed approval.

"He came in, slugged back a coffee, grabbed a muffin, and took off." The young woman fanned herself. "Can't you just see him in a black leather jacket on the back of a Harley?"

"I can." Or on a fluffy white mat on the bathroom floor. The memory sent a rush of heat through her, and her sore internal muscles clutched. She gave the other woman an assessing look. Sounded as if she was hot for Logan. She was pretty, with red hair, a killer figure, and a style that was sexy, not wholesome. Logan might well go for her.

Except Maddie had her secret weapon. Those three magic words.

She savored a mouthful of creamy scrambled eggs, then looked up when her brother came over. "Hey, Tom. Big excitement you and Shelley arranged for your wedding guests. I always knew your fiancée liked drama."

He gave a fond laugh. "She does, but not that much. Her idiot cousin and his wife are lucky they got sent to the hospital, or she'd have put them there herself."

It had taken Maddie a while to warm to Shelley, who was a drama queen. But she'd come to see that Tom's fiancée had a caring heart and lots of potential; she was just immature. On the plus side, she'd gotten Tom to loosen up—kind of like Logan had done when they were teens—and she truly seemed to love him.

"Can I talk to you for a minute?" he asked Maddie.

"Sure. Go ahead."

"I mean . . . Want to bring your breakfast and join me?"

Wedding stuff, she figured. To the other women, she said, "Thanks for the ski invitation. I'll let you know."

She picked up her plate and coffee cup then joined Tom at a table in a quiet corner. "Did the fire disrupt plans?"

He shook his head. "For poor Inger and Gord, and a bit for Andi, but they have things under control."

"Good." Was it odd to enjoy scrambled eggs dragged through maple syrup? she wondered as she munched contentedly. And where had Logan gone? When would he be back?

"Maddie?"

"Sorry. I'm a little tired after last night." She smiled a secret smile.

"Speaking of which," he said disapprovingly, "I saw you with Logan, almost sitting on his lap."

Trying not to blush, she said, "Sitting on his *chair* and catching up." She glared at him. "By the way, he informed me that I'm seriously dating someone. According to you."

He shrugged it off. "You should stay away from Logan."

She rolled her eyes. "Jesus, Tom, that story got old when I was fifteen. *You* got to be friends with him, but you didn't want me to? Give me a break."

A reminiscent smile twitched his lips. "He said and did things no one else would. He had a dangerous edge. Yeah, that had its appeal, but—"

"Tell me about it," she broke in. That appeal hadn't faded.

"I was two years older than you, and a guy. I could handle being with him. You weren't that tough."

"Tough?" She rolled her eyes. "Oh yeah, you're a tough guy, Tommy."

He pointed a finger at her. "Don't call me that, Madeleine."

She pointed a finger back. "I'm not a kid now. If you can be friends with Logan again, then so can I."

"I'm not—" He bit off whatever he'd been going to say.

"Not friends?" she guessed. "But you invited him to your wedding. Or were you just looking for free investment advice?"

For a moment, he looked startled, then he said, "I don't need investment advice from Logan Carver."

"Seems he's done okay for himself."

His face tightened. "I'm not so sure."

"What do you mean?"

"Look, these investments of his—" He broke off. "Trust me, sis, you should stay away from him. He's no better for you now than he was in high school."

"Because . . . ?"

"Can't you ever just take my word for anything?" he said in an exasperated tone. "He's not the kind of man who's going to settle down, marry, buy a house, start a family. And that's all the stuff you're looking for. You should be with a guy like Michael."

Temporarily sidetracked, she stared at him. "Wait a minute. Did you invite Michael because of me?"

"He's a good guy. When the two of you met before, you hit it off, but neither of you did anything about it."

"I can find my own dates, thanks very much. As for Logan, you don't know who he is now. You hadn't seen him in ten years. And it's only been a couple of weeks since you bumped into each other in that coffee shop, so I'm guessing you haven't shared a whole lot of boy talk."

Troubled eyes scanned her face. "No, but I'm not sure he's changed, and I'm beginning to wish I hadn't invited him." He ran a hand through his hair, the way he did when he was stressed. "Look, Maddie, I've got all I can handle right now. I'm getting married on Saturday, this place could have burned down, I'm worried about Brianna, and—"

"You're worried about Brianna?"

"She's pushing herself too hard. The U.S. syndication thing is getting to her, and it's starting to show. She needs a break, fresh energy, some perspective. I hope this week helps." Again he shoved his hair back from his forehead. "What I'm saying is, I don't need to be worrying about you, too."

"Then don't." God. Didn't anyone *get* that she was an adult?

She forced herself to keep eating, though her appetite was pretty much gone. If she hung out with Logan this week—even if they kept the sex part secret—Tom would worry, and so would her parents. And they wouldn't worry in silence; they'd give her flack.

Yet she couldn't lose this opportunity to get to know Logan again.

She had to talk to him. Much as she loved her family, she wasn't going to let them rule her life. It was up to her and Logan to decide what they wanted to do.

LATE in the afternoon, Logan drove the Hummer back to the Alpine Hideaway.

He'd spent the day acting like a man with too much money to burn who wouldn't mind getting into some trouble. Mostly, he'd hung out with his informant, Harvey Binder, the high-flying lawyer with a taste for cocaine, who'd set up the meet with Eddie Tran last night.

Binder had been charged with driving impaired, high on cocaine—on the way to court, no less—and negotiated getting the charges dropped in exchange for information about his source. His dealer was small potatoes, but the lawyer said his dealer had hooked him up with a "colleague," Tran, ostensibly as poker buddies.

Binder'd played a few times with Tran, and his gut instinct said the man was crooked. His instincts matched up with other intelligence from the streets. Tran could be the local kingpin, the man who was importing cocaine, heroin, and other drugs from Asia and distributing them through people like Binder's source.

If Logan's undercover recon bore out those suspicions, Project Takedown would assign an undercover cop to try to infiltrate Tran's operation, identify the North American and overseas members, and bust the whole gang. Depending on how it went with Tran this week, Logan might be that operative. He could be the one who brought down an international network of drug dealers.

But he was getting ahead of himself. The next step was tonight's game. He'd been invited back. Moving too fast could set up red flags, but among these assholes there was a "mine's bigger than yours" vibe that let him flash his gaudy diamond ring, talk about his Hummer, make bold bets, and boast about his luck with unspecified "investments."

The wedding had given Logan a pretext for being in Whistler

for the week, but he would disassociate himself from the wedding group as much as possible, so as to ensure their safety. What he'd tell Eddie Tran, his henchman Joe Lee, and anyone else who cared to listen was that his old pal Tom had lost his edge, the rest of the guests were lame, and Logan was fucking bored.

Bored. Like he could possibly be bored with Maddie.

What was she thinking, after last night? Had those two quickies convinced her he was a crappy lover? He should keep his distance, but hell, he wanted to see her.

When he entered the chalet, he glanced into the lounge. A number of guests were there, dressed for dinner and having drinks, but not her.

Behind him, the front door opened, and Andi, the wedding planner, rushed in, cheeks flushed. "Logan, hi," she said with little enthusiasm. "Are you coming to dinner tonight?"

"Remind me?"

"The Italian restaurant in Whistler Village? The whole group's going. I imagine Tom would appreciate your being there."

No, he wouldn't. But would Maddie? "Not sure yet."

Her jaw tightened. "People are gathering for drinks in the lounge. Be there if you want to come. I have to go change." She hurried down the hall.

He followed, deliberating, and reached his door just as Maddie came down the stairs with some redheaded woman he didn't really notice because he was busy staring at Maddie. Her blue scoop-necked blouse was made of some clingy fabric that hugged her breasts and exposed lots and lots of creamy skin, and she'd matched it with a slim skirt and tall black boots.

He'd always been a sucker for boots. Especially black ones.

Hell, he'd always been a sucker for Maddie. Now, they'd been lovers, and all he could think about was holding her again. His cock throbbed to life.

"Well, there you are," she said with a smile. "I thought you'd deserted us, Logan."

He stared at those innocent-looking pink lips and imagined

them saying, "Fuck me, Logan." His cock hardened, and he was glad his jacket covered the front of his jeans. "Had some business to take care of."

"Hi," her companion said. "I'm Samantha."

"Hi," he muttered, wishing she'd leave.

Maddie's eyes were even more vivid than usual as they searched his face. "Coming to dinner with the group?" she asked.

"Are you?" Was there any way they could sneak off together?

"I—" She broke off as Tom and Shelley came down the stairs, and Tom called her name in a tone that sounded disapproving. "Yes, of course," she said. "Well, Samantha and I are meeting friends for a drink, so I'll see you around."

The two women walked down the hall, and he admired the sultry sway of Maddie's hips and ass.

"Logan?" Tom's voice made him turn. "Stay away from her," his old friend said.

"Seems to me I've heard that before." Ten years ago he'd listened, but that was a whole different story. Maddie'd been an infatuated kid with stars in her eyes. "Your sister's grown up, and it's her business who she sees." And hooks up with.

Tom took his upper arm in a firm grip. "You and me. In your room. Shelley, I'll meet up with you in the lounge."

The pretty blonde's eyes widened in surprise, but she turned and walked away.

Logan unlocked his door, and they went inside. "What?" he demanded, yanking away from Tom's grip. Normally, his friend was easygoing, but he sure was protective of his sister.

"Leave Maddie out of this. I saw how the two of you were talking last night. She said you were just catching up, but I know what I saw."

"Jesus, you've been on Maddie's case, too? Besides, I thought she was *seriously involved* with someone. Or so you said."

"She will be. With Michael. If you stay out of her life. You're not the right kind of guy for her."

Logan gritted his teeth. He'd told her that himself. And she'd told him to get over himself. "Are you sure you know your sister?"

"I know she's warmhearted, sometimes too warmhearted, and I know she's looking for a husband, one who'll build a home and family with her. You're not the right man for her, Logan."

"Can't argue with that." But if what she wanted right now was a fuck buddy, he sure as hell didn't want that guy Michael filling the role.

Eyes troubled, Tom said, "We've been friends all these years, man. I was impressed when you became a cop. Folks who knew you back then figured you'd end up on the other side of the law."

Logan shrugged. Maddie'd known better.

"I didn't tell Maddie. She didn't know we were in touch. I wanted her to forget about you. Then you told me you were going undercover, might be out of touch for months or even years, and I shouldn't try to track you down. Damn it, Logan, you're not husband material. Don't get her hopes up."

He might have worried about that himself, if Maddie hadn't so casually walked out on him last night. No more stars in that girl's eyes.

Tom gripped his arm again. "And keep us—Maddie and all of us—out of this job you're doing."

"I intend to." Did Tom actually think Logan would risk Maddie's or anyone else's life?

After Tom stalked out, Logan went to the window and stared out, debating what to do.

Point one: Maddie's sex life was her own business, not her brother's. Point two: if the two of them had sex in private, she'd be in no danger from Eddie Tran.

Point three: from the messages she'd been giving, she might not even want to see him again.

He had to find out. Besides, a man had to eat.

He dressed in black pants and a light cashmere sweater the color of a cat's golden eyes. Had to love an undercover assignment where they outfitted him in designer labels rather than grungy gang-type clothes.

The guests were milling in the entrance hall, getting ready to leave, when he joined them. When Shelley sent Tom running up to their room for something she'd forgotten, Logan seized the opportunity to tug Maddie around a corner. "Your brother warned me off," he said quietly.

"He's worried." Her mouth twisted. "I don't want to worry him, but . . . " Her clear blue eyes gazed up at him.

He said it straight out. "I want to see you again."

A quick smile flashed, warming her eyes. "Me, too."

The simple words sent a rush of pleasure through him, and he took a step closer, almost but not quite touching her. "We'll keep it our secret."

Heat glittered in her eyes. "It'll be foreplay, watching each other at dinner. When you look at me, Logan, know I'm counting the minutes until you fuck me."

His cock surged. "I'll be hard all night. But Maddie, there's somewhere I have to be after dinner. I could be out late."

The warmth left her face. "Oh, really?"

"It's, uh, business."

"I see. Then how about you leave your room unlocked. And maybe, when you get back, there'll be a woman in your bed." She flicked her hair back so it rippled in glossy waves. "And maybe there won't." Then she strode away from him with that hip-swinging walk.

There damned well better be a woman in his bed.

Chapter 5

WHEN the group returned to the Alpine Hideaway later that night, Maddie pretended not to notice or care that Logan went straight to the parking lot. There, he climbed into a huge, ostentatious black vehicle. A Hummer? He drove a Hummer? A gas-guzzling muscle car? The old Logan had driven an ancient Ducati motorbike and wouldn't have been caught dead in a vehicle like a Hummer.

Grimacing, she went inside.

Michael was waiting for her. "Are you feeling all right, Maddie? You barely ate. Or don't you care for Italian food?" He'd been seated at the same table but at the opposite end, so they hadn't been able to talk.

"No, I love it. I just wasn't hungry tonight." She'd picked at her seafood linguine while casting glances over at Logan. Andi's seating plan had put him with Samantha, the sexy redhead, who'd sat next to him and flirted during the entire meal.

It was hard to blame her, because he'd looked eminently flirtable, in another gorgeous sweater that showed off his great build and this time even matched his tawny eyes. The expensive clothes, together with the longish dark hair, stubble, and gold earring, might have looked all *GQ* on a less masculine guy, but Logan had a raw edge, a sense of barely controlled power.

He was so sexy and she wanted him so badly, her body was twitchy with frustration and need.

What was he doing tonight that was more important than being with her? Business, he'd said. Yeah, at this hour? It was probably another stupid poker game.

Poker, a shiny new Hummer, a flashy diamond ring . . . Who, exactly, was the new Logan Carver? Was he really an investment guy, or was that a fancy word for gambler? She remembered Tom's reticence about Logan's job. Did he suspect something?

She let Michael guide her toward the lounge, where they joined her parents in a game of Scrabble. Scrabble, rather than a booty call. Oh no, she wasn't impressed. Even if she'd told Logan they were just fuck buddies, she still deserved respect.

Michael gave her that. He was attentive, funny, smart, and he got along great with her parents, which Logan never had. She was annoyed about Tom's match-making, but she had to admit, if Logan hadn't reentered her life, she'd be paying serious attention to Michael. She'd bet he didn't gamble nor drive a Hummer.

By the time she retired at eleven and Logan still hadn't returned, she was annoyed enough that she locked her door, dialed his room, and left voice mail. In a sugar-sweet tone, she said, "I decided I wouldn't fuck you tonight, Logan. I found something better to do. Pleasant dreams."

Then she ran a steamy bubble bath and climbed into it with a romance novel, which only depressed her. Yes, she wanted romance and a happy ending, but it seemed Logan's wasn't the face that belonged in her dreams or her future.

Disappointed and frustrated, she pulled on her jammies and went to bed. There, she thrashed around, unable to get comfortable, and it took her more than an hour to get to sleep.

*   *   *

MADDIE woke to a jangling noise. Another fire alarm? No, the phone. Logan. The alarm clock read two fifteen. The nerve of the man.

She grabbed up the phone. "What?"

"What was better to do?"

Huh? Oh, right. She remembered her message. And the fact that he, too, had had something *better* to do. "What was yours? What was better than spending the evening in bed with me?"

"You're pissed off."

If she admitted to it, she'd be telling him he was important enough to piss her off. "No, I'm just saying we're both entitled to our privacy."

"Are you with that blond guy?"

Michael? Logan thought she'd go to bed with a man she'd barely met, the night after having sex with him? "Get a grip," she said angrily, then hung up the phone. Loudly.

Sitting up in bed, she waited, holding her breath. If he wanted her badly enough, if she mattered to him, he'd call back. He'd have a good excuse; he'd tell her how much she mattered.

Yeah, right. Logan? As if.

The phone didn't ring. Of course it didn't. That told her exactly where she stood. She flopped back into the nest of bedding and switched pillows to put fresh linen against her heated cheek.

The phone rang again. She jerked upright and snatched it. "What now?"

"I'm coming up."

"You are not!"

"I am. And either you let me in, or I'll knock on the door and wake everyone."

"Damn it, Logan, you—" She realized she was talking to dead air.

Heart racing, she hung up. He wouldn't. Would he? It would be totally embarrassing, and Tom would be furious. But she felt a secret thrill.

In the darkness, she stared toward the door. Was that a creak of floorboards in the hallway? There was another sound. Maybe the knob turning? Then two taps, like the tip of a finger firmly hitting wood.

"Oh!" She leaped out of bed and rushed toward the door, where she flipped off the lock.

The door opened, and the doorway filled with a solid male presence smelling like a damp pine forest. He closed the door behind him and flipped on the light.

She glared at Logan, yet she couldn't help but appreciate the picture he made. His hair was wet and uncombed, dripping water onto a white T-shirt that hung loose over jeans. The tail of the dragon tattoo curved around his arm below the sleeve. Her gaze traveled down. "Bare feet? It's the middle of winter."

"Cute pj's."

Why hadn't she changed into black lace? "I wasn't expecting company." She kept her voice low, so it wouldn't carry to the surrounding rooms. "I didn't *want* company."

"Why weren't you in my bed?" He crossed his arms over his chest, and his tone was challenging, but at least he had the courtesy to keep his voice down.

She retreated back to the bed and hopped under the covers. Sitting, she stuffed a pillow behind her back and pulled the duvet to her shoulders. "Because I was in mine. I didn't feel like fucking you tonight."

"You did earlier, before I said there was someplace I had to go." He paced over to stand by the bed, looming above her.

"A poker game, right?" When he didn't deny it, she went on. "So, I take second place to gambling. Sorry. *You* take second place to a good night's sleep."

"Fuck. It's not like that." He sank down on the bed, and she felt the press of his jean-clad thigh through the duvet.

She moved her leg away and tried not to notice how delicious he smelled, fresh from the shower. "What's it like then?"

"It's not about poker. There's an investment opportunity with some of the players."

"Investment opportunity?" So it really was business. All the same, that wasn't a lot better than coming second to poker.

"A big one."

"That's the business you were doing today, when you were out all day?"

He nodded.

She shook her head, bewildered. "You just stumbled across this big opportunity the first day you were in Whistler?" What a strange coincidence. Or was it? Her eyes widened. "Did you know about it ahead of time? Is that why you came to the wedding?" Immediately she'd said it, she shook her head. "That doesn't make sense. You could have come to Whistler anyhow, to meet up with these people."

His eyes flicked shut then opened again.

"Logan?"

"I wanted to make it look like it happened by accident, rather than being planned."

"Jesus, Logan. So when Tom invited you to the wedding, you saw a way to stage this?"

Something flashed in his eyes that looked like regret. "Shh."

Realizing her voice had risen, she lowered it to a heated whisper. "You're not even bothering to deny it."

He ran a hand through his hair, and drops of water flicked on the duvet. "I had a good reason."

"Yeah, right. Getting richer." She shook her head in disgust. "Ten years without ever once talking to Tom or me, then you go and use him like this?" And her, too. If she'd known he was such an asshole, she'd never have seduced him. Never have let herself think about caring for him again.

Again, that flicker in his eyes, deeper this time. It looked like . . . pain.

Well, tough shit if she'd hurt his feelings. He'd not only hurt hers, she felt as if he'd betrayed her all over again.

He rose and walked to the window, where he pulled back the curtain and stared out for what seemed like a very long time. Then he turned and came back to the bed. Standing, he gazed down at her, expression indecisive, almost . . . tormented.

She glared back.

He bent down and touched her cheek with gentle fingers.

She knew she should jerk away, even tried to do it, but her body wouldn't move. Despite everything, his touch made her flesh tingle and her heart race. The ghost of old love, she figured, making its final appearance before she nailed the lid on the coffin. "Logan, you should go."

"Maddie," he sighed. Then, "Fuck, Maddie," on a note of anger. Then another sigh. "I hate this."

Finally, she found the strength to bat his hand away. "Believe me, I'm not enjoying it, either."

Again he sank down on the bed.

"Get off," she snapped. "Go away."

"No."

FEELING like crap, Logan stared into her lovely face, innocent of makeup, her expression hurt and angry. Brown hair tumbled every which way. She'd bundled the duvet around her all the way up to her neck, and the collar of her pajamas stuck up. White sheep on a blue background, a blue that was drab compared to the bright shade of her eyes.

She'd looked cute in those pj's, though. Like winter nights by the fire, buttons being undone one by one to reveal creamy skin and soft curves. Slow, sensual lovemaking in flickering candlelight. His groin tightened.

Ignoring it, he focused on her eyes. "I'm going to tell you something. I shouldn't. It goes against all my training."

"Training?" She eyed him as if he'd gone nuts.

Which he had. Telling Tom the bare bones had been essential to putting his cover in place. On a need-to-know basis, Maddie had no need to hear this, and telling her broke all the rules.

But he'd always been a rule breaker, and he had a need to tell her.

A deeply personal need to replace the expression of betrayal in her eyes. He'd hurt her again, and this time he wouldn't walk away.

"I'm with the RCMP, Maddie. I'm here doing reconnaissance. Undercover."

She gaped. "What? You're a cop?"

"Yeah. Can't show you proof because, like I said, I'm undercover, but—"

She'd been staring at him, eyes growing wider as he spoke, and now she interrupted. "I believe you."

"You do?" The cold, sick feeling inside him began to ease.

She nodded firmly, the light in her eyes warming. "Yes. I can see it. Oh, Logan, you can fight crime and put away bad guys, but you don't have to do it in a suit, in an office."

Just as had happened when they were teens, he got the feeling Maddie understood him. "Everyone thought I'd end up on the wrong side of the law."

"Not me."

"I know." Memory and emotion threatened to swamp him for a moment. He cleared his throat. "You were the only one who ever believed in me. Though God knows what I did to deserve it."

And, God knows, it might well have been her belief that had kept him on the right path. People talked about the self-fulfilling prophecy, that a person became what you expected them to. One person's opinion—Maddie's, and her faith in him—had outweighed everyone else's dire predictions.

Suddenly she launched herself out from under the duvet and into his arms. "Oh, Logan, I'm so impressed. So relieved, so happy!"

He hugged her tight, feeling pretty relieved and happy himself. But then, with a bundle of sweet curves and soft flannel in his arms, a fresh worry hit him. Yeah, he was a law enforcer rather than a lawbreaker, but he was still the wrong kind of man for her. She wasn't getting starry-eyed, was she?

He had another concern, too, an even more important one: her safety.

Easing her away from him, he said, "I can't tell you any details. And you can't let on to anyone. This is dangerous, Maddie. You have to keep quiet for your own safety. The only person who knows is Tom, but don't even talk to him about it. Try to forget I told you and just act naturally."

Sitting up in bed in her sheep pajama top, the duvet heaped over the lower half of her body, she nodded solemnly. "For your safety, too. I understand."

"In public, pretend you barely know me. Say you're not surprised I turned out to be an asshole."

"I hate to . . . Yeah, I'm getting it." She frowned. "Undercover. Does that mean you do things like infiltrate the Hell's Angels?"

"Yeah. Though this isn't that kind of job, Maddie. Not yet. It's just preliminary reconnaissance, and it won't touch you and Tom and the wedding guests." She had to understand the bigger picture, though, and how wrong he was for her. "But yeah, I can vanish undercover for months, potentially years, on an assignment. Living with the kind of criminals I hope you never in your life meet."

She grabbed his hands and clung. "I hate to think of you in danger."

He gave a wry grin. "It fits though, doesn't it? Better than being in a law office."

Frowning, she studied him, then slowly said, "It's an important job, and someone has to do it."

"Yeah. But it's hell on a guy's personal life," he said, just to make sure she got the point and didn't start romanticizing him and what he did.

She nodded slowly. "I can see that."

"So where does that leave us?" It made no sense to be with her, but he wanted it. A few hours in Maddie's arms. Memories to savor in the long, lonely nights undercover. But only if it was really okay with her. "You said you just wanted casual sex." Tonight, to sweet, sexy Maddie in flannel pj's, he couldn't say "fuck buddy." "I'd like to be with you, but it's got to be secret. And I'll be working most nights."

He touched her flannel-clad arm. "It's not much to offer. And I know I've handed you some pretty heavy stuff."

Chapter 6

MADDIE dropped her gaze to Logan's hand, not wanting to meet his eyes while she tried to sort out how she felt.

Strong fingers, a few scars. Now she could guess how he'd gotten that scar on his rib cage. An undercover cop. On the one hand, she was proud and thrilled. Yet, as he'd said, it was one hell of a way to live. The opposite of what she was looking for: a conventional family and home. Now she understood why Tom was trying so hard to steer her away from him.

But this was Logan. She'd wanted to find out who he'd become and whether she might still care for him. Now she knew. He was a good man, a lonely man who fought crime. And yes, she still cared and could so easily care more deeply.

But, thinking long term—because she'd always dreamed of long term with Logan—could she envision loving a man who disappeared into the world of gangs and criminals for months on end? Who might lose his life there? No. She couldn't live like that. Couldn't have kids with a man like that.

"Maddie?"

She'd told him she wanted a fuck buddy. That had been a lie. She'd wanted more. But he had no more to give.

No, she knew that wasn't true. He cared for her. He might never say it, but he'd just shown it. He'd gone against all he'd been taught, even risked his own safety, to stop her from feeling hurt.

He'd never offer her a future. This might be the only time she'd have with him, so she'd damned well take it. After, she wouldn't walk away empty-handed. She'd have memories. Memories of being with a man who, had circumstances been different, she could have loved with all her heart.

She rested her hand atop his. "I understand, Logan. And yes, I want to be with you."

"Thanks, Maddie." He leaned toward her, angling his head for a kiss.

She met him halfway, melting into his arms. "Thanks for trusting me with the truth." Then she met his lips with hers.

This kiss felt almost like their first one all those years ago: a gentle exploration, a heartfelt release of all the emotions she'd been storing up. With her kiss, almost-sixteen Maddie had tried to tell Logan all the things she'd never dared put in words. And now, twenty-five-year-old Maddie did the very same thing.

She sensed that Logan was, too.

Tenderness turned to passion, gentle kisses became deep, demanding ones that robbed her of breath and sent flames of arousal licking through her blood. She longed for the touch of his naked flesh against hers, to seal this bond between them.

She fumbled for the bottom of his T-shirt and hauled it upward. He took over and yanked it over his head, and her fingers went to work on his jeans. He'd left the button undone and, when she pulled down the zipper, she realized he wore no underwear. His penis, already full, sprang into her hand the moment she released it.

He gave a moan of pleasure, then pulled away to take off his jeans.

She reached for the hem of her pajama top.

"Leave it. I want to unbutton you. Lie back, Maddie."

She obeyed, trembling with anticipation.

Despite the rigidity of his erection, he didn't rush as he unbuttoned the first button at her neck then moved to the next. As he progressed downward, he parted the fabric, but only slightly, and his fingers caressed the line of flesh he revealed. Though he didn't touch her breasts, only skimmed the cleavage between, her nipples tightened.

She watched his face, not his hands.

He was gazing at her with desire and something that looked like wonder. When he undid the last button, he thrust the fabric aside, baring her breasts.

His smile reminded her of the one she'd seen on his face the day he'd finally saved enough to buy his Ducati bike. She knew that, whatever the emotional cost later, she'd made the right decision in not sending him away.

A moment later, he drove the capacity to think straight out of her head when he leaned over and sucked one nipple into his mouth as neatly as if it were a ripe strawberry. Sensation shuddered through her, straight to her sex, and she didn't try to hold back a gasp of pleasure.

His tongue laved the swollen bud with gentle abrasion, his erection thrust insistently against her thigh, and he made wordless sounds of pleasure as he suckled her breast.

She stretched luxuriously, feeling sensual and wanton as she let him pleasure her. Gradually, he worked his way down her body, licking, tasting, dropping kisses, and she encouraged him with murmurs and sighs. When he reached the waistband that hung low on her hips, he didn't peel off the pajama bottoms, only eased them down to kiss her bared flesh.

The air was cool enough to make her naked torso prickle, but below the waist his touch heated her, outside and in. Inch by inch he dragged her jammies down her belly, trailing kisses as he went. This was so unlike last night's urgency. Somehow, in all her fantasies about Logan, she'd never imagined him being so gentle.

Or playful, as he puffed air into her navel, making her giggle.

He glanced up, golden eyes warm, then bent again to his task.

She tensed as he moved down, his breath warm against the sensitive flesh of her waxed mound. He'd only peeled the pajama bottoms to her thighs, so her legs were trapped together. Wanting to separate them to give him better access, she moaned in frustration when she couldn't. "Take them off, please take them off."

"Your wish . . . " He pulled off the pajamas and tossed them aside.

Quivering with need and anticipation, she bent and spread her legs, inviting him between them.

"Oh, yeah, Maddie. So pretty." He gave her what she ached for, his tongue firm and tantalizing as he licked her sensitive flesh, dragging response from every cell he touched, making her want more.

She twisted against his tongue, arousal building toward the need for release. He'd give her an orgasm, she knew it, but now she was hungry for something else. Logan, in her arms. "I want you inside me. M—" Quickly she stopped herself. She'd been going to say, "Make love to me," but that might scare him. Instead, she said, "Now, Logan."

His tongue gave one last, lovely swipe, then he reached for his jeans and fumbled in the pocket.

Impatiently, she raised her arms to him then clasped them around his back when he lowered himself atop her. Almost simultaneously, his lips came down on hers and his penis surged inside her. "Yes," she sighed against him and followed the sigh with her tongue, teasing his lips into opening, then darting inside his mouth.

Her tongue made love to his mouth as his penis dipped and surged in and out of her. This was so perfect, being joined, feeling him fill her. He filled places that had been empty, lonely, waiting. Waiting, she knew now, for him and only him.

She tangled her fingers in his still-damp hair, tugged gently on the small hoop in his ear, stroked down his back to squeeze the pulsing muscles of his taut butt. Her nostrils filled with a heady scent. She was vanilla, he was pine, and the accent notes were the salty tang of sweat, the musk of arousal.

His body was so tough and hard, hers soft and curvy as she cushioned him and absorbed every thrust, taking him deeper and deeper still.

He broke the kiss and pushed himself up to his knees, clasping her around the waist and bringing her with him. Groins locked together, she arched back, away from him, and lifted her legs, wrapping them around his waist and locking her feet together behind him.

He held her there, hands on her hips, plunging into her while his eyes burned with a passion so intense his gaze almost singed her. A tilt of his hips angled his penis just right to brush her swollen clit each time he thrust into her.

She cried out with surprise and pleasure. "I want . . . " she gasped, unable to find words. So close, arousal intensifying until it was almost pain. "I need . . . "

Faster, he moved faster, each stroke harder and deeper, rubbing that sensitive bundle of nerves, giving her exactly what she needed, making the tension spiral higher, making it crest, and then . . .

Orgasm surged through her in deep, pulsing waves of pleasure, and she had to cry out, though she muffled the cry against the back of her hand.

Logan's body jerked, too, in his own climax, and he let out a guttural moan.

Their bodies pulsed together, then the tension slowly eased out of her body and her legs relaxed their grip on him. He let go of her hips as she sank down to lie flat, then he followed her down until he lay atop her, weight on his forearms. He gazed into her eyes. "You're really something."

"You, too."

"Hope we weren't too noisy."

She grinned. "If anyone comments in the morning, I'll say I had a nightmare."

He faked an evil grin. "That's me, your worst nightmare." Then his face sobered, and he slowly rolled off her to lie on his back. "Guess I am. I mean, I'm the last kind of man you want in your life long-term."

She curled onto her side to face him, unsure what to say. "I know you're not marriage material. But we were friends ten years ago and . . . it feels like we're friends again, as well as lovers. I like it."

He moved onto his side, too. "Me, too. You're special, Maddie Daniels. Always have been."

Her heart warmed. "So . . . " She spoke slowly, testing the words as she said them. "Maybe, long-term, we can hold on to that friendship."

He wove his fingers through hers. "That sounds good for me. But maybe not so good for you. I disappear for long stretches of time. Besides, you'll . . . " He swallowed. "You'll get married, have kids." Was that regret in his voice?

"That doesn't mean I'd give up my friends."

FRIENDS. He gazed into her solemn eyes. Yeah, he and Tom had kind of kept in touch. And occasionally, when he wasn't undercover, he'd go for beers with some other cops, tell war stories. That kind of camaraderie helped keep him sane when he spent so much time among the scum of the earth.

But this, the kind of friendship Maddie was talking about, was different. Softer. Deeper. It was like . . . coming home.

Except he'd never had a home. And he never would. He wasn't that kind of guy.

But maybe he was a guy who had a real friend. He squeezed her hand. "Maddie, I was a shit, leaving Vancouver and not saying anything. Tom said—"

"Tom? What did he have to do with it?"

"He saw us kiss that night."

Her mouth opened in a big oh. "And he said you should leave me alone."

"Yeah, and he made a good case. I knew he was right."

"He wasn't—"

"He was right that you were getting all starry-eyed over a guy who was no good for you." Hell, the night they'd kissed, he'd seen those stars in her eyes, and it wasn't just a reflection from the night sky. "But he was wrong when he told me not to say good-bye. He was wrong about telling me not to call, wrong when he let you think I'd disappeared and forgotten all about you."

"But . . . you did."

"He and I kept in touch. Once, twice a year. I always asked about you. He always said you were doing great. Happy, busy, dating." Wryly he added, "Dating *seriously*."

"Rarely was that true."

"He knew when I became a cop. Knew when I went undercover."

She shook her head, looking stunned. "I don't know what to say." Her voice rose, and she pulled her hand free from his. "What were you both thinking?"

"We wanted what was best for you. Maddie, you were fifteen when I left."

"Yeah. Then I was sixteen. Eighteen. Twenty-one." She kept her voice low, but her tone was bitter. "Were either of you ever going to realize I could think for myself? Maybe when I was *fifty*?"

He winced. "Sorry. Don't know what else to say."

She huffed. "I'll think about accepting your apology."

He smothered a grin. Maddie'd never been able to hold a grudge. Then his gaze lit on the clock beside her bed. "It's three thirty. I should go." The idea of staying, of holding her as they fell asleep, was tempting. But the Alpine Hideaway came to life early in the morning. It would be almost impossible to sneak out of her room without being seen. He forced himself out of bed.

"Yeah." She yawned and stretched. "Sure wish I could sleep in, but it would look strange if I didn't show up for breakfast. And then there are ski lessons." She frowned up at him as he pulled on his jeans. "Are you going to do anything with the group?"

"Not much. Have to give the impression that the big reunion with Tom and me is a bust. That I'm looking for something more exciting than this group has to offer. If my subject checks me out, I don't want him thinking I'm close to any of you. Could be dangerous for all of us."

Her eyes had gone dark with concern. Knowing Maddie, it was more for him than herself. "I'll pretend I barely know you and only say bad things about you."

"Good. And tonight . . . " He pulled his T-shirt over his head. "There's another game. I'll be late again."

"I understand."

He grimaced. "Hate to do things this way, Maddie, but it seems like the only way." It sure wasn't like he took her for granted. She was the best thing to happen to him in . . . well, in ten years.

"I'll catch some sleep and leave my door unlocked." She yawned again.

"I don't deserve you."

He expected a jokey comeback, agreeing with him. Instead, she gave him a soft smile and said, "Maybe you do."

How about that? That was the nicest thing anyone had ever said to him.

He bent to press a kiss to her forehead. "Sleep well."

LATER on Monday, Logan decided it'd be good to make a brief appearance among the wedding guests and stage a quarrel with Tom.

Most of the guests were gathered in the lounge. It was that in-between time. They'd been doing outdoor stuff all day and were rehashing their adventures over drinks before dinner. No Tom yet, so he'd hang out and wait for him to appear.

As usual, the guests had formed groups, and he was an outsider. Though his cover required that role, he still felt an absurd twinge. What would it be like to walk into a room like this and be welcomed?

A female voice called, "Logan Carver, it's time you came and said hello. Have you totally lost what few manners you ever had?" He recognized the admonishing voice before he gazed over at Maddie and Tom's grandmother, sitting with her husband.

He walked over. She and her husband had aged some—her hair was pure silver now, and he'd lost a good deal of his—but they still looked healthy and attractive. "Mrs. Daniels, Mr. Daniels. It's been a while. Sorry," he said gruffly, not wanting to be too polite but hating to be totally rude to a woman who'd been kind to him. "Manners never were my strong suit."

"Can say that again," Mr. Daniels said coolly.

A flash of color by the door caught Logan's attention, and he glanced over as Maddie came in. A coral-colored sweater hugged her breasts, reminding him of a rose in full bloom. Her gaze caught his, and a smile lit her face. A spontaneous one, which she quickly turned to a frown.

The woman would never survive undercover.

When he turned back to Mrs. Daniels, her eyes, a lighter version of Maddie's blue ones, were narrowed with curiosity. "I didn't know you were still friends with Tom and Maddie."

"We lost touch, but I bumped into Tom a little while ago. Hadn't seen Maddie in ten years, though."

"She had a crush a mile high on you when she was a girl," she said, and her husband made a *hmph* sound.

"Yeah, well."

"You could have exploited it, but you didn't," she said.

Embarrassed, he shrugged. "She was a kid."

"She was." Her gaze drifted past him, then her eyes danced and her mouth crinkled at the corners. "Yes, she was."

"Logan," Maddie's voice said as she came up beside him, "you looked like you needed a drink."

She shouldn't have done that. Shouldn't even be speaking to him. He turned to her as she handed him a highball glass with something peachy and girly looking inside it. Ice clinked and the glass was cold and damp as he took it, but his fingers brushed Maddie's, and heat rushed through him. "Uh, thanks. What is it?"

Her eyes twinkled. She lifted her matching glass and clicked it against his. "It's called a bad boy."

He gave a surprised laugh, which was echoed by Mrs. Daniels as Maddie turned and walked away.

He tasted the drink, which was fruity and refreshing. A bad boy. He loved her sense of humor. But she was distracting him from his cover story. Refocusing on Mrs. Daniels, he said gruffly, "Guess she's got my number."

"I do believe she might." Humor tinged her voice.

He saw Tom come in and was about to excuse himself when Mrs. Daniels beamed at him. "Logan, I've had the best day. I went skiing."

"Oh, yeah?" Seemed to him she was on the old side, but good for her for staying active. Not that he should be making nice with her.

"This was my first time. It's something I always wanted to do," she said with relish, "and it was as good as I'd ever imagined. It was like flying."

"Damn fool woman," her husband put in. "You could have broken your neck." His words were gruff, but Logan saw tenderness in the gray eyes behind his wire-rimmed glasses.

"You're just jealous that another man had his arms around me," she shot back.

Logan's brows went up. Should he ask? Before he could decide, Mrs. Daniels glanced past him and raised a beckoning hand. "Brianna, you tell my recalcitrant old husband."

Shit. He'd hoped to avoid the TV host. The woman was smart, perceptive, and she had a way of nosing out the story behind the story.

"Tell him what?" she asked, coming to join them. Then she held out her hand to Logan. "Hello. We haven't met. Brianna George."

"Logan Carver."

"Tom's friend." She looked skeptical. "Are you—"

"Mrs. Daniels asked you something," he cut her off.

She gazed at him curiously then turned to the older woman. "Right. Sorry. What was it, Joan?"

"I keep telling Walter I didn't run the slightest risk of falling on the ski hill."

Brianna smiled. "I think you were pretty safe."

"He's just jealous of that ski instructor." The older woman turned to Logan. "He skied me down the hill, holding on to me from behind." Then she tilted her head, looking flirtatious and almost young. "And he was cute. Right, Brianna?"

Her husband made another *hmph* sound, but the younger woman's dark eyes sparkled, and she said, "Definitely."

"What was his name again?"

"Zack."

"That's right. He spent a fair bit of time with you, too, didn't he, dear?"

"I think he, uh, did a great job teaching all of us." Surprisingly, she sounded a bit flustered.

"How was your lesson?" Mrs. Daniels asked. "Did you have fun?"

"Fun?" Brianna echoed.

Logan wondered if her successful career allowed much time for fun. But she gave a quick smile and said, "Yes. It was fun. And now I must go. I have a conference call with my team. I just came in to remind Andi I can't make it for dinner."

Mrs. Daniels tsk-tsked. "You're always working. Didn't this morning show you there's more to life than work? It's good to have fun every now and then."

"I'll take that under advisement." As Brianna turned to go, Logan thought he saw a spark of mischief in her eyes.

Whatever was on her mind, he was glad for it. She'd been too distracted to pay much attention to him.

He took a swallow of the fruity drink, not looking forward to another night of scotch and cigars.

"What's the name of that drink again?" Maddie's grandmother asked.

"A bad boy."

"Hmm. Deceptive name, isn't it? It looks rather sweet to me."

"It is, kind of." Wondering why her eyes were twinkling, he said. "Gotta go."

"Haven't learned respect, have you?" Mr. Daniels grumbled. "People accept Tom and Shelley's invitation to this party, then run off hither and yon."

His wife patted his arm. "Some people have busier lives than us, Walter. Let's not judge." But the gaze she turned toward Logan held a challenge.

He hated to disappoint her, but there was nothing he could say without blowing his cover. So he shrugged. "See you around."

Tom, Shelley, and the wedding planner were talking near the door. He stalked over, raising his voice enough so people standing nearby could hear. "This party's a waste of time. I've got better things to do."

Tom's eyes widened in surprise, then he caught on. "Then get lost. It's not like we want your company."

"That cuts two ways."

He left without letting his gaze meet Maddie's. He didn't want to think about how many hours it would be until he could hold her again. For now, he had to focus on his job. It was time for the flashy, loudmouthed poker player to step things up a notch. He needed to let a thing or two slip about his criminal past and connections. He wanted Tran to trust him enough to loosen up. Like, to take cell phone calls in front of him rather than leaving the room.

The man was a slimy asshole, and Logan's instincts told him he was crooked, but he needed more than instinct if Project Takedown was going to invest resources by sending in an undercover cop. Besides, the time spent winning Tran's confidence might well result in Logan being chosen for that undercover assignment. He'd love to be the one who took the bastard down.

Chapter 7

THE next night—Tuesday—Maddie stood inside the entrance of the French restaurant where the group had dined, deliberating. Andi and a number of the guests were heading back to the Alpine Hideaway, and the thought of curling up in bed was appealing after three nights with lots of great sex but little rest. But would she sleep or just worry about Logan?

He'd told her he was only in the initial reconnaissance stage of an investigation, but still she worried. It was a good lesson for her. If he disappeared for months inside a gang like Hell's Angels, she'd go insane.

"Coming, sis?" Tom broke into her thoughts.

"Yeah, Maddie, come with us," Michael added, catching her arm.

Most of the other younger guests were going clubbing. Whistler had some great night spots, and the music and conversation would be a distraction, so she said, "Sure."

Bundled up against the cold, they strolled the short distance, laughing and talking. When Maddie turned to say something to her friend Kim behind her, she noticed an Asian man on his own. He was drifting along behind their meandering group, content to follow and not pass them. Was he spying on them? She shook her head. She was getting paranoid.

MAXX FISH, one of Whistler's most popular clubs, was a good antidote for her nerves, with its cheerful crowd and pounding music. She danced with Michael, who was a good dancer, then begged off to get a drink. They sat with some of the other Alpine Hideaway crowd, and before long Tom and Shelley, who'd been dancing since the group arrived, left the floor and came over.

"Hey guys," Shelley said. "Want to stay here or move on to another club?"

Her question led to a debate. In the middle of it, a short, muscular Asian guy who looked to be in his late twenties approached their group. "Excuse me," he said politely. "I believe you are friends of Logan Carver? I saw you with him at dinner a couple of nights ago."

Maddie tensed. It was the man who'd been behind them when they walked over here.

Tom's face froze for a moment, then he nodded stiffly. "We know Logan. Why?"

"I just met him, and he's been talking about an investment opportunity. Don't want to go into the details, if you know what I mean." The man winked. "Just wondered if someone could, you know, give him a reference. It's hard to trust your money to a stranger,"

Tom said, "I hear you, but I'm not sure I can help. I've never invested with him. We were friends in high school, then lost touch. I only ran into him again two or three weeks ago, so there's not much I can tell you. And no one else here knows him at all."

"I knew him in high school," Maddie put in.

Tom quickly said, "Maddie, I—"

She interrupted. "He was a troublemaker back then. This week . . . Well, let's just say I don't think he's changed much."

Tom's eyebrows rose, but he jumped in to say, "I was hoping he'd settled down, but it doesn't look like it. I guess . . . if I was looking for a, uh, legitimate investment, he's not necessarily the first person I'd talk to."

The other man's black eyes glittered. "Gotcha. Thanks." Then he frowned. "Thought he was a cop or something."

"What?" Maddie gasped.

Tom gave a quick, forced laugh. "Yeah to the 'or something.' When he was a lot younger, he was a cop for a few months. He said he quit because they were a bunch of losers. That's when he got into the, uh, investment business."

Maddie gaped at him. Was he supposed to admit Logan had joined the police?

"Quit, huh?" the guy said. "Heard a rumor they caught him stealing drugs during a bust, and he went to jail for it."

Her mouth opened in a silent "Oh." Was that part of Logan's cover story?

Face hard, Tom shrugged. "I guess that wouldn't surprise me too much."

When the man had gone, Kim said, "Wow, you two. That was harsh."

Telling herself she was helping Logan, Maddie said, "Oh, come on. It's not like he has a lot of time for us these days."

"Yeah," Shelley said, sounding annoyed. "He accepted Tom's invitation to the wedding, and all he's done is blow us off. Do you really think he's into some shady investment scheme?"

Tom nodded. "I wasn't going to say anything, but he tried to interest me in an investment, and it did sound questionable. I wish I'd never invited him."

"Sorry, hon," Shelley said. "It's nasty when a friend turns out to be a loser." She tossed her hair in a blonde swirl, as if she was dismissing the topic. "Let's go check out another club. I vote for Garfinkel's, and I'm the bride, so I get my way."

As everyone rose and went to get their coats, Maddie caught Tom's arm. "I'm tired. I'm going to catch a cab and head back to the chalet."

He hugged her quickly. "I'm glad you came to your senses about Logan."

"Right." She wished she could talk to Tom about Logan and his cover story, but Logan had made her promise not to.

Michael took her arm. "I'll come back with you."

"Sure." She forced a smile. She did enjoy his company, but right now she'd rather have been alone with her worries.

Where had that guy gotten the idea Logan had been arrested? If it was part of his cover, why hadn't he mentioned it to her?

She took a deep breath then let it out. He must have his reasons. She trusted Logan.

THAT didn't mean she couldn't give him flack, though.

Last night, when he'd slipped into her room, she'd had candles burning and been wearing a black lace camisole and a thong. Tonight, she was in bed in pink flannel, and flipped on the bedside light as he crossed the room.

"Hey," he said softly. "Sorry I'm so late."

Sitting up in bed, arms crossed over her chest, she said, "I hear that once upon a time you were a cop, and it didn't work out."

His eyes widened, then narrowed again as he came to sit beside her on the bed. "Who told you that?"

"Tom. He was sullying your reputation."

"Okay, good." When she scowled, he said, "Maddie, it's part of my cover story."

"I figured. But why didn't you tell me? Don't you trust me?"

"The less you know, the better. For your own safety."

She gave a soft huff. Okay, maybe in this case he did get to be protective. When he tugged on her crossed arms, she let him pull them apart and hug her. Mmm, he was fresh and warm from the shower again. She put her arms around him and snuggled her face into the shoulder of his T-shirt. Voice muffled by cotton, she complained, "You told Tom."

"I told him some stuff he could feed to people."

He eased back slightly. "How did the cop thing come up?"

"I'm getting to that. But come into bed first."

Smiling, he quickly stripped off his shirt and jeans, taking a couple of condoms from his pocket and tossing them on the bedside table.

She slid over to let him in, giving up the warm spot she'd created, then twined herself around him. Against her leg, she felt his penis twitch and begin to grow.

Trying to ignore it and the answering pulses of arousal throughout her own body, she said, "A man came up to us at a nightclub and asked about you."

He tensed. "Did he give a name?"

She shook her head. "He was Asian, maybe in his late twenties. On the short side. Muscular. Pays too much attention to his hair. Do you know him?"

"Yeah." He tightened his arms around her. "Steer clear of him, Maddie. What did he say?"

Lying curled in each other's arms, heads sharing one pillow, she filled him in on what the man had said and how she and Tom had responded.

"Okay, that's good."

"What's the bit about going to jail? You arranged for that rumor to get spread?"

"No rumor; it's the truth."

"What? Logan!" Shocked, she started to jerk upright.

He tugged her down. "I'll tell you about it."

"You'd better." She settled back into his arms. He'd never have stolen drugs, so what was this all about?

"After high school I kicked around on my bike, ended up in Manitoba. Went to Assiniboine Community College and studied criminology."

The boy who'd wanted to fight crime. She caressed his arm.

"I applied to the RCMP and got hired. After nine, ten months, they talked to me about working undercover. Seems they'd picked me as a possibility when I applied. No family or friends, no ties to any community, and a kind of questionable record."

How sad that sounded.

"They kept a close eye on me during training and on the job. I had some problems with authority, but that wasn't a bad thing for undercover work. What they needed to know was that I was honest, not corruptible."

She nodded, knowing he'd have passed that test.

"We talked about how I'd transition into undercover. Discussed different scenarios. Long story short, it ended in me stealing heroin during a bust and getting sent to jail."

She frowned. "Seriously?"

"Gave me immediate street cred. I made connections in jail, and when I got out, I started working undercover in Ontario."

"But you got a criminal record? Is that really what it takes to go undercover?"

"It's not necessary. But for me, why not?"

Why not get a criminal record? Was the man crazy? "What happens when you want to stop working undercover?"

He shrugged. "If I ever did, the RCMP would take care of it."

If. Not when. The life span couldn't be very long for an undercover cop. She shivered and bit her lip. Could she even bear to have him as a friend? If he died on the job, how long until she found out?

She didn't believe Logan really wanted that kind of life. Yes, he was a loner, but that was due to circumstances. It wasn't his basic personality. As a teen, the product of foster homes, he'd had no idea how to fit in, yet he'd hung around the Daniels home. She knew he'd wanted to belong. She'd seen that same wistful expression on his face a time or two here in Whistler.

His fingers tugged the collar of her pajamas. "Time to undo some unbuttons."

She decided to drop the subject for now. Later, when he was mellowed out from sex, she'd pick it up again.

"You really have a thing about buttons, don't you?" she teased.

"On you. Especially with your pj's. It's such a contrast. This innocent little-girl flannel"—his fingers toyed with the fabric—"then the sexy woman underneath."

"Are you sure that's what's underneath? Maybe you'd better check."

"That's exactly what I was planning." Deftly he slipped the top button through its buttonhole.

She lay back, enjoying his slow, sure touch, the deliberate, tantalizing brush of his fingers across her skin. Logan was such a considerate lover.

So considerate, she hadn't had a chance to explore his body as thoroughly as she'd like. Now seemed like a good time, when he'd just pulled off her pajama bottoms. If she let him bury his face between her legs, she'd be gone.

"Lie back," she told him.

When he obeyed, she flicked off the bedside light. It was too bright and unromantic. She hadn't drawn the curtains, and dim light from the carriage lamps outside the Alpine Hideaway filtered into the room. When she tossed back the covers, she could see Logan clearly.

Such a hard, muscled, purely masculine body, with that sexy tattoo covering one shoulder and upper arm. Perfection from head to toe, except for the scar. She hated to think about his scar and the life it symbolized.

Instead, she focused on the centerpiece: his lovely penis. When she grasped it gently, it jerked and swelled in her hand.

His foreskin covered the crown. There was something symbolic about him being uncircumcised. The man was so guarded, even his penis had a protective shield. This one, though, she knew would readily yield to her.

She stroked up to the top and down again, barely skimming the surface. Delicately, she slid the foreskin down to reveal the swollen crown. His moan of pleasure encouraged her.

Circling him, firming her grip a little, she slid her hand up and down his shaft. Tenderly she teased his sensitive foreskin, easing it up over the head then down again with each stroke. Pulsing heat, tensile strength, satin over steel.

"So good, Maddie," he murmured.

Needing to taste him, she bent lower, inhaling the delicious scent of male arousal. She slid his foreskin all the way up to cover the crown and took him in her mouth.

He pulsed and groaned.

As she sucked, the thin membrane retracted slowly, and she followed it with soft licks and swirls of her tongue. His muscles tensed, and his breathing was audible, ragged. Was it from arousal, or was her touch too much for this extra-sensitive flesh?

She released him. "Is this okay?" He'd given her so much sensual pleasure, she wanted to return the favor.

"God, yes. Don't stop." He threaded his fingers through her hair.

She went back to her ministrations, exploring his shaft with her fingers, teasing his glans and foreskin with her lips and tongue, delicately licking salty drops from the eye. This was their fourth night together. How could it have taken her so long to learn him in this intimate detail?

Feeling him in her mouth, in her hands, made Maddie remember how he'd felt inside her. Her sex clenched and throbbed, wanting him. But he'd given her so many climaxes with his mouth, his fingers. If he wanted to come in her mouth, that was more than okay with her.

Logan tugged gently on her hair, pulling her head away. "I want to be inside you."

"Really? I'm happy to—"

"Really." He took one of the condom packages he'd dropped on her bedside table and ripped it open. "Climb on top of me, Maddie."

She straddled his hips and sheathed him. Then she raised up on her knees, gripping his shaft in one hand, lifting herself until the tip of his penis probed the slick folds of her pussy. A shudder of pleasure rippled through her. Logan, this was Logan. It still stunned her that they were lovers. Gradually, she lowered herself, taking him in bit by bit.

He held still, not thrusting, and she had the sense he wasn't even breathing. When he was fully inside, he said, "I want to kiss you."

Oh, yes. She leaned forward, walking her hands up the bed until their lips touched.

His arms circled her, pulling her flush against his body. As he parted her lips with his tongue, his penis thrust into her in slow, steady strokes.

His kiss was lazy, too, exploratory and sensual, as if they had all night. She also sensed emotion in it, something sweeter and more tender than pure sexual need.

Logan seemed convinced that he wasn't the kind of man who could love and be loved, but she believed that deep in his heart he craved exactly what she did. Could he ever bring himself to acknowledge it?

She tried to tell him, through her lips and tongue, that he deserved everything his heart secretly desired.

He answered her in kind, as if he was taking, needing, everything she offered. And as their mouths mated, their bodies kept pumping together in that soft, easy rhythm.

Because Maddie was using her arms to brace herself, her hands weren't free to roam. His, however, massaged the back of her head, stroked the long lines of her back, cupped her butt, and teased the crease between her cheeks.

His thrusts might have been slow, but each one brushed sensitive flesh and went deep. Each one heightened her arousal. So did the fact that she knew—because his body was telling her with each sensual movement—that this was more than sex.

Breaking the kiss, he rolled them onto their sides, facing each other. He lifted her top leg so it wrapped around him, letting him penetrate even more deeply.

Their heads rested side by side on one pillow. He stroked the side of her face, trailed his fingers down her neck, then drifted featherlight over her breasts.

Her areolas and nipples pricked to attention. "Oh, Logan."

"You're beautiful, Maddie."

His hips still pumped, his penis slip-sliding in and out of her slick, sensitive pussy, keeping her near the edge of orgasm but not sending her over the top.

She stroked his hip, then down to the base of his shaft.

He caught a nipple between his fingers and squeezed lightly. Tingles shot straight to her clit, taking her even closer to the peak.

She caressed his balls, hoping to speed the action.

He captured her hand. "What's the rush?"

She gave a mock groan of frustration.

Then, finally, his fingers slid between her legs. He captured her clit between thumb and forefinger.

"Oh, yes." Close, she was so close.

He squeezed gently and rolled the tiny bud in a circular motion. "More," she whispered.

He complied, giving her exactly what she needed, and then she was climaxing in waves of relief and pleasure.

He kept thrusting, even more slowly now, and the pressure prolonged her orgasm.

When the waves finally ebbed, he rolled again, onto his back so that once more she lay atop him. He kissed her deeply, then put his hands on her shoulders. "Sit up and ride me. Take what you want."

Her limbs were heavy with satiation as she forced herself upright to the position she'd started out in. She began to rise and fall on him, lifting to the top of his shaft then sliding back down. Moving as slowly as he'd done, almost trancelike in the afterglow of orgasm. Her body was so deliciously exhausted, she couldn't imagine summoning the energy to climax again, but she'd make sure he had a good one.

Reaching behind her, she fingered his balls, and this time he didn't stop her. He began to lift his hips, thrusting up each time she lowered herself, catching her rhythm and speeding it. His breath rasped, and his golden eyes glittered in the dim light.

He was staring at the place where their bodies joined, and she followed his gaze. Oh yeah, that was sexy, mesmerizing.

Arousal shivered through her again. Tiredness forgotten, she hurried the pace. Each time their bodies met, she ground hard against him, maximizing the delicious pressure.

His fingers found her clit, and she whimpered as need flooded through her. "Logan, oh God."

Their bodies slammed together, and the room was silent but for his harsh pants and the wet suck-and-slap sounds their bodies made as they joined.

In the dim light, she saw the white flash of his teeth. "You're so hot," he rasped. "So perfect."

His balls tightened in her hand, and he strummed her clit.

She arched, closing her eyes, throwing her head back, abandoning herself to sensation as he gave a wrenching groan and let loose in frenzied thrusts that filled her, claimed her, that demanded the orgasm that ripped through her body.

Vaguely, she was aware of his hands grasping her waist, holding her while her body shook. Of feeling boneless as he eased her down to the bed.

Of him lying beside her and gathering her close so her head rested on his shoulder, and tucking the duvet around them.

Of his kiss on the top of her head.

It would be so easy to drift to sleep. She'd slept so little the past few nights, and she'd never felt so sexually satisfied. She'd never felt so content and at home as she did in Logan's arms.

"I guess I should go," he said regretfully, interrupting her reverie.

She hated that he had to leave. And before he did, there were things she needed to say. Under the covers, she stroked his bare skin and let her fingers follow the line of his scar. "Logan, you've been working undercover for quite a while, haven't you?"

"Huh? Yeah."

"Do you ever think about making a change? Like, being a regular police officer? You could settle down in one place. Have friends, a home, a family." With her. If he did that, she could let herself love him.

He jerked away, freeing his body from hers, and sat up in bed. Brow creased, he stared down at her. "Don't go there, Maddie. Why are you doing this?"

"It's a fair question, Logan."

"I told you from the start, I'm not that kind of guy. You want a fuck buddy? I'm him. You want a husband? Find another guy."

His harsh words could have pierced her, but she knew they didn't come from his heart. Why was he so afraid of caring, of being the man she knew he could be? "You want me to do that?" she asked calmly, gazing up at him. "To shower with another man? To be so hot for each other we have sex on the bath mat? To cuddle up in bed with another man and let him unbutton me?"

He crossed his arms over his chest.

"Do you?"

"No, I don't." He bit the words out. "Okay, I'm jealous. Are you happy? Yeah, this week—being with you—it's one of the best things that ever happened to me."

Her heart surged. If he could admit that, there was hope.

Unfortunately, he followed it with, "But it can't be more than that."

She sat up, too, hugging the duvet to her for warmth. "Yes, it can."

He shook his head. "Damn, Maddie. I should've known. When you said 'fuck buddy,' it wasn't the real you."

"It was." Though discovering that had been a surprise to her, too. "It is. But so's the girl who likes flannel pajamas. And so's the woman who *sees* you, Logan. Who sees inside your head and heart better than you see yourself."

"Yeah, right," he said sarcastically. Then something flickered in his eyes, a hint of vulnerability. Words dragged out slowly, reluctantly. "What do you see?"

"A boy who never knew who his father was. Whose mom was an addict who didn't, probably couldn't, look after him." She rested her hand on his arm. "Social services took you away from her when you were five. You went into in a foster home. But you didn't fit in. You'd learned how to be tough, how to survive, but not how to play nice. Not how to give and receive affection."

"My heart bleeds," he scoffed.

Her lips twitched. He was proving her point very nicely. "Foster home after foster home, always causing trouble. You learned that it was better not to want a family, a home, love. Better to reject other people, to reject even the idea of home, than be rejected."

An edge to his voice, he said, "Whatever. I am what I am, however I got that way."

"You are." She nodded. "And it's time to change. You're no longer a vulnerable kid whose only tool for survival is putting on a tough shell. You're a man, one who's risked his life to make the world a better place. It's time to go after the things you've always secretly wanted."

She slid her hand down his arm and twined her fingers in his, then leaned forward to wrap her other arm around him and rest her head against his chest. His heart was hammering as if it wanted to escape.

LOGAN couldn't move. Maddie was all around him, hugging him, gripping his hand, resting her head on his chest. Her scent—vanilla and sex—was all he could breathe.

He knew about the fight-or-flight adrenaline response to threat, and that's exactly what he felt now. Some deep instinct told him to run. But another even deeper instinct held him there in her embrace.

This girl—woman, now— had a habit of handing him crap he couldn't handle. What was she talking about? Things he'd secretly wanted? Yeah, he'd envied her and Tom their life. And yeah, this week when he'd held Maddie, he'd felt . . . Oh, fuck. There was no point to dreaming about things he couldn't have.

Slowly, he pulled back from her embrace and freed his hand from hers. "Maddie, you mean well, but you have too soft a heart. Don't go seeing things—wanting things—in me that can't exist. I don't want you to get hurt."

She smiled sadly. "And I want you to be happy. Just think about what I said."

When he pulled on his clothes and snuck back to his room, he had trouble thinking of anything else.

Chapter 8

WEDNESDAY morning, when Logan went into the dining room to grab a coffee and breakfast, Maddie was seated with Tom and Andi, talking intently to her brother, who looked troubled. Wedding glitches? Whatever the problem, the two of them would handle it together. They were there for each other, loving each other, whatever happened.

What made Maddie think he could be like that? As a teen, she'd been a naive dreamer. At twenty-five, she should know better.

Maybe he should stop seeing her. She didn't need a friend like him, and she sure as hell shouldn't be getting all romantic over him, if that's what last night had been about. If he wasn't such a selfish bastard, he'd encourage her to date that blond guy who was always hanging around her.

As he stood by the coffee urn sipping the Alpine Hideaway's special blend, Maddie hugged her brother then rose. When she came toward the door, she, too, looked upset.

She saw Logan and drifted casually toward him. "Morning."

"What's wrong?"

"Tom and Shelley had a fight. But don't tell anyone. I'm sure they'll work it out. I'm going to go talk to her mom."

Shit. He wanted Tom to be happy. And he hated seeing Maddie upset. His arms ached with the desire to hug her and offer comfort.

"See you later?" she asked.

"I'd like that."

Her face lightened, and he felt ridiculously pleased.

A few minutes after she'd gone, Tom came toward him. Bracing for another "stay away from my sister" lecture, he quickly realized his friend wasn't noticing anything but his own distress.

"What's wrong?" Logan asked.

"Shelley." He sounded frustrated. "Sometimes it's like she doesn't even see me."

"Huh?"

"She gets these ideas and never thinks how they affect me. It's like I don't exist."

Tom had always been a better follower than a leader. The only time he got assertive was when he tried to protect Maddie. "Uh . . . maybe you need to tell her."

"Tell her what?" Tom snapped.

"What you want. What you think. Or do you think . . . "

"What?"

"Do you think she doesn't care?" Maybe Shelley wasn't caring and generous like Maddie. Maybe she was a bitch. He'd barely met the woman.

"N-no," Tom said slowly. "I think she does."

"Then you need to tell her that stuff. Make her see you."

Tom's face, like Maddie's a few minutes ago, brightened a bit. "Yeah. Thanks, man."

Glancing past him, Logan realized a couple of the guests were watching them with curious expressions. "Shit. There's eyes on us. Say something nasty."

Tom's lips quirked in a quick grin, then, loudly, he snarled, "Asshole!"

"Back at ya." Logan slammed down his coffee mug and abruptly stalked out.

LATER that afternoon, Maddie climbed into a big sleigh pulled by giant, friendly looking horses, and took a seat beside her friend Kim. She pulled a rug around her and wished Logan was there to keep her warm. Had he paid any attention to what she'd said last night, or had he dismissed it out of hand?

She glanced over to Tom and Shelley, settling into in a much smaller sleigh. Just the two of them. Though Shelley was quieter than usual and Tom looked tired, they had their arms around each other and were smiling private smiles.

How wonderful that their love was strong enough that they were willing to work through their problems. They were opposites in many ways, but as she'd told Tom at breakfast, they balanced each other. Both had become better people since they'd gotten together.

That would happen with her and Logan, too, if he'd give them a chance. Would they ever be the couple in the romantic sleigh built for two?

"You're looking wistful," Kim commented. "There's nothing like a wedding to make a single girl feel really, really single, is there?"

"You said it."

"There's this guy I dated a couple times. We got along well, but we're both busy at work and had trouble matching up our schedules, so it didn't go anywhere. I'm thinking it might be worth trying a little harder."

"It sure couldn't hurt. Who knows? Maybe he's the one for you."

Kim nodded thoughtfully. "He's really smart. Sexy, too, though we never got further than a kiss." A smile twitched her lips. "It was a really good kiss. I can't believe I didn't try harder to make it work."

Maddie nodded. "Much as we'd like to believe we're going to find that one perfect person, and it'll all be a bed of roses, it's rarely that easy." It sure wasn't for her and Logan. He was far from perfect, and so was she. Their romance—if she dared call it that—was definitely no bed of roses. She grinned to herself. Well, maybe it was, only she'd picked a rose with a whole lot of thorns.

"You could try harder, too," Kim said. "He really likes you."

She started. "What? He does?" She and Logan had tried so hard to keep their relationship a secret.

"Yeah, and here you are sitting beside me when you could be in that other sleigh cuddling up with him." She gestured toward another big sleigh.

"Oh. Michael." Maddie had deliberately chosen a different sleigh. It wasn't that she didn't like Michael, but he was getting friendlier, taking her arm, kissing her on the cheek when they said good night. If she'd sat beside him in a sleigh, he'd have put his arm around her, and that wouldn't have felt right. "He's a good guy, but I like taking things slow."

The sleigh jingled along, and she snuggled under the warm rug, enjoying the crisp air and stunning scenery. This week she'd been outdoors a lot: skiing, skating, snowshoeing, and going on a snowmobile ride. All fun activities, but how much better they'd have been if Logan had been by her side.

The sleighs delivered them to a rustically charming log restaurant, where Andi had scheduled a fondue dinner. The hostess gushed all over Brianna, and Maddie smiled, quite happy not to have a high-profile, high-pressure career such as Brianna's or Shelley's. She loved being a healer. Not only did she give massages, but she encouraged good health, taught exercises, and even did a little informal counseling. When a person was semi-naked on a massage table, warm hands kneading out their aches, their normal defenses and barriers tended to ease away. People opened up in a way they wouldn't ordinarily do.

Hmm. She'd never given Logan a massage . . .

ON the drive back to the Alpine Hideaway, Logan was pumped over his progress. Eddie Tran had gone to the suite's small kitchen to speak on his cell, and Logan had followed a moment later, ostensibly to get ice for his scotch. Tran had watched him, but he kept talking about a shipment that should be available for distribution next week. "Shipment" could have meant anything, of course.

Later, Tran's henchman Lee had offered Logan and the other player, an associate of Tran's, cocaine. The other man had indulged. Logan had passed, saying he didn't use drugs, and he figured the smart people were the ones who made money off the drug trade.

"Smart and wealthy," Tran had said. "Just like in your . . . investment business."

"Just like that," Logan had agreed, and their gazes had met for a long, meaningful moment.

Oh yeah, Tran was definitely in the drug trade. What's more, Logan was building a rapport over cigars and poker. He was setting himself up nicely to be the agent who infiltrated this international gang and took them all down.

As he parked at the Alpine Hideaway, his thoughts turned to Maddie. He hoped she had come to her senses and wasn't still thinking a leopard could change its spots. Yeah, he wanted to be with her, but not if she was going to get hurt.

A few minutes later, freshly showered, he snuck into her room. Tonight, she was awake. She sat on the bed in black leggings and a white T-shirt, legs crossed in the lotus position. Some kind of relaxing nature-sounding instrumental music was playing.

She hopped off the bed. "Hey, you." Her shirt had a logo with a pair of hands and the words, Put Yourself in My Hands.

He gestured to it. "Happily." Then he caught her up in a warm hug.

She chuckled. "Massage therapist tee." She'd told him about her job, the office she shared with another massage therapist, her varied clientele, and the satisfaction she took in her work.

She planted a quick kiss on his mouth, then pulled out of his arms. "Come to bed. I have something special planned for you."

"That sounds promising." He let her pull him toward the bed— the back of her shirt read, Every Body Needs Massage—and began to strip.

"I've never given you a massage."

His cock pulsed. "I recall you massaging a certain portion of my anatomy. I'm definitely up for more of that."

She eyed his growing erection, and a flush of arousal pinked her cheeks. "Tempting, but not yet. Lie down on your stomach." A grin flashed. "While you still can."

He obeyed. So she meant business and had the T-shirt to prove it. The only time he'd ever had a massage, it had been therapeutic, after he'd torn up his shoulder pretty badly on the job. The masseur had been a guy, and what he'd done had helped, but it had hurt like hell. Of course, Maddie had small, soft hands. She couldn't cause him much pain. Hopefully, what she had in mind was a sexy massage as foreplay.

A scent filled the air, flowery and old-fashioned but pleasant. "What's that?"

"Massage oil with lavender for relaxation and arnica for easing sore muscles."

"Smells nice."

And her hands certainly felt nice as, warm and silky with oil, they touched his shoulders. For a few minutes, she stroked lightly and probed here and there, occasionally making him wince. "Want to move lower?" he suggested, wriggling his ass. "Or I could roll over, because there's another part of me that would really like some attention." Though her touch wasn't blatantly erotic, the simple fact of her touching his naked body kept him semierect.

"Be patient." Now her fingers dug into his shoulder muscles and began to work them, and he tightened involuntarily. "Relax," she said. "If it hurts, breathe through it."

"You want to hurt me?" he joked. "Didn't know you had a streak of sadism in you."

"If it doesn't hurt, it's not doing any good." She kept kneading. "Breathe into my hands and visualize the tension releasing."

He could stare at a crime scene and visualize the events that had occurred. But visualize tension releasing? Still, this was Maddie's job, so he tried to follow her instructions. Why hadn't he realized how locked up his shoulders had become?

"That's it," she murmured.

He breathed the way she'd told him, and asked, "How are Tom and Shelley?"

"They're talking. Sharing their feelings. Not just the love, but their fears, doubts, hopes. I think they're going to be okay."

"Hope so. Tom's a good guy. He deserves to be happy."

Her hands paused a moment, then resumed their kneading, working down both sides of his spine. "Yes, and it's not so bad that he's having to work for it. Things have come easily for him, and when they didn't, he pretended he didn't want them anyhow. He's a smoother-over rather than a confronter."

"A follower, not a leader."

"That's true. He's realizing he needs to be more honest with himself and the people who love him. As for Shelley, she speaks and acts before she thinks about other people's feelings. She's learning, too."

"She's going to be your sister-in-law. That must feel strange. Bringing someone else into that close family of yours."

A hand tapped his ass. "We did that with you."

He shook his head. "You and Tom did, but your parents never accepted me."

"Your fault," she said briskly. "You were so determined to be the tough guy."

"It was all I knew, Maddie." And it still was.

As if she'd heard the unspoken words, she said, "Sure. And all Tom knew was being the nice guy who didn't speak up when he got mad or hurt. Today, he learned that isn't working for him, and he's changing."

Last night she'd told him he could change. But even if he wanted to, he didn't have a clue how.

"You're tensing up again." She dug her thumbs into the hollow at the base of his spine. If her touch had been lighter, it would have been sexy, but this hurt. Her hands might be small, but they were powerful.

No pain, no gain, his massage therapist had told him as he tortured him.

"You did add some spice to Tom's and my lives when we were kids," Maddie said. "Things were dull before you came along."

"Dull? I thought your lives were great."

"Yeah? What things did you like?"

He smiled, remembering. "Your clean, comfortable house, lemonade and hot chocolate, popcorn in front of the TV. The way your parents were interested in what you and Tom were doing. Even when you screwed up, they never yelled at you. And when you or Tom were mad at them, you never, I mean . . . There was never any doubt . . . "

"Never any doubt they loved us or we loved them? No, there wasn't. It was unconditional love."

"Never understood what that means." Or, in fact, what love meant. No one had ever loved him.

"That you love someone no matter what. You don't say, 'I'll love you if you do this or that.'" Her hands stilled, and for a long moment the only sound in the room was that ripply nature music. Then, so softly he could barely hear, she said, "You don't say, 'I'll love you if you turn into a certain kind of person.'"

He mulled that over. The way he felt about Maddie had always been just . . . there. She could be an annoying brat or do the sweetest thing imaginable, and she was Maddie. She'd been—and was again—the bright spot in his life.

Her fingers dug into his ass, then it was her knuckles, and he groaned. "God, woman, you're a sadist."

She didn't speak, just continued to pummel him. He sucked it up and remembered sitting on the back steps of the Daniels house with her, watching the stars come out. Telling her that crap about wanting to be some great crime fighter. And listening to her share her dream of living in a big, rambling house like the one she'd grown up in, where she planned to have two kids, a fox terrier, and a calico cat.

"And a husband?" he'd teased, though for some crazy reason the idea of her married to some other guy—a better guy—hurt. "Some perfect guy who goes to the office every day, brings you flowers every night, and takes you to Hawaii every year?"

"The perfect guy," she'd echoed, turning those big blue eyes on him. Yeah, her crush had been obvious. He should have done more to discourage her. He shouldn't have let her kiss him.

He shouldn't have kissed her back.

He shouldn't be with her now, except Maddie was the one person in the world he could never resist. Suddenly, he didn't need a massage therapist; he wanted his lover in his arms. He rolled away from her, and she let out a squeak of surprise.

"Enough beating up on me," he said, wrapping his arms around her. He eased her down until she was lying flat and his body blanketed her. Then he kissed her.

She sighed against his mouth, "Oh, Logan." Her arms came around him, and she opened her lips to him.

Chapter 9

MADDIE clung to Logan as he nibbled her lips and his penis nudged her thigh. She stroked the back she'd massaged, feeling the shift of his powerful muscles.

She'd had the bright idea that massaging him might make him open up to his emotions. Him, not her. But, as she'd feasted her eyes on his gorgeous body, felt the strong muscles, and worked to ease knots of tension, her own emotional truth had been so obvious.

This week, she'd fooled herself. She'd told herself she needed to find out who he'd become and how she felt about him. She'd pretended she could decide how much to care.

But all along, she'd loved him. From the age of thirteen she'd loved him, and she still did.

A few minutes ago, they'd talked about her family, and she'd blithely said their love was unconditional. That's when it had hit her, a revelation that stole her breath and froze her fingers.

If she loved Logan—and of course she did—she had to accept him the way he was. Not just as the lover whose tongue was tracing the rim of her lips, drawing her own out to meet it. But as an undercover cop, a man who had a highly dangerous job and disappeared for months at a time into the criminal underworld.

So much for her dream of a conventional home and family. If she wanted that, she should forget about Logan and date Michael, the safe, good guy with the normal job and no cart full of emotional baggage. Her brother and Logan had been right all along in warning her Logan wasn't the right man for her.

Not that she'd ever have listened. Apparently, she had a one-man heart, and it had chosen Logan.

He nipped her bottom lip, then sucked on it, and her nipples and clit throbbed in response.

Of course, part of the reason she loved him was his bad-boy vibe, his edginess, and the fact that he wanted to catch criminals and make the world a better place.

She didn't have a clue what to do. Except, right this moment she was in bed with the man she loved. There was only one thing to do: make love with him.

She pulled him closer, deepening the kiss, pressing her breasts against his chest, shifting her hips, then raising her legs until his penis was nudging between them.

Rather than entering her, he slid back and forth across her sensitive folds, brushing her clit until she was slick with arousal. "Oh yeah, Maddie, this is good," he murmured with satisfaction; then he sheathed himself and eased slowly inside her.

Worn out from tiredness and emotion, she dropped her legs to the bed. She and Logan rocked together in slow, small motions that pressed her breasts against his lightly haired chest, his hips against the tender insides of her thighs, his firm organ against her most sensitive, intimate flesh.

Yes, this was making love. It was sensual, blissful, and she wished it could last forever. She wished they'd fall asleep like this and wake up like this, merged together as if they were one being.

But orgasm snuck up on her and claimed her in shivering ripples that in turn made Logan climax deep, deep inside her.

And on the heels of her orgasm came another urge, an ache behind her eyes that told Maddie tears were as inevitable as her climax had been. She had to be alone. She couldn't dump all her emotional baggage on him, or he'd freak out.

Struggling to hold back the tears, she shifted her hips. "You're heavy. And I'm tired. Time to go, Logan."

He gave a regretful sigh and eased off her. "Yeah."

She managed to hold it together as he got dressed, dropped a kiss on her forehead, and murmured good night.

Before he'd reached the door, tears were beginning to slip down her cheeks. As soon as he'd gone out, she rushed over to flip the lock, then heaved herself back into bed with a sob.

What an idiot she was. She buried her face in a pillow to muffle the sobs.

All week, as she'd skied and skated in the crisp beauty of Whistler, she'd wished Logan was there with her. Earlier today, she'd looked at Tom and Shelley in the sleigh and envied them. When she'd eaten fondue, she'd wanted Logan beside her sharing tidbits.

But even if by some miracle he did admit to loving her, to wanting and deserving love, she might never share special times like that with him. She couldn't ask him to give up the job he'd devoted himself to. Their lives would be a bigger version of this week: stolen hours together, mostly spent in secret.

If they had kids, she'd be the one going to parent-teacher meetings, taking them to lessons, playing on the beach with them. He'd be gone, and she wouldn't even know where.

She wouldn't know if he was alive.

THE next morning, Maddie woke from a troubled, unrefreshing sleep and tried to cold shower herself to alertness. The chilly water didn't do much for her state of mind, but at least it reduced the puffiness of her tear-swollen face.

Still, she had no desire to go downstairs and try to act normal. Instead, she sat by the window, telling herself she wasn't watching to see Logan leave. And in fact, she didn't see him. Was he having breakfast, sleeping in, or already gone for the day?

She did see Andi go, climbing into a silver 4x4, no doubt off to make final arrangements for the rehearsal tomorrow or the wedding itself. Two couples with ski gear climbed into an SUV and headed off. Maddie's parents, skates slung over their shoulders, climbed into their car, and she smiled fondly. They'd been so active, she'd barely seen them. Shortly after, Brianna emerged and strode quickly down the road. Other guests either got into vehicles or headed off on foot.

Maddie's stomach rumbled. By now, the dining room would have pretty much cleared out. Smoothing down her favorite blue sweater, which she'd worn in a futile attempt to cheer herself up, she headed downstairs.

In the entrance hall, Tom and Shelley were pulling on jackets. "Morning, Maddie," Shelley said cheerfully. Then she peered more closely at Maddie's face. "Hey, soon-to-be sis, you look down. Want to come skating with Tom and me?"

Maddie gave her a quick hug. Yeah, there was a lot to like about Shelley. "Thanks, but I'm tired. Hope I'm not coming down with something." Like a case of heartbreak.

Tom put an arm around her shoulder and squeezed. "Take care of yourself. Can't have our maid of honor getting sick."

She forced a smile. "I'll be fine. Go have fun."

When she entered the dining room, it was almost empty. Her grandparents sat at a table by the window, him half hidden behind a newspaper and her absorbed in a novel.

Deciding against a hot breakfast, Maddie selected a cranberry bran muffin and a bunch of grapes, then poured herself coffee. When she turned away from the coffee urn, her grandmother was beckoning to her.

Much as Maddie loved her parents, she had a real soft spot for her gram. The woman had a way of sensing her moods and providing the kind of support she needed. Smiling affectionately, she walked over. "Good morning. Looks like we're all having a lazy one."

Her grandfather put down the *Whistler Pique* to greet her, and she waved a hand. "It's okay, Gramps, go back to your reading."

"You're a good girl," he said, a twinkle in his eye, then lifted the paper again.

"Do you have a cold, dear?" her grandmother asked, studying her face.

"I think I'm fighting one." Maddie took a bite of the muffin, wishing she'd gone for something more decadent like pancakes slathered with maple syrup.

"Is everything all right with Tom and Shelley? I've caught a . . . vibe, as you young folks say."

"They had a spat, but they've worked it through."

"That's a good sign. Put a man and a woman together in a marriage, and there are going to be disagreements."

From behind the paper came a snort.

Gram tossed a wry look in her husband's direction and raised her voice. "The important thing is that you work them out. Of course, it helps if the man has the sense to realize he's mostly always wrong."

This time the sound was a chuckle.

Maddie smiled. Her grandparents had many differences and sometimes they aggravated each other, but their love was strong. "In this case, there was some wrong on both sides. They each owned up and are trying to do better."

"That says a lot for both of them and the strength of their love," Gram said approvingly.

"It helps that their issues aren't major."

"When a couple's fighting, the issues always seem major."

"At least to the woman," came from behind the paper. "If you females could only learn a little perspective . . . "

The two women caught each other's eye and laughed. "Men," Gram said.

Maddie winked at her. "I don't know how you can live with him."

"I often wonder myself." But her eyes softened. "And the answer is always the same. I love the old coot."

This time the sound from behind the *Pique* was half snort, half chuckle. "Love you back," he said. His hand emerged to rest on her sweater-clad arm.

"Does love make everything worthwhile?" Maddie asked. "Like, what if the two of you had some really huge differences?"

Her grandmother's gaze sharpened. "Such as?"

"Oh, say one of you had wanted children and the other didn't. Or you had strong religious differences. Or . . . what if Gramps had had a job where he traveled a lot and was rarely home?"

Those light blue eyes studied her intently, and Maddie knew she was trying to read between the lines.

To her surprise, Gramps lowered his paper and also focused on Maddie's face. His hand slid down his wife's arm until it clasped her hand. "You ask if you can live without her," he said gruffly. "Whatever the problem, however much she drives you crazy, can you live without her?"

Gram squeezed his hand. "An excellent sentiment. Except, you can. You always can. But do you want to? For example, if you want children and he doesn't, is it better to have the children or to have the man? Yes, there are some hard decisions. That's where compromises and sacrifices come in." She glanced at her husband. "Right, Walter?"

"Like going to the opera when you hate it," he said promptly.

"Oh yes, that's so hard on you," she teased. "No, I meant bigger sacrifices. Like retiring early when you really didn't want to."

Startled, Maddie gazed at him. "You didn't want to, Gramps?"

He shook his head. "But your gram, she said she didn't want me dying in the harness, or some such nonsense."

"I wanted us to spend our golden years together, not with him off at a high-stress job. I wanted him going for walks with me, getting more fit. And he saw reason."

"It was hard at first," he said, "but I do feel like I got a new lease on life."

"So, I was right," his wife said promptly.

"You're wrong about the opera." He lifted the paper and re-treated behind it again.

"Is this about Logan?" Gram asked.

Maddie sighed.

"You always had a thing for that boy."

"Still do. But he's . . . " She shrugged. Of course she couldn't tell Gram the truth, not without jeopardizing Logan's cover.

"I always thought he had a good heart."

"So did I." But, much as she wanted to, she shouldn't let her grandmother think well of Logan. She forced herself to say, "The way he's acting this week makes me think we were wrong."

The edge of the paper folded down, and her grandfather fixed her with a steely gaze. "That boy always wanted something from this family."

He was right. Logan had wanted something and still did: acceptance, belonging, love. She could give him that, if only the price she'd have to pay wasn't so high.

Then again, wasn't giving him up an even higher price?

Chapter 10

BY late afternoon, Maddie had a headache. She'd spent hours tormenting herself with visions of what her life would be like with Logan—and without him. She'd even imagined life with Michael, in a rambling home with a couple of kids and a couple of pets. Why couldn't she have both the life she wanted *and* the man she wanted?

Then she'd spent more hours beating herself up for being so presumptuous as to think that either of those wonderful men might ever love her.

Finally, sick to death of her own thoughts, she headed down to the lounge for distraction and alcohol.

The first person she saw when she stepped through the door was Logan. Holding a steaming mug in one hand, he sat across from her grandparents. Her grandmother said something, and Logan gave a soft chuckle and replied.

And Maddie knew.

Logan was in her heart, and no amount of analyzing was going to change that. If all she could have with him were moments like this, by the fire with him and her grandparents, she'd take them.

She walked over to them. There was so much she wanted to say, but they were in public, and she had to keep things casual. "Hot chocolate by the fire? Taking a break from being the bad boy?"

His eyes twinkled. "Oh, we're being bad. We're enjoying a little sex on the slopes."

"It's almost as good as skiing," Gram said. "Logan, go get Maddie a drink."

"Yes, ma'am." When he'd been a teen, his tone had varied between belligerent, defensive, and snarky. Now he sounded relaxed and at ease. As he put down his mug, he made sure his arm brushed Maddie's.

When he'd gone, she said, "Logan's minding his manners tonight."

Her grandmother's gaze followed him as he walked over to the bar. "I don't know what's going on with him this week. He's himself, then he's not."

"Gram, you haven't seen him in ten years. How do you know who his 'self' is?"

She huffed. "I know perfectly well, and so do you. I just figured he'd outgrow the need to put on that rebel without a cause act."

"Who says it's an act?" Gramps said.

"Oh, Walter. Open your eyes."

"They're open. So're my ears. I've heard some rumors about him, and they're not pretty."

"Gram," Maddie said carefully, "if Logan's acting like a rebel without a cause, maybe there's a reason for it. I think it's better if you go along with it and don't, uh, try to salvage his reputation."

Two sets of beady eyes stared at her, then her grandparents looked at each other. Gram tilted her head, Gramps gave a shrug, then they both picked up their drinks.

When Logan returned with a mug for Maddie, he said, "Sorry, but I need to go." He picked up his own drink, then, gazing at her over the rim, drained it.

She lifted her own in a silent toast and took a sip, savoring the sweet, rich taste as she watched him walk away. *Be safe*, she thought.

Then she reminded herself, people got hit by cars crossing the street. No one was ever truly safe.

All the same . . . "Be back in a sec," she told her grandparents and then hurried after him. She caught up to him in the hall as he was unlocking the door to his room.

"Maddie?" He glanced around to ensure they were alone, then opened the door. "Want to come in?"

She shook her head. "Not a good idea." She gazed into the face she'd adored ever since she first started noticing boys. "Logan, I just wanted to say . . . " She took a breath and spoke the three magic words. "I love you."

Surprise and wonder lit his face. "Maddie, I don't—"

"Sshh. We'll talk later."

MADDIE'S words had rung in Logan's head all night. Words no one had ever said to him before.

Words that made him feel strong, valued, like there was finally a place in the world where he belonged: in her arms. But, how could that be? He wasn't the kind of man she needed.

Her words gave him a different perspective as he played his role with Eddie Tran. Yeah, taking down criminals was important, but did he really want to spend his life undercover, among the scum of the earth—and in all likelihood end up dying alone with a knife or bullet in his guts?

By the time he'd made it back to the Alpine Hideaway and showered, all he knew was that he had to bare his heart to Maddie. She was the only person he'd ever been able to talk to. Now he had things to say that he doubted he even had words to express.

When he slipped into her room, she greeted him with a welcoming smile that sank into him like spring sunshine after a frozen winter. He drank in the sight of her in pink pj's, sitting in the lotus position on top of the bed. Candlelight flickered, and instrumental music rippled around him.

He walked over to the bed, thinking that, much as he loved her in sexy lingerie, those buttoned-up pj's did it for him every time. But he wasn't going to unbutton her. Not until they talked.

He pulled a chair toward the bed and sat down facing her. Reaching over, he took her hands and held them.

"Logan?" She gazed at him questioningly.

He had to blurt it out, no matter how awkward he felt. "Maddie, what you said this afternoon . . . I don't know what love is. But I do know that the way I feel about you is something I've never felt for anyone else."

Her blue eyes studied him, soft but intent. "How do you feel?"

"Like I'd do anything for you. Like you're the only person in the world I've ever been able to talk to. Like I could climb into bed with you every night and never get tired of holding you in my arms. If I had any idea what *home* was, I'd say it's being with you."

Moisture glazed her eyes, and she squeezed his hands. "You can have that, Logan. A home with me. You deserve it."

The fact that she seemed to genuinely believe it almost made him believe it, too. "You deserve more than me."

"There's only you," she said with certainty. "I know I'll never love anyone else the way I do you."

"Wow." She stunned him. How could she feel that way about a guy like him? "Hell, Maddie. I didn't mean for this to happen." He blew out air in a long breath. "But I've been thinking. You said, maybe I should give up undercover work and become a normal cop."

"You should do what you need—want—to do. I'll love you regardless. I'll be here for you. No terms and conditions." Her lips trembled. "I won't pretend it wouldn't be hard, but I'd do it."

Her shoulders had slumped, but now she straightened them. "Though, yes, of course I'd like it better if you were a regular cop. Logan, you could have a normal life. A home, friends, family."

"I never thought I would."

"I know. But you always wanted them."

"*Growing Pains.*"

"Pardon?"

"That silly old TV show? That's the kind of life I wanted." He paused. "Still want. But I'd be crappy at it."

She gave him a sweet, misty-eyed smile. "Nobody's perfect at it. You mess up, argue, apologize, muddle through. Make some compromises and sacrifices."

"I guess. You really think I could do this?"

"I do." Her lips curved mischievously. "Gram and Gramps would give advice."

He chuckled. "I bet they would."

"I know what Gram would say first. You have to tell the girl you love her." Maddie firmed her jaw and tilted her head, but he saw vulnerability in her eyes.

He'd never in his life said those words or even thought them. Still, when he opened his mouth, they flowed out as if they were the most natural words in the world. "I love you, Maddie."

Her eyes flooded with tears. "Oh, Logan, I thought I'd never hear you say that."

"You might have to get used to it. Like, maybe . . . " He took a deep breath. "Like maybe every day of your life." Why the hell would he want to hang out undercover with criminals like Tran if he had Maddie to come home to? And maybe, one day down the road, a cute little girl who took after her mom. Maybe even a little boy who'd know, from the day he was born, that he was loved and would always have a safe home.

"Every day?" Her cheeks were damp with tears, but she didn't release his hands to wipe them away. "What are you saying?"

"You said maybe I was ready for a change. I didn't realize it until tonight, but you're right. I'm going to put my undercover days behind me."

"It's time?" she asked hopefully.

"Has nothing to do with time. And everything to do with you."

She gazed at him, and he saw her heart in her eyes. He knew she must see the same thing in his. "Oh my God, Logan," she said softly. "That would be so wonderful. I can hardly believe it."

"Me, either. But Maddie, if you'll take a chance on me, this is what I want."

"It's what I want, too." She leaned forward, he bent to meet her, and their lips touched in a soft kiss. Like a promise for the future.

Then she eased away. "How long would it take? What about the job you're working on now?"

"The reconnaissance finishes this week. I'll go back to Vancouver, make my report. They'll send in another cop undercover, to carry on."

She studied his face, frowning slightly. "Will that jeopardize the job? Were you supposed to be the one who went undercover?"

"Could have been, but that hadn't been decided. We'll find a way of getting someone else in there."

"You're sure? I mean, if you want to finish this job . . . "

"Thanks, Maddie, but no." An undercover cop never knew when that bullet or knife would hit, and now he had so much to live for. He'd find other, safer ways of catching criminals. "What I want is to be with you. The sooner, the better."

"Oh, Logan." A smile spread on her face. "There are so many things I want to do with you."

"Me, too. Though I'm not looking forward to your parents' and Tom's reaction."

"It'll take some time. But Logan, you really will be part of the family."

"That sounds good." Almost unbelievably good. A thought crossed his mind. "You do know I want you for you, right? Not for your family?"

She ginned. "Yeah, I kind of got that."

"I love you, Maddie."

"I love you, too." She gave his hands a gentle tug. "Make love to me, Logan."

He remembered how the week had started, with Maddie saying, "Fuck me, Logan." Those words had made him hard.

The ones she spoke now were better, so much better. Yes, they sent a surge of lust to his groin, but they also turned his tough old heart to pure mush.

He sat by her on the bed and took her into his arms. Soft flannel, warm curves, bright blue eyes. The woman he loved. "Oh yeah, Maddie, that's exactly what I'm going to do. Make love to you. For the rest of our lives."

Chapter 11

MADDIE walked down the petal-strewn aisle in her off-the-shoulder rose-colored gown, feeling as if she were floating. The church was decorated with pink roses and creamy orchids, faces beamed at her from both sides, and organ music buoyed her. She grinned at the waiting groom and he smiled back, then he looked past her, face bright with expectation.

At the front of the church, she took her place beside the rest of the wedding party. The music stopped, there was a rustle and buzz as everyone turned to face the back of the church, then the organ struck those four notes. Here comes the bride.

Shelley stepped into the doorway, lovely in ivory lace, and began her walk down the aisle. She restrained her normally lithe, athletic stride to match the music, but the glow on her face showed how eager she was to reach her groom. When she arrived at the front of the church, she thrust the bouquet toward Maddie, then she and Tom gripped each other's hands tightly.

Maddie clasped the bridal bouquet and looked out at the fifty or so beaming faces. Everyone's gaze was fixed on Shelly and Tom. Everyone's except Logan's. She gave him a private smile.

He looked so handsome in a classic black suit, crisp white shirt, and tie striped in black and gold. This morning, amid the pre-wedding bustle, he'd managed to take her aside for a few minutes to tell her that his transfer from undercover work to a regular police job was under way. For a few more days, he had to maintain his cover, but soon he'd be free.

She tore her gaze away and focused again on the bride and groom. This moment was theirs. She and Logan would have many, many moments of their own. As many as there were stars in the sky.

IT felt right to have the wedding reception at the Alpine Hideaway, Maddie thought later that day. It had come to feel like a home away from home, and Inger, Gord, and their staff took such good care of them.

Yes, space in the cleared-out lounge was a little tight for dancing, but why should she care? Logan had thought it best to avoid the reception, not wanting his undercover role to spoil the mood. She'd quietly told Michael that, while she thought he was a great guy, she wasn't interested in dating him. So, aside from dancing with her brother and dad, she spent most of her time fulfilling her maid of honor duties and helping Andi, the wedding planner.

Andi was distracted, and no wonder. Turned out, she was actually dating the hot firefighter who'd swept her out of the snow that first night. Throughout the wedding dinner and the party afterward, she'd clearly been torn between her usual responsible self and a head-over-heels romantic. Maddie could definitely empathize with the latter.

The other big surprise of the day was that Brianna had brought a date. She'd met Zack, an incredibly cute, charming Aussie ski instructor when she took a lesson earlier in the week. Tom had told Maddie he was worried about Brianna working too hard and getting stressed out, but today she looked young and carefree—and quite possibly head over heels herself.

Humming, Maddie wandered around the room, chatting with friends and family, gathering empty champagne bottles and fetching new ones, and dreaming of the day she and Logan could acknowledge their relationship in public.

Shelley's dad's voice broke into her thoughts as he called, "Okay, all you single girls, come on up. My beautiful daughter's going to toss the wedding bouquet."

Maddie grinned. Earlier, when she'd been helping Shelley into her wedding gown, the bride had said, "Get up at the front when I toss the bouquet. I'm aiming for you, sis."

Maddie had said, "I have my love life well in hand. Throw it to someone who needs the luck."

Shelley'd shot her a curious look and said, "We are *so* talking when I get back from my honeymoon."

Now, Maddie's friend Kim towed her toward the group of eight or so other single women, but Maddie managed to stand behind her as Shelley got ready for the toss.

With a sparkling grin, the bride hurled her bouquet of pink sweetheart roses and creamy white orchids straight into the arms of Brianna George.

Epilogue

INSIDE the entrance of the Alpine Hideaway, the reception desk was vacant. "Inger? Gord?" Maddie called.

"Coming," Inger's cheerful voice called from the direction of the kitchen.

Leaving Logan with their luggage, Maddie went down the hall to meet her.

Inger gave her a big hug. "Maddie Daniels. It's so good to have you back with us."

"It's wonderful to be here. Come see who I've brought with me."

Together they walked back to reception, and Inger said, "Oh. Oh, it's him."

"Not exactly a warm greeting," Logan commented, a twinkle in his eye.

"It's a long story, Inger," Maddie said, stepping into the curve of the arm he held out. "My bad boy is actually one of the good guys."

The older woman gave her a look that said, *You poor, deluded child.*

Maddie put her arm around Logan's waist and hugged him. It was up to him to decide how much of the story to tell.

"I'm with the RCMP," he told Inger. "I was working undercover. Had to play a role."

Maddie gazed up at his strong, handsome face, framed in longish dark hair, accented by the gleaming gold hoop in his ear. She'd never get tired of seeing him smile, hearing him laugh. In the past weeks he'd started to come out of that tough-guy loner shell he'd carried around all his life.

"Hmm," Inger said. She opened the register with a whack. "That's a hard job, going undercover. Hard on you and on friends and family."

"I've given it up," he said. "I'm just a plain old cop these days."

"Oh?" She glanced up, eyes brighter. Then she turned to Maddie. "Guess you had something to do with that?"

"Guess I did." She stretched up to kiss Logan's cheek. His decision had gone a long way to winning over Tom and her parents, too. Her gram, on learning the truth, had merely winked and said, "I always knew there was more to you than met the eye, Logan Carver." Gramps had said, "Guess this is a time I'll let my wife say, 'I told you so.'" Oh yes, Logan was going to have the family he'd always longed for.

One day before too long, she suspected he'd even become an official member, but she was in no hurry. She and her true love had their whole lives ahead of them.

He filled out the register, then they got their key and carried their luggage to their room. Sentimentally, she'd reserved the same one she'd occupied before.

She spun around—everything looked the same, yet everything was so different—and gave a sigh of delight. "We can actually go to bed together and get up together."

He nudged her in the direction of the bed. "Want to try out that first part now? You did pack your pj's, right?" His lips touched hers, lazily, luxuriously, and she gave herself up to the kiss. Being with Logan was everything she'd dreamed of, and more.

But then she pulled away. "Later. Jammies and all. I told you, right now we have other plans." Ever since she'd seen those horse-drawn sleighs for two, she'd longed to snuggle up in one with Logan. When they'd decided to spend this weekend at Whistler, she'd told him it was an opportunity to do all of the things they hadn't been able to before, starting with a sleigh ride.

"You're such a romantic," he teased.

"And you love it. Don't ever say you don't."

He raised his hands. "Never. I love it, and I love you, Maddie Daniels. Now, let's go for a sleigh ride."

She grinned at him. "I love you, too, Logan. And I did tell you they have big snuggly blankets, right?

"Mmm, that opens up all sorts of possibilities."

BRIANNA gave Zack a final kiss, then climbed out of bed and pulled on a robe. "Well, that was very nice. You obviously missed me." She'd cut her workday short and driven up from Vancouver, arriving just as he got home after his last ski lesson. They'd barely said hello before tumbling into bed.

He sat up and stacked a couple of pillows behind his back. "Bet on it. Four days is a long time." The past weekend, he'd been down in Vancouver with her but had returned first thing Monday.

She gazed at him for a long moment, just enjoying the sight. Spring skiing had given him a tan and lightened the tips of his hair to pale gold. His sparkling green eyes looked even more vivid.

When news had broken about her and Zack being a couple, she'd endured a fair bit of teasing, but she'd survived, and so had her career. In fact, there was a lot to be said for having a gorgeous man by her side at the last fund-raiser.

With some difficulty, she tore her gaze away and went over to the desk in his studio apartment, an apartment they'd found after a determined hunt and one he shared with no one but her. "I want to see the latest. You've been doing the revisions your agent suggested?" She powered up his laptop.

After some research, he'd contacted several literary agents and two had offered representation. The one he'd chosen was young and enthusiastic and had given him great suggestions for making his stories even stronger before she sent them out to publishers.

"I'll show you later," he said, climbing out of bed, all rippling muscles and athletic grace, and coming to hug her. "Let's grab a quick shower, then I've got something planned."

"Are we getting together with your Aussie mates?" They'd been to the Down Under pub a few times, hanging out with his friends. The simple fact that she was with Zack had been her entrée to acceptance.

With his friends, she was Zack's lady rather than a TV star. After all these years of striving to build a career, it was fun to sit back and relax. Not that people weren't interested in her show. A number of the gang from the Down Under had turned into fans, particularly since she'd pulled out of the U.S. deal and was able to concentrate on the kind of local interest stories she'd always loved the most.

Her favorite new feature was The Scoop on Romance. Tom and Shelley's segment had proven so popular that now, once a week, she did a romance feature. Her guests ranged from high-powered celebrities to regular folks like Tom's grandmother and grandfather, each sharing their real-life romance and the lessons they'd learned along the way.

Who'd have ever guessed Brianna George would be promoting romance?

Oh yes, she was happy. She was happy in her work life as well as her personal life, truly happy for the first time ever.

"Nah, not the pub tonight," Zack said. "Last weekend, you were talking about that first week you were in Whistler, remember? You told me about the night you realized romance might not be such a bad thing."

"When I saw the couples on the sleigh ride." She gazed at him, excitement filling her. "We're going for a sleigh ride?"

"You got it. Just the two of us. And a thermos of Slippery Slopes."

She chuckled. "You know what happens when you get me started on a slippery slope."

"Too right. There's just no stopping you."

And there wasn't. With him, she was flying.

He caught her face between his hands. "I love you, Bree."

"I love you, too, Zack." She'd never believed she'd say those words to a man, but they felt totally right.

Two months ago, when Shelley had hurled her bridal bouquet straight into her arms, Brianna had been stunned. Now, she had a feeling that before too long, Tom's new wife would be saying, "I told you so."

ANDI stood in the center of the stripped-bare living room of Jared's house. "I know I've asked this a million times, but the whole thing feels so real right now. Are you sure you're okay with this?"

"I'm not selling. It's just a two-year lease." He put a big box stuffed with keepers by the door.

She admired the way the muscles flexed under his T-shirt and the tautness of his butt as he squatted, then rose. "So many changes," she murmured. Two weeks ago, he'd been notified that he'd been accepted for a firefighter job in Vancouver. He'd advertised his house for rent on the Internet, and it had been snapped up.

He came over to her and took her hands. "For you, too. Are you okay with all this? Acquiring a roommate and all?"

She smiled up into his silver gray eyes. "A roommate? Is that what you call it?"

"A live-in lover?"

"So far, you're proving pretty handy. You can cook, you're tidy, and you mix a great Fire and Ice."

"That's it?" He gave her a mock scowl. "The full catalog of my virtues?"

"I can think of one or two others." Like being a phenomenal lover and an all-round good guy. He'd easily won the approval of her parents and friends.

In fact, her partner Sarah—who'd been delighted her aimed bridal bouquet toss had netted such prompt results—was already discussing wedding plans. Andi had told her to relax; she and Jared were in no hurry. The way things were going, she had a feeling they'd have years and years ahead of them, so right now she was just enjoying the process of falling more in love each day.

Hand in hand, she and Jared walked to the door. "You've lived in Whistler all your life," she said, thinking how hard it must be to leave.

"Whistler's great, but I'm ready for a change. We'll come back and visit."

"Your parents were so sweet to say we could stay with them." His parents—all of his family that she'd met so far—were wonderful.

"They love you as much as I do, and they're happy for me. But I'd rather stay at the Alpine Hideaway. More privacy."

"Did you tell your folks we're staying there tonight?"

"Nope. Just said we'd be packing up then heading down to Vancouver. They don't need to know we're not leaving until tomorrow."

"Our last night in Whistler should be on our own," she agreed. "Now, hurry up, or we'll be late."

They both put on sweaters and jackets, then he shouldered the last box. He put his hand on the light switch, and they stood in silence for a moment. Andi sent a silent message to his deceased wife. *If you're here, Beth, know that I love him, too. I'll take good care of him.*

She was pretty sure he was sending his own message to Beth, too, and kept quiet until he flicked off the light switch and opened the door.

After he locked up, she put her arm around his waist and, still not speaking, they walked to his 4x4. She climbed into the front while he finished securing the load in the back, then he drove away without a backward look.

A few blocks down the road, he said, "Starting to snow. Won't be many more snows left this season."

She gazed out at the flakes drifting down. "It was like this back in January when the wedding group went on the sleigh ride. I kept wishing I was with you."

"And now you are."

"You and me, a big fluffy robe, snowflakes drifting down, and lights glowing beside the trail . . . I've really been looking forward to this."

As they pulled into the parking lot near the sleigh ride base, the headlights caught another couple in their beam.

"My gosh, I think that's Brianna George." Andi squinted through the snow. "Brianna and Zack, the ski instructor she brought to the wedding."

"Yeah?"

Their arms were woven around each other's waists. "Looks like things are working out for them, too." She smiled, thinking back to Tom and Shelley's wedding. It had gone off perfectly in the end, the wedding vows even more meaningful after what the bride and groom had gone through in the days leading up to the wedding.

As for her, she'd been less than efficient, because she'd been so thrilled to have Jared there at her side. But it hadn't mattered; everyone had been having too much fun.

"Let's go say hi," she said, climbing out of the truck.

He came around and dropped a kiss on her lips. "Okay, but we're not sharing a sleigh with them."

She laughed up at him. "No way. I want you all to myself."

Holding hands, they hurried to where people were gathering around a group of sleighs. Giant Percheron horses snorted and sent puffs of vapor into the chill air, and bells jingled each time they tossed their heads.

They caught up with Brianna and Zack just in time to hear Brianna exclaim, "Maddie?"

Maddie? Maddie Daniels? Andi tugged Jared forward and saw Tom's little sister nestled up against a tall, handsome man with a big smile on his face.

He looked familiar, but it took her a moment to place him. And then . . . "Logan?" She gaped. Had Maddie actually hooked up with that bad boy?

Maddie let out a bell-like laugh. "Wow, it's like a reunion. I can't believe we're all here, and on the same night."

"Logan?" Andi demanded. "You're with Logan?"

"I am," she said blithely.

Hmm. Maddie did look glowingly happy, and in fact, so did Logan. The smile was the reason Andi hadn't recognized him.

"Want to hear a story?" Maddie asked. "A romantic one?"

"I like romantic stories," Brianna said.

Andi didn't bother pointing out how much the TV host had changed in the last two months. "So do I. Okay, Maddie. Tell us a story. Just so long as it ends with a happily ever after."

"Oh, absolutely. Now, this is a story about a girl who kissed a boy on a starry night, and from that moment they were destined to be together . . . "

As Maddie continued, smiling in the shelter of Logan's arm, Andi snuggled closer to Jared. Destiny. Yes, maybe it was destiny. But destiny wasn't all it took. Love wasn't always easy, and didn't you value it all the more for having to work for it?

Maddie and Logan clearly knew that, and she guessed that the TV host and her Aussie boyfriend did, too.

Maybe there was a magic recipe for love. Mix destiny and hard work, then throw in a splash of sex on the slopes.

And this time, she wasn't talking about the drink!

ABOUT THE AUTHOR

Susan Lyons writes sexy contemporary romance that's intense, passionate, heartwarming, and fun. Her books have won Booksellers Best, Aspen Gold, Golden Quill, and More than Magic awards, and have been nominated for the Romantic Times Reviewers' Choice award. She lives in Vancouver, British Columbia. She has law and psychology degrees, and has also studied anthropology, sociology, and counseling. Her careers have been varied, including perennial student, grad-school dropout, job creation project administrator, computer consultant, and legal editor. Fiction writer is by far her favorite career. Writing gives her a perfect outlet to demonstrate her belief in the power of love, friendship, and a sense of humor.

Visit Susan's website at www.susanlyons.ca for excerpts, discussion questions, writing-process notes, articles, and giveaways. Susan can be contacted at susan@susanlyons.ca.